ALSO BY DAVID BALDACCI

STANDALONES
Absolute Power
Total Control
The Winner
The Simple Truth
Saving Faith
Wish You Well
Last Man Standing
The Christmas Train
True Blue
One Summer
One Good Deed

MEMORY MAN SERIES
Memory Man
The Last Mile
The Fix
The Fallen
Redemption

ATLEE PINE SERIES
Long Road to Mercy

WILL ROBIE SERIES
The Innocent
The Hit
The Target
The Guilty
End Game

JOHN PULLER SERIES
Zero Day
The Forgotten
The Escape
No Man's Land

KING & MAXWELL SERIES
Split Second
Hour Game
Simple Genius
First Family
The Sixth Man
King and Maxwell

THE CAMEL CLUB SERIES
The Camel Club
The Collectors
Stone Cold
Divine Justice
Hell's Corner

THE SHAW SERIES
The Whole Truth
Deliver Us from Evil

SHORT STORIES
Waiting for Santa
No Time Left
Bullseye

DAVID BALDACCI

ONE GOOD DEED

GRAND CENTRAL
PUBLISHING

LARGE PRINT

New York   Boston

Copyright © 2019 by Columbus Rose, Ltd.

Cover design by David Litman. Cover copyright © 2019 by Hachette Book Group, Inc.

Grand Central Publishing

Hachette Book Group

1290 Avenue of the Americas, New York, NY 10104

grandcentralpublishing.com

twitter.com/grandcentralpub

First Edition: July 2019

Grand Central Publishing is a division of Hachette Book Group, Inc. The Grand Central Publishing name and logo is a trademark of Hachette Book Group, Inc.

The publisher is not responsible for websites (or their content) that are not owned by the publisher.

The Hachette Speakers Bureau provides a wide range of authors for speaking events. To find out more, go to www.hachettespeakersbureau.com or call (866) 376-6591.

Library of Congress Cataloging-in-Publication Data has been applied for.

ISBNs: 978-1-5387-5056-8 (hardcover), 978-1-5387-5057-5 (large print), 978-1-5387-0146-1 (international), 978-1-5387-5055-1 (ebook)

To Ben Sevier, for believing
in both me and Aloysius Archer

ONE GOOD DEED

CHAPTER

I

It was a good day to be free of prison.

The mechanical whoosh and greasy smell of the opening bus doors greeted Aloysius Archer, as he breathed free air for the first time in a while. He wore a threadbare single-breasted brown Victory suit with peak lapels that he'd bought from the Sears, Roebuck catalogue before heading off to war. The jacket was shorter than normal and there were no pleats or cuffs to the pants because that all took up more material than the war would allow; there was no belt for the same reason. A string tie, a fraying, wrinkled white shirt, and scuffed lace-up size twelve plain Oxford shoes completed the only wardrobe he owned. Small clouds of dust rose off his footwear as he trudged to the bus.

His pointed chocolate brown fedora with the dented crown had a loop of faded burgundy silk around it. He'd bought the hat after coming back from the war. One of the few times he'd splurged on anything. But a global victory over evil had seemed to warrant it.

These were the clothes he'd worn to prison. And now he was leaving in them. He comically lamented that in all this time, the good folks of the correctional world had not seen fit to clean or even press them. And his hat held stains that he hadn't brought with him to incarceration. Yet a man couldn't go around without a hat.

The pants hung loosely around his waist, a waist grown slimmer and harder while he'd been locked up. He was fully twenty-five pounds heavier than when he'd gone into prison, but the extra weight was all muscle, grafted onto his arms, shoulders, chest, back, and legs, like thickened vines on a mature tree. In his socks he was exactly six feet one and a quarter. The Army had measured him years before. They were quite adept at calculating height. Though they had too frequently failed to supply him with enough ammunition for his M1 rifle or food for his belly, while he and his fellow soldiers were trying to free large patches of the world from an oddball collection of deranged men.

The prison had a rudimentary gym, of which he'd taken full advantage. It wasn't just to build up his body. When he was pumping weights or running or working his gut, it allowed him to forget for a precious hour or two that he was squirreled away in a cage with felonious men. The prison also held a book depository teeming with tattered, coverless books that sported missing pages at inopportune times, but they were precious to him nonetheless. His favorites had been Westerns where the man got the gal. And detective novels, where the man got the gal and also caught the bad guy. Which he supposed was a funny sort of way for a prisoner to be entertained. Yet he liked the puzzle component of the mystery novels. He tried to solve them before he got to the end, and found that as time went on, he had happened upon the correct solution more often than not.

The jail grub he had pretty much done without. What wasn't spoiled or wormy held no discernible taste to persuade him to ingest it. He'd gotten by on a variety of fruits picked from a nearby orchard, vegetables harvested from the small garden inside the prison walls, and the occasional piece of fried chicken or soft bread and clots of warm apple fritters that arrived at the prison in mysterious ways. Some said they were dropped off by compassionate ladies either looking to do good, or else hoping for a husband in three to five years. The rest of his time was spent either busting big rocks into smaller ones using sledgehammers, collecting trash along the side of the roads, only to see it back the next day, or else digging ditches to nowhere fast because a man with a double-barreled shotgun, sunglasses, a wide-brimmed hat, and a stone-cold stare told him that was all he was good for.

He was not yet thirty, was never married, and had no children, but one glance in the mirror showed a man who seemed older, his skin baked brown by the sun and further aged by being behind bars the rest of the time. A world war coupled with the brutal experience of losing one's liberty had left their indelible marks on him. These two experiences had successfully robbed him of the remainder of his youth but hardened him in ways that might at some point work out in his favor.

His hair had been long going into prison. On the first day they had cut it Army short. Then he'd tried to grow a beard. They'd shaved that off, too. They said something about lice and hiding places for contraband.

He vowed never to cut his hair again, or at least

to go as long as possible without doing so. It was a small thing, to be sure. He had started out life concentrated only on achieving large goals. Now he was focused on just getting by. The impossibly difficult ambitions had been driven from him. On the other hand, the mundane seemed reasonably doable for Archer.

He ducked his head and swept off his fedora to avoid colliding with the ceiling of the rickety vehicle. The bus doors closed with a hiss and a thud, and he walked down the center aisle, a suddenly free man looking for unencumbered space. The rocking bus was surprisingly full. Well, perhaps not surprisingly. He assumed this mode of transport was the only way to get around. This was not the sort of land where they built airfields or train depots. And those black ribbons of state highways never seemed to get rolled out in these places. It was the sort of area where folks did not own a vehicle that could travel more than fifty miles at any given time. Nor did the folks driving said vehicles ever want to go that far anyway. They might fall off the edge of the earth.

The other passengers looked as bedraggled as he, perhaps more so. Maybe they'd been behind their own sorts of bars that day, while he was leaving his. They were all dressed in prewar clothes or close to it, with dirty nails, raw eyes, hungry looks, and not even a glimmer of hope in the bunch. That surprised him, since they were now a few years removed from a wondrous global victory and things were settling down. But then again, victory did not mean that prosperity had suddenly rained down upon all parts of the country. Like anything else, some fared better than others. It seemed he was currently riding with the "others."

They all stared up at him with fear, or suspicion, or sometimes both running seamlessly together. He saw not one friendly expression in the crowd. Perhaps humankind had changed while he'd been away. Or then again, maybe it was the same as it'd always been. He couldn't tell just yet. He hadn't gotten his land legs back.

Archer spotted an empty seat next to an older man in threadbare overalls over a stained undershirt, a stubby straw hat perched in his lap, brogans the size of babies on his feet, and a large canvas bag clutched in one callused hand. He had watched Archer, bug-eyed, for the whole time it took him to reach his seat. An instant before Archer's bottom hit the stained fabric of the chair, the other man let himself go wide, splaying out like a pot boiling over, forcing Archer to ride on the edge and uncomfortably so.

Still, he didn't mind. While his prison cell had been bigger than the space he was now occupying, he had shared it with four other men, and not a single one of them was going anywhere.

But now, now I'm going somewhere.

"Joint stop?"

"What's that?" asked Archer, eyeballing the man looking at him now. His seatmate's hair was going white, and his mustache and beard had already gone all the way there.

"You got on at the prison stop."

"Did I now?"

"Yeah you did. How long did you do in the can?"

Archer turned away and looked out the windshield into the painful glare of sunshine and the vast sky over the broad plains ahead that was unblemished by a single cloud.

"Long enough. Hey, you don't happen to have a smoke I can bum?"

"You can't really *borrow* a smoke, now can you? And you can't smoke on here anyways."

"The hell you say."

The man pointed to a handwritten sign on cardboard hanging overhead that said this very thing.

More rules.

Archer shook his head. "I've smoked on a

train, on a Navy ship. *And* in a damn church. My old man smoked in the waiting room when I was being born, so they told me. And he said my mom had a Pall Mall in her mouth when I came out. What's the deal here, friend?"

"They've had trouble before, see?"

"Like what?"

"Like some knucklehead fell asleep smoking and caught a whole dang bus on fire."

"Right, ruin it for everybody else."

"Ain't good for you anyway, I believe," said the man.

"Most things not good for me I enjoy every now and again."

"What'd you do to get locked up? Kill a man?"

Archer shook his head. "Never killed anybody."

"Guess they all say that."

"Guess they do."

"Guess you were innocent."

"No, I did it," admitted Archer.

"Did what?"

"Killed a man."

"Why?"

"He was asking too many questions of me."

But Archer smiled, so the man didn't appear too alarmed at the veiled threat.

"Where you headed?"

"Somewhere that's not here," said Archer. He took off his jacket, carefully folded it, and laid it on his lap with his hat on top.

"Is all you got the clothes on your back?"

"All I got."

"What's your ticket say?"

Archer dug into his pocket and pulled it out.

It was eighty and dry outside and about a hundred inside the bus, even with the windows half-down. The created breeze was like oven heat and the mingled odors were...peculiar. And yet Archer didn't really sweat, not anymore. Prison had been far hotter, far more...peculiar. His pores and sense of smell had apparently recalibrated.

"Poca City," he read off the flimsy ticket.

"Never been there, but I hear it's growing like gangbusters. Used to be the boondocks. But then it went from cattle pasture to a real town. People coming out this way after the war, you see."

"And what do they do once they get there?"

"Anything they can, brother, to make ends meet."

"Sounds like a plan good as another."

The older man studied him. "Were you in the war? You look like you were."

"I was."

"Seen a lot of the world, I bet?"

"I have. Not always places I wanted to be."

"I been outta this state exactly one time. Went to Texas to buy some cattle."

"Never been to Texas."

"Hey, you been to New York City?"

"Yes, I have."

The man sat up straighter. "You have?"

Archer casually nodded his head. "Passed through there on account of the war. Seen the Statue of Liberty. Been to the top of the Empire State Building. Rode the rides over at Coney Island. Even seen some Rockettes walking down the street in their getups and all."

The man licked his lips. "Tell me something. Are their legs like they say, friend?"

"Better. Gams like Betty Grable and faces like Lana Turner."

"Damn, what else?" he asked eagerly.

"Had a box lunch in the middle of Central Park. Sat on a blanket with a honey worked at Macy's department store. We drank sodas and then she slipped out a flask from the top of her stocking. What was in there? Well, it was better'n grape soda, I can tell you that. We had a nice day. And a better night."

The man scratched his cheek. "So, what are you doing all the way out here then?"

"Life has a crazy path sometimes. And like you said, folks heading this way after the war."

The man, evidently intrigued now by his companion, sat up straighter, allowing Archer more purchase on his seat.

"And the war was a long time ago, or seems it anyway," said Archer, stretching out. "But you got one life, right? Less somebody's been lying to me."

"Hold on now, Church says we get *two* lives. One now, one after we're dead. Eternal."

"Don't think that's in the cards for me."

"Man never knows."

"Oh, I think I know."

Archer tipped his head back, closed his eyes, and grabbed his first bit of shut-eye as a free man in a long time.

2

ARCHER GOT OFF at Poca City seven hours later and too many stops in between to remember. People had gotten on and people had gotten off. They'd had a dinner and bathroom break at a roadside diner with an outhouse in the back, both of which looked only a stiff breeze away from falling over. It was nearly eight in the evening now. He stood there as the bus and the rube with too many queries and the remaining nervous folks clutching all they owned sped off into the night chasing pots of gold along dusty roads with nary a helpful leprechaun in sight.

Good riddance to them all, thought Archer. And then, a second later, his more charitable consideration was, *Well, good luck to them.*

We all needed luck now and then, was his firm

belief. And maybe right now he needed it more than most. The point was, would he get it?

Or will I have to make my own damn luck? And hope for no bad luck as a chaser?

He put on his hat and then his jacket and looked around. He was in Poca City because the DOP said it was here he had to serve his parole. He dragged out the pages he'd been given. In fat, bold typeface at the top of the page was "Department of Prisons," or the DOP. Below that was a long list of "don'ts" and a far shorter list of "dos." These rules would govern his life for the next three years. Though he was free, it was a liberty with lassoes attached, with so-called legal conditions that he mostly could make neither head nor tail of. Who knew prison could stick to you, like running into a spider's web in the morning, flailing about, just wanting to be free of the tendrils, while alarmed that a poisonous thing was coming for you.

Archer had been released from prison well before he served his full sentence due to time off for good behavior and also for passing muster at his first parole board meeting. He had ventured into the little stuffy room that held a flimsy table with three chairs behind and one chair in front and him not knowing what to expect. Two burly prison guards had accompanied him to this meeting. He had been dressed in his prison duds, which seemed to shriek "guilt" and "continued danger" from each pore of the sweat-stained fabric.

Behind the table were three people, two men and one woman. The men were short and stout and freely perspiring in the closeness of the room. They looked self-important and bored as they greedily puffed on their fat cigars. The woman, who sat in the middle of this little band of freedom givers or takers, was tall and matronly with an elaborate hat on which a fabric bird clung to one side, and with a dead fox around her blocky shoulders.

Archer had instantly seized on her as the real power, and thus had focused all of his attention there. His contriteness was genuine, his remorse complete. He stared into her large, brown eyes and said his piece with heartfelt emphasis contained in each word, until he saw quivering at the corners of those eyes, the false bird and fox start to shake. When he'd finished and then answered all her questions, the consultation among the board was swift and in his favor as the men quickly capitulated to the woman's magisterial decree.

And that had been the price of freedom, which he had gladly paid.

The Derby Hotel was where the DOP said it would be. Point for those folks, grudgingly. Its architecture reminded him of places he'd seen in Germany. That did not sit particularly well with him. Archer hadn't fought all those years to come home and see any elements of the vanquished settled here. He trudged across the macadam, the collected heat of the day wicking up into his long feet. Though the sky was now dark, it was still cloudless and clear. The air was so dry he felt his skin try to pull back into itself. Archer also thought he saw dust exhaled along with breath. A pair of old, withered men were bent over a checkerboard table incongruously perched in the shadow of a large fountain. The thing was built principally of gray-and-white marble with naked, fat cherubs suspended in the middle holding harps and flutes, and not a drop of water coming out of the myriad spouts.

With furtive glances, the old men watched him coming. Archer shuffled along rather than walked. For long distances in prison, meaning longer than a walk to the john, you had your feet shackled. And so, you shuffled along. It was demeaning, to be sure, and that was the whole purpose behind it. Archer meant to rid himself of the motion, but it was easier said than done.

He could feel their gazes tracking him, like

silent parasites sucking the life out of him at a distance, him in his cheap, wrinkled clothes with his awkward gait.

Prison stop. Look out, gents, ex-con shuffling on by.

He nodded to them as he and his filthy shoes grew closer to the cherubic fountain and the bent checker-playing men. Neither nodded in return. Poca City apparently was not that sort of place.

He reached the harder pavement in front of the hotel, swung the front door wide and let it bang shut behind him. He crossed the floor, the plush carpet sucking him in, and tapped a bell set on the front desk. As its ringing died down, he gazed at a sign on the wall promising shined shoes fast for a good rate. That and a shave and a haircut, and a masculine aftershave included.

A middle-aged man with a chrome dome and wearing a not overly clean white shirt with a gray vest over it and faded corduroy trousers came out from behind a frayed burgundy curtain to greet him. His sleeves were rolled up and his forearms were about as hairy as any Archer had ever seen. It was like fat, fuzzy caterpillars had colonized there. His nails could have used a scrubbing, and he seemed to have the same coating of dust as Archer.

"Yes?" he said, running an appraising glance

over Archer and clearly coming away not in any way, shape, or form satisfied.

"Need a room."

"Figgered that. Rates on the wall right there. You okay with that?"

"Do I have a choice?"

The man gave him a look while Archer felt for the wrinkled dollars in his pocket.

"Three nights."

The man put out his hand and Archer passed him the money. He put it in the till and swung a stiff ledger around.

"Please sign, complete with a current address."

"Do I have to?"

"Yes."

"Why?"

"It's the law."

The law seemed to be everywhere these days.

Archer reluctantly took up the chubby pen the man handed him. "What's the address of this place?"

"Why?"

"Because that's my *current* address, is why."

The man harrumphed and told him.

Archer dutifully wrote it down and signed his name in a flourish of cursive.

The man eyed the signature upside down. "That's really your name?"

"Why? You mostly get Smiths and Jones here with ladies on their arms for short stays?"

"Hey, fella, this ain't that kind of a place."

"Yeah, I know, you're all class. Like the naked babies set in marble outside."

"Look it, where you from?" said the man, a scowl now crowding his face.

"Here and there. Now, here."

The man slid open a drawer and pulled out a fat, brass key.

"Number 610. Top floor. Elevator's that way." He pointed to his left.

"Stairs?"

"Same way."

As Archer started off, the man said, "Wait, don't you have no bags?"

"Wearing 'em instead of carrying 'em," replied Archer over his shoulder.

He took the stairs, not the elevator. Elevators were really little prison cells, was his opinion. And maybe the doors wouldn't open when he wanted them to. What then?

One thing prison took away from you, hard and clear, was simple trust.

He unlocked the door to 610 and surveyed it, taking his time. He had all the time in the world now. After counting every minute of every hour of every day for the last few years, he no longer had to. But still, it was a tough habit to break. He figured he might actually miss it.

He checked the bed: flimsy, squeaky. His in prison had been concrete masquerading as a mattress, so this was just fine. He opened a drawer and saw the Gideon Bible there along with stationery and a ballpoint pen.

Well, Jesus and letter writing are covered.

He took off his jacket and hung it on a peg, placing his hat on top of it. He slipped out his folding money. He laid the bills out precisely on the bed, divided by denomination. There was not much there after he'd laid out the dough for the room. The DOP had been stingy, but in an effective way.

He would have to work to survive. This would keep him from mischief. He wasn't guessing about this.

Archer took out his parole papers. It was right there in the very first paragraph.

Gainful employment will keep you from returning to your wayward ways, and thus to prison. DO NOT FORGET THIS.

He continued running his eye down the page.

First meeting was tomorrow morning at nine a.m. sharp. At the Poca City Courts and Municipality Building. That was a long name, and it somehow stoked fear in Archer. Of rules and regulations and too many things for him to contemplate readily. Or adhere to consistently.

Ernestine Crabtree was her name. His parole officer.

Ernestine Crabtree. It sounded like quite a fine name.

For a parole officer.

He opened his window for one reason only. His window had never opened in prison. He sucked in the hot, dry air and surveyed Poca City. Poca City looked back at him without a lick of interest. Archer wondered if that would always be the case no matter where he went.

He lay back on the bed. But his Elgin wristwatch told him it was too early to go to bed. Probably too late to get a drink, though number 14 on his DOP don't list was no bars and no drink. Number 15 was no women. So was number 16, at least in a way, though it more specifically referred to no "loose" women. The DOP probably had amassed a vast collection of statistics that clearly showed why the confluence of parolees and alcohol in close proximity to others drinking likewise was not a good thing. And when you threw in women, and more to the point, *loose* women, an apocalypse was the only likely outcome.

Of course, right now, he dearly wished for a libation of risky proportion.

Archer put on his jacket and his hat, scooped up his cash, and went in search of one.

And maybe the loose women, too.

A man in his position could not afford to be choosy. Or withholding of his desires.

On his first day of freedom he deemed life just too damn short for that.

CHAPTER

3

HE FOUND IT only a short distance from the hotel. Not on the main drag of Poca City, but down a side street that was only half the length of the one he'd left—but it was far more interesting, at least to Archer's mind.

If the main street was for checker playing and marble musical babies, this was where the adults got their jollies. And Archer had always been a fan of the underdog with weaknesses of the flesh, considering how often he fell on that side of the ledger.

The marquee was neon blue and green with a smattering of sputtering red. He hadn't seen the likes of such since New York City, where it had been ubiquitous. Yet he hadn't expected a smidge of it in Poca City.

THE CAT'S MEOW.

That's what the neon spelled out along with the outline of a feline in full, luxurious stretch that seemed erotic in nature. To Archer, Poca City was getting more interesting by the minute.

He pushed open the red door and walked in.

The first thing he noted was the floor. Planked and nailed and slimed with the slop of what they'd been serving here since the place opened, he reckoned. His one shoe stuck a bit, and then so did the other. Archer compensated by picking up the force of his steps.

The next thing of note was the crowd, or the size of it anyway. He didn't know the population of the town, but if it had any more people than were in here, it might qualify as a metropolis.

The bar nearly ran the length of one wall. And like on the bows of old ships, sculpted into the corner support posts of the bar were the heads and exposed bosoms of women—he supposed loose ones. And every stool had a butt firmly planted on it. Against one wall fiddle and guitar players plucked and strummed, while one gal was singing for all she was worth. She had red curly hair, a pink, freckled face, and slim hips with stiff dungarees on over them. Her notes seemed to hit the ceiling so hard they ricocheted off with the force of combat shrapnel.

Behind the bar was a wall of shelves holding every type of bottled liquor Archer had ever seen and then some, by a considerable margin. He reckoned a man could live his whole life here and never grow thirsty, so long as the coin of the realm kept up.

Indeed, happening on this place after being behind bars this morning and enduring a long, dusty bus ride and encountering less than friendly citizens hereabouts, Archer considered he might be in a dream. With three years of probation to endure, he felt like a large fish with a hook in its mouth. He could be yanked back at any moment, and that lent force to a man's whims. Thus, he decided to take full advantage while he could.

Sidling up to the bar, he wedged in between what seemed a colossus of a farmer with a rowdy beard and hands the width of Archer's head, and a short, thick, late-fifties-something, slick-haired banker type in a creamy white three-piece suit far nicer than Archer's. He also had a knotted blue-and-white-striped tie, with reptile leather two-tone shoes on his feet, a fully realized smirk in his eye, and a woman less than half his age on his arm. Resting on the bar in front of the man was a flat-crowned Panama hat with a yellow band of silk.

Archer caught the bartender's attention and held up two horizontally stacked fingers and tacked on the words "Bourbon, straight up."

The gent, old, spent, and thin as a strand of rope, nodded, retrieved the liquor from the vast stacks, poured it neat into a short glass, and held it out with one hand, while the other presented itself palm up for payment. It was a practiced motion that a man like Archer could appreciate.

"How much you charging for that?" he asked.

"Fifty cents for two fingers, take it or leave it, son."

"What's the bourbon again, pops?"

"Only one bourbon in these parts, young feller. Rebel Yell. Wheat, not rye. You don't like Rebel, you best pick another type of alcohol or another part of the state. Give me an answer, 'cause I ain't getting any younger and I got thirsty folks with *folding* money want my attention."

"Rebel sounds fine to me."

He passed over the two quarters and settled his elbows on the bar with the short glass cupped in both hands. He hadn't had a drink in a while. He'd banged one back the day before prison, just for good luck, so he reckoned it was a certain symmetry to have one the day he left prison. He was into balance if nothing else these days. And moderation, too, until it proved inconvenient, which it very often did to a man like him.

The banker eyed Archer, while his lady ran her tongue over full lips painted as warm a red as a sky hosting a setting sun.

"You're not from here," said the banker. His silver hair was cut, combed, and styled with the precision available only to a man who had the dollars and leisure time for such tasks. His face was as flabby as the rest of him, and also tanned and creased with lines in a way that women might or might not find attractive. For such a man, the thickness of his wallet and not the fitness of his torso was his main and perhaps only aphrodisiac for the ladies.

"I know I'm not," replied Archer, sipping the Rebel and letting it go down slow, the only way to drink bourbon, or so his granddad had informed him. And not only informed but demonstrated on more than one occasion. He tipped his hat back, turned around, bony elbows on the bar, his long torso angled off it, and studied the banker, then flitted his gaze to the lady.

The banker's smirk broadened—he was reading Archer's mind, no doubt.

"I like this town," said the banker. "And everything in it."

He patted the lady's behind and then his hand remained perched there. She seemed not to mind or else had grown accustomed to this fondling, or both. As the man's fingers stroked her, she took a moment to powder her nose while looking in a mirror attached to a shiny compact. The lady next shook out a tube of lipstick from her clutch purse and repainted her mouth before once more taking up what looked to be a murky martini with three fat olives lurking mostly below the surface, like gators in a bog.

"Been in Poca City long, have you?" inquired Archer.

"Long enough to see what's good and what needs changing. And then changing it."

He closed his mouth and eyed Archer from under tilted tufts of eyebrow.

"You gonna keep me in suspense?" said Archer finally.

The banker laughed and swallowed some of his whiskey. His eyes flickered just a bit as the drink went down, like wobbly lights in a storm.

Archer's mouth eased into a smile at this weakness, but the man didn't seem to notice. Or care.

"Poca's growing. This used to be just cattle land. And farming. Now that's changing.

Business and money coming in. Not too much riffraff."

"How do you decide about riffraff? See, I might fall into that category and then where do we go with this happy conversation?"

The lady laughed at this, but the banker did not. She shut her mouth and sipped her bog.

The banker intoned, "Fact is, a man can make money here if he's willing to work. With the war over, we have winners and losers. I aim to make certain Poca falls on the winner's side of the ledger. See, I was here before the war, trying to make things work. Place was an armpit then. Now the country is rebuilding, hell, we're putting the bricks and glass back up all over Europe, too. Had that damn Berlin Airlift feeding all them folks. Commies taking over in China. That Stalin fella getting half o' Europe under his iron thumb and testing them damn nuclear bombs. Now, Truman said we'd all be getting a fair deal here, but I don't take no man's word for that, president or not. Folks are heading west again, making their way to new lives, new fortunes. And in Poca, we're sort of at the crossroads of all that. Betwixt old America where most now still live and new America that lies west of here. People pass through. Some stay. Most keep going because we can't compete with the likes of Los Angeles and Frisco and that gambling haven in Las Vegas. But opportunities still abound here. And I'm well positioned to take advantage of every one of them. And I am, by God."

Archer listened to all this, nodding, his mouth twitching back and forth as he processed the man's many words.

He said, "Saw the fountain with the babies, and the geezers playing checkers. Kinda odd sight."

The man laughed. "Old and the new. Before long there won't be time for people to be sitting around playing checkers."

"No water coming out the fountain though."

"We've had a drought," the man said. "For a long time now."

"People gonna come to a place where there's no water?"

"Not if your livelihood depends on raising cattle and crops. That's why we're changing our ways. We use the water for drinking and bathing and such and not cattle and crops, we'll be fine. You know how damn much a cow drinks?" He laughed.

Archer nodded and took another sip of the Rebel and let it slide down his throat like lava over fresh dirt. "I guess I can see that," he replied.

"Look, where you coming in from?"

"A seven-hour slow, dusty bus ride from the east."

The banker squinted as he calculated. "That's a fair stretch of road, mister."

"I figure you for a banker type, but I'd like to be sure."

"Why, you looking to rob me?"

They all three had a laugh at that, but Archer's died out before the other two had finished guffawing.

Archer glanced at the woman, who was doing the tongue-on-lip thing again. She was in her late twenties with silky, dark hair in a Veronica Lake peekaboo. The sheet of hair fell off the side of her head like a waterfall at night, which contrasted sharply with her pale complexion. Archer could smell her scent across the span of the banker's cologne. It was spicy and warm and tapped something in him that prison had never inspired. She had on a tight, late-day, thunder-blue dress with a wide, deep neckline that revealed things she evidently wanted to reveal, and a black dog leash belt encircling her small waist. She had on white wrist-length gloves, and a matching narrow-brimmed hat with a small bow. Her heels were high enough to muscle her calves. She wore a small necklace with a rock of diamond in the center. She kept fingering it like she wanted to make sure it was still there.

Archer slowly drew his gaze away from her. "So you came here all those years ago and the town starts to make something of itself at the same time. Am I to imply a connection?"

The other man chuckled. "I like you. I like how you handle yourself."

"Man favors a compliment same as a woman," said Archer, tipping his hat at the lady.

"Fact is, I've been instrumental in putting Poca City on the map. Got my finger in all the pies worth anything. Saw its potential, you could say. And now that potential is being realized."

The man ran his gaze over Archer's long, broad-shouldered, muscular frame.

"You look like you can handle yourself just fine. Bet you were in the Army."

"I did my bit. About three years without ever seeing America once. Why?"

"A strong and brave man, then, who knows how to survive difficult circumstances. Which means you're just the hombre for me." He took out a wad of cash as big as any fist Archer had ever made in prison or seen coming his way.

The man trimmed five twenties off the pile and laid the bills on the bar within easy reach.

Archer made no move to pick them up.

"Well?" said the man.

"Fellow hands out cash like that, something's expected. I'm just waiting on details."

The man guffawed again and slapped Archer on the shoulder a bit harder than was necessary. He immediately grimaced and shook out his hand.

"Damn, you made of rock or what, soldier?"

"Or what," said Archer.

"I like to pay for potential. And I trust my instincts. Maybe we can do some business."

Archer still did not pick up the money. He finished the last finger of his drink and set it down. He said nothing and neither did the man, for a bit.

All around them gazes flitted to this little group and then away. Maybe it was the money in plain sight. Maybe it was something of a visceral nature between the two men, with the woman hanging on as the lovely sidekick to whatever was going on here.

The man took his time removing a cigar from his pocket, efficiently slitting the cellophane band with a switchblade, trimmed the end with the same tool, put the knife away, dropped the cellophane on the bar—the bartender swept it up—and then he lit the cigar with a platinum lighter. He puffed luxuriously on the stogie a couple times until it was drawing properly, put the lighter away, and eyed Archer, who'd been watching the deliberateness of the man's actions with fascination.

The man held up the smoke and said, "This here's from Cuba. Finest in the world. I like all my things that way."

Archer glanced once more at the woman. "I can see that."

"Now to business. You can do a job for me. That money there will be your payment."

"I'm listening."

"A man owes me something. I'd like you to collect it for me."

"What man and what something?"

"His name is Lucas Tuttle. Lives down the road a ways. And the something is his Cadillac."

"Why does he owe that to you?"

"I made him a loan and he failed to repay it. The Caddy's the collateral."

"Maybe he forgot. These things happen."

The man pointed to the cash. "Hundred dollars. Take it or leave it."

He tapped his ash free right on the wood grain of the bar. The skinny bartender once more swooped in and cleared the mess with a cloth.

Archer snagged an ashtray from in front of

the big farmer who was draining highballs at an alarming rate. He placed it right under the fellow's stogie, drawing a sneer from the banker man.

Archer said, "I have to know some more. Like, how do I know he owes you anything? I go there and take his car, that's stealing. You go to the joint for that in a heartbeat. You understand me? So I need to know if you're giving me a bum steer or what."

The man nodded appreciatively. "I like a man who's cautious. I'm one myself." He glanced at his lady. "Am I not cautious, Jackie?" He gave her right buttock a hard squeeze that made her wince a bit and then removed his hand.

The creature named Jackie glanced at Archer, maybe to show she still counted for something here, and then dutifully turned her attention to her man before saying, "Cautious as a young woman with a drunken man in close proximity." Her voice was surprisingly husky and assured. It starkly emboldened every fantasy of her Archer was holding.

The man perched his cigar on the ashtray and pulled something from his pocket. It was a mess of wrinkled papers. He unfolded and straightened them out, placing them on the bar. On the pages was a swath of tiny, printed writing.

"This is a promissory note. For five thousand dollars. See, this is the amount I loaned Tuttle. In good faith and everything. Man needed the money and he came to me. I loaned him the cash from my own pocket. You can see the amount here and his signature there. Now, on this page." He flipped through to a second one. "This is the security that I required for the loan and which he provided. You read your way right down there." He paused. "Hold on, you *can* read, can't you? Things might not work out between us if you can't."

"I can read," said Archer, with a touch of impatience because he was feeling it. "Even did two years of college before the war came calling."

He caught the woman's eye on this. She seemed to be calculating him in a new and maybe more favorable light.

He ran his eye over the paper.

"Nineteen forty-seven Cadillac Series 62 sedan painted dark green. And the license plate number is listed."

The man pointed to the page. "That's right. *That's* the collateral for the loan that was not repaid. That's what I want you to get for me."

Archer scratched his chin. "Okay, got a question."

"Shoot."

"Nothing personal, but how do I know he didn't repay you?"

"Now you're thinking. I like that. Well, here's how. If the man had paid the loan, this note would be returned to him. Fact that I still got it shows that never happened. Tuttle's a smart man and he'd never have let his money go without getting this in return. See, this is same as cash money, mister. Same as those five twenties right there. And you see the date the loan was due." He shuffled back to the first page and stabbed at a line with his finger. "Right there. You read that. Go on."

Archer did so, doing the numbers in his head. "That date's exactly two months ago yesterday."

"That's right."

"Got me another question."

"You like your questions," said the man, and Jackie giggled.

"How come it's two months past due, and you don't have the money or the Caddy yet? You don't strike me as a man overly full of generosity."

The man looked at Jackie. "This gent is a keeper, Jackie, I'm telling you."

Jackie commenced shooting admiring glances Archer's way and giggled once more.

"She your wife?" asked Archer, though he saw no ring on her.

"I got me a wife, but she ain't it," said the man offhandedly.

Jackie's giggle died in her throat as she glanced, embarrassed, at Archer. She took a sip of her gator bog drink and said, "There's no need to be like that."

The man glanced at her, a look on his mug that Archer had seen many times before on gents, especially in bars, and one he had never once liked.

"Did I ask for your opinion, sweet cheeks?"

"Well, no, but—"

His hand shot out, gripped her wrist, and squeezed. "Then keep it to your goddamn self, you hear me?"

Archer tensed and was about to jerk the man's hand off her, when he caught a look from Jackie that silently pleaded with him to do no such thing. Archer relaxed back against the bar as the fellow gave Jackie's wrist one more grind and then flung her hand away as he drilled her with a look of quiet satisfaction. "Just so we understand each other, honey." He turned back to Archer like nothing had just happened.

"So?" asked Archer expectantly, masking his anger.

"The truth is I've *tried* to collect on this debt, only Mr. Tuttle is not amenable to honoring the debt."

"And how many men have you paid a hundred dollars to try for you?"

"Well, I will concede that you are not the first. The exact number I prefer to keep private. But I will say that Lucas Tuttle is not a man you want to crowd."

"And suppose I try and fail? Do I keep the money?"

"Depends on the effort expended. I mean, you can't just waltz on down the road and make a feeble attempt at obtaining my collateral and then expect to get the cash, now can you?"

"I don't expect so, no. Then, you would be the judge of that?"

"I would be, but I'm a reasonable man. Wouldn't be in business for long if I weren't."

"And if I failed your expectations, I'd have to give this back?"

"Well, the fact of the matter is, soldier, till you deliver me the car or show me the efforts you undertook to my reasonable satisfaction, you don't walk out of here with that money. I just put it there as what they call an inducement."

"Supposing I have expenses in gaining back

your collateral? How am I to pay for them with nothing up front? You see my problem?"

"What sort of expenses?"

"Till I see the lay of the land and this Mr. Tuttle in particular, how should I know?"

The man looked warily at Archer, then at the money, and then back at Archer.

"You're the first one to lay out that issue."

"Well, I'm looking ahead. Maybe I get this done for you, there's more opportunity for me in Poca City, like you said."

"How much front money are we talking about then?" asked the man warily.

"I'd say two Jacksons would do amply."

The man picked up a pair of bills and handed them to him. "I'm placing my faith in you. Now, see here, what's your name, soldier?"

"Aloysius Archer."

"That's a heckuva name. You go by your Christian name, son?"

Archer shook his head. "Too hard to spell and most folks can't pronounce it. I go by Archer."

The man put out his hand. "I'm Hank, Hank Pittleman."

"Well, Mr. Pittleman, let me see what I can do. Now, if I get the car for you, doesn't that mean he gets that paper you showed me marked paid? So, do I need to take that with me?"

Pittleman smiled, took a long puff on his stogie, and shook his head. "Oh, no. That's not how this works, Archer."

Squinting through the man's wispy curtain of cigar smoke, Archer said, "Well, tell me how it does work then."

"Like your expenses, how can I know what I'm gonna get for a 1947 Cadillac? I *might* get five thousand for it, though I sure as hell doubt it. I was crazy in the head for not asking for more collateral." He glanced here at Jackie. "Maybe my heart is just too soft. The point is, Archer, even if a miracle happened and I got some poor sucker to fork over five grand for the Caddy, the debt still isn't paid in full because there's interest on top. I got to make a profit on my money. You see that, don't you? Money neither is nor should be free."

"I always like to make a profit off my money too." He rubbed his fingers over the twenties.

"Say I sell the Caddy for three thousand, then Tuttle still owes me another two thousand plus interest, plus my incidental costs of collection." He tapped the pile of twenties. "Like this. Adds up."

"Mr. Tuttle has dug himself one deep hole."

A smile creased Pittleman's face. "Hell, I didn't make him take my money, did I?"

"You have his address, and directions there? I don't know the area."

Pittleman took out a thick pencil and wrote something down on a bar napkin and slid it over to Archer. "When do you expect to do this then?" he asked, pocketing the pencil.

"Soon."

"What does soon mean?"

"Pretty soon."

He put the twenties in his jacket pocket.

Pittleman watched this move. "Now, so you know, I have technically just made a loan to you. Though not a scrap of paper has passed between us to legally memorialize that arrangement. But my money has long strings attached. Same as Tuttle's. And I demand honesty and integrity in my associates. Expect the same of myself."

"Well, I aim to deliver both, Mr. Pittleman."

In response, Pittleman drew the switchblade from his coat pocket once more, sprung it open, and speared the remaining twenties lying there, pinning them to the wood of the bar. The knife quivered there like a pine tree in the wind.

"I'll hold you to that."

Archer didn't even look at the blade or the stabbed twenties. "Now, where can I reach you most times?"

"Right here at this time will do, every day except Saturday and the Sabbath."

"And then you'll be at worship?"

"No, then I'll be with my dear, beloved wife."

Pittleman suddenly clutched his head and grimaced in pain.

"Hey, you okay?" asked Archer, gripping him by the shoulder.

"Must be all this cheap hooch."

Recovered, Pittleman unpinned his knife and thrust it back inside his pocket after closing it. "I trust I will hear good news from you, Archer."

Archer tipped his hat first to Jackie and then to Pittleman.

"I will do my best."

"For *me* you will, you mean?"

"Well, can you see it any other way?"

Archer headed to the door while most of those at the bar, and Pittleman and Jackie in particular, watched him go.

He was no longer shuffling. He was walking upright, springy and brisk, like any free man with serious folding money in his pocket would.

CHAPTER

4

IT WAS FIVE MINUTES before nine in the morning. The sun was scaling the sky, which was a dazzling blue without a single cloud marring its surface. As Archer stood there on the pavement, looking up, he had started to doubt that cumulus was even allowed here.

Then he lowered his gaze and turned it to the Poca City Courts and Municipality Building. Done in the rococo style and also decidedly on the cheap, the structure was easily big enough for the unwieldy name chiseled across its imitation stone front that was bracketed by false spindle turrets and its middle filled in with even more curious architectural elements. It looked to Archer like it had been dropped from a fairy tale into their midst. A castle without a king or queen; he wondered what they had done with the moat.

Archer spat on his hand and wiped it through his hair before replacing his hat there. He had sink-washed his shirt, undershorts, and socks the night before, letting the breeze dry them fine. His worn and dusty Oxfords had been spit-polished. He'd even found an iron at the hotel, and for a nickel's worth of rental time had done the best he could on his suit and shirt; he'd even given his slender tie a few passes. He'd stopped by a barbershop and splurged for a shave overseen by a tiny, wrinkled black man with no teeth, who wielded his strap and razor like a musketeer. His jaw and chin had never been this smooth since he'd dropped from the womb.

He was as smart-looking as he was ever likely to be, he figured.

The lobby had marble floor tiles in swirls of emerald green and fat columns holding up a ceiling with murals depicting things close to the musical infants stuck in the fountain, just with more color and poorer taste. He quickly found the proper department, emblazoned as it was on a black-backed directory, in a lobby that was full of strays looking for direction, as he was.

The elevator was a grill-door operation, which

Archer still did not cotton to. So he walked two floors up and headed down the hall counting office numbers as he went. He neared the sheriff's haunts and also that of the tax revenue bureau. A uniformed man in his fifties came out of the former's door as he passed by and gave Archer the once-over. He had on a big Stetson hat, a Colt long-barreled revolver in a waist holster, and sported a gut that one would see coming around the corner before one did its owner. Pinned to his broad chest was a shiny pointed star.

"Where you headed, son?"

"Parole Office," said Archer.

The man's eyes gleamed with condescension. "Carderock?"

Archer nodded, fingering his hat.

"Ernestine Crabtree's the parole officer," said the man.

"That's what my paper says."

"She's a damn fine-looking woman." The man tongued his lips and his eyes tightened and his nostrils flared. "Damn fine."

"Okay," said Archer.

"But she don't mess with your kind, son."

"I'm not looking to mess with anyone, least of all my parole officer."

"She likes men with badges," he said, pointing

to his own. "You tell her Deputy Sheriff Willie Free says hello."

"Will do, Sheriff Free."

Archer watched the man saunter down the hall before he turned and walked on.

The door was half-frosted glass above, transom over that, stained and scraped pine down below.

Engraved across the glass was: PAROLE OFFICE: ERNESTINE J. CRABTREE.

Archer drew a calming breath and wondered what the next few minutes would hold for him. He gripped the knob and pushed the door open.

The room inside was small. Varnished parquetry floor, walls painted white, whirly fan going above, the smell of cigarette smoke enticingly lingered as did a trail of its vapor in the air. Well, this place had the bus beat by a mile just on the tobacco issue, he thought. There was a hat tree in the corner from which dangled a woman's trim, green pillbox hat.

He closed the door behind him, glanced down at the floor, and saw the piece of folded paper that apparently had been slipped under the door. He bent down and picked it up.

He read the words on the page. They were crude and mostly misspelled. And they were all of a sexual and violent nature directed at Ernestine Crabtree.

Archer's mouth curled in disgust as he scrunched up the paper and put it in his pocket.

A plain wooden desk sat in the middle of the room, a straight back chair not built for comfort was lined up behind it and perched in the kneehole, and a weighty and ponderous, dull gray Royal typewriter dominated the top of the desk, with a preprinted form wound into it. A pulled-out leaf was on the left side of the desk and had several files on it. A blue fountain pen lay in its cradle, its brass nib sparkling from the overhead light.

Archer ducked down to take a look at the page in progress. It looked official, and the typed comments on another poor parolee soul held phrases like, "unacceptable attitude," "overly aggressive," and "devious." He looked for the name of the person she was reporting about, but it must have been on another page.

A fat black phone sat to the right of the typewriter, its cord snaking into the kneehole. Next to the phone was a speckled glass ashtray, with a spent, unfiltered butt lingering, and a chrome lighter parallel to it.

He twirled his hat and waited, until the clock on the wall overhead hit nine a.m.

The door he'd come through opened and there stood, apparently, Miss Ernestine J. Crabtree.

His first thought was she looked nothing like her name. His second impression was the name did her justice just fine.

She was around his age more or less and tall for a woman, about five-eight barefoot, he estimated. She wore a black skirt that stopped below the knee and was flared out by a petti- coat underneath that widened her hips, and a white blouse with ruffles down the front and a schoolmarm Peter Pan collar.

Despite the fullness of the skirt, he could gauge her figure, which was shapely, perhaps more than that now that he thought about it. She had on flesh-colored stockings—and no doubt the seams would be lined up perfectly in back—and grim, low-heeled pumps. Her blond hair was done up in so tight a bun that it pulled at her face. Her chin was sharply defined, the cheeks nicely formed and riding high, the lips full, with not a trace of lipstick, which he'd already figured on because there had been none on the cigarette end. Behind black shell glasses, her eyes were blue and wide, the irises plump, with the overall effect being what he thought some might call *vivacious*. At least they held the potential if she let her hair down, in more ways than one. All in all, quite a looker, he concluded. And then he thought about the sick note residing in his pocket and he stopped thinking about the woman in that way.

Her countenance *did* fit her name, he concluded. It was a slab of granite with nothing behind it. The baby blue eyes, now that he studied them again, seemed bound to the surface of the fleshy sockets only. It was a cold and untrusting face peering back at him.

"You are Mr. Archer?" she said, coming forward after shutting the door.

"Yes, ma'am, I am."

"I am Ernestine Crabtree."

"I figured, from the name on the door." He put out his hand. "Been here a couple of minutes."

She did not return the gesture. "Then you're two minutes early."

"I guess my watch has the runs."

The granite only deepened a notch at his poor joke.

"Let's get down to it then," she said sharply.

She motioned to a chair set against the wall. "Pull that up across from the desk," she commanded as she sat down in front of the typewriter, her back straight as a two-by-four.

She spun out the page in there and rolled in a fresh sheet with a few firm cranks of the wheel as he sat down across from her, his legs splayed wide, his hat dangling in one hand.

"Full name?"

"Aloysius Archer."

"Middle name?"

"Never had one."

"Really?" she said incredulously.

"I think they believed one name was good enough, and certainly Aloysius might, under some circumstances, be quite as good as two names."

She stared at him for a long moment with what he thought were lips fighting to become a smile. In the end, the granite won out.

She asked for more personal information, which he readily gave, and that Crabtree promptly typed on the form.

"You have your parole papers?"

He presented the pages and she dutifully looked over them.

"I trust you have studied your list of dos and don'ts?"

"Yes ma'am."

"And you have adhered to these instructions since leaving prison?"

"Yes ma'am."

"No drinking, no carousing?"

"And no women, loose or otherwise."

She looked up from the papers. "I think you're taking this matter far too frivolously, Mr. Archer. This is a serious business."

"I can guarantee you that I'm giving it a lot of weight, ma'am. I don't want to go back to prison. That life is not for me. It was worse than fighting in the war, and that's saying something."

The granite receded a bit, as she seemed pleased by his candid admission. "That's the proper attitude." She used a rubber stamp to imprint the seal of her office across the top of the first page and placed her initials and the date on a line provided by the stamp and passed the pages back to him.

"A fellow I met in the hall asked me to say hello to you," he said.

She glanced up at him. "What fellow?"

"Willie Free. He's with the law."

Archer watched closely for her reaction. She did not smile; instead the woman grimaced. That told him a lot, maybe that he had already suspected from the way Free had looked and talked about her.

She cleared her throat. "I have some job interviews for you to go on. Gainful employment is absolutely vital to achieving your goal of never returning to prison."

"Thing is, I already have a job."

Her fingers paused over the drawer she was about to open.

"Excuse me?"

"I had an interview with a gent last night. He hired me."

"To do what, exactly?"

"Man's in the business of loaning money. He hired me to collect a debt he's owed."

"This is highly irregular. I'm not sure—"

He pulled the two twenties from his pocket and held the bills up. "He already gave me an advance."

She eyed the cash, her eyes widening a bit. "That's a lot of money just for an advance. What do you get when you complete the job?"

"Another sixty dollars."

A moment of silence passed as Archer slowly put the money away. When he looked up, the woman seemed to be appraising him in a different light.

"All right, but if that position does not work out, you will be required to go on three job interviews in the next week. And have gainful employment by that time. There's plenty of work here if you apply yourself."

"Fine, but let's hope it doesn't come to that."

"You'll need to report in once a week for the next two months. If your progress is satisfactory, the visits can fall back to once a month, though I can perform spot checks on you at my discretion."

"I'm in Room 610 at the Derby Hotel. You're welcome anytime."

Her frown deepened. "I'm readily aware that you're staying at the Derby Hotel as that is where all parolees go initially. But I will *not* be visiting you in your room there. This is a professional relationship. I'm sure you can appreciate that."

"Sorry, ma'am. No offense. And I do appreciate that."

"When you do change your place of residence you are required to immediately notify me of same, do you understand?"

"You'll be the first to know."

"I need you to sign this form evidencing that you were here today. I'll place it in your file and communicate the fact of your attendance to the proper authorities. And I'll see you in a week's time." She held up the pen.

"Right." He stood, came around to her side of the desk, took the pen, and signed the document. He took a moment to breathe in her scent, which, frankly, intrigued him far more than Jackie's had the prior night. Then he thought of the misspelled note and the repulsive comments, and the cocksure manner of Deputy Sheriff Willie Free, and he quickly straightened and laid down the pen.

"Um, you can't spare a smoke, can you?" he asked.

She glanced at the ashtray and appeared to bristle a bit.

"No, I can't. It's against the rules for me to provide that sort of thing to parolees under my jurisdiction. It could be viewed as improper."

"That's okay. Someone told me they were bad for you anyway."

She gave him a condescending look. "Really, Mr. Archer, I highly doubt that if cigarettes were really bad for you the companies making them would continue to do so."

"Well, I guess that's the difference in our thinking."

She looked startled again by his words. "How do you mean?"

"My way of looking at the world is that some folks do what they want, and they don't care what happens to others, so long as it's good for them."

"I try to be more optimistic."

He twirled his hat between his fingers. "See you in a week, Miss Crabtree."

She returned to her typing and started clacking

away. He walked to the door and looked back in time to see her watching him.

"Hope you're saying good things about me."

"Good-bye, Mr. Archer."

She immediately went back to her typing.

As Archer was coming down the front steps of the Courts and Municipality Building, he saw on the street someone he recognized. Archer would have kept walking, but the man saw him, too.

"Archer, by God, tell me it ain't you and I still won't believe it. What a damn sight for sore eyes. So, you're out then?"

The speaker was short and reedy with a neck too long for his body, and an Adam's apple the size of a ripe peach. He was in his late forties, and his hair was graying rapidly and thinning even faster. His sideburns were long and curled inward at the bottom. Physically unimposing, he still seemed to take up more space on earth than his stature warranted.

"Dickie Dill," said Archer, reluctantly coming over to him. "Never expected to see your mug again."

Dill put out a thin hand with fingers like little scythe blades. Archer had seen those same hands wrap around the neck of a fellow inmate who was three times Dill's size and come close to strangling the life out of him. It took four guards to pull the little man off the far larger one. After that, prisoners and guards at Carderock Prison let Dickie Dill be.

Archer had thankfully never had a beef with the man, but there was something about Dill that just struck him as peculiar enough to be avoided if possible.

The men shook hands.

"Hellfire, boy, I think we all come through Poca. Been here three months now. Ain't too bad."

"Yeah, wondered what happened to you."

"Got me out and I'll be staying out this time. Third time's the charm, they say. I'll kill a man to keep from going back if I have to." He cracked his knuckles and gave Archer a look that made him conclude that Dickie Dill ever *not* being behind bars was not a good thing for the rest of humanity.

He wore faded dungarees and what looked to be a homespun shirt tucked in with dusty brogans on his feet. His belt was a length of braided rope, and his old porkpie hat was creased, worn, and stained. The few teeth he had were displayed in a perpetual snarl.

"You checking in with Miss Crabtree, were you?" asked Dill, eyeing the building behind them. "I was in there not mor'n half hour ago. She's a looker all right, but a cold fish. Gal needs a man to warm her up."

Archer briefly wondered if Dill was the subject of the comments on the page in the typewriter. He could see all of them fairly applying. He put his hand in his pocket and felt the balled-up note. And was Dill also the author of that? Archer could see that being the case, too, particularly given the violence and misspellings.

"Just finished up. A woman as a parole officer? What's her story anyway?"

"Ain't you never heard of Carson Crabtree?"

"Doesn't ring any bells. Guess he's related?"

"Her daddy."

"Okay, everybody's got a daddy."

"Yeah, but Carson Crabtree done killed three people down in Texas, oh, been more than a dozen years gone by now."

Archer processed this. "Three people. What for?"

"Man was just mean. They 'lectrocuted his ass."

"Being mean doesn't sound like enough reason to murder three people."

Dill thumped his thumb against his temple. "Touched in the head, more like. You know, crazy, I 'spose. To kill a man you got to be, or else he done you a wrong and you're just settlin' matters. Not a damn thing wrong with that and I got experience that way."

"Not sure the law would agree with that, Dickie."

"That's your goddamn problem, Archer, you think rules is all there is."

"More or less what the Army taught me."

"Hellfire, boy, you ain't in uniform no more. Live life and kick you some ass now and then."

Archer looked thoughtful as he glanced back at the steps he'd just come down. "Maybe Miss Crabtree is overcompensating then." He said this more to himself than Dill.

"Come again?" said Dill, eyes twitching and his sideburns doing the same. "What's that mean?"

"Her father was a criminal, so now she's working to help other criminals turn away from their bad ways."

"Oh, right, I see. Hey, I'm thinking 'bout maybe having a go at her. Like I said, gal needs a man to tell her what's what."

Archer emphatically shook his head. "You do not want to do that, Dickie, trust me."

"Why not? I think she might cotton to me after a while."

"You do anything, touch one hair on her head,

say one word out of line, and they'll send your butt right back to Carderock, and you won't be getting out ever."

Dill eyed him funny, but there was alarm in the man's eyes, too.

"You sure 'bout that?"

"Damn sure, Dickie. Don't try it. Promise me now. I'm looking out for you."

"Oh, all right then. I promise. Thanks for the advice, Archer."

"You working?"

"Yeah, got me a job at the slaughterhouse. Would be there already 'cept I had my talk with Miss Crabtree and then lined my belly over at a diner. Truck's gonna take me out now."

"What's it you do there?"

Dill grinned ferociously. "Kill the dang hogs."

"How do you do that?"

"Smack 'em in the head with a sledgehammer." He pointed to a spot on his own skull. "Right about here. They don't feel no pain. Less I don't kill 'em with the first pop. I try to, though. Hell, man, you know how much pork this here country eats?"

"Never gave it a minute's thought."

"A lot. Bacon and sausage and something called cutlets. Me, I can't stomach it. I'm up to my ass in blood and hog brains all day long.

Gets to you after a while. But it pays good. Got dollars in my pocket. Got three other ex-cons from Carderock working there."

"Miss Crabtree's suggestion?"

"Yep. Got the job same day. They need skull crushers. I don't mind it. I mean, somebody's got to do it, if you want your bacon, right?"

"Where are you living?"

"Little room over the mercantile on the west side of town, bath and shower down the hall. Dollar a day. You?"

"The Derby. But I'll be moving, I 'spect."

"Yeah, I started out there, too. Guess we all do, but then I moved on. Can't afford the damn Derby. *You* working yet?"

Archer hesitated. "Looking around. You know a man name of Hank Pittleman?"

"Pittleman? Yeah, heard 'a him. He's some big wheel around town."

"Saw him coming out of a place called the Cat's Meow last night and we struck up a conversation."

Dill's face scrunched up like a frost-bit flower. "You listen up, Archer. Don't you go near that place."

"Well, I know we're not supposed to."

"No, what I mean is they check for our kind there, boy."

"Come again?"

"They got, what you call, *plants* in there. They look for ex-cons breaking parole there. It's a temptation, like. Send your ass right back to prison in a heartbeat, same as you just now told me if I messed with Ernestine Crabtree."

Archer's features remained inscrutable. "Is that right? Well, thanks for the warning. Won't catch me in there." Yet Archer wondered if he already had been caught. But then wouldn't Crabtree have mentioned it?

"Sure thing. Hey, maybe we ought to get together some time."

Archer shook his head. "No can do, Dickie."

"Huh, why's that?"

"Rule Number 2."

"Come again?"

"Rule Number 2 on our parole list. You can't be hanging around with other ex-cons. Didn't you read the papers?"

Dill looked chagrined. "Well, reading ain't never been my strong suit, boy."

"They had a book depository at Carderock."

"Book depository, what's that then?"

"Like a library."

"Ain't nobody told me about that. But then again, I don't much like books."

Archer nodded. "Well, good luck," he said, without any enthusiasm.

He left Dill there and walked off into the sunshine with forty dollars in his pocket and the rest of the day to figure out.

CHAPTER

5

POCA CITY HAD A REASONABLE NUMBER of distractions fraught with legal and other peril; however, Archer managed to avoid them all that day. He wasn't sure about the next day, though. His natural defenses *did* have their limits. And when he was presented squarely with choices of right and wrong, Archer could be reasonably counted on to miss the angel's cue about 20 percent of the time on a good day. But then again, he had been truthful with Ernestine Crabtree—he did not want to return to prison.

He mostly walked the pavements, halting to eat a ham and cheese sandwich for his lunch outside while sitting on a turned-over box, and later an ice cream cone bought from a uniformed Good Humor man perched in his blue-and-white

truck. They jawed about matters both important and frivolous. He looked for but never saw
Miss Ernestine Crabtree with the murderous
father, though he kept a constant sight line on
the court building. He thought she might come
out to enjoy the sunshine and perhaps smoke
one or two, but that never happened. He didn't
know why he wanted this. He was not going
to have anything other than a professional relationship with the woman, but the note he'd
found and the lawman's leer and Dill's telling
him about the woman's violent past made him
curious about her.

His spending spree had cost him all of fifty
cents, with the twin Jacksons lying in the depths
of his pocket undiminished. He managed to
scrounge a cigarette off a passing stranger, and
he sat on a bench near the town square taking
his time whittling it down and watching all who
passed by in front of him. There was prosperity
in the air, comingling with those clearly in economic despair. But those on that woeful side of
the equation would no doubt work hard to get
to the "other side" with all due speed, rising
to the mountaintop to look down on others
scrambling madly for their piece of the pie.
And that, to Archer, was the fledgling American dream in a nutshell, particularly after a war

that had knocked the stuffing out of just about everyone.

Archer had good reason to soak in as much of Poca City as he possibly could. This would be his home, at least for the foreseeable future, and he had made friendly with as many folks as he could on his walking tour, at the same time foraging for information to the extent he could without raising their suspicions. He had learned that some had short fuses, and he was not looking to make enemies of any sort.

Like Dill, many had heard of Mr. Hank Pittleman, though the opinions of these folks varied greatly. He was either a devil or a benefactor, with not one commentator occupying the middle ground. Archer took in all this with a grain of salt and let it marinate as he smoked. Many had also heard of Lucas Tuttle. He was described as a farmer of fierce devotion to the soil and a provocateur of skilled debate. He was also a seasoned hunter, as comfortable with firearms as he was skewering, with his impressive vocabulary and agile wits, those who did not align with his points of view on myriad subjects. These ranged from local crop rotation theories to the efficacy of the Marshall Plan to the question of the gold standard versus all other benchmarks.

A curious combination and perhaps the ear-marks of a formidable person from whom to collect a debt. This was possibly why all efforts heretofore employed by Mr. Pittleman had suffered failure in their execution, with perhaps the stark *execution* of the poor debt collector having followed.

On this very point, Archer said to one man, wearing an aged Hoover collar, a greasy felt hat, and an intense expression, "Tell me something, has this man Tuttle ever killed anybody in a dispute?"

"Well," said the fellow, his teeth gnawing at his top lip. "If he has, it never reached a court of law. And that's a fact. For I am a member of the local bar and would be in a position to know of such."

"Would you reasonably expect that it would have *reached* a court of law?" Archer had per-sisted.

"I would expect that in Poca City, all results are possible, except for consistent rain and politi-cians who keep their promises. And a man with influence can achieve things unavailable to the *rabble*. I trust you recognize the both of us as part of that unfortunate clan, mister."

Archer could not doubt that the man spoke the bold truth.

After his smoke, Archer flicked a shard of tobacco off his tongue, made a decision, rose, and set out to the west at a steady pace, his long legs energetically eating up distance. He wanted to explore new territory. It was in his blood.

After he'd gotten out of the Army, someone had asked him if he was good, bad, or indifferent to having once been a person fighting a world war now consigned to a normal existence. Archer had answered that he was all of those things, or could be, depending on the opportunity.

"You mean the circumstance," the man had corrected.

"No, I think I got it right the first time," Archer had re-corrected.

And his thinking in Poca City had not been changed by recent events.

It led him to march out to the road he'd taken the prison stop bus in on and lift his thumb to the sky. In the Army, he'd often served as a scout, going ahead to see where the enemy might be and what sort of killing assets they might have. It was rough going and dangerous because he often found himself behind enemy lines outnumbered forty to one. But in his opinion, it was always better to know than not know. Which was why he was standing on a dusty road with a cloudless sky overhead and his thumb pointed to Heaven. Or at least in the kingdom's vicinity. Archer never seemed to know the exact location of God, because the fellow never seemed to stay still long enough to allow Archer to make his acquaintance.

The beanpole, ginger-haired farmer in the truck who stopped to pick him up made no inquiries other than to ask where Archer was headed. He told him, the man nodded, pointed to the rear, shifted his gears, and they set off. Archer rode in the back with a bale of hay and a baby goat curled up asleep on a pile of rags.

The air remained intensely dry. Archer had it on good authority from at least a half-dozen folks in town that Poca City saw rain about as often as one viewed a rich man in a soup line.

"You telling me it never rains here?" he'd asked one bright-eyed citizen.

"No, it does. But if you're asleep when it commences, there might not be any evidence of it remaining the next morning when you wake up and make inquiries."

"But don't they grow crops here?"

"Absolutely," the same gent had volunteered. "But just the kind that fertilizes itself on wind and dust, of which we have an abundance."

The ride took nearly an hour, and as soon as

he bid the farmer, the hay bale, and the still-sleeping baby goat adieu, Archer wondered how he was going to get back. But like most things, he decided he would tackle that when the time came and not before. He was a man who lived each moment as though it would surely be his last. War just did that to you. And prison had piled on that notion, forcing it bone deep into Archer. He figured he would never be free of it now.

He eyed the name on the mailbox that leaned toward the road, like it was giving an edge to the postman coming.

L. TUTTLE.

The farm stretched as far as Archer could see. He didn't know if that qualified it as a big farm or not; he was not versed in such matters. He'd grown up far from here, in a home of glass, brick, and vertical quality. Grass had not been included in the deal. There was not a cow that he knew of within twenty miles of his birthplace. Here, though, the bovines were everywhere, dotting the land like a foraging army bivouacked for a stretch till the time for fighting would come along.

He saw the gravel road that led out of sight and figured the home of L. Tuttle would be just along that way. He eyed the sky, and the sun told him it was now nearer to four than three. He checked his watch, although he trusted the sky more than he did his windup.

He saw dust kicking up in the distance: either a tornado, or a tractor working away. As he squinted, Archer could make out it was the latter. He took off his hat, slapped it against his pants leg to dispel the dust that clung to every bit of him, and headed up the road.

He'd been right; the one road branched off, like the sweep of a river, to three o'clock, and a quarter mile down this fork he saw the house and the outbuildings.

It occurred to him that Tuttle was a prosperous man, which made the matter of the debt more problematic, at least in his mind. But a promissory note signed, with collateral laid against it, was a serious thing, he was finding. While perhaps some would see it as a small issue, the fact was, if debts remained unpaid, whatever followed would genuinely be the collapse of civilization as any of them would know it, Archer included. And he and millions of others had just fought a world war to ensure that neither anarchy nor fascism nor anything else would replace the reasonable screwing over of people without money by those who possessed damn near all of it.

Archer had come back from the war feeling lucky to be alive. He had not come back to seek a fortune. He wanted his share, to be sure, but it constituted a small ambition, and would not move mountains or deprive others of theirs. He had undertaken a years-long, small detour due to a profound lack of judgment over a concern that he had no sooner deemed of little importance, when it rose up and smote him with the power of a king and his legions crossing the Rubicon. And that mistake had caused his ass to be dragged right to Carderock Prison.

His two years of college had included readings in ancient history. He didn't know that material would have applied so readily to him in the year 1949.

He picked up his pace as he went in search of Lucas Tuttle. He had a plan. Whether it would work or not was anyone's guess. But something tickled at the back of his head, same as when he was a scout looking first for Italians and later for Germans. He had found the Italians the far easier of the pair. They didn't really want to fight, he reckoned, because every time he'd run into some, they were either drunk or eating their dinner. He wasn't surprised they'd turned on Mussolini and stuck his head up on a pike. They probably wanted to simply get back to their pasta and bottles of wine and their women. The Germans, on the other hand, seemed to like killing about as much as Dickie Dill liked strangling folks or smashing hogs in the head just so till they died. Archer had never ventured to the Pacific Theater, but he'd heard the Japanese were worse than the Germans.

As he drew closer, he saw that the house was a large, neat, one-story made of stained plank siding, with quarry stone chimneys, plenty of windows, and a wide porch on which sat two rocking chairs. The thing looked well built, trim and tight as a drum. He supposed there was no dust inside.

He rapped on the single door with his knuckles. He could hear the footsteps coming. Something was about to happen. And you couldn't ask more from life than that.

CHAPTER

6

THE FRONT DOOR swung wide open in an inviting way, until the twin barrels of the Remington twelve-gauge over-under greeted Archer; they were aimed at his belly and he could see no easy way around that.

He looked at the fellow holding the advantage on him.

He was around fifty-five with about as interesting a face as Archer had ever beheld. The large head was topped by a great crown of white hair that toppled downward like a snow avalanche off a mountaintop. The tanned brow was thickly furrowed, and the chin was a V of bone, while the jutting jaw seemed a flesh-and-blood version of the over-under's muzzle. But what really caught his attention were the green eyes hovering in stark contrast to the tumble of white hair. They occupied their sockets with the intensity of twin machine guns in a bunker. The impression was mesmerizing and appalling to Archer all at the same time.

"Can I help you, mister?" the man said politely, belying the ominous threat held in his hands.

"Are you Mr. Lucas Tuttle?"

"What do you want, pray tell?" His benign look hardened several notches, the eyes now seemed an emerald fire. "And you might indeed want to start praying, son."

"Well, right now, all I want is some separation from me and that Remington."

"Oh, no. That may well be premature. State your business or your belly will grow quite familiar with the intrinsic purpose of this firearm."

"I was hired by Hank Pittleman to come here and relieve you of your 1947 dark green Cadillac sedan."

The machine gun eyes narrowed a bit. "You are not endearing yourself to me, stranger. You seem like a fine young man, though a bit rough around the edges. It would be a shame to end things for you right here and now."

"I had determined to come out here at night

when you were asleep and see if I could take back your Cadillac without you knowing. But then I decided to approach the matter on a more direct footing."

The muzzle lowered to a part of Archer's anatomy that was even more precious to him than his stomach.

"To answer your query, I *am* Lucas Tuttle, sir. Now explain yourself further, but you best tell me your full, legal name first. That way it can go on the tombstone properly."

"Aloysius Archer, but just call me Archer."

Tuttle looked him up and down with a practiced stare. "You're the right age. And you look like a tough cookie, for sure. Did you serve, Archer? Did you do your patriotic duty?"

Archer thought this an odd departure, but if it kept the man's mind off the Remington? "I did my bit. Over three years in Europe."

"Who under?"

"For most of the war, the Fifth Army, General Mark Clark. I was part of Second Corps, Thirty-Fourth Infantry Division."

"That was the Mediterranean Theater, was it not?"

"Yes, sir. Salerno, Bologna, Genoa, Milan, the Barbara, Volturno and Gustav Lines, Anzio Beach. Names I couldn't say before, and places

I never thought I'd be. And I truly have no desire to go back."

"That was some fierce fighting, I understand."

"You could say. The Fifth had over a hundred thousand casualties when all was said and done. Lost a lot of good men and good friends."

"Were you wounded, Archer, fighting?"

"Most everybody was wounded, Mr. Tuttle, and I was no exception."

"Your medals, sir? Did you distinguish yourself? Be detailed."

Now Archer's features set firm, like cement going from fluid to hard. "I killed folks I didn't know, because they were trying to kill me. I left the Army with metal inside me I didn't start out life with. I got a box of medals and ribbons somewhere, and they don't amount to a hill of beans now. That's my piece, so you can just pull the damn trigger if you got to and be done with it."

The muzzle dropped a shade lower but then held on Archer's knees.

"I like your spirit, Archer. What I do not understand is your alliance with that scoundrel Pittleman."

"I needed a job and he gave me one. A hundred dollars if I deliver the Cadillac to him.

He advanced me forty dollars with the rest to come on him getting that car."

"He has sent others before you."

"That I've heard."

"They came at night. They did not wish to face me."

Archer eyed the over-under. "I can see why they might have done it that way."

"Trespassing is a crime hereabouts, as it should be in every democratic union that holds property rights as sacred. Thus, I furnished them exactly what they deserved."

"Okay. I'm one who doesn't think property is worth a man's life, but that may just be me."

The emerald eyes blazed at this comment. "However, you, sir, show up in broad daylight and knock on my door and admit your mission to my face. Explain yourself."

"Pretty simple. I wanted you to tell me to *my* face whether you owe that debt or not."

"Why is that important to you?"

"Well, if you don't owe it, I have no further business here."

"And if I *do* owe the debt?"

Archer said nothing.

Tuttle appraised him, running his gaze from the top of the hat to the heels of the shoes.

"Come on inside, Archer, and let's talk."

He moved aside so Archer could enter and led him down a long, tiled hallway to a small, plainly furnished room with wood paneling and a plank floor with a colorful rug laid over it.

"Sit down over there," he said, motioning with his shotgun to a chair.

Tuttle took the chair opposite, his shotgun muzzle pointed to the floor.

"I borrowed the money from Hank Pittleman. I had need to do so at the time."

"Do you owe the man five thousand dollars plus interest?"

"Yes. And it's also true that I gave my 1947 Cadillac as collateral for that loan."

"Why'd you do that? Seems like you have a good deal of prosperity going on here."

"Prosperity sometimes does not equal folding money, Archer. And my suppliers do not barter in wishful thinking."

"So you owe the debt but won't pay it back?"

"Do you think life is that simple?"

"Life has never struck me as being simple unless you're determined to make it so."

"Pittleman has stolen from me. That is why I have not repaid the money."

"What's he taken from you?"

"Something far more precious than the sum of five thousand dollars."

"Can you be more specific?"

"He has taken my daughter."

That was a new one on Archer, and his face showed it to be so. "How's that exactly?"

"He has convinced my beautiful daughter that she should no longer be a part of her father's life. She has fallen in with his evil and sick ways. For all of her life, I saw her sweet face every day. Now, I have not seen her for over a year."

"How'd he do that?"

"By giving her things, Archer. By turning her head with materialistic offers. By introducing her to the shallow pleasures of his hedonistic lifestyle. And he treats her roughly, or so I have been told."

"What's her name?" Archer asked, though he was reasonably confident of the answer.

"Jackie."

"I've met her."

"Indeed? And she was no doubt in the company of this heathen."

"Then you won't pay back the debt because he's turned your daughter against you?"

"You said before that property is not worth a man's life. Well, why is a debt, though legally owed, more important than a father's love for his daughter?"

"And you said you hadn't seen her for over a year?"

"That is so."

"Well, why not try talking to her?"

"I can't, Archer. She refuses to see me."

"Why?"

"That is my business."

"When I saw her, she didn't act like she was being held against her will. And you're talking to a man who has seen that up close and personal."

Tuttle shook his head dismissively at this comment. "He has her trapped in a prison of the mind's making, Archer. Far stronger than steel bars with no predetermined release date, and no judge to whom to appeal."

Archer rubbed his chin, thinking about his sixty dollars. "Just to be clear, you have the money for the repayment?"

"I have, but not one penny will the man receive so long as my daughter remains absent from her home. I can only imagine the ways in which he has defiled her."

Archer glanced at the Remington. "I have to say I'm kind of surprised you haven't taken out your anger on him directly."

"And with what result, Archer? Do you think me a simpleton?"

"You want to explain that?"

"If I were to shoot that foul being, my freedom would be forfeited, if not my life. And if I did not succeed in killing him, he would sue me for all I have. Then, he would have not only my Jackie, but all my worldly possessions *and* the land that my father and his father before him have built into a tidy industry. Indeed, in the depths of my mind, I think it no coincidence that he has seduced my daughter in such a manner in the hopes that I would attempt to take out any murderous intentions I might have, just so he could confiscate it all."

"You're saying he planned all this?" Archer said skeptically.

"To me, the connection is as inevitable as the eastern rise of the sun on the rotation of the earth's axis."

"I understand from Mr. Pittleman that he's currently married."

"That is indeed the case."

"And his wife has no issue with her husband being with your daughter?"

"I think Marjorie Pittleman takes great issue, but her options are limited, seeing that he controls the purse strings."

"Hank Pittleman does seem to be the controlling type. And he does have a lot of money apparently."

Tuttle raised the over-under to its original position. "So, what are your current intentions?"

"Seems to me there's only one solution."

"What's that, I wonder, Archer?"

"If I can get your daughter to leave Pittleman, will you repay the loan?"

"And exactly how do you propose to do that?"

"You'll have to let me work through it."

"And then you'll be able to collect your commission?"

"About that, got a question."

"I'm listening, Archer."

"What's it worth to you, to have your daughter away from this man?"

Tuttle's features turned a shade darker and the pair of green eyes flamed with phosphorous intensity. "You would charge money to a father to free his daughter of an abomination?"

Archer sat forward and twirled his hat. "Look at it my way. From what you're telling me, Pittleman is not a man of his word. Now, suppose I get the loan repaid. Why do I think the forty dollars in my pocket will be the last cash I ever see from him? Don't get me wrong, I don't mind doing the right thing for the right thing's sake. Hell, I did that over in Italy and Germany.

But a man has to eat. And he has to have a roof over his head. You see my point?"

Tuttle's finger danced over the trigger of the Remington.

"How much then?"

"Let's make it sixty dollars. That way, I'll be made whole in case Pittleman doesn't come through. I think that's fair and square."

"But if he *does* come through, do I get a refund of my contribution to your economic stability?"

Archer rubbed at his cheek and glanced at the Remington. "Well, that would come under the title of risk, Mr. Tuttle. And a man has to be fairly compensated for accepting it."

"So, no refund then?"

"Honestly, no sir."

"I'll give you three days. Then I'll come looking for Pittleman *and* you."

"I'll be sure to hold you to that, sir."

It was an unexpected reply that made Tuttle fully lower his shotgun.

"Desiree here will show you out, Archer."

Archer turned to see a woman standing there as Tuttle passed by them both and disappeared down the hall.

Desiree was in her forties, medium height, bland, brown hair with black framed specs over dull eyes, but her facial features were etched in stone and she had an air of efficiency about her. She was dressed in a quiet gray jacket and skirt and black pumps with heels sharp enough to pierce his skull. A small string of fake pearls lay against her light blue blouse.

"Mr. Archer," she said, putting out a hand. He rose and shook it. "This way, sir."

As they walked along Archer said, "So what is it that you do here, ma'am?"

"I assist Mr. Tuttle as his secretary."

"He seems like a real sweetheart, when he's not pointing his shotgun at my privates."

"It pays well, and it requires little interaction with anything other than my typewriter."

"You know Jackie Tuttle?"

"I knew her when she was here, yes."

"I met her in town last night. She was with Hank Pittleman."

The eyes behind the lenses swelled a bit. "I expect she was."

"Mr. Tuttle wants her back. He doesn't want her with Pittleman."

"I am well aware of that."

"I bet you are. So, if you don't mind my asking, why'd she leave home?"

"I *do* mind you asking."

"Well, to explain things, Mr. Tuttle wants me

to convince Jackie to leave Pittleman. If I knew a little more about the situation, I might be able to accomplish that."

Desiree stopped and looked up at him. "And bring her back here?"

"I never said I would bring her back here. I just said I'd try to get her to leave Pittleman. I mean, he's married and all anyway. Doesn't seem right."

"How refreshingly moral of you, Mr. Archer."

"You can drop the mister. I'm just Archer."

"All right, Archer. I appreciate your honesty and frankness. The fact is Jackie never told me why she was leaving. Though it was around the time her mother died."

"What was her name?"

"Isabel."

"Pretty name. What's that, Spanish?"

"She was from Brazil. Mr. Tuttle traveled there for business when he was younger, and they met. They married and came back here, where they had Miss Tuttle."

"Was Isabel sick? Is that how she died?"

"No. She died in an accident."

"Sorry to hear that. What kinda accident?"

"It was just a horrible, horrible accident. I'll leave it at that."

"Were she and Jackie close?"

"Isabel adored her daughter and that adoration was returned."

"Maybe that's why she left. Because she was so heartbroken about her mother."

Desiree looked at him funny and said, "I'm sure that was part of it." She hesitated. "Would you like to see a picture of Isabel?"

"Sure."

Desiree led him down another hall and opened a door into a large and comfortable sitting room with several oval windows that looked out onto the stark fields behind the house.

Archer took it all in. Big, solid furniture, colorful rug on the Spanish tile floor, paintings on the wall depicting countryside and wildlife, and a stone fireplace that rose to the ceiling. A mantel of petrified wood fronted the stone with a framed photo on it.

"Mr. Tuttle sure has nice things," he noted.

"He's had his ups and downs, but now things are looking up."

Archer didn't think the woman sounded too happy about that.

"This is Isabel."

Desiree had lifted the framed photo off the mantel and held it out to him.

Archer gripped the frame and stared at the woman in the snapshot. She was dark-haired

and olive-skinned, and Archer could not remember seeing a lovelier countenance. It wasn't
just the beautiful features, it was the spark of
life in the eyes that made his own pair seem dull
and unresponsive by comparison.

"So she died about a year ago? That's when
Mr. Tuttle said Jackie had left home."

"Yes, that's right."

She took the photo from him and replaced it
on the mantel.

Twirling his hat, Archer said, "Why'd you really
bring me in here and show me that picture?"

"I just thought you'd like to see Miss Tuttle's
mother."

"Okay," said Archer. "And I'm Harry Truman."

She looked him up and down. "I thought
Truman was older and shorter."

He fiddled with his hat some more. "What do
you think about Mr. Tuttle wanting her to come
back home?"

"I haven't thought about it."

"And if you did?"

"She's a grown woman. She should be able to
make her own decisions."

"What sort of accident again?"

"I told you that—"

"I know Jackie and I like her, and I was just
wondering, that's all."

"Well, I don't really know all the details. Just that it was very tragic. Now, I have some dictation to type up. I'll show you out."

"I can find my own way, thanks. You should probably get to your typewriter. Don't want Tuttle pointing his shotgun at you because you got behind in your typing. It's a little unsettling."

Archer left the tidy house, put on his hat, and wondered what the hell all that had been about.

CHAPTER

7

A HITCHED RIDE BACK with a mother and her bucktoothed, runny-nosed son in a dented Studebaker, with no wheel caps and a rattling sound that signaled the engine was close to throwing a rod, brought Archer to Poca City before the dinner hour. He used the down-the-hall shower to clean off the dust and put his only clothes back on. He set off now to do something about that wardrobe predicament. His long legs took him down the street to a haberdashery about three blocks from his hotel that he had passed on his earlier ramblings.

The old gent in there seemed to be thinking about closing up for the day and contemplating his dinner when Archer strolled in.

"Need some fresh duds," he said.

The fellow was dressed like a walking bill-board for his line of business, down to the cufflinks and the pocket square aligned with an engineer's precision. "I can sure see that, young man. What can I do you for?"

"To start, let's get a copy of what I got on now, only better."

"Well, that's fine, since I only got better. But can I see your money first? Just a common courtesy from folks I don't know, is all. This is a respectable establishment."

"I deal with no other kind."

The show of the twin twenties was all it took to capture the man's undivided interest. And it took only an hour to complete the selling and buying. With Archer's physique and height, nothing needed to be altered, and the man had his girl cuff both pairs of pants on her sewing machine right then and there.

"That's a damn sight miracle," said the man of the fine fit. It was a single-breasted Hart, Schaffner & Marx model of a medium blue color with narrow pinstripes. His wide-knotted tie was a bloodred, and the command collar on his Alden dress shirt softened the thickness of his neck. The leather belt holding up his pants was black and braided.

"I like the hat," said Archer as he peered in

the mirror at his new felt snap-brim with a dented crown and a burgundy silk band. He had bypassed the recommendation of a rabbit hair trilby headpiece. His white pocket square had a two-point fold.

"Shoes good? Those wingtips are the very finest leather. You'll need to keep them conditioned and shined regularly."

"I'll break 'em in."

The man handed him a bag and a hanger with the extra pair of slacks on them. "Two pairs of underwear, same number of socks. And the extra pair of trousers, pleated and cuffed."

"Right," said Archer. "I'm good to go."

His Jacksons had been drastically reduced, although Archer had been surprised that he'd been able to afford the new clothes and shoes for less than forty dollars. The man told him he hadn't been open that long and was looking to build up his business and thus was giving Archer a deal.

"You look fine in the new duds, so talk my place up to everybody, you hear me?" said the man, and Archer promised that he would. He walked out the door wearing his new clothes. The girl had put his old suit, shirt, and shoes in another bag.

He dropped all this off at the Derby, hung up

his old things and new spare pants, and headed out to eat some dinner. The restaurant was named the Checkered Past. Whoever had come up with the names of the places here had a sense of humor, Archer would grant them that.

The sign out front promised steaks and fat potatoes at good prices and coffee until midnight. He entered and took his seat at a table with a red-and-white-checkered cloth covering it and matching napkins. He ordered his steak rare and his coffee piping hot, and afterward sampled the peach cobbler, which was good, the best he'd ever had perhaps. He laid down his coins for the meal, and then plotted out his next steps on the way back to the Derby.

He got up the next morning, cleaned up in the bath down the hall, and headed down to the front desk. "You know where Hank Pittleman has his house?"

The clerk, the same gent who had checked him in the first night, scratched his furry forearms and said, "Why you want to know that?"

"Have business with the man and he told me he spends Saturday and the Sabbath at his home with his wife."

"Well?"

"I need a way to get out there."

"Can always walk."

"How far is it?"

"Take you a good four hours."

"Any way I can hitch a ride with somebody?"

The man stroked his chin and looked Archer up and down. "Actually, got a delivery going out there this morning. You help with that, it'll pay for the price of the ride. I can fix it up."

"When does it leave?"

"Hour from now."

"Where from?"

"Alley behind the hotel."

"Okay, I'm gonna grab some breakfast then."

"Do what you want. Hey, now, where'd you get those clothes? Those sure ain't the duds you were wearing when you got here."

"I bought some new things."

"With what?"

"Same what I paid for the room. Cash."

"Where'd you get that kind of moolah?"

"Department of Prisons gave it to me."

"Thought you was one of them when you checked in. But are you shitting me? They give prisoners money?"

"Well, I promised 'em I wouldn't kill anybody else if they did."

Archer fell silent and stared at the man with a look that he hoped meant business.

"W-well, you be at the alley in an hour."

"I will, friend."

Archer got a cup of coffee and a fried egg and toast at a hole-in-the-wall a block down from the hotel and read a discarded newspaper while doing so. The Soviet Union had recently detonated its first nuclear weapon. While Archer had been in prison, something called NATO had been established. The newspaper Archer had been reading at the time said the creation of NATO would make sure there were no more wars.

They must have forgotten to tell old Joe Stalin that, thought Archer.

He met the truck and driver behind the hotel.

The man told him his name was Sid Duckett. Around sixty years old, he was about three inches taller than Archer and outweighed him by maybe fifty pounds. He looked like he could lift the truck he'd be driving, but then told Archer he'd thrown out his back and welcomed the help in exchange for a ride out. He had on faded jeans that showed off his wide hips and bow legs, a cotton shirt tucked in, a wide leather belt with a buckle the size of a paperweight, dusty boots, and a greasy snap-brim hat with a fake bird feather sticking from the band.

"Well, get to it then while I check my paperwork," said Duckett.

"What are we hauling?"

He pointed to a large stack of wooden crates piled next to the hotel's tradesmen entrance.

"What, all that?"

"All that, buddy, if you want the ride."

Archer took off his hat and coat, and rolled up his sleeves. A half hour later, after much grunting and heaving, and words of unhelpful advice from Duckett, the truck was loaded.

Archer rolled down his sleeves and picked up his jacket and hat.

"Let's go," hollered Duckett from the front seat. "Time's a-wasting, fella."

Archer climbed in next to him and they set off.

"Guess you folks don't use much talcum powder around here," noted Archer.

"What's that?" replied Duckett, looking puzzled.

"Just worked my butt off, but the air's so dry I didn't even break a sweat."

They drove for an hour and not once did the landscape change from flat and brown, or the sky from clear to something else. Archer didn't recall even seeing a bird passing over.

Archer eyed this for a while before saying, "See here, does it always look this way?"

"What?"

Archer pointed out the windshield. "The land around here."

Duckett eyeballed what they were passing. "Sometimes we get a bit of snow."

"But other than that?"

"I don't like change," said Duckett gruffly. "When things are the same, you got no surprises."

"I'm into variety myself," replied Archer.

"Well, you're in the wrong damn place, brother, least when it comes to the weather."

"Does that mean there are surprises around here not having to do with the weather?"

Duckett eyed him suspiciously. "You ask a lot of questions."

"My momma told me that was the only way to learn."

"Maybe your momma should have told you not to be so damn nosy."

They pulled off the road and shortly came to a set of wrought iron gates.

Duckett honked the horn and a dark-skinned, strongly built man with small features, dressed in worn olive-green dungarees, a faded striped shirt, and work boots, rushed out from somewhere and opened them.

"Holy Lord," exclaimed Archer. "This is one man's home?" He stared up at the behemoth that loomed before them like the rise of mountains from the plains.

Duckett nodded. "Yeah, why?"

"What does one man want with all that?" said Archer.

Duckett aimed a glare his way. "Don't tell a man what to do or not do with his money. Mr. Pittleman wants a place like this, well then he can damn well build it. And he did."

"I wasn't saying otherwise. Just voicing an opinion."

"Man single-handedly made Poca City into something. I grew up here. Wasn't shit here. Man changed that. Why I got a job. Don't be bad-mouthing him with your *opinions* less you want trouble."

"I'm the sort who doesn't care for trouble, pal. Had enough of that to last a lifetime."

"Damn good thing, because the trouble I'm talking about starts with a capital *T*."

"Well, if a man's going there, he better make it count," replied Archer, drawing a sharp glance from Duckett.

"Thanks, Manuel," Duckett called out to the man who'd opened the gates.

After he drove through, Duckett said, "You can get out here if you want."

"What about unloading the truck?" said Archer.

"I do that at the trucking warehouse Mr.

Pittleman has. It's about a quarter mile away. You can see it from the rear of the house. Has its own road off the main one, but I can get to it from here. They got men there to help unload."

"Well, the deal was I help you at *both* ends, so let's get to it."

Duckett looked at him with an odd expression. "Didn't expect that. Thought you'd duck out if you could."

"I didn't duck out fighting a war. Not starting now."

Duckett said defensively, "I was too old to fight. But did my part here."

"I'm sure you did."

"What was it like over there?"

"Not too bad if you didn't end up dying."

They drove to the warehouse, which was a large sprawling structure about forty feet high with an A-framed shingle roof. Two double metal slide doors fronted it. Over the doors was stenciled, HP TRUCKING.

"For Hank Pittleman?" noted Archer.

"Well, ain't you a smart one," said Duckett. "You must 'a gone to college." He backed the truck up and they climbed out.

A smaller door set next to the double ones opened, and a medium-height, sturdily built man around forty with a pencil mustache riding over a slash of mouth came out. He shook hands with Duckett and was introduced as Malcolm Draper, Pittleman's business manager. Duckett told him why Archer was there. Draper wore a slick three-piece worsted wool suit, polished shoes, and a gray hat with a black band. His eyes were beady enough to make Archer instantly distrust the gent. And the Smith & Wesson .38 Special revolver he carried in a holster dangling near his crotch didn't endear him, either.

Archer pointed at the gun. "Never seen a man in a three-piece suit and collared shirt wear a holstered gun like that."

Draper said, "We have valuable property in there. We take precautions."

"Archer fought in the war," noted Duckett.

"So did a lot of men," said Draper dismissively. "Ain't nothing special."

"Did you fight in the war?" Archer asked him.

"I got asthma."

"Well, ain't that special," replied Archer.

The metal doors slid open and two men came out with a metal-and-wood trolley, and they all helped unload the truck. Then the men rolled the loaded trolley through the open double doors and into the warehouse.

Archer caught a glimpse of boxes and crates stacked nearly as high as the ceiling.

"Lotta stuff," he commented to Duckett and Draper.

Draper said, "No railroad lines near here. Only way to haul freight is by truck."

"I can see that."

A few minutes later Duckett dropped Archer off at Pittleman's house and said, "How you getting back?"

"Figure that out later. Thanks for the ride."

Duckett said, "Can I give you a dollar for the help?"

Archer waved this off. "I'm good, friend. But thanks anyway."

Duckett flipped him two Walking Liberty half-dollar coins. "Don't never turn down money, *friend*."

Duckett put the truck in gear and drove off.

Archer watched Manuel close the gates behind him.

Then he slapped his hat against his thigh to knock off the dust and headed to the house.

CHAPTER

8

THE PLACE SEEMED EVEN LARGER than Poca City's Courts and Municipality Building, with more imagination in the design and better materials, Archer observed. The layout was not so much medieval-castle-like, at least to Archer's limited familiarity with architecture, as it was similar to the grand mansions he'd seen pictures of and built by the likes of the Vanderbilts and Rockefellers.

Wide, curving flower beds were planted on both sides of the walk going up to the house. Yellow and red and pink buds cascaded all around these beds, so they must be getting water from somewhere, he figured. It seemed like vast attention had been paid to all the landscaping outside, and Archer assumed that attention to detail would carry through to the interior.

He knocked on the door and a few moments later could hear footsteps approaching.

An elderly woman with stringy gray hair dangling from under a cap and attired in a black-and-white maid's uniform opened the door.

"Yes?" she asked dully, her face as fine a representation of a sourpuss as he was ever likely to eyeball. And he had seen plenty in his time.

"I'm here to see Mr. Pittleman. Name's Archer. He knows me."

"Just wait here," she said without a sliver of interest.

She stalked off after leaving the door open. Archer took the opportunity to step through and look around. Archer had never seen such opulence, even when he'd been in the Waldorf Astoria Hotel in New York, before the doorman had run a uniformed Archer out for loitering around with a female guest apparently beyond the boundaries of good taste.

He was confronted by tapestry-shrouded and gilt-tasseled chairs set against the far wall; curtained French doors leading off to who knew where; a row of grandfather clocks with fancy faces and fancier inner workings that he could see; and marble tables with flower-filled, hand-painted vases topping them. Twin suits of armor, a foot taller than him, were set on pedestals on either side of the front door. Far above him were other doors set in the wall with iron grilles fronting them. He imagined they were like fake balconies to look down from, but the first wrong step would be a doozy. Long grass and Oriental rugs covered stretches of the stone and timbered floor. The walls were covered with paper that looked like silk, though Archer couldn't imagine even someone like Pittleman being able to afford acres of that commodity, but what did he know about such things?

Unfortunately, despite the vast size of the space, he could feel the walls closing in on him. The oxygen seemed sucked from around him and replaced with pure carbon dioxide. He hadn't had so much trouble making his lungs function since a German sniper had missed Archer's head by the width of the Lucky Strike he'd been in the process of lighting. He had dipped his head to ignite his smoke at the exact moment the bullet struck. That slight change in position meant the round entered and exited his helmet instead of finishing its business in his brain. Realizing his near death, he'd laughed for a good ten minutes and then chucked up vomit into a bucket for ten minutes more. He'd never smoked any other brand from that day forward, since those smokes had more than lived up to their name.

He heard footsteps approaching again, but these were planted more firmly than the old woman's. Pittleman came into view. He was dressed casually in pleated and cuffed gray slacks and an open-collared shirt, which showed a glimpse of his undershirt and also high-lighted his bloated belly and soft shoulders. His trousers were held up by a braided leather belt that looked expensive and probably was. He was holding a newspaper in one hand and a cup of coffee in the other. His hair was just as neatly combed, but in the light of day Archer could see clearly the sun splotches spread over the man's face like clumps of dirt on an otherwise pristine, if saggy, carpet. And under his eyes were pouches filled with blue veined wrinkles, like the tracings on a dime store map.

He doubted Jackie Tuttle would look any less alluring in the daytime instead of in a dark, smoky bar. But still, that was reason enough to drink in the absence of light.

"What in the hell are you doing here, Archer?"

"Came to report on Mr. Tuttle."

"You got the Cadillac, boy?" He glanced toward the front door.

"No, sir, but I'm working on it. Mr. Tuttle told me a few things and I just wanted to run them by you."

Pittleman looked him up and down. "New clothes?"

"Yes sir."

"I guess I see where my forty dollars went. You gonna disappoint me?"

"I hope not to."

"Come on back."

He turned and led Archer down a broad hallway festooned with paintings, murals, and the heads of unfortunate animals.

"You hunt?" asked Archer, looking at the frozen countenance of what appeared to be a water buffalo.

"I do, just not critters."

Archer looked confused until Pittleman saw this and laughed. "Lots of things in life more important than these here things to hunt, Archer."

"Like what?"

"I'll let you find out for yourself. Hope it's not a lesson you come to regret."

He led him into a room with glass walls and a glass ceiling, all supported by steel beams. In the center of the room was a table and three upholstered chairs with medieval scenes stitched on them. Leggy potted plants were arrayed around the room. A dark davenport was against one wall with light-colored pillows, and a menagerie of birds printed upon them. Floor lamps with shirred paper shades and graced with various designs both architectural and animal were strategically placed.

Sitting in one of the chairs was, Archer supposed, Mrs. Pittleman. She was around sixty, white-haired, large, big-boned, and matronly with flat cheeks, a chunk of nose, and ears that stuck out. Her eyes, covered by a pair of pince-nez, were set too close together for symmetry. She wore a dress of little style and shape; it might as well have been a blanket laid over her. But it probably cost a small fortune, Archer thought, just like everything else in the place. Archer doubted she had been beautiful even in her youth, but there was refinement and intelligence in her eyes and features. He believed her soul might be far more attractive than the outside of her. But that might just be wishful thinking. Thinking the best of people often was, he had learned.

"Marjorie, honey, this is Archer. He's been doing some work for me."

She inclined her head but offered no verbal greeting.

Pittleman sat down, drank his coffee, and folded up his newspaper.

"Take a seat, Archer."

Archer sat uncomfortably on two knights jousting.

Pittleman said, "So you been out there and *talked* to him? Why? Did he catch you trying to take the Cadillac? If so, why aren't you dead or at least gravely injured? I don't pay good money for a half-ass effort, soldier."

"I went yesterday afternoon. Knocked on the door and talked to him."

Pittleman shook his head in confusion and poured another cup of coffee from a silver-plated pot with a long, curved spout. A platinum cigarette case was on the table lying open. Inside were gold-tipped, needle-thin smokes. Next to that was a nickel-plated Smith & Wesson snub-nosed revolver with walnut grips and a hair trigger manually filed down to make it so.

"You like that little belly gun?" asked Archer.

"Nice gat. Drops what I hit, can't ask for more."

With hiked eyebrows Archer said, "How often do you *drop* things?"

"Depends on the target and my mood."

"With that hair trigger do you even bother fanning the hammer?"

"I shoot slow, but I don't miss. Isn't that right, Marjorie?"

She didn't respond, but Archer didn't think Pittleman expected her to.

Pittleman took a drink of his coffee and the movement revealed on his wrist a watch encrusted with six diamonds and twin sapphires. Archer saw the name LONGINES etched on the face underneath the glass. He looked down at his own timepiece and reminded himself that they both told the same story despite being separated by a truckload of dollars.

Pittleman said, "So why the hell did you go out there and see Tuttle in broad daylight? You think he was going to just hand you the keys to the damn Caddy? You can't be that cockeyed, boy!"

"No, sir. I just wanted to verify that he owed the money."

"I already *verified* that to you, son. Are you simple? Did I make a mistake hiring you?"

"Well, he *did* verify it. And he has the money to pay the debt off. Which I think you probably want more than the car. Am I right about that? I mean, you said it wouldn't come close to paying off the debt and interest and such."

"You are right about that. So what?"

"Well, there's one little sticking point on the debt."

"And what might that be?"

Archer glanced at Marjorie and did not proceed.

Pittleman looked confused for a moment before exclaiming, "Good Lord, is it Jackie we're talking about?"

Archer shot another glance at Marjorie, who was now drinking her coffee and leafing through a magazine with a placid expression. She could be in church marching silently through her catechisms, he thought.

"That's what he said. He wants her back."

"She's an adult, in case you and her daddy didn't notice. She can decide on her own."

"But he won't pay back—"

"Which is why I told you to get the goddamn *car*, Archer. Hell, boy, I didn't need you to go out there and ask the man what his problem was in paying me back my money. I *know* what it was. He doesn't like the fact that his daughter is now seeing me. Now go paste that in your new hat bought with *my* money."

"So you know all that then?"

"Let me tell you something else I know, son. Jackie's current status doesn't give Lucas Tuttle a pot to piss in when it comes to a legal obligation owed to yours truly."

"Why not take him to court then?" asked Archer.

Pittleman sat back in stark wonderment. "What, and subject my dear wife here to gossip of a perverse nature? To dredging up facts in a court of law that might prove painful to her? No sir." He patted his wife's hand. "I love her too much to put her through that."

"I can see that," said Archer slowly, when in truth he could see none of it. He eyed the three-initial monogram on the man's shirt cuff.

"Got a problem with something?" said Pittleman when he caught him looking there.

"You afraid you might put on another man's shirt by mistake?"

"Funny guy, huh? If I'd known that when I hired you, maybe I wouldn't have. Now get your ass out there, Archer, and take back my collateral by hook or crook. And if you don't, you're going to owe me forty dollars *with interest*. And I might leave you naked on the street, son, with more wounds than you got fighting the Krauts. Where you staying?"

"Derby Hotel."

"Mighty fine place," said Pittleman, with another sly glance in Marjorie's direction. "You need money to keep staying there. And you sure know how to get it, don't you?"

He turned back to his paper.

"Got another question," said Archer.

"We're done here," replied Pittleman as he picked up the belly gun and examined it, the barrel pointing in Archer's general direction.

Archer next looked at Marjorie, who was still leafing through her *Saturday Evening Post* magazine, apparently mesmerized more by the words therein than by her husband's admitted adultery.

Pittleman glanced at her. "You need anything, honey? Just tell me, if you do now."

She graced him with a smile. "I'm just fine, Hank."

"Hell, I know you're fine. Just ask any man." He glanced at Archer. "And why are you still here, son? Have I not made myself as clear as the sky outside?"

Archer rose and tipped his hat at the woman. "Nice to meet you, Mrs. Pittleman."

She nodded absently at him, her gaze holding on the magazine.

He walked to the door, looked back at the odd couple, and could only shake his head.

On his way out, he glimpsed a young woman in a maid's uniform scampering up the stairs. She looked back, saw him watching, and gave him a wide smile. He tipped his hat and returned the smile. She hiked her eyebrows fetchingly, then disappeared from sight.

He waved to Manuel, who opened the gate for him. He passed through and headed for the road. He walked for a while, the dust collecting on him like metal fragments to a magnet. He finally hitched a ride on a slow-moving Model A heading to Poca City and driven by a man dressed all in black who said he was a circuit preacher. He told Archer he needed to repent his ways, regardless of what they were, and gave him a pamphlet from a wooden box in the back that was entitled "The Devil Is Inside You."

Archer got back to town over an hour later and threw the pamphlet away in the first trash can he spotted.

I know the devil's inside me and maybe I like it that way.

He went back to the Derby and washed off the dust in the hall bath. He went in search of and bought a bottle of Blue Bird gin and two packs of Lucky Strikes and a box of matches. He walked back to his room and debated what to do.

Tuttle was not giving up the money if Jackie stayed with Pittleman.

Pittleman was going to do nothing about that situation.

So the only way for Archer to make any money off this was to take the damn Cadillac.

But all the others who had attempted it had failed. Or maybe died trying if the Remington had anything to say about it. He didn't even know where the man kept the sedan. Maybe in one of the outbuildings he'd glimpsed when he was there.

Tuttle would be on his guard for another attempt, and while Archer would die for his country, and almost had, he didn't relish kicking the bucket via buckshot simply trying to earn a living. But if he didn't get the car, Pittleman, who he assumed was a man of his word, would probably tar and feather Archer before running him out of town. And if he could argue that Archer had taken his money and not done what he promised, that constituted a crime and he'd be right back in Carderock.

He smoked a Lucky right down to nothing, drank his gin slow and easy, and pondered why he had not taken the simpler route and become a hog-brain basher like Dickie Dill. This made him think of the scrawled note he'd found in Ernestine Crabtree's office. He pulled it out of his old jacket, read it again, found it even more disturbing, and put it back where it had been.

Maybe there was one person who could help him with his dilemma.

Jackie Tuttle. But he had no idea where she even lived.

But Poca wasn't that big a place. He waited until the darkness was about to fall, put on his new hat, and then set out to find her.

CHAPTER

9

His search ended abruptly in the lobby of the Derby Hotel, where Jackie was sitting in a cane back chair in front of an empty fireplace topped by a slab of marble collecting still more dust. He stopped and looked down at her as Jackie smiled up at him.

"Well, get a load of you," said Archer.

"Surprised?" she said.

"You can see that for yourself."

She eyed his new clothes. "Nice duds."

"Yeah, lot better than what I had."

"I can see *that* for *myself*."

"What are you doing here?"

"Waiting for you to come down. What else?"

"Why?"

"Hank phoned and said you'd come by today. And he told me where you were staying."

"Why would he call you about that?"

"Hank tells me most things." She rose. "Let's go eat. I'm starving."

She wore a skintight dark blue cocktail dress, a white scarf around her neck, and a black, fitted pillbox hat with a bit of frilly lace tacked up. Her shoes were black with low heels and bows on the toes. Her costly nylon stockings gleamed over her shapely calves. Gold chandelier hoops hung from her ears, and she held a small clutch purse in her gloved hands.

"You do look sharp," she said, running her hand along his lapel and then clutching his tie and pulling on it for good measure, bending him down to near her height. "With a little work you might be approaching dreamboat status. Sort of like Cary Grant and Clark Gable all rolled into one."

"You're nice on the eyes too," he said appreciatively. "Prettier than any gal I've seen at the movies."

"Glad we got all that out of the way. But don't say that in front of Hank. He's a jealous man. And that knife isn't the only weapon he carries."

"Yeah, I saw his belly gun up close and personal

today. But his wife doesn't seem to be the jealous type. In fact, she doesn't seem to give a whit."

As they walked out into the fading light and headed down the street, Jackie said, "Oh, Marjorie gives a whit, trust me."

"Care to explain?"

"Not really. And I'm not sure you're set up to understand even if I did."

They slid into a shallow booth with red vinyl seats at the Checkered Past.

Jackie ordered a gin and tonic with a twist of lime.

Archer went with a ginger ale.

She looked at him oddly. "You lost your thirst or are you waiting to tell them the rest of the ingredients for a highball? They do a nice Seven and Seven here in case you're interested."

"No, just trying to watch my p's and q's."

"How is not drinking doing that?"

"If I get sauced, I might say or do something with you I might regret."

"Hell, Archer, that's half the fun."

She sipped her drink when it came, while he chugged his.

"So, Marjorie?" began Archer.

"What about her?"

"She knows about you and Hank."

"I know she does."

"You're really not going to enlighten me, then?"

She took off her pillbox and set it on the table next to her place setting. "And why exactly do you feel the need to be enlightened?"

"I don't like not knowing things. Gets under my skin."

"That's a good attribute, but it doesn't persuade me. I hear you talked to Lucas Tuttle."

"You mean your *father*, yeah, I did."

She shrugged. "And what did the old gasbag say?"

"Why ask me? Pittleman must've told you, since I told him."

"I'm not going back home, Archer, if that's what you want to know."

"Okay. But your father truly seems to miss you."

She looked at her menu. "What're you in the mood for?"

"Steak and potatoes, coffee, black. Piece of the cobbler to finish."

She glanced up at him. "You sound certain about that and you haven't even looked at the menu."

"I am sure."

"You've eaten here before?"

"Last night."

"What'd you have?"

"Same as what I just said."

"You don't like variety?"

"Two things in a row *is* variety, of a sort."

"You'd make an intriguing study, Archer."

"Of what kind?"

She pulled out a pack of Chesterfields and offered him one, which he took. She lit his with her metal lighter, cupping her gloved hand around his, and then did the same for herself. Jackie blew out a cloud of smoke and said, "Hell, just about any kind of study."

He turned his head and released smoke from his nostrils. With all the other tables similarly engaged, the restaurant looked like it might be on fire.

"I heard your mother died in an accident. I'm truly sorry about that."

She tapped ash into the chromium ashtray and positioned her elbow on the table so that her cigarette pointed to the ceiling like she was putting up her hand to swear an oath; her flippant expression was gone. "Who told you? Surely not my father."

"Lady named Desiree."

She nodded. "Desiree Lankford."

"Efficient-looking woman."

"She *is* very efficient."

She finished her cigarette early and ground it out in the chromium ashtray.

"Your daddy said he had the money to pay back the debt, only he won't so long as you're with Pittleman."

"Then I guess you're going to have to take the Cadillac, like Hank told you to in the first place. You need to keep up, Archer. Hank doesn't suffer fools gladly."

"And get shot for my troubles?"

"Did my father answer the door with the Remington, then?"

"Does he usually?"

"My father's not a trusting man."

"Yeah, it was pointed at all parts of me that I find important and necessary."

"Well, why would he point at the *unnecessary* ones? You say he had the money?"

"What he told me. Why?"

"Just wondering. What's your plan now?"

"Why?"

"I'll tell you this. Hank isn't happy you already spent his money without getting his collateral." She once more eyed his new clothes.

"Is that why you sought me out? You sort of his spy? I won't hold it against you. A gal's got to do what a gal's got to do."

"I have better things to do with my time, Archer, than spy on folks. I 'sought' you out because you're new in town and I thought you might like some companionship."

"Okay, sorry about that. As to the plan, I'll think of something. Always do."

"I like a man with confidence in himself. I just hope yours isn't misplaced, because it won't turn out well for you."

"I know about the Remington now."

"Not talking about that. I know for a fact that Hank was angry when the other men came back empty-handed. And he took it out on them, for sure."

"You don't think I can hold my own with Pittleman?"

"It's not Hank you have to worry about. He employs a lot of men. And some of them are even bigger and stronger than you." She added sweetly, "And I suspect that *most* of them aren't nearly as nice as you are."

"Thanks for the warning."

"Don't say I never gave you anything. Hey, where are you coming in from? You said seven hours from the east?"

"Just wandering. Have been for a while."

"You mentioned you did two years of college?"

"That's right."

"Where?"

"Not anywhere near here."

"Why didn't you finish?"

"Little thing called a world war came calling and interrupted my studies."

"Right, you said you fought."

"Every man my age did unless they had bad eyes, bad feet, or a bum ticker."

"I hear the sons of some rich or influential men didn't have to suit up."

"Well, my old man wasn't rich or influential, and, anyway, I volunteered."

"Why?"

"Do my part, why else?"

"Were you brave?"

"More lucky than brave, probably."

"Why don't I believe that?"

"Believe what you will."

They ordered their food when the waitress came over.

"Steak and potatoes for you, too?" he said after Jackie finished her dinner request and the waitress had gone off.

She gave a surprised Archer a coy smile. "I like variety as much as the next person."

"You left home right after your mom died?"

"Why do you care about that?" she said with a frown.

"I'm just a curious soul, always have been."

"Well, it's my business, not yours. So tell your curiosity to scram."

Archer looked around the dining room, and his gaze alighted and held on Ernestine Crabtree, who was eating her dinner in a far corner of the restaurant. She had a book next to her and a pad of paper in front of her and was writing something down with a pen.

"What is it?" asked Jackie, glancing that way. "You know her?"

"Just looking around, seeing what's what."

"Eye for the ladies, Archer? Don't be afraid to confess it."

"Look, I'm no better or worse than other men on that score. *You* know her?"

Jackie sat back and ran a finger down her glass of gin. "Not really. Seen her around. She seems a little—"

"—wound like a clock? Yeah, seems that way to me, too."

"It's sad she's all by herself with only a book to keep her company."

"Books can be good for you."

"You don't strike me as a book reader, Archer, despite your two years in college," she said skeptically.

"You're wrong there. I been reading books

a lot lately. Good friends to help pass the time."

"Did you have time you wanted to pass?"

"Don't we all?"

"What'd you study in college?"

"Mostly the co-eds."

"You're a laugh a minute until you're not."

Archer looked around once more and flinched when he saw three men sitting at a table in another corner of the restaurant. Two of them were hardened, uncouth types with greasy hats and slovenly chins. The other one was Dickie Dill. He was eating his steak blood-rare and cutting it not with the restaurant's cutlery but with a switchblade. That was disturbing enough, but all three men were also snatching glances at Crabtree, and then talking and laughing. That all set Archer's nerves on edge.

When one of the men rose and headed toward Crabtree's table, Archer said to Jackie, "Excuse me for a minute."

He beat the gent to the table by a half second. Crabtree looked up first at the man and then at Archer.

"Mr. Archer, what are you doing here?" she said.

"Saw you sitting here and came over to say hello." Archer glanced at the man. "Hey, friend, you know Miss Crabtree, too?"

"Not as well as I want to," barked the man. "Three's company, so beat it, pal." He was larger than Archer, with a broad chest and thick arms.

Archer said, "I would beat it, but I also have business with the lady."

"What sort of business?"

"The personal kind."

"Like I give a damn." The man reached out to grip Archer's shoulder, but Archer deftly blocked the man's thrust and took the hand in a firm shake. So firm, in fact, that the man's eyes started to wince. With his other hand Archer held the man's other arm tight against his side.

"Mr. Archer," said Crabtree. "What are you doing?"

"Just having a gab with this nice man."

"It looks like you're hurting him."

"Naw. I'm not hurting you, am I, fella?"

"You better let go before I get riled," said the man, his eyes watering now with the pressure Archer was applying.

Archer glanced over at Dill to see the little man watching him intently, his blade held point up.

"I mean no harm, friend. But I sort of have to insist on you going back to your table and I'll do the same. You can see that Miss Crabtree is busy right now, so the respectful thing to do is walk away." Archer gave the hand another firm squeeze, and the look in his eyes was of a man who was not going to be denied.

The man looked down at the paper and the pen as Archer increased the pressure on the gent's fingers.

"I'll come back 'nuther time then," he said hoarsely.

Archer slowly let go and stepped back. "Well, you might want to find somebody else to talk to. Dickie over there is a nice one. I know you're eating with him and all already."

Crabtree jerked her head to look in that direction, then she glanced up wide-eyed at Archer.

Before the man left, Archer pulled him close and said into his ear, "I'm just outta Carderock myself, pal. One thing I learned about Miss Crabtree, they got the law watching her all the time, case people like you and me make a move like you just tried to do. Dickie gave me the same advice about the Cat's Meow. Just trying to help you out, friend. You take care."

The man looked goggle-eyed at Archer, gave a searching glance around the restaurant, turned, and hurried back to his table, where he sat and immediately entered into a serious discussion with the other two while shooting glances back at Archer.

Archer looked down at Crabtree. "Sorry about that, ma'am. Didn't mean to interrupt your meal."

"No, um, that's fine. I, well, thank you, Mr. Archer." She paused. "What did you just tell him?"

"Nothing important. I take it he's one of your parolees."

"How did you know that?"

"He's not drinking."

"Oh, yes. Dan Bullock. He was released three weeks ago."

"Right. Well, I was just wishing him luck in his new life." Before she could respond he glanced down at the paper and saw the writing there along with a title at the top of the page.

"You a writer? You working on a story?"

She covered the page with her hand. "I…just scribble."

"Well, okay. See you at our next meeting."

"Yes."

He walked back to join Jackie.

"What was all that about?" she exclaimed as he sat down.

"Just heading off a little bit of trouble."

"Seemed like you knew her."

"Didn't I say? I just met her walking around town. Nice lady."

She glanced at the table with the three men. "I think you might have made some enemies, Archer."

"Wouldn't be the first time. But I think it'll be okay."

"A woman like that is a target, unfortunately."

"Why's that?"

"She doesn't have a man with her," said Jackie matter-of-factly.

He stubbed out his Chesterfield when their food came. They ate their meal mostly in silence. Archer had things he wanted to ask but was afraid to, something he usually wasn't, especially with a woman. But this was a woman the likes of which he had never really encountered before. He had an unsettling notion that she might be more than a match for him. Ernestine Crabtree, too. Poca City seemed to have its share of independent women designed to scare the bejesus out of him.

Jackie insisted on paying and Archer didn't protest too much, since he would have had to dig into the dregs of his remaining cash to do so. Still, a woman should not pay for a man's meal. It just wasn't done.

"You have any work needs doing, let me know. I can pay off the meal."

She ran an appraising eye over him. "Oh, I'll

let you know all right. You might come in very handy for what I *need*."

Jackie then gave him such a look that Archer felt himself blush for one of the few times in his life.

As they walked out, Archer thought he saw Ernestine glance at him, but that also might have been his imagination. Dickie and his pals had long since left. Archer kept a sharp eye out for them on the street but saw neither hide nor hair of the terrible trio.

It was warm, the air still bone dry as they walked along.

"Does any moisture ever creep into the ether here?" he asked.

"Now and again, but not so you'd notice much. We're pretty far from the ocean."

"Guess so."

"It does brittle your skin. I have to slather on moisturizer after I get out of the bathtub."

Okay, thought Archer, that was a deliberately low blow, designed to knock him off his stride. And it succeeded beautifully. He nearly ran into a lamppost.

Jackie entwined his arm with hers and said, "You want to head over to the Cat's Meow? We could do some dancing and quench our thirst for real. No bender, just a couple of highballs."

"Aren't you Pittleman's gal?"

"We see each other from time to time. But I'm not his 'gal.' He provides for me."

"Okay."

"So you want to go drinking and dancing?"

"I'll have to take a rain check on that."

She did not look pleased by his refusal. "I might not ask again."

"I understand that. Look, you have any idea where your father keeps the Caddy?"

She stepped away from him. "Do I look like a patsy? First, you give me the cold shoulder, and now you ask me to make your job easier, Archer? Why should I? Give me one reason."

"I can't think of a single one, Jackie."

This frank answer seemed to soften the hardened edge she had adopted. "Well, he used to keep it in the barn."

"Used to?"

"Would you keep it in the same place if a bunch of men had tried to take it?"

"Right. So where, then?"

She put a fist on her hip and stared at him. "There's a building about a quarter mile behind the barn. My father stores old farm equipment there. If I were you, I'd look there."

"Any idea where he might keep the car keys?"

"No."

"That's okay. I know how to hotwire a car."

"Do you now? How is that, I wonder?"

"The Germans weren't always good about leaving the keys behind when they abandoned their vehicles, so the Army taught me what to do."

"Good old Army," she said. "Providing skills you can use your whole felonious life."

"Thanks, Jackie, for the information."

"Don't thank me, Archer, it's your funeral."

He thought she would just turn and leave, but she didn't. She rose up on her heeled tiptoes, hugged him tight, and pressed her ruby-red lips against his cheek, leaving her mark upon him. She smelled of gin and lime, and also lavender and maybe the moisturizer she used after climbing naked from the bathtub. She slowly withdrew her body from his, her hands sliding down his shoulders, along his obliques, and then around his waist.

"See you around, Archer."

"Yeah."

She turned and left him there on the street.

Right now, he couldn't have hit a German with a bazooka at a foot's distance. He took off his new hat and slapped it hard against his thigh, giving himself a sting from the blow. Not so much to rid himself of the ubiquitous dust, but to make himself feel some hurt for allowing a lovely young woman who wanted to drink and dance and maybe do other things with him get off scot-free thinking he was a lame SOB from the east of here.

He went back to the hotel and slept until one in the afternoon dreaming of tubs and moisturizer and a host of college co-eds applying same and who all looked like Jackie Tuttle. He had dinner at a place cheaper than the Checkered Past. After that he stopped at a hardware store, where he bought a clasp knife and a Ray-O-Vac flashlight with batteries for the grand total of a buck-fifty from a man in a dirty undershirt with a bib tucked in gnawing on a chicken leg and holding a Pabst Blue Ribbon in the other mitt. Both these tools would come in handy.

Later that night, he glanced at the still cloudless sky, wondering if actual weather had been somehow suspended over Poca City. He then turned to look at the road where the bus had dropped him. It seemed like at least a year ago, but not in the way of accomplishment, since he had none. He set off to see about taking back a 1947 Cadillac sedan without dying in the face of the Remington.

He had had the good sense to change into his old clothes from prison. He reasoned that if he did get killed they could bury him in the new duds instead of the old, blood-splattered ones, and there'd be nothing Hank Pittleman could do about it.

Archer angled his hat just so and set off to snatch a Caddy.

CHAPTER

IO

He managed to hitch a ride on a Peterbilt long-haul truck. The tobacco-chewing driver said he was taking freight all the way to Nevada and could do with some company for a bit. For a good hour he and Archer sat in the cab and talked about the war—the driver had served in the Navy—and the New York Yankees probably winning the World Series again.

"Hell, I can see 'em winning a bunch in a row, the lineup they got," said the driver.

"What about that player with the Dodgers?" said Archer. "Jackie Robinson?"

The man nodded. "That colored boy can hit something fierce, I'll give him that, and run like the durn wind." He spit his chew into a Maxwell

House coffee can riding next to him on the seat. "Won Rookie of the Year in '47."

"Heard he might be the National League MVP this year," said Archer.

"Maybe so, fella, maybe so."

Then they had turned to politics, speculating that maybe Dwight D. Eisenhower would run for president when Truman was all said and done.

"I like old Ike," said the driver.

"Make a good campaign slogan," opined Archer.

He had the man drop him off about a mile before Tuttle's, figuring he didn't want any witnesses to what he was planning.

Archer walked the rest of the way. A silky darkness had fallen by the time he got to the mailbox, with the air turning chilly. He made the turn at the fork and squatted down, studying the house and the barn and the flat, tilled fields beyond. Channeling his instincts as an Army scout, Archer looked at what needed looking at and formulated a plan. The Caddy clearly wasn't in the house. The barn was the next logical choice, but Jackie had warned him off that. But still. He had to be sure.

He skittered over to the barn, found the door unlocked, which did not give him any ease, and decided to approach the place from another entry point. A side window succumbed to the nudges of his knife, and he entered there and shone his Ray-O-Vac flashlight around. It was quickly apparent that the car wasn't in here. But there was another vehicle. He ran his light over it. It was a four-door, long-hooded, burgundy automobile with a beige cloth top and white-wall tires. He opened the door and looked at the license and registration cards on the steering post. It was in Tuttle's name, and the car was a 1938 Cadillac LaSalle. It was a beautiful car, just not the Cadillac he was looking for.

After a bit of a trudge over uneven ground, he found the outbuilding right where Jackie said it would be. But there was nothing inside except ancient pieces of farm equipment, including a strange-looking device that had several cone-shaped nodules fronting it. He shone his flashlight over it and read off the words, ALLIS-CHALMERS CORN-PICKER. This farming business was more complicated than he had thought. Frustrated now, he left the shed, and squatted on his haunches, pondering what to do next.

His nostrils twitched due to some disturbance in the air. He took a long whiff and then gave a short cough. He rose and followed this scent down a dirt road that wended its way through the shallow-rooted Loblolly pine trees. The smell grew stronger the further in he went.

He finally arrived at a wide clearing, with dirt underfoot. And smack in the middle of this flat blackened ground was the source of the smell.

The vehicle had been set aflame. The chassis was still there, but the tires had burned away, as had the interior. What was left wasn't much, to be sure.

Archer walked over to it and looked around. The original color of the vehicle couldn't be determined, the paint also having burned away. The license and registration cards on the steering post had long since been consumed. He hustled around to the back and knelt down. He had to use his knife to scrape away burned fragments, which allowed him to read the plate number.

It was the 1947 Cadillac, all right.

He stood, an undeniable truth now vexing him: Pittleman's collateral no longer existed.

His trip had been wasted.

Well, that was a kick in the gut, almost near to what the over-under shotgun could have provided. He walked back to the main road and looked around. He didn't see a vehicle light in either direction. He took to his heels and returned to the Derby after midnight.

In his agitation, Archer took the stairs two at a time. He unlocked the door to his room, tossed his old hat down in the corner, opened the window, drew his chair up to it, lit a Lucky Strike, and sat there looking out while he smoked. If he couldn't get the Cadillac, and Tuttle wouldn't repay the loan without his daughter back, Archer was fresh out of ideas as to how to earn his commission. And he wasn't certain that this latest calamity might not cost him his life, at either the muzzle of Pittleman's snub-nosed gat or the twin barrels of Tuttle's Remington.

He burned down two more Luckys and took more than a swallow of his Blue Bird gin, and ended up sleeping in his old clothes. He awoke the following morning with no plan going forward. With his money dwindling and his prospects bleak, he opted for coffee and a slice of toast and a fried egg in the little café attached to the hotel.

He strolled around town as Poca City woke up, thinking about the burned-out Caddy. He figured that Tuttle must have done the deed to spite Pittleman. It seemed to Archer that the sedan had been burned some time ago. It had been cold to the touch, only the burned smell had lingered. That odor could stay for a very long time, Archer knew from his combat days. Archer was certain it had been destroyed before he'd even gone out to meet with Tuttle. The man must have had a nice laugh at his expense, knowing that the loan collateral no longer existed.

Whether consciously or not, his strides took him to the blocky Poca City Courts and Municipality Building. He walked up to the correct floor and knocked on the door.

"Enter," said the stern voice.

He swung the door open, and there sat Ernestine Crabtree clacking away on her Royal typewriter. She had a pencil stuck through her hair bun. She stopped typing when she saw him.

"What are you doing here?" she asked. "It's not your time yet."

She was attired in a similar fashion as before. Prim dress, same shell glasses, low chunky heels that he could once more see through the knee-hole, thick stockings, but very nice ankles and calves.

He noted a cigarette smoldering in the ashtray.

He came in, pulled the chair in front of her, and sat down.

"I could use some advice, Miss Crabtree."

"About what?"

He eyed the lit smoke.

She saw this and said, "No, I can't. I'm sorry."

"No problem, brought my own."

He pulled out his pack of Luckys, tapped it against the desk, shook out a cigarette, and lit it. She took her smoke from the ashtray and had a puff, too.

"What advice?" she said curiously.

"You know my debt collection job?"

"Yes, you mentioned it."

"Well, I've gone out there twice now."

"Who owes the debt?"

"Lucas Tuttle."

"Wait, the other night, weren't you with—"

"That's right. Jackie Tuttle. You know her?"

She shook her head. "Not really. Did you collect the money?"

"Well, no. Lucas Tuttle says he has the money to pay Hank Pittleman back."

"Hank Pittleman?"

"You know him?"

She shook her head a second time. "But I know he is very wealthy and owns a lot of property around town."

"Anyway, Tuttle won't pay back the debt unless Jackie comes back home."

"And she doesn't want to do this?"

"No."

"Then how will you collect the money?"

"Well, Mr. Tuttle signed over as collateral for the loan his 1947 Cadillac." He added, "It's all legal. Pittleman showed me the papers. And Mr. Tuttle confessed to owing the money."

"So you could take the car in repayment of the loan?"

"I could, except I found out last night the man burned it up."

She sat forward and put her cigarette down. "He burned up his own car?"

"Looks that way."

"Where does that leave you?"

"In a pickle of sorts. You know Mr. Pittleman advanced me forty dollars. And if I can't get the loan repaid or the car now, I'm sort of up the creek, so to speak."

"You mean Pittleman will want his forty dollars back?"

"Right."

"But surely you still have the money."

"Well, I spent some of it."

"How much?"

"Actually, most of it."

She looked at him in disbelief. "You spent nearly forty dollars since we last met!"

"Well, I bought some new clothes to replace these. I wore these to prison some years ago.

And I have to eat and all. Though I earned a dollar doing some lifting, I'm not eager to use my back for my daily bread."

She shook her head and looked cross. "See, this is why I was prepared to have you go out on job interviews. If you had, you wouldn't be in this kind of dilemma."

"Yeah, I see that. But I can't take it back now."

"But it's not too late, you know. You can earn money other ways. I can help you with that."

"Yes, ma'am. And it may come to that. And for that I thank you." He smoked down his Lucky and then ground it in the speckled glass ashtray. "What book were you reading at dinner?"

"It was by Virginia Woolf. Have you ever heard of her?"

Archer shook his head.

"She was from England. She died back in 1941. I admire her work greatly. And her, personally."

"I might try something of hers then."

"I could loan you a book here and there. If you'll really read it."

"I guarantee you I will. I like detective stuff the best. But I'll read most anything. So you're trying to write, too?"

"Again, I just…scribble." She paused and considered him in an appraising light. "Dan

Bullock? You were afraid he was going to try something with me, weren't you?"

"Well, he was, wasn't he?"

"It wasn't the first time a parolee has... approached me."

"I would expect not. But that doesn't make it right. And, well, there's something else."

"What?"

In answer, he took out the paper he'd found on her office floor and explained that fact to her before handing it over. "I wouldn't normally give such trash to a lady, but maybe it's best you know about it."

She only briefly glanced at it before tossing it into the waste bin next to her desk.

"You're right, it is trash."

"You get many of those?" he asked quietly.

She glanced up at him. "It unfortunately comes with the territory. Please don't give it another thought."

He nodded, sensing that she was done with this topic. "So any advice for me?"

"Mr. Archer, it's not my job to get you out of jams you got yourself into."

He cracked a grin.

"I'm being serious."

"I know you are. It's just that I've been in jams mostly my whole life." He rose and put his hat on. "I'll get outta this one, too." He tipped his hat. "Hope you have a nice day."

She half rose from her seat and started to say something, but Archer was already gone. Crabtree rushed over to the door, opened it, and watched him walk with purpose down the hall and out of sight. She slowly closed the door and went back to her typewriter. But the Royal never clacked once, because she never touched the keys.

CHAPTER

11

THAT NIGHT, ARCHER, dressed in his new clothes, walked down the street and took up his post across the street from the Cat's Meow. It was near on eight, and he assumed that Pittleman and Jackie might already be in there. After having had dinner with the woman he felt a pang of jealousy that she was in the company of another man, particularly a man like Hank Pittleman.

While he stood there, Archer thought about what he would discuss with Pittleman when he came out of the bar. He wanted the man to have a few drinks in him before he did so. He didn't think he was going to get a second chance with the gent. But the fact was the collateral was no more, so perhaps Pittleman would have another plan. At the very least, he couldn't blame Archer for Tuttle's torching his own Caddy.

Like any good scout, Archer was prepared for the unexpected, but he had not anticipated what would happen next.

"Mr. Archer?" said the surprised voice.

He turned to find Ernestine Crabtree standing there on the pavement, not six feet away, staring at him. Like his, her clothes were different from what she had started the day with.

The dress that had fallen well below the knee had been replaced with a fresher model in a startling petrol blue paired with a black jacket with a high-back collar. Her dimpled knees showed clearly below the starkly raised hem. And the thick nylons had been replaced with their sheer, silk cousins. The low heels were gone, and her height had shot up to within about two inches of his by virtue of her spiked, strappy footwear. The knotted bun had vanished, and she had on a black fascinator hat with a sticking-up bow and attached short veil. Her blond tresses fell straight down and skimmed her shoulders like a stage curtain against the floor. Her face, freed from being pulled at by the hair and covered by the shell glasses, had now relaxed into a thing of startling beauty, the eyes wide and holding considerable depth. And the paint on her face, lips, and nails rivaled Jackie's for its vitality.

Archer could only stare openmouthed at her for a few seconds. "Miss Crabtree, what in the world are you...? Well, you look...different."

She glanced down at herself, and the woman's pleased look gave her inner feeling away.

"I'm...meeting someone."

"Where would that be, I wonder?" said Archer as he made a show of eyeing the Cat's Meow, which was the only place down this way worth going to, and that still had its lights on and its door unlocked.

"Where that would be is none of your business. What are *you* doing here?"

"Just stretching my legs and getting some fresh air."

"You wouldn't possibly be thinking of going into that bar?"

"What bar would that be?"

"The Cat's Meow, right there."

"Oh, is that what that is, a bar?"

"Of course, it's a—" She paled a bit and looked down at her peep toe shoes.

Archer said, "I guess you've been in to see for yourself. I wouldn't know."

She squeezed her black envelope handbag and

continued to study the toes of her high heels with evident concern. "There is no law against me enjoying a drink, every now and again."

"No law at all, ma'am. I would join you if I could, but it would violate Rule Number 14, and possibly 15 and 16, depending on how things turned out. There might be others, but those will surely do."

She eyed his clothes. "Your new suit fits you... very well."

"And that dress is very pretty. And your hair down that way gives your face a nice framing."

She touched her hair and tried, but could not manage, to suffocate the smile that appeared on her face.

"Thank you," she said with a level of shyness that he had a hard time reconciling with the unyielding parole officer. "Are you working on your pickle of a problem?"

"I am indeed. It's why I'm here at this particular spot."

She glanced at the bar. "You think he might show up here? Mr. Pittleman, I mean?"

"Well, the man told me he's here every day except Saturday and the Sabbath, when he's with his wife. And I know that for a fact since I was at his house on Saturday."

"Why did you go there?"

"He's paying me, so I thought it right to explain things to him."

"But from what you told me this morning, he wasn't very understanding."

"No, but he was very clear on what I needed to do if I wanted to get paid. But now with the collateral all burned up, we have to go in a different direction. I've been thinking about some options to give him. And see if he has any ideas. Always a good thing to give a man options and let him know what's what."

"Yes, I agree, that *is* smart."

"Well, I have to be smart, since he pretty much told me he was going to hurt me bad if I didn't finish the job."

"He threatened you with bodily harm? That's a crime."

"Who's gonna call him on that? From what I've heard he owns just about anything worth owning around here."

"Well, he doesn't own the law. Or me."

"Never figured he could afford you, Miss Crabtree."

She smiled at this comment but then caught herself and her expression returned to neutral. "So, what will you do when you see him tonight?"

"Tell him the truth. Tell him about the burned-out car and give him some ideas going forward. At the least I figure it'll buy me a little time to sort things out. I mean, I can't collect what doesn't exist anymore." He paused and eyed the bar. "Well, don't let me keep you. Is the person you're meeting already in there, or are you meeting him out here?"

She ignored this and said, "If things don't work out with Mr. Pittleman, I have other positions, as I said. You can earn money to pay him back what you owe."

"I really do appreciate that, Miss Crabtree. More than you can know. But the fact is, the slaughterhouse job doesn't really appeal to me. Now, old Dickie Dill might favor bashing hog skulls in for cash in his pocket, but it's not something I'm suited for, being human and all."

He thought she might laugh at this last part, but she fought it long and hard and her cold side won the day. "A job is a job. You think everybody loves what they do for a living?"

"Do you?"

"I do not have to answer that."

"I know that. I'm just making conversation, since you're still here."

This seemed to sting her a bit, something he had clearly not intended.

"Well, I'll let you get on with your 'thinking' then."

Hiding his self-inflicted chagrin, he tipped his new hat at her and watched as the woman crossed the street and entered the Cat's Meow without a backward glance at him.

He was cursing himself for having now messed up twice with beautiful young women, when he saw the pair navigating down the street.

Pittleman was dressed in a seersucker suit with a boater hat sporting a red-and-blue band, and brown and white wingtip shoes. Jackie Tuttle rode on his left arm and was bedecked in a tight lavender dress and a short-waisted white jacket with narrow lapels over it. Her legs were encased in black seamed stockings, and her feet in black heels with fancy laces around her ankles, the mere sight of which gave Archer the spine shivers. She wore a lavender beret over her dark hair.

He had never seen a more beautiful woman, other than Ernestine Crabtree minutes before. If someone had told him a place like Poca City could hold *two* such alluring women, he would have called the person either a liar or cockeyed beyond belief.

He slunk back behind a conveniently placed sycamore growing up out of the street as they passed, and so they did not see him as they entered the bar.

About two hours later Ernestine Crabtree exited the premises. Archer looked for but failed to see the companion to whom she had referred. He kept behind the tree as she looked around, perhaps for him, or possibly others. Then, despite the height of her heels, she began walking quickly down the street with elegant strides of her long legs.

He watched her go until she was nearly out of sight. He was about to turn back when Archer saw something that made him leave his post outside the bar and take up following Crabtree.

CHAPTER

12

THESE BOYS JUST don't take a hint, thought Archer.

The subject of his frustration was the burly and unkempt Dan Bullock, who was currently following Crabtree. This was why Archer had left his post at the Cat's Meow. His fellow ex-con was stealthily making his way from cover point to cover point as the woman walked along.

Archer felt he was back in Italy threading his way through a bombed-out village as he slipped along in the hopes of uncovering some information to help him and his fellow soldiers. He knew very well what Bullock was doing. He just didn't know the *exact* particulars of his intentions in following a woman late at night. But he knew that none of them were good for Crabtree.

They had entered a neighborhood of cute bungalows with little shutters on the windows and tiny brown lawns. Archer thought it seemed like a nice place to call home. Bullock seemed to like these surroundings better for his purposes; he picked up his pace, closing the distance between him and his prey. There was no one else around.

Except for Archer, twenty yards behind.

Bullock took something from his pocket. Under the moonlight, Archer saw a flash of metal.

It was a knife.

Archer started to sprint forward.

He needn't have bothered.

When Bullock was still five feet from his target, Crabtree turned. From her sizeable envelope purse the woman had taken a walnut-gripped .38 Colt Detective Special snub-nosed with a three-inch barrel. She took aim at Bullock's broad chest as the big man came to a stop so fast he nearly toppled over.

"What in the hell!" he cried out.

Crabtree calmly looked him over and noted the knife in his right hand. "Mr. Bullock, first, drop the knife before I put a large hole in you."

He immediately did so.

"Second, I hope you see that this means your

parole is hereby revoked. The authorities will be coming to arrest you just as soon as I tell them what you've done."

A pale Bullock took a step back. "Look here, ma'am, I don't want to go back to no Carderock."

"Then why were you following me, with a knife?"

"I—"

"Clear out!" she barked, startling the man. "Now!"

He turned and sprinted off.

Crabtree watched him go until she could see him no longer. She bent down and, using a handkerchief, picked up the knife and put it in her purse. She continued on into one of the bungalows. A light came on in the hall, and then another in the front room on the right side of the bungalow.

Archer drew closer and assumed this was probably her bedroom. He could see her silhouette against a lowered window shade. Then she drew the curtains across it, cutting off his view.

He turned and hustled back to the Cat's Meow, his already high respect for Crabtree growing immeasurably.

* * *

He had barely taken up position behind the sycamore tree when the door to the bar opened and out staggered Hank Pittleman, with Jackie on his arm. Yet, she seemed to be carrying him more than he was carrying himself, and it was apparently a struggle for the woman.

While Archer was standing there, Pittleman turned and slapped her across the face, knocking her beret off. The sudden blow almost caused Jackie to fall over and take him with her.

Archer had stayed his hand in the bar when Pittleman had acted the same. And he'd held his objection because of the look Jackie had given him. But not this time, he decided. He rushed across the street and came up beside the pair.

Pittleman didn't seem to have the capacity to recognize him or anyone else, but as he lifted his hand to take another swing at Jackie, Archer smoothly put his hand under the man's arm, blocking him from doing so. Jackie, her cheek reddened where he'd struck her, looked over, smiled, and mouthed, *Thank you*.

She bent down and retrieved her hat. Instead of attempting to put it back on, she simply shoved it into her jacket pocket.

"What the hell!" snapped Pittleman. Then he clutched at his head and spit something up. Archer had to move his foot out of the way to avoid getting his new shoes besmirched by the man's vomit.

"Too much to drink?" he asked Jackie as Pittleman started to rattle nonsense once more.

"How'd you guess?"

"You okay where he—"

"I'm fine. I've been hit a lot harder than that." They lurched along with Pittleman talking mostly incomprehensibly.

"Where are we taking him?" asked Archer.

"He's got a place in town."

He nodded, and they kept walking, cradling the gimpy-legged Pittleman between them.

It surprised Archer when Jackie led him to the Derby Hotel.

"What, this is where he stays?"

"Yes. He's on the top floor."

Archer's jaw slackened another few degrees. "What room?"

"Two of them they've put together for him: 615 and 617."

"I'm in 610."

Jackie looked over at him, her features full of possibility. "Why, that's right down the hall, Archer."

When Pittleman failed completely to continue standing even with assistance, Archer took off his hat and said, "Hold this for me, Jackie."

He squatted down and hefted Pittleman into the air over his shoulder with one clean thrust of his legs.

"You *are* a strong man, Archer," she said approvingly.

"Yeah, well, at least I'm something. Lead the way."

With the load he was carrying, Archer forced himself to ride the elevator up, though he closed his eyes while doing so. They got to the room and Jackie dug into her purse for the key. She stuck it in the lock while Archer stood there with Pittleman slung over his shoulder like a carcass kill. Jackie swung the door wide and waved Archer in.

He strode in, saw the bed, and deposited Pittleman there. Quiet snores were now emanating from him. Archer looked around as Jackie handed him back his hat.

"What's he need two rooms for?"

"He doesn't need them. He just wanted them."

"Well, that makes no sense whatsoever."

"Makes sense to him. And didn't you know?"

"Know what?"

"Hank owns the hotel."

Archer took a step back and looked down at the sleeping mess of a man. "Hell, what doesn't he own?"

"Not much."

Archer looked her over. If anything, her dress was even tighter and more revealing than the one from the other night. Jackie caught him eyeing her and sat on the edge of the bed, taking all the time in the world to cross one gleaming stockinged leg over the other.

"Well, he's taken care of, now what?"

He looked down at her. "Any ideas?"

"We can go to your room for a drink."

"I had some gin, but it's gone now."

She reached into her purse and pulled out a small flask. "Problem solved."

"Last gal I saw with a flask pulled it out of her stockings."

Her smile was wide, warm, and inviting and caused Archer to go weak-kneed.

She edged her skirt high enough to get his undivided attention. "Well, as you can see, I *am* wearing stockings. But, I'll keep that in mind for next time, Archer."

"You're counting on a next time?"

"I like math. I can count really high." She rose. "In fact, to 610. Let's go."

"Okay to leave him like that?"

"I leave him like that all the time."

They made the short walk to Archer's room after she locked Pittleman's door behind them.

He opened the door to his room and let her go in first. He shut the door behind him and pocketed the key.

She picked up two short glasses off the scarred dresser and poured out a portion of the contents of the flask into each one. Archer observed that she measured with precision.

"You like things just so," he noted.

"Just so," she replied, handing him a glass and then clinking hers against his.

She pressed the glass against her injured cheek.

"You're gonna have a bruise there," he said.

"Wouldn't be the first time."

"Back in the bar that night?" He looked down at her wrist.

"Men have to show off, Archer. If they can't do it with their brains, and most often they can't, they do it with the fact that they're stronger than women. Hank's not stupid, but he's no better than most men when it comes to that."

"Doesn't make it right."

"Are you telling me you've never struck a woman?"

"Never even thought about hitting one."

She raised her glass to him. "Glad to hear it." She took a drink and looked him up and down. "So you never told me why you got the new clothes."

"Want to look the part."

"What part is that?"

"Professional debt collector for one drunk asshole."

He grinned and took a swallow of his drink, while she laughed loud and long, something that both surprised and pleased him.

She ran a hand up and down his jacket, while he tossed his new hat down on the bed.

"Where do we go from here?" he wanted to know.

Jackie moved slowly around the room while she sipped her drink, swaying maybe to some tune in her head. She reached the window, drew back the curtain, and looked out onto the dryness of Poca City.

"I have no plan, Archer. I'm just feeling my way. What were you doing outside the bar tonight?"

"Waiting for you to come out with Mr. Pittleman."

"Why?"

"Needed to update him on things."

"Like what?"

"Like your daddy torched his 1947 Cadillac, so there's no way for me to get it back."

"And how do you know this?" she said, looking at him with interest.

"I went out there last night with the idea of getting the car. It wasn't where you thought it might be. I found it in a little clearing not too far from there, in the middle of a bunch of pine trees."

She continued to gaze at him, her hand perched on one hip. "That used to be my secret spot, Archer, when I was little. I'd go there and pretend to be all sorts of things. A princess, Amelia Earhart, Jean Harlow, and Madame Curie."

"Well, right now it's got a mess of a burned-up car. And it's been there a while, long before I went out there asking about it."

"I wonder why he did that?"

"To spite Pittleman. Make sure the man's never gonna collect so long as you're with him."

"Then he's a fool."

"Not sure about that. Pittleman told me he's not taking Tuttle to court because it might cause embarrassment for his wife."

Jackie smiled and said, "He really told you that?"

"I went out there to see him and that's what he said. You don't think he was telling the truth?"

"Who knows? I find the truth coming out of folks' mouths less and less these days."

He sat on the one chair while she slipped off

her shoes, taking so long to undo the straps around her ankles that it forced Archer to look down into his drink before something happened he might later come to regret. But that water might already be over the dam.

She dropped her heels on the floor, took her legs up under her haunches, and perched there like a queen on her throne. But it wasn't a throne; it was Archer's bed.

"This is getting interesting, Archer, don't you think?" she said in that husky and now whiskey-draped voice.

He looked up, cradling his drink and taking another short swallow.

"Could be."

"You know, all the others just tried to steal that damn Caddy in the middle of the night."

"May they rest in peace. I took a different tack. Just my nature."

"You're the path-less-traveled sort of man, are you?"

"It seems to me that if I just follow along with everybody else, my life will always be crowded with folks I don't necessarily care to spend time with."

"Now you can't accede to my father's request, and you can't fulfill Hank's, either. And you spent money and you can't pay Hank back."

"You seem different than you did in the bar that first night. I mean, the way you talk and all."

"Hank likes me a certain way. So, I'm that certain way when I'm around him."

"What way is that?"

"You're a college boy. Do you know what chattel is?"

"Like property."

"Right. That's what Hank likes, owning things. And he also likes girlish giggles, flighty, flirty, his hand freely grabbing my ass, and all that goes with it. That also includes the occasional insult, slap, or punch."

"And you're okay with that?"

"If I weren't, I wouldn't let him do it."

"You're educated, aren't you? I mean, you sound it."

"I went to college, too. Only *I* graduated." She tacked on a smile and eyebrow hike to this.

"What'd you study?"

"Psychology."

"How's that work for you?"

"I can read people pretty well. Now, Hank, he's easy. You, not so much."

"Always thought I wore it on my sleeve."

"You might be wearing something, but it's not *you*, Archer. Not by a long shot."

"Why do you want to be around a man like that? He's more than twice your age. And he's married, too. Marjorie Pittleman seems nice and respectable."

"That's not my issue, that's his and his wife's. As to my reasons, Hank treats me pretty well for the most part. We go out, we have a good time, and then I have my own time."

"Where do you live?"

"In a house on Eldorado. Number 27. Hank got it for me."

"A house, huh, then you're a kept woman of sorts."

"You got that from a book, I think."

"I think you're right about that. You have long-term plans with old Hank?"

"I don't really think past tomorrow. I only live in the moment. Spontaneous."

He shook his head and finished his drink. "I don't think I believe that."

"Believe what you will or won't. But let me give you an example." She set her drink down, stood, and slipped off her jacket, revealing her dress straps and bare shoulders. She pulled down the straps, reached around to the back of her neck, undid a clasp there, pulled down the zipper, and commenced to wiggle herself free from the dress's constraints while Archer could only watch with rapt attention. Finally, the fabric hit the floor. She stepped out of the pile of dress and stood there with not much on except her stockings, garter belt, and underwear.

Archer found he could not look away, not even if a regiment of Nazis were bearing down on him with Hitler leading the pack. He had seen naked or nearly naked women before, in four different countries. He had never seen one that stirred his heart like this woman. Her body was icy pale and soft in every place that mattered to a man. Her mouth was infinitely kissable. And her contrasting Veronica Lake dark peekaboo had never seemed more in reach for a man like him.

She put an exclamation point on this by twirling around for him.

"Are my intentions now made clear?" she said, coming to face him. "Because I'm not sure what else I can do, quite honestly."

"I think I get the point."

"I'm truly relieved."

"And Hank?"

"He's not here now, is he?"

"Do I have a say in this?"

Her face fell. "I think that's a given, but if you're not interested?"

She bent down to pick up her dress, but

he gripped her by the shoulders, pulling her straight up.

"You're taller without my shoes on," she said, looking up at him.

"I suppose I am."

"You have a nice mug, Archer. Good bones. Not too handsome and not too scary."

"Moderation is a good thing."

"But not all of the time."

He looked down at her and noticed the bruises on her arms, upper thighs, and obliques.

His features darkening, he said, "What the hell happened there? You fall?"

She didn't even look at where he was staring. "Nothing important, Archer. Nothing at all."

"You sure? I mean, if Pittleman did—"

She put a hand over his mouth.

"Focus. I need you to focus. The night's not getting any younger and neither are we."

She stood on her tippy-toes and put her lips against his.

A moment later, they toppled, as one, onto the bed.

CHAPTER

13

WHEN HE WOKE EARLY the next morning, she was gone, and Archer wasn't surprised. She seemed like a cat to him. Affectionate when she wanted to be, and off again when she had gotten her fill.

A loud noise from somewhere out in the hall had catapulted him groggily from his slumbers. He rolled out of bed and saw it. She'd left her flask behind, perched on the dresser. He hefted it and heard the slosh of contents inside. Maybe she'd left it here because she intended to come back and retrieve it at some point. That was a thought to both spur and trouble a man.

He washed up in the toilet down the hall, put on his new clothes, and stepped out of his room. Pittleman's room was just down there. Archer wondered if that was where Jackie had gone for the duration of the night. The thought that she had left his bed to inhabit Pittleman's gave him a pang of jealousy that within the span of two strides he decided he had no right to feel.

Still.

He walked briskly down the hall to Number 615 and was surprised to see the door slightly ajar. He gripped the knob and opened it just a crack, so he could see inside. With the light streaming in from the windows, he gazed around the room and saw Pittleman still stretched out on the bed. He smiled when he thought about the hangover the man was going to wake up to. But despite his earlier thoughts, there was no sign of Jackie. He was about to leave when he saw it. The towel on the floor. And next to it, something that glinted in the creeping glow of sunlight, but that he couldn't make out precisely.

He gave a searching look up and down the hall. No one was about yet, for it was still early. He swung the door all the way in, stepped inside, and closed it behind him. The last thing he wanted was to disturb the sleeping man, but he thought of a ready explanation if Pittleman woke up and saw him.

He scurried over to the towel and squatted

down. The object next to it was a switchblade, like the one he had seen Pittleman use at the bar to spear the twenties and not so subtly threaten him. The blade was open. Archer looked at the towel and knife more closely and then became rigid. They were both coated with blood. He stood, walked over to the bed, and looked down at Pittleman.

The man wasn't asleep. Nor was he awake. He was just dead.

The slit under his throat was wide and deep. The person wielding the knife had driven the blade in to its full length, and then worked it jaggedly from side to side, like opening a can of soup. This wasn't necessary to kill the man. It was done to mutilate, and that thought sickened Archer. The dead man, his clothes, and the bed-covers under him were soaked in dried blood. It must have been a gusher when the blade had hit the big arteries. He knew this for certain.

Archer had killed a German near Salerno in hand-to-hand fighting. He'd been lucky to get the advantage, and the German had been un-lucky to lose his grip in what might have been the coldest winter Italy had ever seen. Though he hadn't been nearly as vicious as the person who had dispatched Pittleman to the here-after, Archer had slit the German's throat from basically ear to ear, just as he'd been taught. That way you didn't have to worry about your opponent's having a second opportunity to take your life. Archer had been covered in the German's blood when twin geysers had erupted from the severed arteries feeding his brain. He thought whoever had killed Pittleman would have the same foul coating.

His next thought was one of self-interest. He rummaged in the man's pocket and pulled out the thick wad of cash, which seemed about as hefty as the last time Archer had seen it. Well, it didn't look like robbery had been the reason to kill the man. And yet for Archer now to peel a few twenties off would not diminish it a jot. The man's widow would have plenty left over. And Archer might have indeed done so, for he was no better than most when it came to levels of selfishness, but he made the mistake of looking at the man's eyes.

They were wide open and seemed to be staring intensely up at him, carrying with them a look not of disapproval, but of betrayal. If a dead man's eyes could really convey that emotion, they had just done so to Aloysius Archer.

He slowly put the wad back, with not a single twenty plucked from its hide, and then used his fingers to close the man's flat, glassy eyes.

Archer had done this very thing on battlefields more times than he ever cared to remember. It had been gospel among American soldiers that a dead comrade with open eyes could still see the violent carnage of his own death and would therefore never have a restful afterlife. Archer wasn't particularly fond of Pittleman—he really didn't know the man—and what he had learned about him was not especially heartwarming. Yet he could see no reason to deprive him an element of peace in death.

But then something occurred to him. He looked in the other pocket and pulled out the promissory note papers given by one Lucas Tuttle to, now, a dead man. He slipped these in his jacket pocket. They might come in handy down the road.

A moment later, and after fully realizing the peril of his current situation, Archer stepped away from the bed, backed to the door, and left the room of the murdered man, after giving another look up and down the hall.

Slightly dazed by what he'd seen, though he had viewed deaths far more horrible than Pittleman's, and in far greater numbers, Archer hurried back to his room and had himself a nip from the flask. There was a difference between killing on the battlefield, where it was expected, and murder in a hotel room, where it wasn't or at least shouldn't be a common occurrence.

He took out the papers and studied the legal writing there. He looked at the amount owed and the signature of Lucas Tuttle. He flipped back to the page with the collateral listed and saw the Cadillac's description. That collateral no longer existed, but that didn't matter now. These papers were worth five thousand dollars plus interest to, he supposed, Pittleman's widow, and at least sixty dollars to him. But Archer wasn't sure what to do with them right now. He put the papers away in his jacket pocket.

His nerves steadied a bit, he walked down the stairs to the hotel lobby, sat in the same cane back chair Jackie had, stared at the empty fireplace, and thought about what to do.

There was one prime suspect, at least to his mind.

He knew that Jackie Tuttle was well aware of the dead man's location last night, having helped transport him to that very spot. And Archer had no idea how early she had left his room, him being sound asleep after their lovemaking. And he had no clue as to how long Pittleman had been dead, though it was not a recent death, the blood having dried, and the body having cooled considerably. Archer knew that they had reached his room at just about the crack of eleven because a clock from somewhere outside had bonged the time. A few hours after that Jackie could have left Archer, done the deed, and departed to her home on Eldorado Street.

But why kill a man who had given her a house and money and all?

He walked over to the front desk, where a different clerk from the one who had signed him in was drinking a cup of coffee. He was small with thin cheeks and dark hair cut close to the scalp. His bowtie was green against a pale white shirt with a wool vest over it. His cheeks and nose carried the red sheen of a heavy drinker, and the heavy pouches under his eyes spoke of many nights with little or no sleep.

"Help you?" asked the man.

"Yeah. I was wondering if you saw a young lady leave early this morning?"

"And who are you?"

"Archer. I'm in Room 610."

"And what young lady would that be?"

Archer described Jackie Tuttle but didn't give her name.

The man looked back at him primly and said, "I didn't see anyone."

"You sure about that? What time did you come on duty?"

"You ask a lot of questions. What's your business with this person?"

"Just making an inquiry about a lady. If you don't know, you don't know."

"Would she have been coming out of *your* room this morning? This ain't that kind of place, mister."

"Well, thanks for telling me. And also thanks for nothing, pal."

As soon as he started walking to the door of the hotel, Archer could feel the man's gaze on his back. He wished he hadn't said what he had. Now there would be a direct line among him, Jackie Tuttle, and the dead Pittleman. As a scout in the army and as an inmate in a prison, Archer had never made an error like that, and he wondered why he had in Poca City of all places. Well, maybe he knew why. A woman was involved. Archer just had a weakness there that disrupted his otherwise flawless instincts at self-preservation.

He walked along, hands drilled into his pockets, wondering if he should break his parole and make a run for it now. Archer decided against that and made a detour after asking a man for directions. Eldorado Street was about a half mile away, nearing the edge of Poca's compact downtown. It was a neighborhood of quaint small homes that looked like something you'd see in a Hollywood picture.

Number 27 was maybe the nicest of them all, he thought, with pretty little white shutters and flowers in both pots and dirt beds already looking for sun at this hour and no doubt thirsting for water. The brick siding was painted white, and the front porch had a little overhang with a metal chair and matching table set near the front door. Unlike some of the other homes, there was no automobile parked in the short gravel driveway.

Archer observed as much of the house as he could, checked around for folks who might be watching him, saw none at this still early hour, and headed up to 27's front door.

He knocked, waited, and knocked again. Then he heard feet padding toward him. The door was opened and there stood Jackie in a thin, form-fitting bathrobe that looked to Archer like something out of Chinatown in New York. It was crimson and had dragons and elongated masks and symbols of other such Oriental influence emblazoned across the fabric. She was barefoot, her face puffy and free of makeup, and her hair looked slept on.

She rubbed her eyes and exclaimed, "Archer, what in the world are you doing here?"

"You were gone when I got up."

"Well, I wasn't going to spend the night there."
She smiled. "Did you like it so much last night
that you came around here for more?"

"Can I come in?"

"I suppose. You want some coffee? Now that
I'm up, I intend to brew some."

"That'll be swell, yeah."

She led him into a small living room and
pointed to a chair.

"Black or something in it?" she asked.

"Just black."

She left, and he looked around. He didn't
know if the furniture had come with the place;
but it looked like it had. It was stuffy and old
and downtrodden, and he couldn't imagine the
stylish young woman picking it on her own. A
few minutes later she came back with a small
wooden tray holding two cups of coffee perched
on delicate saucers. She handed one to him and
took the other. On a plate on the tray were also
a couple pieces of toast, buttered.

"Help yourself," she said, yawning. "You look
hungry. For food or something else?" she added
enticingly.

"Food will do for now." He sipped the coffee,
which was hot and strong and bitter, just the
way he liked it. And the bread and butter felt

good going down with the coffee and helped to settle his rumbling stomach.

"What time did you end up leaving my room?" he asked.

"What? Why?"

He shrugged. "Just wondering. Didn't hear anything when you went."

"Well, I was quiet. Didn't want to wake you. You were sleeping so good." She smiled and stroked his arm. "I wonder why?" She let her hand drop and added, "You were really something last night, Archer. Compared to Hank, well there was no comparison. But he's old."

And not getting any older, Archer thought.

"You check on him before you came here?"

She took some of her coffee and a bite of toast. "Check on him? What for? He was dead asleep when we left him."

Archer managed not to wince at the unintended irony of her word. "Just wondering. You would've passed right by his door and all."

"I came straightaway here and fell into bed. You wore me out."

He abruptly took off his hat and drank his coffee fast enough to where it burned going down.

"You thought any more about how to get that debt paid?"

"Yeah, you can go back home to your daddy."

"Any other way? Because that's not an option."

"Was it really that bad there?"

"What's it to you?"

"I'm just trying to understand things."

"No, you just want your crummy money."

"Okay, that's part of it. And I can understand why you want to be on your own. But your daddy seems nice, when he's not pointing his Remington at you."

"You met my father exactly once. How in the world could you possibly think you know him?"

"That's fair enough. I know you loved your mother. Desiree told me that. Even showed me her picture."

Archer thought this would please the woman, but by her flushed face and angry features, this had been a serious miscalculation on his part.

"I don't like the fact that you're snooping around my business, Archer."

"See here, I didn't ask the woman to tell me that or show me her picture. She just did. And your mom was beautiful. You take after her, not your dad."

Jackie's features softened. "I do take after my mom. And she was beautiful. On the inside, too."

"I can see that. There was a lot of sweetness in the picture."

"But she could get angry, and she never shrank from giving her opinion on anything."

"Like mother, like daughter."

She smiled at this and Archer, heartened by how the conversation was going now, followed that up with a question which he regretted as soon as it left his mouth.

"So how'd your mother die then?"

The flush came back to the face and in her anger Jackie stood and glared down at him.

"Why in the hell does that have anything to do with you? What right do you have to even ask it?"

"I'm…I'm sorry. I have no right at all to ask it. And I didn't mean to—"

She cut him off. "I don't want to talk about it, Archer. And if that's the reason you came, then you can finish your coffee and get the hell out."

"It's not the reason I came."

"What then?"

"Your daddy thinks Pittleman has defiled you."

This did nothing to quell her anger at him. "He *has* defiled me. And it felt good. Why don't you go back there and tell him that, you bastard?"

Archer, getting worked up himself, shook his head disapprovingly. "Look, what do you have against your father?"

"What I have or don't have against him is my business. And only mine."

"Do you love Hank Pittleman or what?"

"Why, do you want to propose?" she snapped.

When he looked stunned by her response, she suddenly laughed and clutched his arm. "Don't go running off, Archer, I was just teasing. And I know you didn't mean to upset me, but sometimes questions like that do."

She sat back down and had another sip of coffee while Archer contemplated the mercurial nature of the so-called gentler sex.

"The fact is, I'm not ready to settle down. And no, I do not love Hank. Chattel does not typically love its patron. We just endure until something better comes along, if it ever does."

"Well, that's something I didn't know till I met you."

"Then I'm good for more than sex in a hotel room."

"You left your flask behind."

"I thought I might come back and get it some time. You mind that?"

Before finding a dead man, the answer would have been easy enough for Archer.

She looked at him peculiarly. "What is up with you? You look like you've seen a ghost or something."

"Nice house you got here. But the furniture doesn't seem to fit you."

"All this was already here. I just brought my clothes."

"You said Pittleman got you this place? So, who does this all belong to? The folks who lived here before?"

"That's right, you don't know. Hank and Marjorie used to live here. Until he built his place outside of town."

"You mean his hotel of a house?"

She was about to reply when a knock came at the front door.

She got up. "Who the hell could that be at this hour?" She added crossly, "Hope you didn't bring any friends."

"Except for you, I don't have any."

She cinched her robe tight and padded to the front door, while Archer rushed to the window and looked out.

CHAPTER

14

THE PATROL CAR WAS PARKED in the gravel
drive of the house. It was a wonder to Archer
that they didn't hear it drive up. It was a four
door, big-grilled Hudson Hornet with a chrome
engine spoiler, a single red light on top, and
a chrome-plated searchlight mounted on the
driver's-side door. It was an intimidating vehicle
that was, unfortunately, painted a dull yellow
with a brown stripe down the side. It might
qualify, Archer thought, for the ugliest damn
car in the whole country.

Archer retook his seat when he heard the
squeak of the front door opening, and the mumbling of words exchanged.

Then he heard Jackie say in a louder voice,
"What?"

Footsteps came down the short hall, and two uniformed men dressed all in brown except for black stripes down the sides of the pant legs appeared behind Jackie. One was short and pudgy and about fifty. His eyes were planted on the woman's backside, accentuated as it was by the tightness of the robe and revealing that she had not a drop of anything on underneath. The other deputy was Archer's height and age. Their faces were both weathered and their hair, when they took off their wide-brimmed tan Stetsons, was smooshed flat.

When they saw Archer, both lawmen's faces creased to frowns.

"Who might this be?" the older one asked.

Archer slowly rose. His manner of dealing with men who wore badges and carried guns was to appear forthright and cooperative, without making sudden moves or giving away anything of importance in the way of information.

"Name's Archer. I was just over visiting my friend."

"Mighty early for a visit," said the younger man.

"I was thinking the same thing, Jeb," said his partner.

Archer looked at Jackie. She looked like she might be sick. "What is it?"

"They just…they just told me that Hank was found dead."

"Dead? How? Where?"

The pudgy deputy said, "So how do you two know each other again?"

"What the hell does that matter, Bart?" snapped a distraught Jackie.

"Now, look, Miss Tuttle, we're just trying to get some information," he said soothingly, now staring at her chest, where, in her distress, the robe had opened, revealing enough cleavage to apparently captivate the lawman.

"How about you find out who killed Hank, how about that?" she snapped.

"Killed?" said Archer. "Somebody killed him?"

"Hell, yes they did!" proclaimed Jeb excitedly. "Bloody as all get out. Never had one like that in Poca before."

"How do you know Hank Pittleman?" Bart wanted to know.

"He hired me to do a job for him."

"What sorta job?" asked Bart.

Archer hesitated, wondering how best to describe what he was doing for Pittleman without getting himself involved in the man's murder.

"Hey, fella," barked Jeb. "You better give us the straight dope or we're taking your butt in for some questions. And we don't ask nice in Poca City."

Before Archer could say anything Jackie blurted out, "Oh, hell, Hank just...he just hired him to collect a debt from my daddy." Jackie now had a good deal more twang to her voice than Archer had previously noted.

"Collect money from your daddy?" said Bart.

Through teary eyes, Jackie said, sharply, "Yes, okay? What the hell does that matter? Hank's dead. You have to find out who did it!" She drilled a finger into Bart's broad chest.

"Okay, okay, we will. Now, this debt? Do you know where the paperwork for it is?"

Archer involuntarily ran his hand along his jacket pocket where these very papers were.

Jackie stifled her sobs, covered her mouth for a moment looking like she might be sick, and said slowly, "He kept them in his coat pocket. Last time I saw them, they were there."

"We didn't find nothing like that in his pockets."

Jackie glared at him. "Then do your job and look somewhere else! How's that for a plan, Bart!"

An angry Bart turned his attention to Archer. "Where you from, son?"

"East of here. Took a bus in."

"From where?" the lawman asked again, his features flexing raw and determined.

No way around it. Archer said, "Tartupa."

Bart and Jeb exchanged glances.

"One thing in Tartupa that I know of," said Bart. "And the bus does come here, sure enough it does."

"What are you going on about?" said Jackie, more tears starting to collect in her eyes.

"Carderock Prison's in Tartupa," volunteered Jeb. "Ex-cons come here for parole."

"Archer isn't an ex-con," she said, turning to him. "Are you?"

Now this was a predicament, Archer had to concede. But it wasn't like he could lie about where he had come from. All they had to do was check his name or go to Ernestine Crabtree and ask her. And you lie to the law, they never seemed to forget. They seemed to take it personally, in fact.

"I did my time," said Archer.

"What?" exclaimed Jackie. "Then you *are* an ex-con?"

Bart looked triumphant, even as his partner's hand stole to the .45 long-barreled pistol riding in his holster. It was a movement not lost on Archer.

"What did they have you busting rocks for?" Bart asked.

"Breaking the law."

Bart's triumphant expression vanished and his hand, too, went to his gun, as Jackie, looking confused, took a step back.

"I'll ask you one more time and one more time only," Bart said.

"The law said I stole something."

"What was that?"

"A car."

Bart snapped, "Shit, they don't send a man to no Carderock Prison for stealing a damn car. You lying to me, boy. I won't have it."

"This was a special car."

"What kind of special car?"

"It was the car belonging to the mayor of the town I was passing through."

"Okay, but still."

"And his daughter was in the car with me."

Jeb guffawed, but Bart didn't look pleased.

"You kidnapped the mayor's daughter?"

"No, she was there voluntarily."

"Oh really?"

"Well, she had her suitcase with her, with all her worldly possessions in it. Fact was, she didn't want to spend her life in some Podunk town, and I was her ticket out. But we didn't have a ride, so we borrowed—"

"You said you *stole* it," interjected Bart.

"No, I said the *law* said I stole it. The daughter was the one who took the car. And since it belonged to her father, I don't see how that could be stealing. We were going to drop it off in the next town over and take the train. Things didn't work out that way."

"What happened then?"

"They caught up to us before we could get on the train, and the mayor got his daughter to say things about me and what happened that weren't true. And that got me sent to Carderock for a spell."

Bart rubbed his cheek while Archer glanced at Jackie to see her staring at him with hurt eyes.

Bart said, "Well, that ain't why we're here. The fact is, Mr. Hank Pittleman was killed and we're here to tell Miss Tuttle."

"Why her?" asked Archer.

"Because they were friends." Something glinted in Bart's eyes. "Hey now, where you staying?"

Archer had wondered when the lawman would get around to that.

Jackie answered for him. "He's staying at the Derby, same as Hank."

Bart wheeled around on Archer. "Oh, you are, are you?"

"Oh, for God's sake, Bart," said Jackie, who

had finally settled down and dried her eyes. "He didn't kill Hank any more than I did. Hank *hired* the man. With him gone, so is Archer's job. How does that make sense?"

Bart's gleeful look faded. "Is that a fact?"

"That's a fact," confirmed Archer.

"Have you told Marjorie yet?" asked Jackie sharply.

When Archer looked at her, he could tell the woman's mind was going a hundred miles an hour.

"We just found the body," said Bart. "Maid walked in on him and almost lost her damn breakfast in the process. You know it's a hike out to their place, but we'll get there. Wanted to come by and tell you since you're closer."

Jackie nodded and managed a brief smile. "Well, I appreciate that, I truly do."

Archer was having a hard time following all this but waited until the lawmen, who each gave him a stern, suspicious look, had departed.

Jackie sat down and looked vacantly across the room, while Archer went to the window to confirm the law was actually leaving him alone. For now.

He sat down opposite the woman and said, "Can you explain something to me?"

"What's that, Archer?" she said wearily.

"The law knows about you and Pittleman?"

"Yes. So?"

"Just strikes me as a little odd. And the fact that they'd come here first and tell you before even letting his widow know."

"Well, like Bart said, I'm a lot closer. It's nearly an hour out to Marjorie's."

"Is this not a God-fearing place?"

"Come again?"

"I mean that people just accept the fact that you and Pittleman have this...arrangement and they're all good with it? Having met his missus, I know that she knows about you, which strikes me as even odder."

"Oh, *that*," said Jackie. "Well, I saved their marriage, in a way. I guess folks appreciate that. Maybe even Marjorie."

Archer could tell by the way that she said this last part, the woman didn't fully believe it.

"In what way would that be?" he said, looking at her funny.

"Hank would have left her for sure if it weren't for me. Everybody knows that."

"I'm not following any of this. So just slow it down and let me have it. Take your time. I want to understand this."

"I don't have time to take my time, Archer," she said curtly. "But I'll tell you this. Hank doesn't—didn't—love Marjorie anymore and would have thrown her over in a minute. I mean, divorced her and married someone else. And there were several eligible ladies waiting in the wings, I can tell you that. But then I came along, and I fed Hank's need. Not just in the bedroom—at his age he wasn't really interested very much—but in having a pretty young thing on his arm to show off to folks in town. You saw that in the bar, certainly?" Archer nodded. "Well, it made him feel, well, more virile. You know that word?"

"I've heard it, yeah."

"Hank spends time with me in town and then he goes home to Marjorie for a couple of days and comes back to town on Mondays. Marjorie knew I had no interest in marrying the man."

"Wait a minute, how did Marjorie find out about all this between you and Pittleman? I suppose he told her?"

"No, I did."

"You!"

"I insisted on it. I'm not going behind another woman's back like that."

When Archer still looked confused, she came over to sit next to him. "I know it's complicated, but it was sort of like a negotiation. I wanted money and a place of my own. Hank wanted a young woman to walk around with and show off. And Marjorie wanted to stay in her big house. In the end, everyone got what they wanted."

"So, are you happy?" asked Archer.

"Well, I was until I found out Hank was dead."

"And now?"

"Now, who knows? I'm sort of left out in the cold."

"Your daddy—" he began.

"—does not figure into the equation of my happiness," she said firmly. Then her expression changed. "I should go out and see Marjorie later today. We'll need to let Bart tell her first, of course. You want to come with me?"

Archer looked at her for the longest time until he nodded yes.

"What in the world do you think happened to Hank?" she said. "Who could have killed him? How did he die? Jeb just said it was bloody."

"Beats me," replied Archer.

CHAPTER

15

WHERE'D YOU GET THIS THING?" asked Archer, as, by prearrangement, he was standing in front of the Derby Hotel later that day. His query had been prompted by Jackie's pulling up in a spanking brand-new four-door Nash Ambassador painted a two-tone blue. It looked like a big-butted bullet about to be launched down the road.

"Hank gave it to me," she said through the open driver's window.

"He gave you a house *and* a car?"

"Well, yes. He wanted me to be able to get around in style after all."

"I didn't see the Nash parked at your house."

"That's because I don't keep it at my house. I keep it in a garage not too far from my place.

Do you know what the sun beating down here can do to a car's paint? And don't get me started on the dust. Get in."

Archer slid into the passenger seat and no more than a second passed between his hitting the fabric and Jackie hitting the gas. The Nash sprung forward so fast, it snapped Archer's head back against the seat.

She glanced over at him in her reflector sunglasses, as he looked at her in annoyance. "I like to move fast, Archer. You'll just have to get used to it."

Archer rolled his window down and kept ahold of his hat, or he would have lost it to the back seat while they were still in downtown Poca City. He ran his gaze over the woman. She was dressed in a below-the-knee black dress, with a dark pyramid coat on over it, a felt hat with a bow on the side, sheer black stockings, and demure shoes with low, clunky heels. He supposed it was the mourning wear of chattel. It was a good look for her, not that anything wouldn't be.

They drove for nearly an hour by the sun, and this was confirmed by his watch. When the house came into view, Archer whistled. "Damn, place looks bigger than when I was here the first time. Maybe it keeps growing all on its own like a tree."

Jackie honked the horn as they pulled up to the gate.

About thirty seconds later, Manuel emerged and opened the gates for them.

"Thank you, Manuel," said Jackie as she drove on through, while Archer studied the house.

"How big is this thing, really?" he asked.

"I have no idea, but it's big enough, don't you think?"

"Whose cars are those?" he asked, pointing to a little park-off where two vehicles sat. "They weren't there last time I came."

"That's Hank's Buick convertible, and Marjorie's Cadillac Coupe de Ville."

"Nice rides, though he won't be needing his anymore."

Jackie pulled to the front of the house and they got out. Archer slapped the dust off his hat and then put it back on as he looked around. He lit up a Lucky, then flicked the spent match into the dirt.

He drew down on the Lucky and said, "Actually, I can see why Pittleman would put up a place like this."

"Why?" she asked.

"He'd want everybody driving by to know that this was his place and only he could build it, that's why."

"I like that about you, Archer."

"What's that?"

"You see things."

"Just have to open your eyes."

She flicked him a knowing look. "Now ain't that the truth?"

Archer had to step back quickly because he had almost crushed some of the encroaching flowers when he had started to head up the flagstone walk. When he regained his balance, he watched Jackie walk right into the house without knocking; Archer tossed his cigarette and quickly followed.

Inside he said, "You think the law's been here to tell her?" Though he had been here before, there were so many things to see, he hadn't glimpsed them all. Now he eyed a vase of silk flowers about as tall as he was. Right next to that was a stuffed fox on a wooden pedestal staring at him, while in a hunting crouch. On the wall above that was a tapestry of a Revolutionary War battle scene hung from an ornately carved piece of what looked to be teak. It depicted gallant men dying gallantly seemingly without a thought as to their personal safety, only elegant, patriotic sacrifice in their dignified countenances. It was something Archer had never once seen in three-plus years of actual combat. For him, it had been a tedious and Spartan existence intersected with chaos, fear, and times of sporadic bravery mingled with anger, panic, hatred, self-pity, and sadness at those who had fallen, followed by a guilty relief at still being alive when the shooting had stopped.

Jackie said, "They have. Otherwise, we wouldn't be here." Then she called out, "Marjorie?"

The same elderly sourpuss woman in a maid's uniform toddled out into view.

"Mrs. Pittleman's in the conservatory, Miss Jackie."

"Thank you, Agnes."

Miss Jackie? thought Archer. One would think his companion was mistress of the place.

Jackie led the way down the same long hall that Pittleman had led Archer on his first visit here. She stopped at a door and took a deep breath, seeming to collect herself for the confrontation ahead.

"You okay?" he asked.

She looked up at him. "You ever felt like you were walking into the lion's den?"

"Yeah, it was called World War II."

"Well, that's how I'm feeling right now."

"But you said Marjorie got what she—"

"That means nothing now, Archer. Not with

Hank dead. I could walk in there and get my ass handed to me."

Archer looked at her in confusion.

"Well, here goes nothing," she said to herself.

Jackie opened the door and strode in. Archer followed and closed the door behind them.

This was the room he'd been in before, only he didn't know it was called a conservatory. In the same chair she'd been perched in before was Marjorie. Sitting in front of the woman was a tall glass with chunky ice in it and an amber-colored liquid halfway up.

Jackie walked right up to the woman and swept her arms around her.

"Oh, God, Marjorie, I am so sorry."

Marjorie Pittleman looked up at her, and then glanced at Archer. Her face was shiny with tears. As he had thought before, while the woman was nothing to write home about in the looks department, Archer was once more struck by the delicate refinement in her features that bespoke of perhaps a sympathetic soul within.

A soul that was clearly in distress right now.

"I can't believe it. I really can't. Why, Hank was just here."

"I know. I know."

"And someone killed him? How could that be? The law won't say much at all."

"I don't understand it either, Marjorie. I was stunned when Bart came to tell me."

She patted the older woman's shoulder and placed a kiss on her flat cheek. "Tell me what you need, and I'll go get it, or do it. Anything, Marjorie, really."

"I can't think of a thing. But with Hank gone, what am I supposed to do?"

"Don't you even think about that now. Not for one second."

Marjorie glanced at Archer. "Where are my manners? Hello. You were here before. Hank had hired you for something or other."

Archer took off his hat and glancing nervously at Jackie said, "Yes, ma'am. Name's Archer. I'm very sorry for your loss, Mrs. Pittleman."

"Thank you, Mr. Archer." She looked back at Jackie. "The whole world seems to be crashing down on me. But it was sweet of you to come visit."

Jackie sat down next to her and took Marjorie's hand in hers. "*We'll* get through this. They're going to find who did this and that person will be punished, as they should be."

Marjorie nodded at these words. "I hope you're right, dear. I hope so."

"Did Bart come by? Or was it someone else?"

"No, it was Bart Coleman and the other one. The tall boy."

"Jeb Daniels."

"I guess they'll be looking into this?" interjected Archer.

Marjorie said, "No, I don't think so. Whenever we have a murder out here, they send in someone from the state police to investigate things."

"How many murders do you folks have?" asked Archer, his eyes growing wide.

"Well, every place has somebody killing somebody else," pointed out Jackie matter-of-factly. "And Poca City is no exception." She patted Marjorie's hand. "We'll find out what we can, and then we'll come see you again. Now you need to get some sleep." She eyed the glass. "You think that's a good idea?"

"Better than pills."

"I suppose."

"But what about all Hank's businesses? He never told me anything. I suppose there are things to do."

"All you need to do right now is get some rest. Here, let me help you up to bed. Archer, I won't be long."

The women departed, and Archer was left to his own devices.

He was about to light another Lucky but changed his mind. He stuck it in his hatband for later. He looked out the window. In the rear he could see numerous outbuildings. And cattle in fenced fields. Crops in other fields. Horses in adjacent paddocks. Men and trucks and tractors and dogs racing to and fro. Crop silos rose up from the dirt like the rocket ships Archer had seen in comic books. He had seen all this on his previous trip, too, and it was just as impressive the second time around. There was a lot of business going on here, and the missus of the house didn't appear to be up for any of it.

He opened the glass door and walked out into the back.

He spotted Sid Duckett holding a clipboard and talking to three other men who looked tired but were listening intently. After the men left, Archer walked over to the big man, who was dressed nearly the same as before, in dirty pants, a tucked-in cotton shirt, dusty boots, and a straw hat.

"Guess you heard the news?"

Duckett nodded.

Archer surveyed all the activity. "A lot going on here."

"Yeah but it's not just here. He's got a lot of businesses. Including a bank."

"A bank?"

"Man owned First City Bank in Poca. And the Derby Hotel *and* the Cat's Meow."

"Damn, didn't know about the Cat's Meow. So, what'll happen to everything now that the man's dead?"

Duckett looked toward the house. "The missus don't really get involved in all that. Maybe sell out?"

Archer scratched his ear. "Hell, who around here can buy all that?"

"Well, there's Lucas Tuttle."

"Jackie's father?"

"That's right. He's got a lot of land. I mean a lot. And he's got money, least so I've heard. So how'd he die, Archer, you know?"

"Law says murder."

"Damn."

"You think of anybody who'd want to do him in?"

Duckett shook his head. "He could drive a man who works for him hard and don't I know that. And cut some tough bargains with other folks. But kill the man?" Duckett took off his hat and slapped it against his leg to clear the dust off. "I can't think of a one."

"There was at least *one*."

He walked back into the conservatory in time for Jackie to reenter the room.

"You ready?" she said.

"I guess so. Was just talking to Sid Duckett out there. He said Pittleman owns a bank and the Cat's Meow."

"That's right. Didn't you know that?"

"How the hell was I supposed to know that?"

"Don't snap at me, Archer. I was just asking a question."

"Anyway, he said Mrs. Pittleman might have to sell out."

"She might, and she might not. That's not our concern right now, is it?"

"He said your daddy may want to buy it."

Jackie looked warily at him. "Is that right?"

"Yeah, why?"

"Nothing."

"How's Mrs. Pittleman doing?"

"Terrible. She just lost her husband."

"Good news is, she seemed to like you."

"I explained that. And, no, she doesn't like me."

"If you say so."

"I *do* say so. Now I would still like to know where those debt papers are. You got any ideas?"

"Not a one," lied Archer because it just seemed the smart thing to do right now.

They stopped on the way back at a roadside

store and got some cold cider and a bag of peanuts still in their shells.

They sat in the Nash's front seat, which was so big it seemed capable of holding Archer's old platoon in its entirety. They ate and drank their fill while an occasional truck or car passed by on the road. They just tossed the shells out the windows. Archer watched as a man on a mule trotted by with a burlap sack over his shoulder.

"What was the war like, Archer?"

He glanced over to see her sweeping peanut skins off the lap of her mourning dress.

"What do you think war's supposed to be like?"

"I've never been to war. It's why I'm asking. You like your questions and so do I."

"It wasn't a lot of fun."

"Were you wounded?"

He finished his cold cider and laid the empty bottle on the floorboard. "I was."

"I saw a scar on your back and another one on your leg when we were in bed. Why didn't they send you home?"

"Because I could still fight."

"You ever kill anyone?"

"That was sort of the point of me being over there."

"How'd you do it?"

"What sort of question is that?"

"I'm just trying to understand you."

"Why's that?"

"I find you interesting."

"Shouldn't you be thinking about the dearly departed Hank Pittleman?"

"I already told you, I'm sorry he's dead, but it's not like I loved the man."

"Do you have to give the house and car back now?"

"It's up to Marjorie. Which means I won't be able to keep them. But back to the killing."

"You won't let it go, will you?"

"Well?"

"Okay, I shot a bunch of Germans and Italians. Then I killed some with my grenades, and some with my bayonet when it came down to man-to-man slogging it out. Slit one's throat with my knife. Killed one man with my bare hands when we both ran out of bullets. Broke his neck the way I'd been taught."

"My God, Archer. That must've done something to you."

"How do you mean?"

"You can't kill all those people and not be affected by it."

"It's what I was trained to do."

"Didn't you feel anything?"

"Yeah, I felt damn lucky I was alive, and they weren't."

She put the Nash in gear. "Well, I don't see how it couldn't have affected you."

"I don't think about it much. Seems to work okay."

"Yeah, well, one day that may not work anymore."

"How do you know about things like that?"

"I told you I studied psychology in college, Archer. After the First World War, men came back with *shellshock*, or so they termed it. The human brain was not designed for war. It changes you. You weren't a killer before you went to war, were you?"

"Never killed anything before I went across the Atlantic. Man or beast."

"Wait a minute, you never hunted, even?"

"Not much to hunt where I'm from."

"But then you became a killer in the war."

"Well, I'm not in the war anymore. And I'm no killer."

She gave him a worried look and steered the Nash onto the road back to Poca City.

CHAPTER

16

AFTER JACKIE DROPPED HIM OFF, Archer
walked down the hall of the Derby Hotel. As
he passed by Number 615, a man in his forties
stepped out dressed in a wrinkled dark blue
three-piece pinstriped suit, worn black leather
shoes, and a solid red tie that could have done
with some laundering. He was about five-ten
and 160 pounds, and looked lean and wiry
and tough, with a face that reminded Archer
of a boxer he had once seen in the ring during
an impromptu match he'd attended during the
war when they'd had a brief respite from fighting. A jutting chin of granite, a nose knocked
off center, two hardened lumps for cheeks, and
flattened, cauliflower ears. His hair was thick,

unkempt, and graying. Over his mouth was a ribbon of dark mustache. He wore a black homburg with a gray band.

Most remarkably for Archer, his eyes were twin darts of crystallized coal, or close to it. They were the calmest pair of eyes Archer had ever seen.

Those eyes now looked at Archer with interest.

"You staying here on this floor, son?" the man said.

"Who's asking?"

The man opened his coat, revealing a silver pointy badge on his vest. "State police. Detective Lieutenant Irving Shaw is asking, Mr.…?"

"Archer. You're a homicide dick, then?"

Shaw ignored this and said, "So *you're* Archer? You were at Miss Jackie Tuttle's residence this morning, correct? The deputies reported that to me."

"I was."

"You two going out or something?"

"Just a friend. Told the same to your deputies."

"A friend who's at her house early in the morning? You sure you didn't spend the night?"

"I slept here last night. I went to see Jackie at her place this morning."

"Why that early?"

"Missed her, I guess."

Shaw took out a worn, small notebook and a stubby pencil and wrote something down. "You say you slept here last night? What room?"

"Number 610."

Shaw eyed the location of Archer's room and his bits of coal eyes lit up like someone had flamed them.

"You hear anything last night?"

"Like what?"

"Anything out of the ordinary."

"I haven't been here that long. So I don't think I know what's ordinary for Poca City yet."

"Just use your common sense then."

"No, I slept pretty hard. Didn't hear anything."

Shaw wrote something else down. "You coulda just told me that to begin with."

"I could've, sure. Sorry about that."

"You're in from Carderock Prison, I hear."

"And I served my time."

"Not all of it. I looked you up. You're on parole now. Ernestine Crabtree?"

"That's right. Already reported in."

"Good for you. So, your story is you were asleep from when to when?"

"Oh, about midnight to six or so."

"You see the deceased last night?"

Archer had been stunned that the two deputies had not earlier asked this question. But this fellow Shaw appeared to be a far superior sort of person. He seemed to like asking questions as much as Archer did.

Shaw had his pencil poised over his note-book.

"You hear me, Mr. Archer?"

"Yeah, I saw him. He was drunk. Outside the Cat's Meow. Me and Miss Tuttle helped him to his bed in there and left."

"So you were at the bar last night with them?"

"I'm not allowed in the bar. Against my parole."

"So it is. Then how'd you run into them?"

"I was passing by the bar last night when I saw them come out. Miss Tuttle was having a struggle holding him up. So, I helped her out."

Shaw rubbed at his mustache with the pencil. "And she let a stranger do that?"

"I had met her before. Both of them, actually."

"Is that right? Where would that have been?"

Archer felt something go hard in the pit of his stomach.

"Around town. My first night here, actually. We struck up a conversation. Interesting man. And she was nice, too."

Shaw wrote something else down and shook his head.

"What?" asked Archer, trying to peer at his scribblings.

"Every question I ask you, it seems to get deeper and deeper."

"What does?"

He ignored this query, too. "The deputies said Mr. Pittleman had hired you to collect a debt owed by one Lucas Tuttle?"

"That's right."

"And you have not been successful?"

"Not yet."

"Would that have been Miss Tuttle who dropped you off in front of the hotel? I just happened to be looking out the window."

Archer felt the stomach pit grow larger. "Yeah, it was. We went out to pay our respects to Mr. Pittleman's widow."

He chuckled. "Short time in town and you met all these folks already. Impressive."

"I'm a friendly sort."

"I'm sure you are, Archer, I'm sure you are. So you and Miss Tuttle helped the deceased from the bar back to here and put him in his bed right there in Room 615? Correct?"

"That's right."

"And what time was that?"

"Eleven or so."

"Eleven or so. And then what'd you two do?"

Archer wanted to lie, desperately wanted to say they had gone their separate ways, but he was unsure what Jackie would say, and once you lied to the law, it was all over.

"We went to my room."

The man's eyebrow went up as he wrote this down. "You went to your room. Number 610 right there? You and Miss Tuttle?"

"That's right."

"What for?"

"We had a drink, well maybe more than one when all was said and done."

"Doesn't your parole forbid the consumption of alcohol?"

"Does it?"

Shaw gave him a patronizing look. "What *else* did you have?"

"Why is that important?"

"Use your common sense again, Archer."

"I didn't have anything to do with that man's death."

"And I don't remember accusing you of it."

"Well, your questions are kind of funny."

"These questions are standard procedure, Archer. Didn't they ask you such when they arrested you before?"

"That wasn't for killing anybody."

"But still."

Archer leaned against the wall. "We spent some time together. I fell asleep. When I woke up, she was gone."

"This time together. Would that be with clothes on or off?"

Archer's features darkened, even as his anxiety rose. "Why's that matter?"

"I can't see how you would think it *doesn't* matter, son."

"I don't know if I want to answer any more of your questions."

"You don't have a choice, Archer. The law is the law."

"Yeah, folks keep telling me that. Okay, we were in bed together. Then she left."

"So, you slept with the dead man's mistress on the night Hank Pittleman was murdered right down the hall from your room?"

"She's not his mistress."

"Really, what is she then?"

"You'll have to ask her."

"Oh, I will, Archer. Rest assured."

"Is that all?"

"No, it's not, son. So, after you left Mr. Pittleman in his room, you never went back there?"

Archer pushed off the wall and gathered his

wits. This fellow Shaw was poking him like a stick to a hornet's nest. Only thing was, he was hitting all the bad spots, for Archer.

"Had no reason to."

"So that's a no, is it?"

"That's a no," Archer lied.

"Understand you were in the Army."

"Who told you that?"

"I don't need to tell you that and I'm not. You know your way around a gun and a knife then?"

"Look, I didn't have nothing—"

"*Were* you in the military, Archer?" interrupted Shaw.

"Were you?"

"Okay, I'll play your game just this one time. I was a pilot in the Army Air Forces. Ninety-three bombing sorties over Europe, then I took my wings to the Pacific and dropped a shitload of TNT on the Japs. Loved every minute of it and was scared to death every minute of it."

Archer judged him in a new, more respectful light. "That's impressive. Lot more complicated flying a plane than firing a rifle."

"I think every man who put on the uniform was impressive. You?"

"Thirty-Fourth Infantry Division. Mostly in

Italy, but we did work our way to Germany eventually. Though we fought more Germans in Italy than we did I-talians."

"Then I think you maybe had it harder than me. That was some damn tough going, I heard. Lot of those GIs never came home from that campaign."

"Sure seemed tough going to me at the time. I liked my foxhole as much as the next man. Only we never got to spend much time there. And the Germans had damn good aim when it came to shelling us when we were hunkered in the dirt."

"You get shot up?"

"We all got shot up. You done with me now?" Shaw put away his notebook and pencil and gave him a bemused look. "You know your way around a gun and a knife, and you were sleeping with the dead man's whatever on the night that he died. And by your own admission you were drinking. And all night you were maybe fifty feet from where he was killed. And you have no alibi for the time he probably died." He paused. "So not only am I not done with you, Archer, I'm just starting." He closed the door to 615 and made a show of locking it.

That was the first time Archer noted the white dust coating the doorknob.

Shaw tipped his hat at Archer and added, "Do not try to leave Poca City, Mr. Archer. That would not be smart. It would make me very unhappy. And you even unhappier than me."

He walked off leaving Archer feeling like he'd just been rolled over twice by a Panzer. He bent down and looked at the doorknob and the white dust coating it. He reached out to touch it but thought better of that notion and retreated down the hall.

Archer went back to his room, picked up the flask, and drained the contents. He wiped his mouth dry, went over to the one window, and looked out at Poca City. He watched as Shaw walked out of the hotel and then stopped. The blood slowly drained from Archer's face as he saw the man Shaw was talking to. It was the front desk clerk Archer had queried about seeing Jackie. The man was gesticulating in the direction of the hotel, while Shaw pulled out his pencil and notebook and wrote it all down. Archer thought he could see the lawman's triumphant look from up here.

Archer sat down on the bed and started to think things through.

None of this was looking particularly good for him. The money in his pocket, the residue from Pittleman's advance, the papers he'd taken from the dead man, all felt like lumps of white-hot coal melting him away from the inside. He knew Shaw was probably going to see Jackie next, and what would she tell him?

You didn't kill the man, Archer.

Yet he hadn't committed the crime he'd been sent to Carderock for, and that hadn't stopped them, had it?

And from what Shaw had said, the motive would be clear.

I slept with Pittleman's mistress.

I'd been drinking.

I knew how to slit someone's throat.

But Pittleman had hired him for a job. Now he had no job, like Jackie had told the deputies. That would cut against any reason he would have to murder Pittleman. But would it be enough? Clearly not if Detective Shaw were the sole arbiter of his guilt or innocence.

He lay back on the bed and wondered if Poca City would be the last stop of his short-lived life.

CHAPTER

17

LATER, ARCHER HEADED OUT. As he passed by the front desk, he looked at the clerk there who had been talking to Shaw outside.

"How you doing, brother?" said Archer.

"Better 'n you, by a long shot, mister."

"Why's that?" asked Archer, marching over to him. "Give me the straight dope, pal."

The smaller man drew back, fear riding in his eyes and the shakes of his limbs.

"Don't mean nothing," said the man. "Just leave me be."

"Take it easy. I mean you no harm."

"Says you," he replied darkly. "Tell that to poor Mr. Pittleman," he added.

Archer wheeled around and walked outside. He took three long breaths, something he had done in the Army before every significant military engagement he and his fellow soldiers had been called up to do. He hadn't been a superstitious person before he'd gone in the Army, but he'd damn well become one while in uniform.

Three long breaths and I came home alive.

His spirits suddenly sagged.

For prison and now this?

He had some decisions to make. There was one area of possibility. With Pittleman dead, Jackie might, despite her words, see the benefit of reconciling with her father. But would Marjorie take Tuttle to court to get the money repaid? If so, Archer wouldn't be getting a dime from that. But maybe Marjorie didn't know, or wouldn't care, about the forty dollars her husband had advanced to him. Yet Shaw could use that as a motive for Archer to have killed Pittleman if he found out about it.

Caught between a rock and a hard place, Archer, so what are you going to do?

He hoofed it to 27 Eldorado Street and knocked on the door. When no one appeared, he tried the door. It was unlocked. He walked in, calling out Jackie's name as he went. He found the woman lying in bed with not a shred of clothing on. She had a glass of something held to her lips.

"You just looking or buying?" she said, taking a swallow of whatever was in the glass.

"I don't know. You tell me."

"I'm hurting, Archer, more than I thought I would be. Come over here and do something about my melancholia."

"What do you want me to do?"

"If I have to tell you, what good are you?"

He crossed the floor, stripped down in record time, and lay alongside her.

"That's better," she said, giving him a kiss.

"I feel funny doing this now."

"Because of Hank? It's because of Hank that I want to do it. Otherwise, I'd just be crying."

"I thought you didn't love him?"

"I didn't. But I can still be sad. I'm no angel, Archer. I'm also thinking that my means of livelihood is about to come to an end. So let me enjoy the moment, damn you."

She gripped a part of him so hard he gasped, then she kissed him roughly and they went from there.

Later, when they were done, she lay her head on Archer's arm and stroked his flat, rigid stomach.

"You have any family, Archer, any brothers and sisters?"

"No. Just me."

"You said you never hit a woman, Archer, like Hank did me?"

"I told you that because it's the truth."

"Oh come on, never? Don't lie to me."

"Like I told you, I never even thought about doing it."

"Why? Because you never had sisters?"

"I'd like to think it's because I see the unfairness of a guy hitting a gal."

"How about your parents? They alive?"

He shook his head and stroked her hair. "They died while I was overseas. Never got a chance to say good-bye, or even see 'em buried."

She rested her chin on his chest and stared at him. "Why not?"

"Couldn't get any leave to go home. My division was in hard fighting with the Germans. The battle for Bologna was, well, it was tough. Good thing the war ended a couple weeks after that because we were beat up bad. So even if I could've gotten leave, there was no way for me to get out. Not that I'd have wanted to."

"Why wouldn't you have wanted to?"

"My parents were dead, Jackie. Nothing was bringing them back. But the Thirty-Fourth needed every soldier it could muster. If we all started taking leave, a lot more men would have died who didn't need to."

"That was very heroic of you."

"No, it wasn't. Heroes are special people who do things they're not expected to do. I was just a grunt doing my job like millions of other grunts. Only I got to come home for no good reason other than I was lucky enough not to die."

"Still, that must have been awful, not even seeing them buried."

"It happened to lots of boys during the war. Why should I be any different?"

"That's extraordinarily magnanimous of you."

"Those are big college words for such a little thing."

"I'm an only child, too. I don't have anyone, either."

"Well, you have your father, like it or not."

Her fingers stopped stroking his belly for a moment before resuming.

"You sure know how to press my buttons, Archer," she said. "And not in a good way."

There were a few moments of silence until Archer said, "Hey, did that detective fellow Shaw come and see you too?"

She sat up and looked down at him, covering her nakedness with the sheet.

"Yes. I didn't like him. He asked a lot of questions."

"What did you tell him?" he asked.

"Well, what did *you* tell him?"

"The truth. Mostly."

"I told him the whole truth. Nothing for it."

"Meaning?"

"He asked where we met, and I told him."

"At the bar?"

"Well, that's the truth, Archer."

Well, there goes my parole. My butt's heading back to Carderock regardless.

"And what did he say?"

"Nothing, but he wrote it all down."

"I'm sure he did. He's a man who likes his pencil and paper. What else?"

"That Hank had hired you to collect a debt from my father. But he already knew that."

"What else?"

"That you had to carry Hank to his room and then we went back to your place for a nightcap."

"Did you tell him what else we did?"

"Not in so many words. Did you tell him we slept together?"

"What else was I supposed to say?"

"A gentleman would not have betrayed a lady's secret. I *do* have a reputation to preserve, Archer."

"Is that right? Well, he called you Hank Pittleman's *mistress*."

"I corrected him on that. Not that he cared. Just looked at me funny."

"Man's a bulldog. He's not going to let this go."

"We have nothing to hide, Archer."

"You and I know that. But what about him?"

"I'm sure it will be fine."

"What about Marjorie?"

"What about her?"

"She may sell out everything."

"She may. It's her right. I told you that."

"So you really think she's going to turn on you then, even after being nice to you today?"

"We're not friends, Archer. We needed each other, that's what I've been telling you, only apparently you weren't listening. With Hank dead, Marjorie Pittleman would love to see me in the street with not a dime to my name. I went over there today trying to buy some time, make her see me in a supportive light." She sighed heavily. "But Marjorie's no dummy. With Hank dead my goose is cooked." She grabbed her pack of cigarettes and lighter off the nightstand and ignited a Chesterfield. Archer declined her offer of one.

She took a puff, blew smoke sideways from her mouth, and said in a funereal tone, "Well, it was fun while it lasted." She pulled the sheet tighter around her with her free hand as she smoked her cigarette. "It's a man's world, Archer. Your kind has all the money and all the power."

"Hold on, now. Don't lump me in with the likes of Hank Pittleman. My pockets are just about empty, and as for power, that's a laugh. I'm an ex-con with about as few prospects as a man can have, even after helping to win a big war."

She tousled his hair. "Well, I can see your point. But it still makes me so mad. It wasn't that long ago where we couldn't even vote. Women have to scrounge around the edges for our share, and let the men think they're so far above us, we're just happy to be along for the ride. It won't always be that way, but it's the way it is now."

"Is that your psychology education talking?"

"That and my common sense and living in this world." She snuffed out her smoke in a tall glass of melted ice. "So now I'm up a creek without a paddle or a damn canoe."

"What will you do now?"

"I'm not going back to my father, if that's what you're suggesting." She lit another cigarette. "What about you?"

"I'm not sure how I collect the debt now and get paid."

"Way I see it, you have options. Hank's dead. My father can pay the money back in good conscience since I'm no longer with Hank. Then you can collect the money Hank promised you from Marjorie. I'll vouch for the deal that Hank made with you. I was there after all. I think she'll listen to reason. I mean, five thousand dollars is a lot of money. And if she wants it back, you have to get paid."

"I could go out and see your father. You think he knows about what happened?"

"Of course he does. But I wouldn't go out there just yet."

"Why not?"

"Hank was *murdered*, Archer. You rushing around trying to cash in on his death will not be missed by Mr. Shaw."

Archer looked at her statement from several angles and pronounced her words starkly plausible. "So maybe I should just lie low for a bit. Shaw already thinks I might've killed Pittleman."

"And you're sure you didn't?"

"You're thinking I'm a killer and yet you just let me in your bed?"

"Well, it was as pleasurable for me as it was for you. And you didn't murder *me*. So let some time pass and then you can take my car while the Nash is *still* my car and go see my father."

"You okay with me seeing your old man?"

"So long as I don't have to go back to the son of a bitch, I'm okay with just about anything, Archer."

CHAPTER

18

THAT NIGHT ARCHER WAS SITTING ALONE at a table in the Checkered Past restaurant looking over his menu. The place was packed, and he had grabbed the last available table. He glanced up from his menu when she walked in. Ernestine Crabtree had reverted to her office look, meaning an exceedingly modest dress in a drab range of charcoal with a coat sporting big flap pockets that widened her hips. Her hair was once more wound in a fiercely tight bun, the shell specs fronted her face, and she had on not a stitch of powder or lipstick. Her tall heels had shrunk by several inches, and her nylons were thick and scratchy looking. She was holding a wide-brimmed cartwheel hat the color of a robin's egg, which served to brighten her appearance a bit. Still, Archer had to almost look twice to make sure it was the same woman.

As there were no empty tables, she looked ready to leave when Archer raised his hand.

"Miss Crabtree," he called out.

The woman glanced sharply in his direction and stiffened when she laid eyes on Archer.

Her gaze darted to the door, but he moved to checkmate her by crying out, "Got a seat for you right here." He indicated the empty chair opposite him.

She vacillated in the doorway of the eatery and, finally, perhaps her hunger taking precedent over her good sense, she strode across the room and sat quickly in the seat he had indicated. She might have thought if she rushed this through, no one would notice that a parole officer was about to eat with a parolee, at least that was Archer's observation.

She set her hat down on the table.

Archer had set his hat on his chairback. He slipped it on, then lifted it off, tipped it in her direction, and returned it to the chairback.

"Good to see you."

"Um, yes."

He passed her his menu.

She avoided looking at him and focused on the choices for dinner.

"You eat here a lot?" asked Archer. "I mean, I saw you the other time of course."

"I eat here *sometimes*."

She seemed to decide on her supper and set the menu down. When it appeared she could no longer avoid setting eyes on him, Crabtree lifted her gaze to his and said, "I heard about Hank Pittleman. They say he was murdered, in his room at the Derby Hotel."

"He was."

"Does that help you or hurt you?" she asked bluntly.

"I was sitting here thinking about that myself."

"And what have you concluded?"

"That it's not a simple answer one way or another."

"I guess I can see that."

He cocked his head. "*Can* you now?"

"The man who is owed the debt is dead. Is the debt still owed? Legally, yes. But pragmatically? And what if his widow isn't aware of the liability? Men often don't tell their wives anything about their business, believing, wrongly, that they won't understand. Now Lucas Tuttle may decide he never has to pay it back. In which case, you probably won't be compensated. But the upside might be that you won't have to pay back the forty dollars to Pittleman's estate."

"Couldn't have said it better myself, ma'am. In fact, you show a right logical mind."

"Are you sure you weren't about to add, 'For a girl'?"

He put a hand over his heart and held the other one up. "So help me God, I was not."

She smiled at this.

"A man named Irving Shaw has already talked to me. Do you know him?"

"I know *of* him. He's a lieutenant detective with the state police. Very highly respected."

"Yeah, I imagine so. He asked a lot of questions."

"Why did he question you?"

"I'm on the same floor as the dead man. Shaw wanted to know if I'd heard or seen anything."

"And did you?"

"No. And I told him so."

"I wonder who could have killed Pittleman?"

"From what I've learned about the man, that list might be pretty long."

"As I said before, he owns a lot of property in town, including the Cat's Meow."

Archer lit up a cigarette and studied her, tapping his ash twice into the ashtray before speaking. "Speaking of the place, Dan Bullock's back in jail, I take it, after coming after you with a knife when you were on your way home from there?"

To her credit, Crabtree didn't even flinch. "So, you followed me?"

"I followed *him* because he was following you. I wouldn't have let him hurt you. Turns out, you didn't need me." He glanced at her purse. "You got the snub-nose in there now?"

"In my line of work, I rarely go anywhere without it."

"Why'd you choose that 'line of work' in the first place?"

She took a few moments to light her smoke, tapping her ash alongside his.

"It's a job. And I *do* help people. The ones like Dickie Dill and Bullock are hopeless cases, I will freely admit that." She paused and took a long draw on her Pall Mall. "But you're not, Archer, not by a long shot, if I'm any judge."

"How's the story you're writing coming?"

"Slowly. But I have a lot of material."

"Where do you get that?"

"Life."

"So, where'd you live before coming here?" he asked, bending his matchstick in half and depositing it in the black ashtray sitting between them.

In response, Crabtree waved the waitress over.

She stood next to the table, pad and pen in hand. She was in her fifties, tired and worn-out looking, with gray hair partially covered by the cap that was part of her uniform—a dark brown short-sleeved one-piece with a frilly, stained apron built into the front.

"What are you all having?" she said curtly.

Archer glanced at Crabtree, who said, "I'll have the beef stew."

"To drink?"

"Lemonade."

She wrote this down and turned to Archer. "You, sir?"

"Steak rare, with the potatoes and green beans. And coffee to drink. Black. And for dessert, how about a slice of that coconut cream pie I see behind the glass over there."

She wrote this down and departed.

Crabtree took another puff of her cigarette. "I was born and raised in Texas. I left when I was seventeen. When the war started, I worked building airplanes."

"Really, which kind?" he said with interest.

"Quite a few actually. The last one I worked on was the B-29 bomber at a plant in Georgia."

He nodded appreciatively. "The Superfortress, they called it. Seen them in the skies when I was over there. And didn't one of them drop the A-bombs on the Japs?"

"Yes, I believe that's right."

"Building airplanes. That's impressive, Miss Crabtree."

"I wanted to do my part, as I'm sure you did."

"You still have family in Texas?"

"No. I have no family left. None." She stared down at the table.

He nodded, felt sorry for her obvious uncom-fortableness, and decided to say no more for now. They waited in silence until their food came. They ate with only the occasional glance at each other. In the middle of it, Archer excused himself to use the washroom.

Later, when he'd finished off his steak and vegetables, he eyed the slice of pie the waitress had set off to the side of the table.

"I'd be honored if you'd split the pie with me," he said.

"No, I really couldn't," said Crabtree, setting down her utensils.

"One bite of pie isn't going to kill anybody."

She sighed and looked unsure but reached for her fork.

"It *is* good," she said as they ate away at it.

"Lot better than what they fed us in the war. It was either rotted or too hard for the teeth."

"What did you do then?"

"Scrounged off the countryside."

"You mean you stole from people?"

"I never stole from anybody. Lots of places were abandoned. If I put a hunk of bread or an apple or some raw carrots in my pocket, I don't think anybody minded."

Crabtree wiped her mouth with a cloth napkin. "Well, I'm just glad the war's over."

"You and me both."

"Thank you for the pie. I should go now. I will pay my bill separately, of course."

"Already paid the bill when I went to use the john."

"Now why did you do that?"

"I knew if I'd offered, you wouldn't let me, so...."

"It's against the rules for me to—"

"You tell me how it's wrong for a man to buy a woman a meal? I mean, you're helping me out with all the parole stuff. This is a way of thanking you."

"It's my job. It's what I'm paid to do. It is not done out of friendship or kindness."

"I paid for your dinner out of an act of kindness. Do you want ex-cons to be kind and thoughtful or not?"

"Well, when you put it that way, the answer

seems obvious, I suppose. So thank you very much for dinner."

"Good, now it's a fine evening. We can walk off dinner."

"I...I really should be—"

"I can at least walk you home."

She glanced at him sharply. "If you saw Dan Bullock, you know where I live."

He nodded. "So what happened to him? You never said."

"He was sent back to prison based on my written account and the knife that he had with his fingerprints on it. I called the police as soon as I got in my house. They picked him up trying to hitch a ride out of town."

"I think he's right where he belongs, then." He stood, put on his hat, and looked down at her. "You ready?"

She picked up her purse and hat, and they set off together.

19

THE AIR WAS CRISP, which was a nice change, though the sky was clear to the horizon and probably beyond. Archer kept glancing at his companion curiously as she walked along rigidly and uncomfortably.

Crabtree said, "So, with Pittleman dead, that means you no longer have a job?"

"The jury's still out on that, so to speak."

"How so?"

"I have an opportunity to still make it pay off, only I have to handle things delicately."

"With Lucas Tuttle?"

"Right. I'm going out to meet with him at some point."

"Why not right away?"

"Well, with Mr. Pittleman being murdered and

all, it's probably smart to let things quiet down a little before I go making money off something connected to him."

"Oh, I guess I can see that." She suddenly eyed him sharply. "Archer, you didn't have anything to do with the man's death, did you?"

"I swear on a stack of Bibles that I didn't."

Her gaze lingered on him for a bit. Her look had told Archer all he needed to know. She and Jackie both thought he might have killed the man.

"Did you finish that book you were reading, by, who was it again?"

"Virginia Woolf. And yes, I did. It was wonderful." She paused. "The writing of hers I like best isn't a novel or a short story, but an essay entitled *A Room of One's Own*."

"What's it about?"

"A woman working in a man's world, essentially."

"Is that how you see it?"

"Perhaps."

"I read a lot in prison. I like detective stories. You heard of Philip Marlowe, Sam Spade, and that little fellow from Belgium?"

"Yes, I have. They're quite entertaining."

"And maybe I can make a living doing that sort of work," said Archer. He had thought of this before and had decided to try it out on her.

"From convict to detective? Quite a leap."

"I was a scout in the Army. My job was to look at things, take in a bunch of information, and then take a course of action. Probably close to what Detective Shaw is doing right now, don't you think?"

She looked impressed with his logic. "I think you might be right."

They eventually arrived at her house.

"You own it?"

"No, I'm renting it for the time being."

"It's really pretty."

She smiled. "It wasn't so *pretty* when I got here, but I've had some things repaired. Though the door to my bedroom still jams. I can never fully close it."

"I can fix that in a jiffy."

She looked alarmed. "What? No, that's all right."

"Ma'am, I'm right here. Probably take me no more than a few minutes."

"Archer, I wouldn't feel comfortable letting you do that."

"Ma'am, let me just say something."

"All right," she said, looking at him warily.

"I spent time in prison with the likes of Dickie

Dill and others like him. They're hard men, and some of them live right here. And one of them followed you home."

"But I took care of that."

"And one of them wrote you that nasty note. So you need to lock your doors—that includes your front door and your bedroom door. Because if they get the jump on you, well...."

She stared at him very deliberately for a long moment.

"I think you're sincere," she said at last.

"That's because I am."

She turned and led him inside.

The interior of the place was Spartanly furnished but it was neat and overly clean, at least to Archer's mind. There were also a goodly number of books on the shelves. From a glance he could see novels by people named Faulkner, Brontë, Whitman, Wharton, Austen, Dickens, Twain, and Steinbeck. And there were quite a few legal tomes, too.

"Got a lot of law books there."

"I actually wanted to be a lawyer once."

"Pardon my ignorance, but can women be lawyers?"

"Of course they can! But I will admit, it's unusual."

"If you want to be one, then I say go for it. Sure you'd make a fine one."

"Thank you, Mr. Archer," she said, evidently pleased by his remark.

"You have relations who are in the law?"

"No, but my father—" She faltered.

"Your father was a lawyer?"

"No, he was—" She broke off and said, "Let me show you the door."

Crabtree led him down a short, plain hall to her bedroom. She took off her hat, dropped it on the bed, and put her purse down on a dresser with a tilt mirror topping it.

"This is the problem, Mr. Archer."

She attempted to close the door, but it caught on the floor.

"Okay, let me see this thing."

He swung it back and forth until the door rubbed like before.

"It's not the door. I believe the floor might be off a bit." Archer took out a nickel and set it on one end on the floor, and they watched it roll right over to the closet door.

"Yep, I'd say the floor is definitely not plumb."

He pointed to the door hinges.

"I think if I tighten the screws up enough on these hinges, it should clear the floor, warped though it is. You got a screwdriver?"

"Let me look. It might take a few minutes."

"I got nowhere to be."

After she left, he looked around and noted the perfectly made bed and the shade on the window that he had watched before she had cut the view off by closing the drapes. He looked in the corner and saw the pair of high heels that she had been wearing the night before.

As he glanced once more at the bed, Archer saw what looked to be the edge of a book poking out from under a pillow. He checked that she wasn't coming back, and then hurried over to the bed. He had no right or business to be doing this, but he couldn't seem to help himself. For Archer, more information was always better than less. And he just thought, at first, that it was a novel. But when he slid it out, he saw that it was a scrapbook. He turned the page and saw the old, yellowed news article. It was from a local newspaper in Amarillo, Texas.

It detailed the trial of Carson Crabtree, who had killed three men in separate encounters. There was a photo of Carson within the news article. It showed a huge man with a bald head and a fierce countenance. He had, surprisingly, worked as a police officer, and curiously enough considering his features and the crimes committed, had the reputation of being kind and considerate to all who knew him. Yet not only had Carson not blamed his actions on mental affliction, the report said, but he also had confessed to the murders. He had died in the electric chair leaving behind a wife, Jewell, and one daughter, Ernestine.

Archer flipped to the next page and saw the grainy image of Ernestine Crabtree, then only fourteen. She looked small, drab, and dour, and it was hard for Archer to believe that she had grown up into the tall, lovely woman he knew her to be. There were a few other stories about this incident, including ones about the three men killed. And their pictures were included, too. Archer studied the men, and then read about their backgrounds. Each was twenty and had been in and out of trouble with the law since their midteens. As Archer read down the list of crimes committed by them, one caught his attention.

Peeping Tom.

Each of the three men had been shot, their bodies left where they fell. The sidearm used was Carson's police-issued one. There had been no trial, what with the man's confession, and no deal worked to avoid the death penalty for that confession. And Archer wondered why.

He heard footsteps coming and he hastily slid

the book back under the pillow exactly as it had been before and stepped over to the door.

A few seconds later she appeared in the doorway. "Here it is, Mr. Archer."

He took the screwdriver from her. "I'm gonna loosen the screws first. When I say so, if you can, just pull up on the edge of the door. Use the knob to grip."

She did so when he told her to, and he tightened the upper hinges. Then he got down on his knees and partially unscrewed the ones there.

"Just pull up as much as you can now."

Crabtree let go of the doorknob, lifted her arms high, and gripped the upper edge of the door and pushed toward the ceiling, which raised the lower right edge of the door about a half inch.

"Just a little higher now. The holes are almost lined up where I need them to be."

She went up on her tippy-toes and stretched out even more.

"Okay, hold it right there."

He glanced over and saw that, with her efforts, the woman's dress had ridden up some. And with him where he was, he had a clear sightline up her dress, revealing her stocking tops and pale thighs above them. He quickly looked away, feeling embarrassed for her. And maybe for himself, too. That was a new one for Archer.

My mother always said I would grow up at some point. And maybe Poca City's the place.

"Okay, that should do it." He got up off the floor. "Try it now."

She did so, and the door swung freely. She smiled. "That's wonderful, Mr. Archer. Thank you."

"And don't forget to lock it now. And you may want to sleep with that gun under your pillow, too."

They went back into the other room, and Archer spotted a bottle and two glasses on a bureau. He picked up the bottle. "Rebel Yell. I hear they make it from wheat, not rye."

"You're not supposed to drink alcohol, Mr. Archer."

"Oh, I know that. Number 14 on the list. I was just wondering. A man does get thirsty here. With all the dang dust."

"Well, you *did* fix my door, and I guess one nip won't hurt."

She poured out two small portions, and they clinked glasses.

"I'm growing to like this town," he said, taking a sip.

"Why's that?"

"You have good people, for one thing. Like yourself. Trying to help others, like me."

She smiled and nodded. "You seem to have come a long way since our first meeting."

"So what does the *J* stand for?"

"I beg your pardon?"

"Ernestine J. Crabtree. It's on your office door. What's the *J* stand for?"

"Oh, um, Jewell. It was my mother's first name."

"Well, it's a pretty name."

"Yes…"

He finished his nip. "Well, I better get on."

"Thank you for a nice evening, Mr. Archer."

He tipped his hat. "My pleasure, Miss Crabtree."

Archer headed back to the hotel, where he ran straight into Detective Irving Shaw.

20

IRVING SHAW WAS LEANING BACK on the front desk in the lobby, staring out toward the main entrance doors, his hat tipped back. His thumbs were tucked into the pockets of his vest. He had an unlit, short-barreled cigar dangling from a corner of his mouth while the rest of his face held a self-satisfied look.

He smiled broadly when he saw Archer walk in. "Just the man I want to see."

Archer came toward him and looked for but did not see the clerk. "Is that right? You're working late hours."

"Hunting a killer ain't a nine-to-five job. Now, I spoke with Miss Tuttle."

"Good for you. And?"

"And she told me some things that I wanted to check out with you."

"Okay. You want to ask me down here or up in my room?"

"Why don't we do it in the room where Hank Pittleman was found dead?"

This surprised Archer, but he followed the man to the elevator. "I'll take the stairs, if you don't mind."

Shaw chuckled. "Seen that before with ex-cons. Small, confined spaces don't feel all that good, do they?"

"No, they don't."

"I'll meet you upstairs. And Archer?"

"Yeah?"

Shaw opened his jacket to show a big-butted Smith & Wesson .45 with iron sights carried in a worn leather shoulder holster. It was a serious piece of ordnance meant for serious business of the killing kind.

"Don't you go screwball and try to bug out on me, okay? I might 'a flown planes in the war, but I'm a damn good shot. Not going to miss anything near as big as you."

"Why would I do that when we're getting all friendly?"

Shaw chuckled again and pushed the elevator button as Archer headed to the fire door and the stairs beyond.

On the sixth floor Shaw used the key to open

the door to Number 615. He and Archer went through and Shaw closed the door behind them. Pittleman's body had long since been taken away, though the bed was still unmade and the cover and pillows bloody.

"Okay," said Archer. "What's on your mind?"

"Miss Tuttle said you carried Pittleman in here and put him down on the bed. Then you two left and went to your room."

"Same as I told you."

"You got a strong back then, because it took two deputies to carry the man out. And you said you never came back in here?"

"That's right."

"And Miss Tuttle said on the way out she opened the door and closed it securely after you both left and then locked it."

"That's right."

"Okay, glad we got that straight, Archer."

"Can I go now?"

"Hardly, son, we're just getting started. Don't be in such a rush."

Next, Shaw pulled something from his pocket. It was a hip flask that Archer recognized.

"Who said you could frisk my place?" he demanded.

"I did."

"You got no right to do that."

"I got every right, son. A man's been killed."

"You mean you can just toss a man's room without permission?"

"I mean exactly that. The law's on my side."

"I wish the law would sometimes be on *my* side."

"Then try not breaking it," Shaw retorted.

"That flask's not even mine."

"I know that. I'm not concerned with the flask per se."

"What then?"

"I also recovered two glasses from your room. With the remains of drink in them."

"Okay, I had a drink with Miss Tuttle, so what? I told you that already."

"Well, the 'so what' is that's a parole violation to be using alcohol, but again, I'm not concerned about that. I've got bigger fish to fry."

"For investigating a man being killed, you don't seem too concerned about much."

"Oh, you'll see that I'm concerned about a great deal. And right now, I'm concerned about *you*. Now, there were fingerprints on the flask and the two glasses. You know about fingerprints?"

Archer looked at his hand. "I know everybody's got 'em."

"Right, and you know everybody's fingerprints are different?"

"If you say so."

"I do. I had Miss Tuttle's fingerprints taken today. I had them compared to the ones on the glasses and the flask."

"She didn't tell me that."

"Well, I didn't tell her why I wanted them."

"Why'd you take her fingerprints?"

"Patience, son, I'm getting there."

Shaw opened the door to the room and pointed at the doorknob. "See that white powder on there?"

"I see it, yeah."

"I had it dusted for fingerprints. That's what the white coating is. Fingerprint dust. Amazing things they can do with fingerprint dust."

"Yeah, sounds exciting."

"Now, there are three fresh sets of fingerprints on there, and only three."

"Okay."

"Miss Tuttle's."

"Well, sure. She opened the door and—"

"The maid who found the body," interjected Shaw.

"Okay, but—"

Now Archer could clearly see the man's line of reasoning, and he felt like he had just been dropped out of a plane and was free-falling to death. And what had Ernestine mentioned? Dan

Bullock's fingerprints on that knife had helped send him back to prison.

"And *your* fingerprints." Shaw shut the door so hard, it caused a bang when the door met the doorjamb. "Which makes me wonder how they got on the doorknob, both coming and going? Since you've confirmed to me that you had never touched them to begin with, and that you had *never* been back to Mr. Pittleman's room after you and Miss Tuttle left him here."

Shaw leaned back against the wall, edged his homburg down a bit, folded his arms over his chest, and stared like a seasoned pointer on a bird at Archer. "So, I'm thinking what you told me before was a load 'a hooey, son. And somebody feeds me baloney, I don't make a sandwich with it, I make an arrest."

"You have a way with words, Mr. Shaw, I'll give you that."

"Now, I want you to start having *your* way with words, Archer, starting and ending with the truth. Anything less than that, the cuffs are going on you right now, son, just so we understand each other."

Archer glanced at the doorknob as his mind processed all of this at a rapid pace. The only problem was, he could see no way around it other *than* the truth. But sometimes not only did the truth not set you free, it could send you right back to prison.

"Okay, I'll level with you. When I passed by here this morning the door was open a crack. I thought Jackie—I mean Miss Tuttle—was maybe in the room. So, I walked in, that's when I touched the doorknob."

"Meaning you lied to me before?"

"I guess you could say that."

"Keep going, Archer, this is mighty fine stuff."

"I saw the man sleeping in the bed. Well, I thought he was sleeping. Then I saw a towel on the floor. With stuff on it. I came closer to see what it was. Then I saw the knife next to the towel; they were both covered in blood. I went over to the bed to see about Mr. Pittleman. But it was too late. He was dead, his throat all butchered."

"Then what did you do?"

Archer decided not to tell him about his debate on relieving some of the dead man's cash because he could not see a way that would remotely benefit his case, which was now for shit anyway. Though he *had* taken the debt papers.

"Then I left. I opened the door and walked out."

"Leaving your fingerprints behind?"

"Yes sir."

"Did you remove anything from this room or the body?"

Archer didn't hesitate, because he knew to a man like Shaw that would be the same as lying.

"No sir."

"You see anybody? Hear anybody?"

"No. It was just me." Archer paused. "Now, I know this doesn't look good."

Shaw unexpectedly chuckled. "Well, you're right about that, son, but it don't take a genius, does it?"

"What happens now?"

"I have more than enough to arrest you, you know that?"

"Look, what would be my reason to kill the man? I was working for him. Him dead, I don't get squat."

Shaw chewed on the butt of his stogie. "Miss Tuttle made the same argument to me earlier."

"Well, she's one smart gal. So?"

"A job and money's not the only reason to kill a man."

"I don't see another, least in my case."

"Sure you do, Archer, think about it."

"Give me a clue."

"How about a woman? Miss Tuttle? You

wanted her and Pittleman had her. For all I know you went to his room, you both argued about the lady, and you did what you did."

"You think I'd kill a man over a woman?"

Now Shaw laughed outright. "Hell, Archer, if I had a dollar for every man who's killed another man over a woman, I'd be a damn Rockefeller."

"Did you check the knife for my prints? 'Cause I can tell you for a fact they aren't on it."

"There were no prints on there because the killer wiped them off, probably on the towel. Otherwise, he wouldn't have left it behind. He just was careless about the doorknob." On this Shaw looked pointedly at Archer. "Meaning maybe *you* were."

"But why not take the knife with him?"

"Then you got a weapon that killed a man to hide or dispose of. Not an easy thing to do."

"You think I brought a knife with me from prison!"

"You took a long bus ride here. For all I know you bought or stole a knife from someone on that bus. Or you coulda done the same while you were here. Miss Tuttle told me Pittleman gave you an advance. Forty dollars cash. How much of that you got left?"

Archer took a quick breath but didn't answer right away. So now Shaw knew about the money Archer owed to Pittleman. Which meant Archer now had a motive to kill the man.

"Well, I bought some stuff, clothes, and food and such."

"Right, but you didn't do your job, Archer. You didn't get the car. So that means you owed Pittleman money. And I been asking around about the man. He is not somebody you want to owe money to. Did you get into an argument with him about that?"

"No, I was going to talk to him about it but never got the chance."

"So you say. And the fact is, you didn't have to bring a knife with you. Jackie Tuttle and two other witnesses have already identified the murder weapon as belonging to Mr. Pittleman himself."

"I know that. He took it out in the—"

"—in the *bar* where you met him? Miss Tuttle told me about that, too. That's another lie you told me. You're ringing up quite a tally. So the fact is you could have used Pittleman's own knife to slit his throat and presto, you don't owe him a dime because he's not around to demand it."

"Lots of other men probably owed him money."

"But lots of other men weren't sleeping with

his lady friend or staying in a room pretty much right down the hall or leaving their prints on a doorknob to the dead man's room. You, and only you, on the other hand, hit the trifecta on that."

Frustrated, Archer fell silent while Shaw's gaze continued to bore into him.

"I've investigated a lot of crimes, Archer. And this isn't my first murder, not by a long shot. Did it before the war and I'm doing it again. Now, it can take a while, but I've never failed to get my man in the end."

"As a law-abiding citizen now, I'm right happy about that."

"We'll see how happy you are when I'm done. This is a hanging state, you know that?"

"Tell the truth, I hadn't bothered to look into it."

"That might change, as time goes on."

"Are you arresting me?"

"Not right now, no."

"So, I can go?"

"For now. But, Archer, don't try to make a run for it, you hear me?"

"You keep telling me that."

"Because I want the message to sink in loud and clear, son."

"I got nowhere to run, and no interest in

running. That's for a guilty man to do, which I'm not."

"You're a funny one."

"Nothing funny about being wrongly hanged."

"I'll grant you that. Now get on out of here."

CHAPTER

21

ARCHER WENT TO HIS ROOM, shed his new
clothes down to his skivvies, opened the window
because he felt claustrophobic and bitter about
what was happening, and lay down on the bed
in the dark and stared at a ceiling he couldn't
really see.

The four walls of his room seemed to be
closing in on him. The feeling of claustrophobia
was, in fact, far stronger than he had felt
at Carderock after the mayor's daughter had
turned all his sincere help into a tale of vicious
kidnapping. He had been simple and naive and
just plain stupid to let that happen to him. The
fact was he had also been trusting, because he
had relied on his comrades-in-arms with his life
during the war. It had never occurred to Archer

that once he was home again in peacetime, his fellow citizens would turn against him.

Still, he was fortunate they hadn't given him life in prison, but Archer would never get back the several years they *had* taken. He would never feel he had gotten the better end of some vague deal.

And here it was happening again.

An hour passed, and Archer never once stopped looking up at nothing.

Then he rose and put his clothes back on.

It took him twenty minutes to walk it. Then he was outside of Number 27 Eldorado Street. Despite the lateness of the hour, there was one light on in what he knew was Jackie's bedroom. He wanted to know what else she had told Shaw.

He walked up to her door and knocked.

"Who is that?"

The voice came from the right of him. He stepped back and looked at the lit, open window.

"It's me, Archer."

"Archer?"

Her voice sounded funny.

"What do you want? I'm in bed." There was nothing inviting in her tone.

"I need to talk. Shaw came by to see me again at the Derby."

"Well, he came by to see me *again*, too. Woke me out of a dead sleep. He only left a bit ago."

"Can I come in? It's important."

A long moment passed before she said, "Give me a sec."

A minute later she opened the door and in the light from inside, he saw she was dressed in a thick light blue robe that went down to her ankles. Her face held a scowl.

She stepped back, and he passed through.

They sat in the living room. She stared at him and he stared down at his hat.

"Shaw is setting up to arrest me for Pittleman's murder," he finally said.

She nodded. "I could tell that by the questions he asked me."

"It would have been nice if you had given me some warning. And he took your fingerprints, too. That would have been good to know," he added accusingly.

As soon as he said this, Archer realized he had made an unforgivable mistake. The scowl turned to something else, something that unnerved Archer maybe as much as fighting the Germans had.

She stood and looked down at him. When she spoke her voice was low and calm and still managed to bristle with menace.

"Let me tell you what would have been 'good to know.'" She paused, but only for a second. "When you came to see me before the cops showed up, you didn't tell me that Hank was dead. But according to what Shaw told me just a bit ago you sure as hell knew he *was* dead. Now, *that* would have been good to know, Archer." She bent down and slapped him hard across the face. The blow stung and reddened his skin and made his eyes water a bit. But Archer didn't move, he didn't say anything. When she raised her hand to strike him again, he assumed no defensive posture, did nothing to stop her.

She looked down at him in some confusion. Then, when it became apparent that Archer was not going to defend himself or fight back, this seemed to take all the energy from her. She dropped her hand and slumped down next to him.

"I should have told you, Jackie," Archer said quietly. "I don't know why I didn't. No, maybe I do. I trusted a gal once and ended up in prison because of it. When I found Pittleman dead, I panicked. I figured the fewer people who knew, the better for me. It was just all about surviving, I guess. And not going back to prison." He fell silent and Jackie said nothing for a few seconds.

"I don't blame you for not trusting, Archer.

It's not like I trust easily or at all. And it's not like I've been an open book with you."

"So where do we go from here?" asked Archer.

"You could start with telling me about Hank. Shaw told me what you told him, but I'd prefer to hear it from you."

Archer nodded, marshalled his thoughts, and said, "I woke up, got dressed, went out in the hall, passed by the door, and saw that it was open. I went inside."

"Why?"

"I thought you might be in there with him. You had left my bed," he added.

"Oh, good Lord, Archer, are all men as dense as you when it comes to that?"

"Probably. Anyway, I saw the man was dead. So, I hightailed it out of there."

"And you never raised the alarm? Never went for help?" Her eyes flashed with suspicion.

"Help? For what? I've seen a lot of dead men in my time, Jackie. No way you were breathing life back into Hank Pittleman."

"Still, you left him like that, Archer? And now Shaw thinks you killed him."

"Did he say that directly?"

"He didn't have to, I could tell from his questions." She paused. "*Did* you kill him? Come on, tell me the truth."

In his agitation Archer stood and paced. "What reason would I have for killing him?"

"Maybe because you didn't like me being with him like you just suggested."

Archer ceased his pacing. "Don't get me wrong, Jackie. You're a wonderful gal and all, but to kill a man I would at least have to know you for longer than a few days and sleep with you more than twice."

"So you say."

"So you really think I did it? Killed a man?"

"It doesn't matter a whit what I think, Archer. It matters what Shaw thinks."

"It matters to *me* what you think."

"I know you can kill because you did that in the war." She paused as he stared her down. "But I guess I don't see you killing Hank, no."

"You *guess*? Well, thanks for nothing."

She gripped his hand and pulled him down on the sofa next to her.

"Don't be that way, okay? You say you don't really know me? Well, that works both ways, Archer, because I don't really know you. You can see that, right?"

Archer didn't want to see that, but what she said made good sense.

She said, "Hell, maybe somebody robbed him. Shaw wouldn't tell me if Hank's wad of cash was missing. He was always waving that around. Everyone knew he carried a lot of money. Stupid thing for him to do. But that could be it."

Archer knew it wasn't robbery. He put his hat back on. "Okay, well, thank you."

"For what?"

"For sort of believing me. You may be the only one in Poca City who does."

"You still going to try to collect that debt?"

"I need the money. I don't want to bash hog brains in."

She looked at him in confusion. "Hog brains?"

"Never mind."

"Now, when you're ready to head out to my daddy's place, let me know. I'll give you the keys to the Nash. It's over in a covered garage on Fulsome Street. You can't miss it." She gave him directions to the place. "Just leave the keys in the glove box when you get back."

"I will. Thanks."

"And Archer? Be careful when you go out there."

"Your old man pulled a shotgun on me last time I was there. Careful is all I'm going to be."

CHAPTER

22

ARCHER ROSE EARLY the next morning, washed his face, armpits, and other strategic locations of his person in the communal bath, put on fresh socks and underwear, and headed down the hall. He halted when he saw the door to 615 standing open.

"Hello?" he said, poking his head in.

The door swung fully open, and there was Shaw eyeballing him. He had on another suit, a faded gray double-breasted with a black-and-white polka-dot tie and a pair of scuffed black moc toe shoes. His hair was neatly combed and his features fresh. He smelled of aftershave and had another unlit stogie perched in his mouth.

"You're up early, Archer."

"Don't like to let the grass grow under my feet.

You never know when you might get yanked off 'em."

"Let me ask you something. Come on in here."

Archer stepped through and Shaw closed the door behind them. He pointed to the connecting door. "You ever been in that room?"

"No. And if my damn fingerprints are on that doorknob then somebody put 'em there."

"Get off your high horse and just listen. We didn't find a single fingerprint on the two doorknobs there, or the two on the hall door to 617."

"Okay."

"You find that puzzling?"

"Should I?"

"Presumably he went into that room on occasion? Why would there be no prints there?"

"You mean someone might have wiped them off?"

"Bingo."

Archer looked at the connecting door. "Jackie told me he had the two rooms, but she didn't tell me what for. Thought it was a waste, a man having two rooms. But she said he wanted 'em, and the man owns the whole hotel, so he can have what he wants."

"Interesting. How's your 'job' coming?"

"Well, I met with Mr. Pittleman and his wife

before he was killed to let them know something."

"Really now, what was that?"

"That Mr. Tuttle had apparently torched the car that was collateral for the loan from Mr. Pittleman that I was trying to collect for him."

"Did he, by God?"

"I didn't see him do it, but I saw the Caddy all burned up."

"What were you doing out there, then?"

"Trying to get the damn car. It was collateral after all. That's legal, right? Pittleman said it was."

"Don't know, Archer. I don't do anything with debts and collateral and such."

"Well, since I didn't touch the car, no harm, no foul regardless."

"Why wouldn't Tuttle pay back the loan if it's owed?"

"His daughter was hanging out with Pittleman, and Lucas Tuttle hated that. Told me he'd pay the loan if Jackie came back home. So long as she was with Pittleman, he wasn't paying."

"So Old Man Tuttle had a grudge against Pittleman, then?"

Archer was alarmed. "Now hold on. Don't go get all riled up about him. He wasn't going to do anything against Pittleman. I told him I was working on it. And, hell, if he was going to kill the man, he wouldn't use a knife. He woulda shot him with the same damn Remington he pointed at me when I went out there."

Shaw shook his head and grinned.

"What?" asked Archer.

"I just right now put up another plausible suspect to have killed Pittleman and you shot it down, boy. Are you dumb or just too honest, or both?"

"I did my time. I'm not looking to have anyone go behind bars if they did nothing wrong. I know how that feels."

"So, you were innocent, were you?"

"Hell, yes, I was."

"If I had a dollar for every time I've heard that."

"Yeah, I know, you'd be as rich as a Rockefeller."

"No, I'd be *richer*." He eyed the connecting door to 617. "Want to see what's in there?"

"You want me to?"

"Maybe you'll see something I missed."

Shaw opened the door and they passed through. It was then that Archer could see why the man wanted two rooms.

"Is this his office?" he said, looking around.

"It is indeed."

There was a large desk with a glass top with a squat black phone sitting on it and a slim white phone book next to it. On the other side of the desk was a tobacco pouch; a briar pipe with a worn mouthpiece was aligned next to it, and a box of Van Dyck cigars sat alongside that. A calendar sat in its own holder on the desk glass with the days ink-filled with appointments and meetings, and a few manila files were next to it. Behind the desk was an oak shelving unit full of stacked paper, files, and an odd book or two having to do with land-title issues, at least that was what Archer gathered from reading off the spines. Against one wall was a four-drawer wooden file cabinet with alphabet ranges written on them from *A* to *Z*, top to bottom. Comfortable chairs and a couch were on the other side of the room. A full bar was set up against one wall, with an empty silver ice bucket and scooper off to the side. Though it was still morning, Archer looked lustfully at the bottles lined up there.

"You poked around already?"

Shaw nodded. "Checked his calendar and such. Didn't find much there. But I did find some interesting things."

"Like what?"

"Man was sick. Dying, actually."

"Who? Pittleman? You got to be kidding?"

Shaw shook his head. "Found some medical reports. Man had a brain tumor. Inoperable, it said. Checked with his doctor. He confirmed it."

"Funny."

"What is?"

"First night I met him, Pittleman clutched at his head. Said it was the bad liquor."

"Nope, it was cancer."

"How long did he have?"

"Not long, the doc said."

"Damn. So why kill the man if he was already dying?"

"That's the question, Archer. But then your motivation would have nothing to do with that. If you wanted Jackie Tuttle, you wouldn't want to wait on it. And by your own admission just now, you didn't know he only had a little time left to live."

"I never wanted a woman bad enough to slit a man's throat, Mr. Shaw."

Shaw perched on the edge of the dead man's desk. "What do you know about Pittleman?"

"Hear he's the richest man around. Owns most of the town. He's got a place outside of Poca almost as big as this hotel. His wife is okay with him seeing Jackie, or at least she knows about it. Mr. Pittleman spoke about it right in front of her while I was there."

"Did he now? What else?"

"I helped haul some stuff from here to his trucking warehouse the other day. Got paid a dollar for it. By a man named Sid Duckett. He works for Pittleman. Met another man there too, name of Malcolm Draper. He works for Pittleman, too. He's his business manager. Man carries a gun."

Shaw rubbed at his thin mustache. "Okay."

"Anything else you find?"

In answer, Shaw picked up some pieces of paper and handed them to Archer.

"Didn't find those in here. Found them in the trash bins behind the hotel."

"You checked the trash bins?"

"You always check the trash bins, Archer. I even looked at the one in your room. Only found a drained gin bottle and empty packs of Lucky Strikes."

Archer looked at the papers. "They're bills of Pittleman's and they're all stamped 'past due.'"

"That's a fact. Man was apparently not paying them."

"But Pittleman was rich."

"Even a rich man can spend more than he's got coming in. And that makes him a poor man."

"Doesn't make much sense."

"It will, eventually."

"Well, I wish you luck. I just hope you're coming to the conclusion that I had nothing to do with the man dying."

"I'm not there yet, Archer. I'm truly not. Just so we know where we stand with each other."

"Okay."

"Why were you up so early the morning Pittleman was found dead?"

"Heard a noise outside in the hall."

"Well, son, I asked you about that, and you said you heard nothing unusual."

"You were asking about unusual sounds in the night. I heard that sound in the morning."

"What time again?"

"Around six. Why?"

Shaw's features turned grave. "Something's going on in this town I don't like. You watch yourself, Archer. You watch yourself close and don't be no fool, son."

As Archer headed to the door, the lawman added one more warning.

"And don't trust nobody." He added warningly, "I don't care how damn pretty they are."

CHAPTER

23

"Hey, fella?"

Archer was crossing the lobby of the Derby when the front desk clerk called out to him. It was the same one who had initially checked him in.

"Yeah?" said Archer, coming over to him.

"You got to pay up if you want to stay here."

This was not what Archer had been expecting. "What's that again, mister?"

The clerk swung the register around. "You only paid for three nights. You been here way longer than that. Woulda caught it before 'cept poor Mr. Pittleman got murdered."

"How much we talking then?" asked Archer, and the clerk told him.

Archer reached into his pocket and counted out his remaining cash, including the two half-dollars he'd gotten for loading the crates.

The clerk snatched all this up and said, "That don't even cover what you owe. And what about going forward?"

"That's all the money I got, brother."

"Then I guess you're gonna have to find other accommodations."

"But if I don't have any more money, how am I gonna do that?"

"Not my problem, fella. Now, go clean out your things. And, see here, I'll be watching. You got ten minutes. Gotta get that room ready for a *paying* guest."

Archer went to his room, collected his few possessions, and marched out of the lobby while the clerk watched him go every step of the way. Archer looked up and down the street and decided he had only one option. He headed over to the Courts building and waited on the steps with his hat tilted over his eyes.

"Mr. Archer?"

Archer pushed his hat back and gazed up at Ernestine Crabtree.

She had on a plain blue A-line skirt with a pleated front, a long-sleeved white blouse, puffy in the arms and tight at the wrists with a wide, open V-neck collar, and low pumps with chunky heels. Her dark hat, made of felt, was narrow brimmed with a band around it and a little bow of ivy green in front. The hair was not done in the usual tight bun. It was actually down around her shoulders, in the same style that he had complimented her on before.

"What are you doing here?"

"Coming to see you about a job."

"You mean you need work to pay back the forty dollars?"

"I mean I got kicked out of the Derby and I'm flat broke, so yeah."

"Come on up."

They took the interior stairs up to her floor and he followed the woman down the hall.

Another man passed them going the other way, leered at Crabtree, and then wolf-whistled. "Woo-wee, baby. You got something I need." Smiling, he eyed Archer. "You're a lucky man getting that skirt all for yourself, pal."

Archer had done this very same thing more times than he could count. But that was before he had read about Ernestine Crabtree's terrible past. And when he glanced at her and saw first embarrassment and then resignation, he wasn't sure which one made him angrier.

"Hey, buddy," said Archer sharply. He dropped

the things he was carrying, grabbed the man by the lapels, and slammed him up against the wall, knocking his porkpie hat off in the process.

"What's your problem, fella?" barked the man.

"Show the lady some respect."

"Respect? You kidding, pal? Dames love when guys do that."

"Not *this* dame. Now apologize to her, right now, before I smash your damn nose in."

Crabtree called out, "Mr. Archer, it's all right. Let it be. Please."

"But—"

"I don't want you to get in trouble on my account. Please."

Archer slowly and reluctantly let the man go. The shaky fellow grabbed his fallen hat and rushed off down the hall.

Archer picked up his things and followed Crabtree down the hall but looked back twice at the man.

"I'm sorry about that idiot," he said.

"Yes, well… Thank you, Mr. Archer, that was very… chivalrous."

She opened the door and let him into the office.

"Have you had anything to eat?" she said. "Or some coffee?"

"No, ma'am, but I'm fine."

"You sure? You look hungry." She opened her

purse and held out two dollars, but Archer put his hand up.

"I'm not taking money from you, ma'am, though I thank you. It'd be against the rules, no doubt, and I'm not gonna put you at risk for losing your job. Back there you said you didn't want me to get into trouble. Well, I feel the same way about you. Just let me get to work and earn some on my own."

She closed her purse and looked up at him with her wide, depthless eyes and said, "Well, I know what you said earlier, but the only thing I have where you can start work immediately is the slaughterhouse."

"I'm in no position to be choosy, so if you could call 'em and tell 'em I'd like the job, that would be good. And how do I get out there?"

She looked at the clock on the wall. "A truck takes the men out there every day. Leaves at eight-thirty sharp right down the street from here. You'll see them gathering."

"Sounds fine."

She looked at his suit. "However, I would not wear your new clothes to do that sort of work."

He looked down. "You're probably right about that. I got my old ones in this bag."

"There's a bathroom down the hall on the right."

He changed his clothes in the bathroom and put the new ones into his bag.

When he came back to the office, Ernestine was just hanging up the phone. "It's all settled." She eyed his new suit in the bag. "Why don't you leave those here? I can hang them up. You can pick them up when the truck brings you back."

"You don't have to do that."

"Like you said, my job is to help people like you. Just come and see me after. I'll wait for you."

"Thank you, Miss Crabtree."

"Well, good luck to you, Mr. Archer. At that place, you, um, you may need it."

* * *

Archer saw the men collecting at the corner and headed over to join them. And, as he had expected, there was old Dickie Dill smack in the middle of them. He and a few other men were engaged in a game of "back alley" craps right there against the front steps of a building. Archer watched this for about a minute while the men were focused on the game and took no note of his presence.

Dill's final roll of the dice brought a curse and

an evil look from the man. Archer saw a dollar bill pass between the ex-con and another fellow.

"Hellfire, Archer, thought I might see your butt out here before long," exclaimed Dill when he spied Archer.

"Hey, Dickie," he said with little enthusiasm.

"This here's Archer, boys," announced Dill to the group of rough-looking gents. Most were smaller than Archer, but a couple were giants who looked like they were put out by having to share the same air with him.

"He's one of us," said Dill.

"What were you in the joint for?" growled one of the giants. His clothes were filthy and so was his thick beard. One eye lurched inward too far, giving him an unsettling expression.

Archer looked up at him. "Something stupid. What were you in for?"

"Killing a man who needed it. And he wasn't the first one who bought the farm with me. Just the only one they caught me on," he added proudly.

"How long did you do?"

"Long enough. This was in the Big House, 'cause the son of a bitch was a snitch for Hoover and the G-men. Woulda done a lot longer 'cept the guards got too scared 'a me." The man did not appear to be joking.

Dill pulled Archer aside. "Buddy 'a mine got put back in Carderock."

"Who might that be?"

"Dan Bullock. You saw him at the Checkered Past. He told me you gave him some good advice. Only the man got all cockeyed and didn't take it."

"Hey, I'm always looking out for people like us."

Dill grinned. "You always were okay in my book, Archer."

But there was something in the little man's features that made the hair on Archer's neck stand up and salute. A man like Dickie Dill did not understand nuance. And when he put his arm around Archer's shoulders, the steely fingers bit in a little too deep, relaying critical information his mouth had not.

An old Ford truck with a sputtering radiator pulled up. Its open rear bed had wood slats on the sides and rough wooden bench seats. The driver came out and dropped the rear gate, and the men climbed on one by one. Dill sat next to Archer as the truck pulled away.

"What'cha gonna be doing at the slaughterhouse?" asked Dill.

"Don't know yet. Guess whatever needs doing."

"If it's killing the hogs, I'll show you how."

"Thanks. Hey, saw you rolling the dice back there."

Dill's friendly expression faded. "So what? You ain't thinkin' 'bout snitchin' on me to Miss Crabtree?"

Dill plucked something from his pocket. Archer saw it was the man's switchblade.

This was the Dickie Dill he remembered and loathed.

Archer leaned over and whispered, "All's I'm saying is you better watch yourself around games of chance. You remember inside Carderock?"

"Hell, that game was fixed by that bastard Riley."

"Yeah, it was. And just like with Riley, you crapped out five times in a row back there except for your first roll, where you got your eleven and sweetened the pot and then crapped out right after. And the man who took your money palmed the dice after each throw. He sees you as a patsy for sure. So next time he asks you to play, just tell him, 'no dice.' Funny, huh?"

Something seemed to go off in Dill's head and he looked viciously over at the man who'd taken his dollar. "I'm gonna cut the bastard up."

"No, you're not. Remember, third time's the

charm. You're not going back to prison. Now, put the blade away. You're not even supposed to have a weapon, Dickie. That'll get you put right back in Carderock."

Dill slowly slid the knife back into his pocket, but he kept shooting looks at the other man the whole ride out.

Archer could smell the place about two miles before they arrived there. The stench made his nostrils seize up. Dill noted this and chuckled, as did two other men on the truck.

"Hellfire, Archer, after a while you can't smell nothin'," said Dill. He touched his nose. "Goes dead in there."

"Well, I like to smell things."

"Like Miss Crabtree's perfume?" said Dill with a wicked look.

"We already talked about that, Dickie."

"Man can damn well dream." He licked his lips, his lascivious look turning Archer's stomach as he thought about what a man like Dill would do to a woman like Ernestine Crabtree given the chance. He was glad he had fixed the woman's bedroom door. But then he heartened himself by thinking that Crabtree might just shoot the little bastard before he could do her any harm.

The slaughterhouse was a large, one-story

cement block building with hog pens on three sides, teeming with very much living stock.

When Archer asked about this, Dill said ominously, "Ain't for much longer," as they marched through a door after climbing off the truck. "This here is where the hogs come to die," he added gleefully.

They were processed in by a burly foreman wearing a long white coat and safety hat. The man told Archer, "Yeah, she called. Pays five dollars a day. Get your money end of the day on Friday."

"Look, can I get an advance, friend?" said Archer.

"You trying to be funny or stupid, or what?"

"Guess so."

"Coat, gloves, helmet, and goggles in that room over there. Find what fits."

"So, what's my job? Not crushing hog skulls, I hope."

"Naw. We got enough of those. You're gonna be sawing up the meat and racking it. You just watch the fellers in there to get the hang of it."

"Why the hat, goggles, and all the rest?"

The man laughed. "You'll see why. Now beat it."

Archer put on a long white coat that was stained with blood, and a helmet, goggles, and gloves.

Dill, similarly dressed, came over to him. "Hey, you wanna watch me bash some hogs in the head? Got a guy who ropes 'em by the neck, holds 'em steady like, then I come in from the rear, so's not to spook 'em, and bam! Hog brains all over."

"No thanks, Dickie, I'll take your word for it."

Archer was led to the room where he'd be working. There were long wooden tables all over and hog parts of all descriptions hanging from ceiling hooks connected to a powered conveyor belt.

An older gent showed him how to use the saws and knives, how to make the cuts, and then how to rack the parts on the hooks.

"They kill 'em and then slit their throats to bleed 'em out. They boil 'em next, that makes the hair and skin a lot easier to get off. Then they split 'em in half and hang 'em up for a while, let the meat get right. Then it comes our way to carve up. When the hooks are full, the belt takes 'em to the cold room."

After watching Archer a few times, he deemed him ready to do the work on his own.

Within the hour, Archer was covered in blood, bits of bone, cartilage, and hog meat. He had to keep wiping his goggles clear from foul things and the film of humidity, for it was uncommonly warm in here. And more than once he suffered a coughing spell because of some foreign matter getting inside him. His gloves were soon soaked in blood and other unsavory detritus. By the end of his shift his arms, back, and legs ached with the sawing and slicing and the lifting of the heavy carcasses onto the hooks.

A horn sounded and the men instantly stopped what they were doing, midslice, or mid–brain bash, for that took place in the next room over. Archer had heard nothing but the squeals and terrified sounds of hogs about to die and then dying, for it was clear that the suffering beasts were not always killed instantly with the first blow from the sledgehammer.

As Archer was taking off his coat, helmet, gloves, and goggles in the locker room, he asked the older man who'd helped him, "How long you been doing this?"

The man closed the door of his locker. "Too damn long, son. Too damn long."

I feel that way after one day.

There was a sudden commotion in the next room. Shouts and cries and the sounds of a struggle.

Archer rushed into the next room with a group of workers to find the man who had cheated Dill at craps holding his shoulder and looking pale and nauseous while Dill circled him holding a sledgehammer.

"You lying, cheating sack 'a shit," bellowed Dill.

Archer looked around and saw the man who had checked him in standing idly by. It was apparent that no one was going to step in and help the injured fellow.

Archer pushed through the crowd and stood in front of the man.

"Dickie, I told you this was a bad idea. Now, put down the sledgehammer and just walk away. Or else your butt is going back to prison. You know what happened with your buddy and Miss Crabtree."

"Yeah, you keep telling me that, Archer. But why do I think you got the hots for that broad yourself? You just calling me off so's you get her all by your lonesome."

"That's got nothing to do with you going after this man."

"Son of a bitch cheated me," Dill snarled. "You said so yourself."

Archer glanced at the man, but kept one eye on Dill. "And I think you taught him his lesson, right, friend?"

The injured fellow mutely nodded. Archer could see that the man's shoulder had been shattered by Dill's blow. "In fact, he needs a hospital."

"What he needs is a grave," barked Dill. "Now get outta my way."

"Not going to do that, Dickie."

"Then you're a dead man too."

Dill came at him, the hammer raised high. Dill was deceptively strong, Archer knew that, and tenacious as hell. But the man had not fought in a world war for years where every day was an act of survival.

Archer didn't retreat from the attack as most would have. He sprang forward and slammed his shoulder into Dill's gut before he could bring the sledgehammer down. Archer was a good sixty pounds heavier than Dill, and the physics of that competition meant that Dill was launched backward into a wall, and the hammer flew from his grasp.

Archer picked it up and stood over the fallen man. Dill put his hands up in a defensive posture, but Archer shook his head and tossed the hammer down.

"I've no intent to hurt you, Dickie. Just wanted to make my point."

He turned to look at the crowd. "Nobody here saw anything." Then he pointed to the manager. "And get that man to a hospital or else there's gonna be trouble."

The man came out of his lethargy, gripped the

injured man's good arm, and hustled him from the room.

Archer helped Dill up. "You okay?"

Dill did not look the least bit friendly. "You better watch yourself."

"I do, all the time."

When the truck dropped Archer off back in Poca City, he walked down the street, still rubbing hog shit off his person.

CHAPTER

24

HE HURRIED UP TO ERNESTINE'S OFFICE after checking the time. She was still there, waiting for him. When he opened the door she rose from her chair.

"You look exhausted," she said, eyeing his stained clothes and haggard features.

"Yeah, well, it's pretty hard work."

"Was it very awful?"

He started to tell her about the fight with Dill, but then decided not to. It would just give the woman something else to worry about. And his well-being really should not be her burden.

"Wasn't too bad. And I appreciate the job."

She held out his bag, and his suit clothes and shirt on a hanger. "Here're your things. I...I took them home at lunchtime and pressed them for you."

"You didn't have to do that, Miss Crabtree, but I thank you for that," he replied, taking the things from her.

"So where will you stay?" she asked.

"That's a good question. They don't pay till the end of the week, so…"

They stood there looking awkwardly at each other.

She dipped her head and said, "This is out of the norm, but…but you're welcome to sleep at my place for a bit. I've got a wall bed in the living room."

"Well, that's really nice of you. But I couldn't put you out like that. It wouldn't be right. And I don't want to get you in trouble."

"You not only paid for my dinner, but you fixed my bedroom door without charge. This will actually settle that debt and make things right."

"Are you…are you sure?"

She looked up at him and attempted a smile. "Yes, Mr. Archer, I am."

"Well, okay." He tacked on a relieved smile.

"I *will* ask that you wait until dark to come over. I…I don't want my neighbors…."

"I can come in through the back door, say around nine?"

"That would be fine. Thank you."

He left her there and headed down to the street. Once his feet hit the pavement he looked around. His stomach was about as empty as it had ever been. The other fellows at the slaughterhouse had brought their lunches in little tins and were allowed exactly fifteen minutes to eat them. And not a one of them, Dill included, had seen fit to offer any to Archer.

He managed to earn fifty cents by helping an elderly man carry some crates up the stairs of his little shop and then swept the room and caulked a window and cleaned and reinstalled the spark plugs on the straight-6 engine of the man's Ford delivery truck. This was another Army-inspired skill that had come in handy off the battlefield.

He used the money to buy a hunk of cheese and a couple rolls that barely dented his hunger. He gulped down two large glasses of water to rid him of the foul taste from the slaughterhouse.

He was walking down the street toward a bench he figured he would sit on until the time came for him to head to Ernestine's. That was when he noticed the four-door, long-hooded burgundy Cadillac rolling slowly by. He had seen the vehicle before, in Tuttle's barn. The driver was a man in his forties wearing a cap and buttoned black vest and pigskin gloves. In the back seat was Lucas Tuttle.

Tuttle must've seen him sitting there because the car came to a stop, the window rolled down, and Tuttle leaned out and waved him over.

Archer left his things on the bench and walked over to the car.

"Mr. Tuttle," he said, eyeing the driver, who was watching him in the side mirror.

"Climb on in here, Archer, want to talk to you."

Archer went around to the other side and got in.

"Damn, son, what have you been doing with yourself?" said Tuttle, holding his nose.

"Earning a living, the hard way."

Tuttle nodded and then sat back against the seat. "Bobby?" he said to the driver. "Go get yourself a Coke. I have business with Archer here."

"Yes, sir, Mr. Tuttle." The man got out and walked off, revealing black breeches covering his legs with dark gaiters below that. A formal chauffeur's getup if ever there was one, thought Archer. It was like you saw at the pictures, where everybody was rich except the servants.

Tuttle was dressed in a worsted wool dark brown suit with a red bow tie and a matching pocket square, and polished brown-and-white shoes.

"You look like you've been to church, though it's not the Sabbath," said Archer.

Tuttle laughed. "Not much of a churchgoer, Archer. Like to rely on myself, not some deity that folks wrote about in a book. I had some business meetings out of town. And business is looking good."

"Glad to hear it."

"So, what's the status of *your* business? You said you were working on it. Are you going to disappoint me, Archer? I will tell you right now I do not like to be disappointed."

Archer scanned the Cadillac's interior looking for the shotgun, but didn't see it.

"Well, I hope not to disappoint you or me, sir."

"So, then?"

"With Pittleman dead, it's gotten a little complicated, so to speak."

"Or perhaps it's gotten easier."

"I don't know about that. I do know that you torched the Caddy."

Tuttle didn't seem fazed by this. "An unfortunate accident. They happen a lot on farms."

"Is that right?" Archer wanted to ask him about Isabel's accident, but decided now was not the right time.

"I want my daughter back home."

"I'm trying, but it might be because her mother died there. She left about the same time. I wonder why."

Tuttle's face darkened. "Do you know *how* my wife died?"

Now that the man had brought up the subject himself, Archer said, "Just that it was an accident, but nobody told me the details."

Tuttle glanced out the window. "Yes, they *say* it was an accident."

"You saying it wasn't?"

Tuttle stared back at him. "I…I don't know, Archer. All I want is my daughter home. And if you can persuade her to do that, you will have earned your money."

"Okay, but Jackie loved her mother and her mother loved her right back."

"And who told you that?" asked Tuttle sharply.

"Your secretary, that Desiree woman."

"Ah, yes. Right. I suppose she would see it that way."

"It's not true?"

"Mr. Archer, there is no more complex relationship in the world than that of a mother and her daughter."

"I think you might be right about that. But are you saying they *didn't* get along?"

"Jackie is supremely headstrong, smart, opinionated, unlike any other woman I know—other than her mother, that is, for my daughter took after Isabel in a fierce way. And women from South America, Archer, are hot-blooded, full of fire and fight. It was what attracted me to her in the first place. She was the only woman of my acquaintance who could hold her own with me. Actually, more than hold her own."

"But if she didn't die in an accident, what happened then?"

Tuttle looked out the window again. "Sometimes it's better not knowing the truth. Do you believe that, Archer?"

"Well, I think the truth is important. But I guess the truth can hurt too."

"You've laid out the dilemma precisely. The truth not only can hurt, but also can have the capacity to destroy. Do you understand that?"

"What sort of truth are you talking about?"

"My wife was a beautiful creature, Archer. Beautiful beyond comparison. I could hardly believe it when she agreed to become my wife, for I was a young man just making his way. But tropical beauty such as she possessed sometimes affects the mind in ways that can be dangerous."

"You mean...?" prompted Archer.

"I mean that sometimes I became frightened of my own wife. You see me with my shotgun, and you think I'm a little touched in the head and prone to violence. But with me it's just bluster, Archer. With Isabel, it was something more." He paused. "And beauty was not the only thing that Jackie inherited from her mother."

"Hold on, now, Jackie is a good person."

"Keep in mind that you've known her a short time. I've known Jackie her entire life."

It was not lost on Archer that Jackie had pretty much said the same thing to him, only in the context of Archer's knowing her father for such a short time. "What exactly are you trying to say, Mr. Tuttle? I'd like the straight dope without all the gobbledygook."

Tuttle poked him in the chest. "Bring my daughter back to me, Archer. And collect your money, which I've just upped to *two hundred dollars.*"

Archer looked stunned. "Why the increase?"

"Don't look a gift horse in the mouth."

He motioned to the door, and Archer slowly climbed out. The chauffeur, who had gotten his Coke and was sipping it while perched on a fire hydrant, observed this, jumped up, and got back into the car, and the Cadillac drove off.

"Archer?"

Archer turned around to see Jackie Tuttle staring at him from across the way.

Jackie Tuttle wasn't really looking at Archer, though. He could see that now. She was looking over his shoulder, at the Cadillac rolling down the street.

She pulled her gaze away and walked over to him. Then she took a whiff and drew back, holding a hand to her nose. "You stink, do you know that?"

He looked down at himself. "Well, butchering hogs doesn't exactly make you smell pretty."

"Is that what you're doing now?"

"Got my butt kicked out of the hotel."

"Where are you staying then?"

"Working on it."

"Look, you can stay with me, Archer."

He shook his head. "No."

"Why not?" She smiled. "It would give us certain advantages of privacy."

"How'd you think that would look, especially to Mr. Shaw with the way things are?"

Her smile faded. "Right, I see your point." She looked down the street. "Was that my father?"

"I think you know it was."

"Did you speak with him?"

"I did."

"And?"

"And he's increased the offer to two hundred dollars if you come back home."

"What else did he say?" she blurted out.

He drew a step back. "What? Nothing."

She lurched forward and grabbed his jacket. "Are you lying to me?"

"No."

She let go of him and her hostile look faded. "Well, good. How about I feed you then? I can see your belly pushing inward from here."

However, he was still reacting to her dizzying emotional swing and didn't answer.

Apparently his unsettled features showed his dilemma, because she smiled disarmingly and said, "My father drives me a little crazy, Archer."

"Yeah, I can see that. Maybe more than a little."

"So, let's go eat."

"I don't have the cash, and I'm not letting you buy me a meal again."

"Then how about I cook for you?"

He looked askance at her.

She said, "You doubt I can?"

"No. I just…Well, what would you be thinking of making?"

"I like my food fried, Archer. So chicken and okra and green tomatoes, for certain. And I have a bottle of wine. You ever have that spirit?"

"Can't say that I have."

"My mother introduced me to it. Wine from Argentina was her favorite. I don't have that. But I have a bottle of red wine from France."

"France! How the hell did you manage that?"

"I didn't. Hank did. He gave it to me."

"You okay with us drinking it?"

"We can toast him, if you want. But I mean to drink it sooner rather than later. He said some people wait years, even decades, to uncork a bottle."

"Never heard of such a thing. Couldn't be any good after all that time."

"They say it is, but I'm not that patient. Why don't you meet me in an hour's time at my house? Then dinner will be ready."

He thought of his arrangement with Ernestine and said, "I'll come up to your back door. And I can't stay all that long. I have to go to work in the morning."

"Right. Killing hogs."

"Well, in my case, just butchering 'em."

"That's a hairsplitter if ever I've heard one, Archer."

CHAPTER

25

IT WAS SIXTY-ONE MINUTES LATER that Archer found himself knocking on the woman's back door. She answered it wearing an apron over her dress.

"Well, if the smell is any factor, this meal will be pretty fine," he said.

He watched her working the skillets on the three-burner stove, which had an electric icebox next to it. When the food was done, shortly after he arrived, they sat down in a small dining room stuffed with too much furniture. She'd lit candles that threw the room into shadowy relief.

The chicken was crispy on the exterior—nearly burned, in fact—and moist on the inside.

"Best chicken I ever had," proclaimed Archer with all honesty.

"Eat what you want, I have plenty."

The okra and tomatoes had been coated in crumbles and fried in lard. After two helpings of everything, Archer finally had to push himself back from the table. "Okay, no more room left and that's a fact."

They had both tried the wine and didn't cotton to it, but when they tried it again later, it tasted different.

"How'd that happen?" Archer wanted to know.

"Hank told me something about it *breathing*."

"Okay."

"He went over there a couple years ago. Took Marjorie with him. They toured some of the wine country in France and Italy."

He looked at her, puzzled. "Didn't think there'd be any left after the war."

"He did say there was damage, for sure. But they managed to bring back a few bottles."

They finished the wine, and Archer rose and put on his hat.

"Sure you don't want to stay?"

"I've made other arrangements."

"Really? Well, excuse me."

"Don't be like that. I already explained why I can't stay here. Shaw would hang me for sure. Thanks for the dinner. It was really nice of you, Jackie."

"Don't start being kind to me when I'm mad at you."

"You ever gonna tell me what happened to your mother?"

Her eyes blazed. "Why? Did my father mention her? Tell me the truth, Archer. I made you dinner after all."

"Okay, Jackie, okay." He leaned against the sideboard and chose his words carefully. "He said she was the most beautiful woman he'd ever laid eyes on, well, something like that. Anyway, he also said that, well, that she could be hot-headed. And sometimes...."

"Yes?"

"Sometimes he was afraid of her."

"What else?"

"And that sometimes you and she didn't get along all that well. That mother-daughter relations are complicated."

"They *are* complicated. But I loved my mother."

"I'm sure you did." He decided to change the subject because he didn't like the direction it was taking, and he wanted to gauge the woman's reaction to something. "Did you know that Pittleman was running out of money?"

Jackie slowly stood. "Who told you that?"

"Shaw. He found a bucketful of past-due bills that Pittleman had tossed into the trash."

"That can't be right."

"Saw it for myself."

"But Hank was rich. Everybody knew that."

Archer shrugged. "Don't know what to tell you."

"You've given me a lot to think about." She fell silent for a few moments, apparently doing that very thing while he watched her closely. "So, are you going back to the slaughterhouse tomorrow?"

"It's my job, till I find something better. And that would be just about anything."

She walked him to the back door. "See you around, Archer." Despite his stench, she gave him a peck on the cheek.

He circled back around and came out on the main road. It took him about thirty minutes to walk over to Ernestine's bungalow. The lights were on, and when he knocked at her back door, she answered it right away. She had changed into a pair of high-waisted royal-blue trousers with buttons on one side and wide cuffs at the bottom, a long-sleeved white blouse with a Peter Pan collar, a light blue cardigan over that, and a pair of dark blue slip-on loafers. The woman's blond hair was still down around her shoulders, though she had clipped part of it back.

"Are you hungry?"

"No, I had my fill, thanks." He took a whiff of himself. "You, um, you mind if I wash up a bit? The...the business today was a little, uh, smelly."

"Of course. I can run a bath for you."

"A bath? You have one of them?"

"Yes. I'll get it going for you. And I have a robe you can wear."

"Thank you, Miss Crabtree."

She said shyly, "Look, we're not in the office now, just call me Ernestine."

"And I'm Archer, no 'mister' necessary."

She ran the bath and told him when it was ready.

He sank into the hot water to which she'd added something that made the water bubble and feel soothing against his skin.

She knocked on the door. "Is everything okay?"

"It's wonderful, Ernestine. I mean really swell. Best I've ever had."

She laughed on the other side of the wood. "It's only a bath, Archer."

"Yeah, well, I haven't had a bath since around 1941."

He finished up and put the robe on. When he came out Ernestine had lowered the wall bed and made it up for him; she was now sitting in an adjacent chair and reading a book. She got up and closed the volume. "It's all ready for you."

He glanced in the direction of her bedroom. "Thank you. Is your, um, bedroom door doing okay?'"

"It's doing just fine, thank you."

He was imagining Ernestine in all sorts of ways, hair down, skirt up, even naked like Jackie. It seemed he just damn well couldn't help doing so. Archer cursed himself. He was no better than the man who'd wolf-whistled at her.

She followed his gaze and said, "Well, I'm sure you're exhausted." She held up her book and said, "I actually wanted to finish this tonight. I'll just do so in my bed."

"What's that you're reading?"

"It just came out recently. It's entitled *1984*. By an English writer, George Orwell. Well, that's his pseudonym. His real name is Eric Blair."

"What's it about?"

"It's a dystopian novel set in 1984, hence the name."

"Long time from here." He added in a puzzled fashion, "Dystopian?"

"It's about life in 1984 as the writer sees it. The people are oppressed, the government knows all. People spy on each other. No one has any free thought."

"I think we just fought a war to stop that from happening."

"I think we did, too. Let's hope it was enough."

"Guess you're right about that." He stared at her for a long moment, his initial lustful desire dying away. Not because he didn't find her attractive, because he did. It was because Archer wasn't sure he deserved anybody as intelligent as she obviously was. And yet he had become perhaps even more intrigued by *who* she was than by what her beauty inspired in him physically.

"Look, Archer, you don't have to check in this week. I obviously know what you're up to...and where you're staying. I'll mark it down as your having reported in and all."

"I appreciate that."

"You're welcome."

"Good night, Ernestine. Hope you enjoy your book."

"Good night, Archer."

CHAPTER

26

THE NEXT MORNING Archer found hot coffee in the percolator waiting for him in the kitchen, a paper bag with an apple, a soft roll, some beef jerky, and a hard chunk of cheese inside, and a note from Ernestine wishing him a good day. He looked around for the woman but didn't see her. She might have already left for work. He wanted to call out to her or go knock on her bedroom door and thank her, but he decided against that. He sat at the table, drank his coffee, and put the note in his pocket.

He took a moment to look around the small space. Then he closed his eyes and, in his mind, allowed himself the fiction of believing that this was his tidy little home and his dear, loving wife had made him this strong cup of coffee and packed him a nice lunch, before he set out to work to earn the daily bread to support him and her and a passel of kids with sensible names and fascinating futures awaiting them all.

He opened his eyes and stared in surprise into his coffee cup. Archer had never before engaged in personal fantasy in any form. He had been raised by stoic God-fearing parents who labored hard and disciplined their only child just as hard. He had volunteered to serve his country, fought in and survived a world war. He had been too busy trying to stay alive to be fantasizing about not dying. Then he had roamed a bit and fallen into a situation that had resulted in his serving time in a rough prison where the rules of civility did not exist, and the guards were sometimes worse than the men they were overseeing. This was the only time he had allowed himself to diverge from the starkness of reality, the good and the bad of it. It felt surprisingly real and personal and satisfying. For about ten seconds.

Then Archer took his paper bag, opened the door, and went to butcher hogs.

Archer did his cutting with a more practiced hand that day. But when he was done, he was as covered with hog fragments as the day before, maybe more so because he had been more productive wielding the knives and saws. He wasn't as sore, though, on the ride home, as his hard muscles had quickly adjusted to his labor.

And the lunch in the paper bag had helped.

Dickie Dill rose from his seat on the truck, stared down the man next to Archer, and took his space when the man vacated it.

"What's up, Dickie?" said Archer, his eyes hooded, but his peripheral vision squarely on the little man, looking for any hint of a knife coming out.

"Guess you think you done me a favor yesterday."

"That's the way I looked at it. You're not back in prison, right?"

"Maybe so. But you do that again, I'll cut you up like you do them hogs."

"Thanks for the fair warning."

That seemed to take all the anger and venom from the man. He settled down, pulled a pickle wrapped in wax paper from his pocket, and started chewing on it.

"We're supposed to get paid tomorrow," said Dill.

"I know. I'm counting on it."

"Thing is, I hear tell there's trouble 'bout that."

Archer glanced sharply at him. "Come again?"

"Word is they ain't got the money to pay all they owe us."

"Where'd you hear that?"

"From folks who'd know, that's where."

"But look at all the hogs going through that place. They must be making money hand over fist."

"Not what I heard."

"Who owns the place, then?"

"Hank Pittleman, least he did."

This didn't come from Dill. It came from the man on Archer's other side who had evidently been listening.

Archer gaped. "Pittleman owned the slaughterhouse?"

"Yes sir, he sure did," said the man, an older gent in filthy coveralls and wearing an equally dirty fedora, an unlit smoke dangling over his plump lower lip, the cigarette jerking up and down as he spoke.

Archer looked at Dill, who had made no comment on this.

The older man added, "And like this here feller just said, folks say they ain't got the money to make full payroll. Heard it too, myself."

"So why are we working then?" said Archer.

"'Cause we ain't got nothing else," said the man simply with a shrug of his broad shoulders. "And they might pay some of what they owe. I ain't walking away from cash money, little though it might be."

"Kick in the nuts, ask me," said Dill, finishing his pickle and wiping his hands on his pants. "I'm gonna cut somebody up they try and pull that shit on me."

Archer didn't even attempt to quash this notion from Dill. Part of him wanted Dill to cut somebody and then end up back in prison, where Archer firmly believed he still belonged.

He got back to town and jumped off the truck.

And found Irving Shaw waiting for him.

The detective was wearing a brown suit and freshly laundered shirt, though his haggard features told of sleepless nights and the burden of solving a murder. He pushed back his homburg and eyed Archer closely.

"Heard you got work at the slaughterhouse. How're the hogs doing?"

"Not too good, actually, considering their only job is to die. Why are you here?"

Shaw caught the eye of Dickie Dill, who was watching him closely, his knifelike hands curled into fists.

Shaw apparently didn't like what he saw in

Dill because he pulled back his jacket so that both his pointed silver star and his .45 were showing prominently.

"Don't I know you, fella?" he said to Dill.

"Nope," said Dill. "Leastways, I ain't know you."

Shaw kept his eye on the little man for an uncomfortably long moment. "Well, I got business with this here gent, so you be on your way then."

Dill turned and walked off with a group from the truck, but Archer caught him glancing back a couple of times and then whispering something to the men with him.

Archer turned back to Shaw.

The lawman said, "Also heard you got kicked out of the Derby. Where you staying?"

"Around."

"But at least you're earning some money."

"Thought I was, but now I'm not sure."

"What do you mean by that?"

"Just heard that the slaughterhouse might not make full payroll tomorrow. And that it's owned, or *was* owned, by Hank Pittleman."

Shaw took off his hat and rubbed at his hair. "Well, that jells squarely with what I've been finding out."

"You mean Pittleman not paying his bills?"

"Not just that. But let's go somewhere and talk. You hungry?"

"If you're buying. I don't have a cent to my name."

Shaw looked at his clothes, took a whiff, and his face contorted.

Archer grimaced. "You try butchering hogs all day and see how the hell you smell."

"Come on then, and let's get your belly full up and my sinuses cleared out."

They each had rare steaks and hard potatoes and coffee and pie at the Checkered Past. As they ate, they talked.

Shaw said in a low voice, "Man was head over heels in debt. Those past-due bills I found in the trash were just the tip of the iceberg."

"How can that be, I wonder?" said Archer.

"Part of it is from gambling."

"Gambling? Where?"

"They got places around here, Archer. None of 'em legal, but they're around. And then we found out Pittleman's been traveling to this place called Las Vegas. You heard of it?"

Archer shook his head. "Hold on a minute. First night I met Pittleman, he mentioned the place. Said the likes of Poca City couldn't compete with Los Angeles and Frisco and that Vegas place."

"That's interesting. Well, it's in Nevada. They got gambling casinos out there. And showgirls. And brothels too."

"Brothels?"

"Prostitution, son. It's legal out there."

"The hell you say. I never knew that."

"And the boys that run those casinos, we're talking criminals, gangsters, make John Dillinger look like a choirboy."

"And Pittleman got in with them? And he owes them money? You think they sent somebody here to kill him then?"

"It's possible, Archer. From what I've learned, those boys don't take no for an answer when it comes to dollars owed. I guess they figure if they let one customer stiff 'em, everybody would try."

"So what are you gonna do? If they sent somebody out from Nevada, doubt they're still around."

"Doubt that, too."

"What now?"

"Figure as soon as we finish up here, we'll take a ride out to see Marjorie Pittleman."

"What for?"

"If her husband was into all these shenanigans, she might know about it. We've been all over his office at the Derby but there might be something helpful at his house. You know the lady. So you game?"

"I'm game for anything that keeps me from going back to prison. But right now this is all clear as mud."

"I've been doing this a long time and it's pretty muddy for me too, son."

27

SHAW HAD A BIG FOUR-DOOR BUICK that he pushed hard as they roared down the road. Earlier, after they'd finished their dinners, he'd escorted Archer to the Derby Hotel and let him wash up in the hall bath. As he was driving, Shaw said, "I called ahead, so the lady's expecting us. Right now, tell me about that fella on the truck with you."

"His name's Dickie Dill."

Shaw's eyes took on a hint of recognition. "Dickie Dill. Damn. I *knew* I'd seen that cuss before."

"Where?"

"Investigating a murder, well, actually two murders, this was way back. Must've been ten years ago, before the war. That Dill killed two women sure as I'm sitting here. But we couldn't prove it."

"I thought you always got your man, Mr. Shaw?"

"Hell, son, even lawmen lie sometimes to make themselves look better."

"Well, any consolation, he was in prison for a long while. Just got out a few months ago, so they must've got him for something else. He's small but mean as hell. He's not a man you want to cross."

"I'll cross him if he steps a foot outta line," said Shaw fiercely.

They reached the gates of the Pittleman estate, and Manuel opened them so they could pass through.

"Hold on," said Archer. He was pointing at a long-hooded car parked in the drive. "That's Lucas Tuttle's car."

"You sure?"

"Sure, I'm sure. That's his driver sitting in the front seat."

"Wonder what he's doing here?"

The front door opened as he said this, and Lucas Tuttle appeared there.

Archer saw that he was putting a sheaf of papers into his suit jacket pocket.

"Let's ask him."

They faced off with Tuttle at the bottom of the steps leading to the front door.

Tuttle had on a checkered sport coat, contrasting charcoal slacks, and black-and-white leather lace-up shoes. His bow tie held a pattern of black-and-white swirls. His crown-dented fedora covered the snowy hair. The bowl end of a pipe stuck out of his breast jacket pocket.

"Archer, what are you doing here?" he asked.

Shaw stepped forward and showed his badge. "He's with me. I'm Lieutenant Detective Irving Shaw, with the state police."

"You certainly look like an officer of the law," said a clearly unimpressed Tuttle.

"Can I inquire as to what you're doing here?"

As he asked this, Archer glanced toward the front of the house. In a window next to the door, he saw Malcolm Draper staring out at them. When he saw that Archer had spotted him, the man abruptly moved away.

Tuttle said, "I was here paying my respects to Marjorie on the death of her husband."

"I understand that you owe her a debt."

"And who do you hear that from?" said Tuttle, glowering at Archer.

"Never mind. Did you pay her?"

"I have Mr. Archer here working on that for

me. So you can ask him about it. Now, if you'll excuse me."

"Just a minute there, fella," said Shaw. "You want to tell me where you were between the hours of midnight and six a.m. on the day Hank Pittleman was found murdered?"

"I was in Houston, Texas, with about ten other gentlemen. We were up conducting business until nearly three in the morning. So unless you think I can fly like that Superman fellow, I think you and I have no further business."

"You get me the names and addresses of these ten gents."

"I'll gladly have my secretary provide them. Never let it be said that Lucas Tuttle was not a good partner to the law."

He tipped his hat, walked to his car, climbed in, and they drove off.

"I don't like that man," said Shaw. "He's too smart and smug for his own good."

"I don't much like him, either," said Archer. "Especially when he's pointing a shotgun at my crotch."

Shaw knocked on the front door while Archer stood beside him looking awkward.

"So those two gals, Marjorie and Jackie, met head-to-head, did they? How'd that work out?"

"Don't try to figure out women, Mr. Shaw. You would just be wasting your time."

"Hell, boy, I know that. I got a wife and a daughter. But see, my job requires me to do just that. Figure people out."

"You been out here before, then?" asked Archer.

"Yeah, how'd you know?"

"Because you didn't start jawing at the size of this place."

Shaw grinned at this comment. "Well, I sure did the first time I came out here. This house looks as big as some of the German factories I dropped bombs on."

The door opened, and the same young maid appeared there.

She smiled when she saw Archer.

"Can I help you?" she said sweetly.

Shaw took out his star once more. "Lieutenant Detective Irving Shaw with the state police to see Mrs. Pittleman. I've been out here before. I called ahead and she's expecting us." He pointed at Archer. "And this here's Archer."

The maid hiked her brows enticingly and smiled. "Oh, I know. I seen Mr. Archer before."

She led them down the same hall as before. The maid opened the door and motioned them in. This was not the conservatory Archer had been in before, but a walnut-paneled library full of books and the smell of wood smoke. Though it was still fairly warm outside, there was a small fire in the fireplace. Marjorie lay on a small hunter green davenport set against one wall. She had on a long, simple beige dress over her husky figure and black shoes with fancy bows. She had just affixed her pince-nez to her nose and peered up at them through the lenses. Archer noted a tall glass of an amber liquid on the rocks on the small table next to her.

She said, "Thank you, Amy, you may leave us now."

Amy gave a little curtsy, glanced with a smile at Archer, and departed.

"Please, gentlemen, sit." She pointed to two chairs upholstered in tiger stripes and gilded wood across from her.

The men took off their hats and sat.

"Mr. Archer, isn't it?" said Marjorie.

"Yes, ma'am. I was out here last time with Jackie."

"Hmm, right, Jackie Tuttle," said Marjorie disapprovingly.

"Ma'am," began Shaw. "Sorry to have to come back and trouble you again."

"Well?"

Archer interjected. "We saw Lucas Tuttle leaving here. He said he came to pay his respects?"

"That's right," she said.

"Sort of surprised me," said Archer. "I didn't think the two men liked each other."

"Perhaps not, but *I* got along fine with Lucas." She turned to Shaw. "Have you found whoever killed Hank?"

"No, ma'am, but we're working hard on it. Now, this is not easy to say, but were you aware that your husband was in, well, money troubles?"

Marjorie tittered. "Don't be ridiculous. Hank was extremely wealthy and as good a businessman as he was a husband to me."

Archer thought to himself that with that analogy, Hank Pittleman might've left his wife dead broke and belly-up.

Shaw continued. "Well, did you know that he had traveled to a place called Las Vegas? It's in Nevada."

"I know where it is, Detective. But, no, I didn't know that Hank had been there. How can you be sure?"

"Well, we had folks out there look into it."

"Why would you do that?"

In answer, Shaw pulled out a sheet of paper. "I have a lawman friend out close to Nevada and he sent some men over to the casinos in Las Vegas. They've determined that your husband owes them about two hundred thousand dollars in gambling debts."

Marjorie's eyes widened at this gigantic sum. "Did you say two hundred thousand dollars!"

"Yes, ma'am."

"My word, I had no idea." Her hand went to her bosom. "Hank, gambling? I can't believe it."

"That's not all, unfortunately."

"What?" she said sharply, her small eyes narrowing behind the specs.

"Your husband had lots of businesses."

"Yes, of course he did. He owned half of Poca City. And now I suppose I do." She seemed pleased by the prospect, thought Archer.

"He owned a lot, sure, but he *owed* a lot, too. This is a list of vendors he has failed to pay over the last eleven months or so. It's a pretty lengthy list. I'm not sure he was paying anybody what they were owed."

Marjorie read down the list, looked at the total dollar amount, turned the color of a cloud, picked up her drink, and drained it in one swallow. She wiped her mouth and Archer noted the shake of her hand as she set it back down.

"There must be some mistake," she said weakly, or maybe hopefully. "I mean, this...this can't be. This is far more than the gambling debts. This...." She faltered and looked up at Shaw in total shock.

"There's no mistake. I'm sorry."

She half rose and looked toward the door, which puzzled Archer, because there was no one there. Then she collapsed back on the davenport and hit a brass button on the wall. A few seconds crawled by, and Amy opened the door.

"Yes, ma'am?"

Marjorie held up her empty glass. "Another of these. Gentlemen, will you drink with me?"

Archer eyed Shaw, who nodded and said, "We'll both be having what the missus is."

"Tell George to make mine a double, and don't bother with any ice," ordered Marjorie.

Amy smiled and skipped out.

Marjorie refocused on Shaw. "This...this is unbelievable."

Archer said, "How come if he owes the boys in Vegas, they haven't gotten paid?"

"I asked my friend that. They said Mr. Pittleman was a good customer and always paid what he owed. So when he asked for credit, they gave it to him."

Marjorie, looking distracted, once more put a

hand to her bosom. "I feel like I've fallen into someone else's life."

"Yes, ma'am. I take it you knew nothing about your husband's businesses, then?"

"I never saw the need, and neither did Hank. I mean, well, he was the man, correct? And I've never had any talent whatsoever when it came to such things. And…and he was so successful. I never dreamt…I mean, I never thought anything was wrong at all." She looked around the grand room. "How could I? I wake up here every day to…this."

Shaw put the paper away. "Well, you wouldn't be the first wife to be kept in the dark about her husband's doings, ma'am."

She glanced warily at Shaw. "These gambling debts? Do you think these people could have had something to do with Hank's death?"

"I certainly think it a possibility. And a two-hundred-thousand-dollar debt is reason enough to kill a man." He paused. "But you would think they'd try to collect the money. With your husband dead, how are they going to get paid?"

Tears gathered in the old woman's eyes. "My poor Hank."

"Yes, ma'am," said Shaw, casting an awkward glance at Archer.

A minute later the door opened, and Amy came in carrying a tray with their drinks. She passed them out and left, but again with a smile cast Archer's way. Shaw noted it this time, elbowed the man, and shook his head, a grave expression on his face.

Marjorie drank a goodly portion of her whiskey while the two men sipped on theirs.

Shaw said, "Has anyone tried to contact you? Phone calls, letters?"

"Pertaining to what?" Marjorie said sharply.

"The debts your husband owed. Gambling or otherwise."

"No, but he had his office at the Derby Hotel, not here."

"Yes, ma'am, we know that. Did he by chance keep any papers here?"

"Not that I know of, but you could talk to Sid Duckett. He might know. Been with us a long time. Hank liked him."

"Is he here?"

"He lives in a cottage over near the trucking warehouse. White house with green shutters."

"Right, but what about Malcolm Draper? I was told he was your husband's business manager of sorts. If anyone knew it would probably be him."

Marjorie took another drink of her whiskey.

"Yes, of course, that's right. I was actually counting on Mr. Draper to help me navigate all of
Hank's affairs. He came on about a year ago. He
would most certainly know."

"Does he live on the grounds?"

"No, he has a room at the Derby."

"Does he?" asked Shaw, who cast another
glance at Archer. "Well, we won't bother you
anymore. We'll go see Duckett and find out
what he might know. And then we'll talk to
Draper in town."

He stood, along with Archer. Marjorie, showing a nimbleness that Archer certainly had not
expected, rose off the davenport, came around
the table, and put a hand on Shaw's arm.

"What am I to do about these debts and such?"

Shaw looked taken aback by the query. "Ma'am,
I don't know. You'd have to check with someone. I suppose your husband had a lawyer."

"I think he did."

"And he owns the bank," added Archer. "They
might know something, too."

Marjorie looked unsure. "Yes, but I've never
had to deal with those people." She gripped
Shaw's arm tighter. "Do you...do you think
these people might come here? These people
from Las Vegas? Am...am I in any danger?"

Shaw said firmly, "If anyone comes here and

makes any threats whatsoever, you let me know immediately. Don't know about Nevada, but we frown on that hereabouts."

"Yes, of course, thank you."

As they walked out of the house Shaw said, "That poor woman looked like she just saw a freight train coming right for her."

"Let's hope it's not coming our way, too," replied Archer.

28

No business papers around here that I know of," said Sid Duckett.

They'd found him sitting on the front stoop of his small cottage smoking a fat cigar.

"So Mr. Pittleman never gave you anything like that? To hold for him or whatnot?"

"Naw. If something needed doing, he just told me, and it got done. For papers and such, you'd have to ask Mr. Draper that."

"And where is Mr. Draper now? At the Derby?" Shaw wanted to know.

"Don't know. Not the man's keeper."

"If you see him, will you let him know I want to talk to him?"

"Sure thing, Detective."

Archer said, "Draper carries a gun. He said it was because of the warehouse."

"That's right."

"But the other guys at the warehouse weren't carrying guns," noted Archer as Shaw looked on.

"Don't know what to tell you about that. Man wants to carry a gun, he can carry a gun."

"You don't," said Archer.

"Never saw a need to."

"Mr. Pittleman ever mention any money troubles to you?" asked Archer.

Duckett laughed. "Money troubles? Hell, he's the richest man around here. Maybe the whole state far as I know. I mean, just eyeball that house 'a his. Look to you like the house of a man with money troubles?"

"Well, looks can be deceiving. Your wages ever been late in coming or not come in full?"

"Not one time."

"Well, rumor has it they might not make full payroll this week at the slaughterhouse," retorted Archer.

Duckett now showed more animation than he ever had before. "The hell you say. What else do you know about that?"

Archer was about to say something when Shaw interrupted. "You tell Draper if you see him, I want to talk to him, you hear?"

"Yes sir."

They drove back to Poca City. Along the way Archer said, "The man was spooked about Pittleman maybe not being rich and the wages not being paid."

"Yeah, he was. But listen, Archer, you can't go around telling folks stuff they don't know unless you got a damn good reason to do so."

Archer shot him a glance. "You think I messed up back there by mentioning the money problems?"

"I don't know, son, maybe so."

Archer looked chagrined and said nothing more on the trip back.

Shaw dropped him off near where he had met him.

"What about Draper?" asked Archer.

"I'll check to see what room he's in. If he's there, I'll talk to him. You go get some rest."

"You mean that, or you just don't want me messing things up any more?"

"Maybe a little of both. You sure you got a place to stay the night?"

"I'm good."

"You gonna go back to butcher hogs tomorrow?"

"Not sure. I don't like working for free."

Shaw rolled an unlit stogie around in his

mouth before sticking it under his hatband. "How about I pay you the same rate as they do, if you go back there?"

"What, why?"

"I checked on your Army record. You were a brave man, Archer. Lots of medals and all. And you were a scout."

"So what?"

"So maybe you can be a scout again. *My* scout. Go back to work at the slaughterhouse tomorrow, and keep your eyes and ears open."

"Well, okay."

"But don't talk unnecessarily," the lawman admonished. "You never know what people are gonna do with what you tell 'em." Shaw opened his wallet and held out five dollars. "Here's an advance. I hear tell you like advances." He cracked a grin.

Archer took the money. "You sure this is kosher, Detective?"

"My job is to catch a killer, Archer. And I'll do it any way I see fit."

Shaw drove off and Archer hoofed it to Ernestine's. However, she didn't answer the door. He looked at his watch. She might be out. Maybe over at the Cat's Meow. Or having a late dinner at the Checkered Past.

He tried the back door, but it was locked.

He took the clasp knife from his pocket and worked the bolt back enough to free it from the doorjamb. He walked into the kitchen and saw pots and pans in the sink. He looked in the fridge and saw a plate wrapped over. The truth occurred to him.

She made me dinner and I never showed up.

Archer felt badly about that but couldn't do anything about it right now.

Despite washing up in the Derby's hall bath earlier, he still stank.

He decided another bath would not be a bad thing.

He went in search of the bathrobe that Ernestine had provided before and found it in her bedroom closet. As he was about to shut the door, he saw it: The scrapbook that had been under the pillow was now on the shelf in the closet.

He hauled it down and sat on the floor and turned the pages slowly past what he'd already seen, until he came to something interesting.

It was a news story about Jewell Crabtree, the widow of Carson and mother of Ernestine. She had climbed into her Chrysler one night, while it was in the garage, and after stuffing a sheet in the tailpipe, started it up and expired on the front seat, leaving behind a note that was addressed to her daughter. There was another picture of Ernestine along with this story, and she was no longer drab or dour. Several years had passed since her father's execution, and her height and beauty had been realized, but her features were stoic—perhaps too stoic, thought Archer. This version of the woman he *could* reconcile with the parole officer as he had first met her.

The last thing in the scrapbook of interest was a letter. Perhaps it was the one mentioned in the news article. It was in a pink envelope with the name Ernestine scrawled in pen on the outside. Archer slipped out the note inside and unfolded it.

Dear Ernestine,

My lovely, lovely child. First and foremost, your father loved you very much. And please do not feel any other way with regard to that. What he did, he did out of his love for you and for no other reason. Any action taken in the past should not affect what you do with the rest of your life. Please live your life with that firmly in mind, and please have a happy life, my dear, dear child. Choices were made by many, Ernestine, and many of them were flawed choices. But choices have consequences, and we all must live with those consequences. But take that sad past and turn it into something positive, my dear child, and don't look back, only forward. Love, your mother.

He sat back against the bed and contemplated all that he had just read. He had to confess that he couldn't really make heads or tails of it, but his heart was mightily saddened by the abundance of tragedies in Ernestine Crabtree's past.

He put the scrapbook back exactly where he had found it.

He went into the kitchen, all thoughts of a bath gone. He washed up the pots and pans and utensils in the sink and put them away. He sat down at the table and thought about last night here. He and Ernestine had been alone in the house. A bottle of bourbon had been at hand. He'd been cleaned up and all, smelling about as good as he was ever likely to. He had done his best to impress upon the woman that he was attracted to her. And she had chosen a book in her bed over *him* in her bed.

While thinking this, he went to the shelf and found an Agatha Christie novel. He walked back into the kitchen and stood at the sink looking out the little window into the darkness, the book still held unopened in his hand.

"How did you get in here?"

Archer spun around to see Ernestine standing there.

"Back door. It was unlocked."

"No, I remember locking it."

"Well, it must be broken, opened easy enough."

She came forward and glanced at the empty sink. "You...you did the dishes?"

"It was the least I could do, considering that you made me a dinner I wasn't here to eat. I'm sorry about that. But I did have the morning coffee and the lunch, and it was much appreciated, Ernestine."

She set her purse down on the table and slipped off her dark blue pillbox hat and took off her black wrist-length gloves.

"Nothing special about feeding a hungry man. As for dinner, I'm sure you had other pressing matters."

"Mr. Shaw met me at the truck, and we went out to the Pittlemans' to talk with his widow."

"Then you haven't eaten dinner?"

"No, Mr. Shaw was good enough to buy me some before we headed out."

She sat down at the table. He did likewise, putting the book in front of him.

"Did you find out anything important?" she asked.

"Just that Pittleman was up to his ears in debt. Guess he had a gambling problem, too. Lost more money than I can count over in that Las

Vegas place. They got gambling houses there. And brothels! I mean, I just don't get it."

"Get what?"

"How women can do that."

"They might not have any choice in the matter."

"I would expect they had a choice and they just made the wrong one. Look at Jackie Tuttle. She told me she chose to be Pittleman's chattel, like it was her job or something. I still can't figure that out."

"So you believe she made the wrong choice then?"

"Well, don't you?"

"I have no right to judge her, as I haven't walked in her shoes."

Archer thought about this for a bit and once more came away with the depth of the woman's wisdom. He nodded. "I guess you're right about that."

Crabtree said, "And now? With Pittleman gone?"

"That ride might have run out for Jackie. And who knows if Pittleman left his wife a dime when all is said and done."

"It sounds like a dilemma all right.'"

"But Jackie is one smart gal. If anyone can survive this, she can."

"You care for her, don't you?"

Archer was startled by this question. "I don't want anything bad to happen to her. I think…"

"You think what?"

"I think she got a raw deal in life and deserves to be happy in spite of that."

Crabtree looked at him with those mile-deep eyes, and for a moment Archer could see himself plunging through their depths to who knew where.

"That speaks well of you, Archer."

He took out his Lucky Strikes and offered her one, but she declined. He lit up and said, "You got a man in your life, Ernestine?" Before she could say anything, he put up a hand. "I know that's a personal question, and you can just tell me to shove off. But I was just wondering. I never had a steady gal. I left home, roamed a bit, then went to college. Then I volunteered and spent years of my life fighting a war across the ocean. Then I got into trouble and there went more years of my life. Now?" He picked up the book. "Maybe these will be my friends. Keep me company at night."

"Books are wonderful, Archer, but they can't be the only things in your life. Humans are built for companionship, at least they should be."

"So, you got somebody?"

"I have someone I care for, yes."

"Does he live in Poca City?"

"Yes."

"He's a lucky man, then." He rose and took the book. "I'm gonna read a bit and then get to bed. Butchering hogs takes it outta you."

"Yes, of course. I'm sure it does."

Ernestine rose and disappeared into her bedroom, while Archer put his smoke out in the sink, stripped down to his skivvies, and lay on the pulled-out wall bed. He put the book on his chest but didn't open it. He just lay there wondering when anything in the world would begin to make sense to him.

29

HOW YOU KNOW THAT MAN, ARCHER?" said Dickie Dill with a snarl accenting his query.

Archer was outside the slaughterhouse eating the lunch that Ernestine had prepared for him. Before he'd left for work, he'd found her in the kitchen making him a hot breakfast, which he'd devoured before heading out. And per Shaw's instructions, he had kept his eyes and ears open while working there.

"What man is that, Dickie?"

Dill was cutting an apple into spirals with his switchblade and somehow managing to do it in a menacing fashion. He stuck a piece into his mouth and chewed with his few tobacco-stained and crooked teeth, mostly gumming the pulp and swallowing it with an effort.

"That policeman what's-his-name."

"Lieutenant Detective Irving Shaw of the state police."

"Yeah, him. What you doing with a cop?"

Dickie tossed the apple core and lit a Chesterfield, blowing his smoke right at Archer.

"Just looking into the murder of Hank Pittleman."

"Shoot, man don't pay his workers, he deserves to die."

"You confessing?"

Dill took a puff of the Chesterfield and looked at him funny, his mouth caught between a grin and a grimace. "You pullin' my leg, ain't'cha?"

"Maybe I am."

"You hang around cops, folks think shit."

"Like what?"

"Like you ain't one of us."

"I'm an ex-con, you're an ex-con. Nothing can change that, Dickie. We're bad boys. Forever."

"But still. Gotta watch out, Archer."

"I'm always watching out."

Especially for you, thought Archer.

"You still at the Derby then?"

Archer started to say no, but then realized Dill would inquire as to where he was lodging, and he didn't want any inkling of his staying

with Ernestine to get out to this loathsome
man. Shaw's telling him about the murders of
two women by Dill's hand had reinforced many
times over his already instinctual desire to keep
the man far away from his parole officer. Or any
woman. Or anybody else, for that matter.

"Yeah, but I'll be moving on soon. So Pittleman owns this place?"

"What about it?" Dill tapped his cigarette out on
the bench next to Archer, uncomfortably close.

"So, you know anybody here that worked
directly for him?"

"What you mean by *directly*?"

"Meaning more than killing and butchering
hogs."

"Why you want to know?"

"Just wondering."

Dill grinned in a way that never came close
to reaching his eyes. "That was you in the
joint too, Archer, thinking 'bout shit too much.
You got to learn to leave things be, boy. Ain't
healthy otherwise."

"So, is that a no?"

Dill made a show of closing up his switchblade. "That means it ain't your business. And
put it outta your goddamn head."

They went back to work, Dill sledgehammer-
ing and Archer cutting and sawing.

The man next to Archer, who had shown Archer the ways with the tools of butchering said, "Heard you talking to Dill."

"That right?"

"You asking about Pittleman?"

"I was, yeah."

"He was an odd bird."

"So you knew him?"

"There were some here who knew him. He had his fingers in lots of pies, they say."

"Man had a lotta businesses, that's true."

"You know a man named Malcolm Draper?"

"I've met him. Why?"

"He's around here a lot too. And he ain't butchering hogs."

"He runs Pittleman's businesses."

"He runs something, all right."

Archer was about to ask another question when Dickie Dill came into Archer's workspace holding his sledgehammer.

"Hey, Archer?"

"Yeah?"

"Thought I'd give you a look-see at what it is I do here."

Another man came in dragging a fat hog by a leather cord. The terrified beast, perhaps sensing what was about to befall it, was squealing and pulling against the tether with all its strength.

Its hooves were digging into the wooden floor and creating an unsettling clatter as it struggled to survive.

All the men in the butchering room, including Archer, stopped what they were doing and looked that way.

The other man faced the hog, knelt down, and pulled the leather cord to the floor, forcing the poor beast's head down and keeping it stationary.

Dill circled around behind the hog and raised his sledgehammer, the look on his face one of unadulterated excitement.

A moment before metal hit skull, Archer closed his eyes.

The sound of the sledgehammer crushing bone was nearly as horrible as the dying squeal made by the unfortunate animal.

When he reopened them, the hog was lying dead on a floor full of hog scraps, bleeding from its crushed head, but also from its nose and mouth. Its one blood-filled and lifeless eye looked up at the man who had just killed it.

Dill held up his homicidal tool in triumph.

"And now you know how it's damn well done, boy."

The message conveyed was perfectly clear to every man in the place. And most particularly to Archer.

"Knowledge is a good thing, Dickie," said Archer, drawing another funny look from Dill.

Archer went back to his butchering.

When pay time came, their wages were short by half. When some of the men began to protest, a couple of large steady-eyed fellows carrying shotguns walked into their midst and calm quickly returned.

Archer had not sat next to Dill during the ride back, but the latter had kept his gaze on Archer the whole way. The men spent the trip back to town complaining about the short wages. The gent who'd taught Archer the cutting method leaned in and whispered, "That man Dill ain't right in the head. Think somebody hit *him* with a sledgehammer maybe when he was a baby."

"Well, if they didn't back then, somebody might want to think about doing it now," replied Archer.

After the truck dropped them off, Archer started walking away, looking once over his shoulder to make sure Dill had headed off in the opposite direction.

Ernestine had arrived at her house ahead of him. She was cooking up some chicken in a pan on her electric stove when he walked in the back door.

"Funny," she said, a smile playing over her

lips. "I had somebody look at the lock today and they said it was just fine. Though it did show signs of being *breached*."

Archer took off his hat, glanced at the lock, and said, "Well, you can never be too careful."

She reached into her apron pocket and pulled out a key. "How about I give you one of these instead?"

After a dinner of fried chicken and corn on the cob and soft peas and doughy rolls washed down with lemonade, Archer proclaimed it one of the best meals of his life.

"How was the slaughterhouse?" she asked, after her smile showed that his compliment had pleased her.

"I have no plans to make it a career, if that's what you're asking."

She laughed. "I hope not. I think you're meant for bigger and better things."

"We only got half our wages, though, so the money problems for Pittleman are real enough."

"That is totally astonishing to me. He seemed so wealthy."

"I've found that looks can be deceiving."

She glanced up to see him staring pointedly at her.

"You have something you want to say?" she asked, giving him a curious glance.

"Look at you. I mean, a man could just see your...well, your beauty and think that was all there was. They wouldn't know anything about all the books you've read, all the things you know. That you want to write a book of your own. And that you help people that need helping, like me. I mean, they wouldn't know any of that."

"You're right, they wouldn't. And what do you think about that?"

"I think it's sad. Like the fellow who wrote those nasty things or the sheriff who wants you to whatever, or the jerk in the hall who wolf-whistled. They just look at you and see one thing."

She leaned forward, and those enormous eyes of hers wrapped themselves around the man. "And how about you, Archer? When you look at me what do you see?"

He didn't hesitate in answering. "I see someone I'd like to be good friends with my whole life."

His answer seemed to startle her for a moment. "I believe you mean that."

"That's because I do." He paused and this line of conversation made him think of something else, something important. "Look here, Ernestine, Dickie Dill?"

"What about him?"

"He's one dangerous man."

"I know that, Archer."

"I don't like the fact that you have to meet with him."

"It's only once a month now. I won't have to see him for quite some time."

"I don't like that you have to *ever* see him."

"It *is* my job." She gave him a piercing look. "Why? Did something happen?"

He started to tell her but then changed his mind. "Next time you have to meet with him, let me know and I'll be there, too."

"You don't have to do that, Archer."

"I'm not doing it because I have to, it's because I *want* to, Ernestine."

"Thank you. That's very...sweet of you."

They spent the rest of the evening listening to music on Crabtree's Emerson radio.

"I like that Sinatra fellow," said Archer. "But give me old Bing Crosby any day."

"I still love listening to the Andrews Sisters," replied Crabtree nostalgically. "After work, in the rooming house I stayed at during the war, we'd lie around, drinking coffee and smoking, and listen to them all night long."

"They came over with the USO while we were fighting in Italy. Them and Bob Hope and some others. 'Boogie Woogie Bugle Boy' always got me stomping my feet. And that Patty Andrews, wow, she was some looker—" Archer caught himself. "And a damn fine singer."

Crabtree looked up at him and smiled. "It's okay to compliment a person's looks, Archer. You're a handsome man, I freely admit that. So long as it's not all we think about each other."

"Right."

Later, they each picked up their books and Ernestine headed off to bed. But about a half hour later Archer put his novel down, picked his hat up, clutched his new key, and left by the back door.

About twenty minutes later, he was knocking on the portal at 27 Eldorado.

Jackie answered his knock dressed in high-waisted jeans, pink slippers, and a checkered shirt tied up high enough to expose her taut midriff. Her hair was curled up in plump rollers.

She did not seem happy to see him. "You think you can just show up any old time and I'll let you in? I got things to do, too, Archer."

"I'm sorry, Jackie. I've been working at the slaughterhouse during the day."

"And staying somewhere you won't tell me at night. I wonder why."

"I need to talk to you about Pittleman. Can I

come in?" He glanced at her rolled-up hair. "Are you getting ready to go out somewhere?"

"No."

"Then what's all that for?" he said, pointing at her hair.

"I'm experimenting with a new hairstyle."

"Women do that?" he said, eyes wide.

"Women do a lot of things to please men. But more so to please other women. At least we like to think so."

She stepped back to allow him to pass inside.

Jackie poured a rum and Coca-Cola over ice for herself without asking him if he wanted one and sat down on the couch across from him.

"What about Hank?" she said bluntly.

Archer lifted his hat off and perched it on his knee, looking uncomfortable. "I came to tell you that Pittleman was a sick man," he said quietly.

"What?"

"He had cancer, up here." Archer tapped his head.

Jackie set her drink down because her hand was shaky. "Is...is that why he had the head-aches?"

"I guess so."

"He never said anything to me about it."

"Well, I don't think he told his wife, either. Doc said he didn't have long."

"He was already dying when someone killed him? Is that what you're saying?"

He nodded. "And there's something else."

She shot him a glance. "That's not enough?"

"Remember I said he had money problems?"

"How could I forget? It's hard to believe, though. I thought Hank was rolling in dough."

"Well, he was also a gambler. And he owed the casinos in Las Vegas two hundred thousand dollars."

She looked stunned by this information. "That is crazy talk, Archer."

"And at the slaughterhouse they could only make half the payroll this week."

"Let me get this all straight. Someone kills a dying man. And then you're telling me that a rich man isn't really rich?"

He nodded again.

Jackie finished off her drink in one gulp and held the cold glass against her cheek.

"And you didn't know about any of this?" said Archer.

"How could I? He gave me a car and a house and spending money. And he told me his headaches were something he'd always suffered from, even as a child."

"Man kept his secrets, I suppose."

Jackie looked at him with a sobering expression. "I guess we all do."

"What were you expecting from Pittleman?"

She set her drink down, crossed her arms, and scowled at him. "What do you mean by that?" she said coldly.

"You couldn't marry the man. He was already hitched to Marjorie. But was it just the use of the house and car and folding money?"

"Why should I tell you?"

"Because the man is dead, Jackie, and we're trying to figure out why. And some folks think I killed him, that's why!"

"You playing at being a shamus?" she said in a bemused fashion.

"It's not playing when you might be looking at a noose around your neck."

"They're not going to hang you, Archer."

"You think the law's never convicted an innocent man before? Because I'm living proof that they have."

She started to say something but then caught herself. "Hank was a hard man, Archer. There are plenty of people who might have wanted to kill him."

"Shaw thinks it might be the Las Vegas crowd because he stiffed them."

"I guess it could be," she said doubtfully.

He looked at her closely. "But you don't think so?"

"I don't know what to think and that's the honest-to-God truth." She looked at him, really looked at him, maybe for the first time tonight. "Do you believe me?"

Archer thought of Shaw's warning about trusting people, especially pretty women. "As much as you believe me," he said evenly.

Her face fell. "Do you want to stay here tonight?"

"Do you want me to?"

"Yes, but…not like that." She sat up. "I'm a little scared, Archer. I mean, I was with Hank a lot, and some people might think…I know things."

His defenses crumbled in the face of this plea. "Sure, I'll sleep here on the couch."

After she went to her bedroom, Archer lay on her couch and stared up at the ceiling. He was now taking his slumber in two different women's homes but not in their beds, and he wasn't sure what to think about that. One thing he was fairly certain of: His life was going to get even more complicated before long.

CHAPTER

30

THE NEXT MORNING, Archer left a note for Jackie and returned to Ernestine's before the woman got up, using his key to get in. He figured she'd be sleeping in, since she didn't work on Saturdays, and he turned out to be right. He opened her bedroom door a crack and saw her still in bed, her novel lying open beside her.

He made his own breakfast, left Ernestine a note, and headed over to the Derby. Shaw had mentioned that he was staying there but hadn't told Archer which room. He wanted to tell the detective what had happened at the slaughterhouse. Archer was afraid that Dill was going to do something at some point. But there was something else bothering Archer about the change in Dill. The little man had become more focused in his aggression, and Archer sensed some purpose behind the man's normally mean-spirited disposition.

Archer walked over to the front desk where the same man who had evicted him was parked behind the counter reading a newspaper. When he saw Archer coming, he dropped the paper and backed away.

"What do you want with me?"

"Hold on, pal. Just want to know if Mr. Shaw's in his room."

"I don't know. Haven't seen him today."

"It was 201?"

"No, 304."

"Oh, that's right. Thanks."

The man picked up his newspaper but shot suspicious glances at Archer as he walked quickly away.

He ran the three flights up and approached Number 304. He knocked on the door and received no answer.

"Hey, Mr. Shaw," he called out, his mouth close to the wood. "It's me, Archer. We have to talk. Found some things out."

No sound. No nothing.

He walked back down the stairs. Shaw had told him he was married and had kids. After this was over, he would presumably go back home to them.

Who do I have to go home to?

First, he didn't have a home. And, second, even if he did, there would be no one in it other than him. He hadn't accomplished much in his life so far. And maybe he was running out of opportunities to improve upon that dismal record.

He checked his watch and left. It was about time for the truck to pick them up. The slaughterhouse worked every day but the Sabbath, he'd been told. Surprisingly, Dill wasn't there. Archer asked around, but no one knew where the little man had gotten to. They just seemed collectively relieved that he was not among them.

Archer worked all day and rode back on the truck with the other exhausted men. At least tomorrow there would be no work. When he got off and was heading down the street, Shaw's big Buick pulled up alongside him.

"Hey, been looking for you," said Archer.

"Been outta town. Get in."

Archer climbed in.

"Why were you looking for me?" asked Shaw.

Archer told him about Dill and the threats and his wanting to know what Archer was doing with Shaw.

The detective took this all in with a few nods.

"Now, where have you been?" asked Archer.

"To see a doctor and an insurance man."

"You sick?"

"Not for me. Hank Pittleman's."

"I'm not following."

"Let's go get some grub. And I could use some coffee."

They again ate at the Checkered Past, this time opting for chicken over steak. And this time Archer paid for the meal with his slaughterhouse money.

When Shaw put down his second cup of coffee and wiped his mouth with his red and white checkered napkin, he eyed Archer closely.

"You been spending time with Miss Crabtree." It wasn't a question.

Archer's face fell. "How do you know that?"

"My job is to know everything, Archer. Sometimes I get there, and sometimes I fall short. But I'm always trying."

"She's letting me stay at her place till I can afford something else. Look, you don't have to tell anybody about this. She's just helping me out. There's no funny business going on."

"I don't doubt that. And from all accounts, Miss Crabtree can take care of herself."

"Now, I went over to Jackie's last night. And

slept there." Before Shaw could say anything, he added, "On the couch, by myself."

"So why'd you go to Jackie's?"

"I told her about Pittleman's cancer."

"And why did you do that?"

"You think I messed up again?"

"Not necessarily, I just want to hear your reasoning is all."

"I guess I wanted to see if she already knew about all that. See her reaction."

"And?"

"And either she's as good an actress as Katharine Hepburn, or the woman didn't know anything about it."

Shaw took this in, rubbing at his jaw.

"And Miss Crabtree?" he said, his tufty eyebrows hiking suggestively. "Despite what you just said, you like her, don't you?"

Archer nodded. "She's a special gal."

"Nothing wrong with liking special gals."

"And the woman has had to deal with some bad stuff."

"Like what?"

Archer was about to tell the lawman about what was in the scrapbook but decided not to. It had nothing to do with the case, and he didn't feel he had the right to share such personal information that he had gained only by looking at something he had no business looking at.

"Just boys being idiots. Catcalls and crummy notes passed under her door. Even a deputy sheriff who's got the hots for her."

"She's a fine-looking woman. Just the way it is. Like you said, boys are boys. Not saying it's right. I got a daughter and two sons. Up to the parents to teach them right. Respect goes both ways, or it don't count."

"That's all I got. What about you?"

"I tell you on the condition that you don't go blabbing it around, you hear me?"

"I hear you. I guess I'm kinda surprised you're even letting me know anything. Or work with you on this thing."

"First time I ever let a suspect help me investigate, Archer, and that's no lie."

"So why me?"

"I got my reasons. And that should be good enough for now."

"Okay."

"Anyway, met with a medical specialist Pittleman was seeing on the south side of the state, good ways from here, I tell you. Put some miles on the Buick."

"What'd the man say?"

"He confirmed that Pittleman was dying.

Incurable. Even cutting him up woulda done no good. This was about six months ago. Told Pittleman he had about a year left to live at that time."

"Okay. But we already knew that."

Shaw held up a finger. "What we didn't know was that the doc told me that Marjorie Pittleman was there with her husband on a couple of occasions."

"So she *knew* he was sick?"

"That's right."

"How'd you even figure to check on that?"

"I don't take nothing people tell me as the truth till I get someone or something else to absolutely confirm it. See, the thing is, people lie, all the time." He gave Archer a hard stare. "We call it *corroboration*."

"Okay. But why is that important?"

"Think about it, Archer. When someone lies, it means they're trying to cover something else up, only reason *to* lie. Hell, son, you should know that, as much as you lied to me! Now, when a husband kills a wife or a wife kills a husband, there are normally only two motivations, least in my experience. First, they have somebody on the side."

"Well, Pittleman had Jackie, but Marjorie knew about that."

"Doesn't mean she was happy about it."

Archer thought back to what Jackie had told him about it and nodded his head in agreement. "And the second motivation?"

"Hell, Archer, ain't it obvious? Money!"

"But we found out that he might not be as rich as some think."

"Which is why I checked with the insurance company that wrote a policy on Hank Pittleman."

"Insurance policy? How'd you hunt that down?"

"It's my dang job, Archer. I got good relations with all the insurance folks. See, they don't want to pay out money any more than you and me would on debts we owe. We find a way to save them the dough, they like that. And they cooperate."

"So what'd they tell you?"

"That a half-million-dollar life insurance policy was taken out on Hank Pittleman about four months ago. His wife's the sole beneficiary."

"Hold on, why would they give a policy to a sick man who's dying?"

"You struck the nail on the damn head there, Archer. I like that. You could be a detective yourself with some training. You got the right nose for it." He motioned over the waitress and ordered another cup of coffee and a piece of the cobbler.

"Here's the thing. They had Pittleman undergo a physical, see. I mean, they all do that. Nurse or a doc comes and does what they do. But they ain't gonna find a tumor in your head by sticking a thermometer under your tongue or putting a stethoscope against your chest." Shaw grinned. "But there's a but. You figure out what it is?"

Archer took only a moment to think about this. "If he was told six months before that he was dying, and they took out the policy four months ago and didn't tell the insurance folks?"

Shaw's grin deepened, and he pointed at Archer. "Bingo. That's insurance fraud. See, on the form they got a little clause that says the applicant knows of no medical or other health condition that would materially alter the risk of the policy being written, or some such legal language like that. Companies do that to cover their ass, and keep the customers honest, and, more important, build in a way not to pay out the money."

"And since they knew he was dying when they got the policy, the Pittlemans committed fraud?"

"Damn right. And it wasn't just the wife's

doing. I mean, Hank Pittleman had to know about the policy, otherwise why would they be sending somebody to check out his health? Now Pittleman's beyond the law, but his wife's not."

"You think she had him killed? I mean, I can't imagine her doing it herself."

"Naw, if she did kill him, she got someone to do it. Now we just have to prove it."

"But you have the motive right here. A half-million bucks."

"Yeah, I can prove insurance fraud all right, and that'll get her a year in prison maybe. But that's not why I'm here, Archer. I'm here to catch a murderer. Whoever killed that man needs to hang. And if his wife paid someone to do it, she needs to go to prison for a long time, maybe the rest of her life. Hell, they might hang her, too."

Archer shook his head.

"What?" said Shaw.

"She just looked like a lost old lady, not a killer."

Shaw wagged a finger at him. "Remember this, son, if you remember nothing else: Sometimes it's the ones that look and act like angels you got to watch out for. People are funny. And sometimes a nice outside covers up a real nasty dark side. Dealt with a lot of folks like that in my time. Smile at you while they're readying the knife to cut your throat."

"I guess you're right."

"No guessing about it. Now, you were saying this Dickie Dill was threatening you 'cause maybe you were working with me?"

"What he said, more or less. And he wasn't at work today."

"Wonder where he got to, then?"

Archer shook his head. "No idea."

Shaw stretched and yawned.

"You look tired, Mr. Shaw."

"During the war they gave us Benzedrine to help us stay awake when we were flying bombing missions. We were popping so many pills, Archer, it was like goddamn candy." Shaw shook his head. "Hardest damn thing I ever had to do, kick that crap."

"Got a question."

"Shoot."

"Why would Marjorie hire someone to kill her husband so she could collect the half-million bucks if he was going to die anyway?"

"Now that's a right good question, Archer. Shows your instincts again. But I'll tell you why, son, and this is called putting the whole picture together based on what we know. What

I figure is she knew about the gambling and was worried he might mess things up so badly that even the life insurance policy wouldn't help her. Or he might not have the dollars to keep the premiums paid up. Policies that big ain't cheap, and you miss one payment, they cancel the policy. So, she doesn't want to wait for him to kick the bucket from the cancer. She speeds up the process." Shaw paused when his coffee and pie came. He shared the slice with Archer.

"Has she tried to collect on the policy?" Archer asked.

"Not so far. I asked the company to let me know. And that Malcolm Draper never tried to get hold of me. I'm thinking we need to pick that man up and make him talk."

"He was looking out the window at us when Lucas Tuttle was leaving after paying his respects to Mrs. Pittleman."

Shaw paused with his fork halfway to his mouth. "He was? Why didn't you tell me then, Archer?"

"I don't know. I mean, the man works there. Didn't see it as odd that he was in the house."

Shaw chewed on his cobbler, took a sip of coffee, and considered this. "How likely do you think it was that Tuttle was over there paying his respects?"

"About as likely as Dickie Dill winning a personality contest."

Shaw snorted at this and then grew serious. "So why was he there?"

Archer looked sheepish.

"What?"

"Tuttle was putting some papers in his pocket when he was coming out of the house."

"What sort of papers?"

"Couldn't tell. But he owed Pittleman five grand plus interest. Maybe he paid it off."

"And the papers might be the promissory note. So Marjorie must have had it."

Archer tried hard not to show his confusion, because Marjorie didn't have those papers. Archer did. Part of him wanted to confess this to Shaw. The other part of him won out.

"Maybe" was all he could manage.

They finished their meal and headed over to the Derby Hotel. They asked at the front desk for Draper's room and whereabouts.

"He went out about an hour ago," said the clerk.

"And what's his room number?" asked Shaw.

"Two fifteen."

"Give me the key."

"But—"

Shaw held up his star. "Right now, mister, 'less

you want to get to know the insides of a jail cell real good."

The clerk nearly threw the key at him.

Instead of taking the elevator, Shaw joined Archer on the stairs. When Archer looked at him inquiringly, Shaw said, "Even a lawman sometimes don't like doors closing on 'im."

CHAPTER

31

DRAPER'S ROOM WAS NEAT and spare, and they found no evidence that the man was involved in any criminal activity whatsoever. In fact, other than the man's clothes and toiletries, they found nothing at all.

"Maybe you were wrong then," said Archer. "Maybe he doesn't know anything."

"No, I think it means I'm right. No man is that tidy without a reason. He doesn't want to leave anything for someone to find."

Archer slowly nodded. "I could see how that might be."

"Then you're learning, son."

They went back downstairs, where Shaw turned the key back over.

"Mr. Draper will probably be back around ten," said the clerk.

Shaw shot him a look. "How do you know that?"

"He most likely went out to the slaughter-house."

"What the hell?" barked Shaw. "You sure?"

"I didn't see him, if that's what you mean, but he goes out there most days after dinner."

Shaw slammed his fist down on the man's counter so hard, the fellow jumped clear back to the wall. "Why in God's name didn't you tell me that before?"

The man stammered, "Y-you d-didn't ask."

Shaw pointed at him. "Don't you go nowhere, fella, less I wanna arrest your ass when I get back."

"What for?" cried out the man.

"For being stupid if nothing else."

He and Archer rushed out and climbed into the Buick.

"Of all the dumb sons of bitches," exclaimed Shaw.

"What's the hurry going out there?" asked Archer.

"I want to see what that man does out there every night. And if we can catch him in the act of doing something wrong, I can use that to get him to rat on the others. Ain't no honor among thieves, Archer. They're just bad folks you got to grab by the neck and shake."

The big Buick roared to throaty life.

With Archer giving directions, they made it to the slaughterhouse far faster than the truck Archer normally rode there on. The place was dark and there were no vehicles out front.

Shaw peered through the Buick's windshield. "You got a gun, Archer?"

"I'm on parole. I can't have a gun, Mr. Shaw."

"Well, I'm making an exception right here and now. Just don't tell nobody."

Shaw hit a button on his dashboard and a little panel dropped down under it. Revealed was a revolver with black walnut grips held in place by pressure clips. Shaw freed it.

"Smith and Wesson .38 Special Victory Model, double action with fixed sights. Carried this baby in the war. Never fired it once." He cracked a grin. "Couldn't hit anything with it on the ground from ten thousand feet up in the air." He handed it over to Archer. "But whatever you hit with that sucker ain't getting back up."

He grabbed a flashlight from the glove box.

"Maybe Draper already came and went," said Archer.

"Maybe. God, this place stinks," said Shaw,

covering his nose with his free hand as they headed to the building.

"Wait'll you get inside," replied Archer. "You'll have to hold your nose *and* your belly."

The door was locked.

"Do we break it in?" said Shaw, tapping on the stout wood.

"Hold on."

Archer stuck the gun into his waistband, took out his knife, and worked away at the lock for about thirty seconds. Then it swung open.

"I won't ask where you learned to do that," Shaw said.

He clicked on the flashlight and they entered the space. Archer, who knew the layout of the building pretty well, led the way.

When they reached the space where the hogs were sledgehammered and the walls and floor were coated with blood and brain matter and Archer explained what went on here, Shaw said firmly, "I ain't never eating another piece 'a pork, long as I live, swear to God."

They moved through the building, listening for any sound of Draper, but there was no noise at all, other than the litany of grunts from the ill-fated hogs penned up outside.

They finished searching the place and went back outside.

"Okay, this is a right puzzle," said Shaw.

Archer wasn't paying attention to him. He was looking over at the hog pens.

"What?" said Shaw, eyeing him.

"Seems to be a ruckus going on over there."

Archer hustled over to the hog pen with Shaw on his heels.

They reached the fence and peered over to where a group of hogs was worrying at something on the ground.

"Give me that light," said Archer. He shone it on the spot.

"What the hell is that?" cried out Shaw.

Archer pointed his pistol in the air and fired two shots. This scattered the hogs, who ran toward the far end of the pen. Archer gripped the top fence rail and swung over, his shoes softly hitting the muck on the other side. Shaw climbed over the fence and landed next to him. They slowly walked over to the spot.

"Holy Lord," said Shaw.

Holy Lord, thought Archer as he stared down at what was left of the body. It was not Malcolm Draper.

It was Sid Duckett. Or what was left of him.

* * *

"His head was bashed in before he died," said the short, rotund coroner, a cigar perched in one side of his mouth, as he rose from beside the body.

Shaw had called in the police and an ambulance and the coroner from a call box down the road. He nodded to the ambulance men, and they took the unfortunate man's remains away on a stretcher.

Shaw tilted his hat back and rubbed his forehead. "I'm man enough to admit I didn't see that one coming."

"You think I maybe spooked him with my talk about Pittleman's money problems?"

"Could be."

While Shaw went over to talk to the coroner, Archer borrowed a flashlight from one of the deputies and examined the dirt in front of the building. He knelt down next to one particular spot.

"Hey, Mr. Shaw."

The lawman hustled over. When he reached Archer, the man was brushing at the dirt. He stepped back and shone his light on this spot.

"See those tire tracks?"

Shaw nodded. "I can see 'em now. Good eye."

"They're fresh, for sure. And I can tell you something else—those tire treads are the same as on the truck Sid Duckett was driving."

"You sure?"

"I saw 'em up close and personal when I was loading those boxes on it. It had two square misaligned patches, just like you see there."

Shaw pulled his Buick keys out. "Okay, we got to find Malcolm Draper, fast."

They drove off, the Buick eating up the miles back to town.

Shaw said, "See, that's the other motivation to kill somebody: Shut 'em up. Duckett might or might not have been involved in all this. But when you told him about Pittleman's money problems, he might've thought he wasn't going to get paid. Or Duckett planned to use that knowledge to make a lot more money from folks who didn't want certain information to get out."

Archer had a sudden thought. "Coroner said his head was bashed in."

Shaw glanced sharply at him. "Right. So?"

"Dickie Dill is an expert head basher."

Shaw eyed him. "You think somebody hired him to kill Duckett?"

"Might be. I mean, Dill would do anything for money. And I've never met a meaner man in my life. And he didn't come to work today."

"Well, Duckett ain't talking to anybody ever again. Loose lips sink ships."

Archer's thoughts went back to a discussion he'd had the previous night and he suddenly felt dizzy in the head and sick in his stomach.

He cried out, "We need to get to 27 Eldorado Street, fast as this damn Buick will go, Mr. Shaw."

32

THE BUICK HAD NOT YET REACHED Jackie's house when Archer told Shaw to pull to the curb.

"Don't want to warn anybody we're coming."

They leapt out and Archer led the way, approaching the house from the back.

It was nearly midnight now, and the silence was complete except for the movements of the two men.

His shoes skimming across the dry grass, Archer quickly reached the back door with Shaw behind him.

"Didn't see Duckett's truck out front," said Shaw.

"Wouldn't expect to."

"You sure you're barking up the right tree here?"

The scream inside the house made Archer put his shoulder to the door and burst the lock from its frame. They both rushed inside, their guns drawn. Another scream was heard, and Archer shot down the hallway and kicked open Jackie's bedroom door. It was pitch-dark inside.

In a flash of illumination from Shaw's flashlight, Archer saw Dickie Dill next to the bed, a raised knife in hand as Jackie cowered below.

"Dickie!" shouted Archer, pointing his gun at the man and firing.

At the same instant, something hit Archer and sent him tumbling against the wall face-first. He felt warm blood gush from his nose and a shiner swell under his eye.

Shaw got off a shot, too, and this time Dill let out a sharp cry. The pilot had hit his target after the infantryman had missed.

"Archer, look out!" screamed Jackie from her bed.

Another shot was fired. This time from the second assailant, who had slammed into Archer when he'd fired at Dickie. After Jackie's warning cry, Archer had ducked. He felt the bullet fly past and then slam into the wall. He kicked out, catching the shooter's arm, and the pistol went flying. Archer lost his balance and fell back against the wall, then turned and pushed off from it.

But this gave the man an opening. He flew forward, his arm encircling Archer's neck. He commenced trying to pull his head backward to a point necks weren't supposed to bend. Archer felt the ligaments in his spine begin to howl and buckle in protest. However, a sharp elbow to the gut, a gasp of air forced from a pair of lungs, and Archer quickly gained the upper hand. A stiff palm strike to the nose drove cartilage back into the man's face, then Archer spun the man around and the thrust of his shoulder slammed the man with force up against the wall. Archer finished him off the way he'd been taught in the military, with a knee to the base of the spine and a hard punch to the kidney. Then he grabbed the man's hair, jerked it back, and then, using all the leverage he could muster, slammed the man face-first into the plaster wall. The fellow fell with a groan, then didn't move.

Archer had no time to dwell on this victory.

Dill had flung his knife across the room and had caught Shaw, betrayed by the beam of his light, in the upper arm. He dropped his gun, groaned, and fell back against the wall.

Dill used the bed as a trampoline and bounced

to the other side of the room, something in his hand.

Jackie screamed and tried to reach for Dill to stop him, but missed, falling out of the bed with the effort.

Dill landed on the floor and lifted the thing high over his head.

It was a sledgehammer.

With a murderous yell he began to drive it downward, but it never reached Shaw's head. Archer tackled him hard and the men tumbled to the floor, slid across it, and hit the wall, leaving them both momentarily stunned. Dill recovered first and tried to wedge the wooden handle of the sledgehammer against Archer's throat, but two rapid punches to the smaller man's face and Archer was able to seize the hammer and throw it clear. Then Archer felt the very thing he'd been afraid of—Dill's steel-like fingers around his throat, trying to suffocate the life out of him. Although Dill had been shot in the arm and was bleeding badly, he still had the upper hand.

"Shoulda killed me when you had the chance, boy," roared Dill gleefully.

Something hit Dill on the head. Archer saw Jackie standing there with a lamp. However, Dill let one hand go from Archer, flung his fist around, and knocked Jackie off her feet. She fell with a thud.

But Dill's actions allowed Archer an opportunity, of which he took full advantage.

Archer reached what he needed in his pocket and then stabbed Dill in the side with the clasp knife, driving it up to the hilt in the man's belly. Then a second time and then a third just for good measure.

Dill coughed up blood in Archer's face, his grip lessened, and he finally let go and fell on his back onto the floor.

Archer stood on unstable legs and looked down at the man, just as Dill gazed up at him and snarled something incomprehensible. He tried to rise up as Archer took a step back, his knife held at the ready. Archer put his foot on the man's chest and pushed him down, holding him there.

Archer had killed even more men in the war than he had let on to Jackie. And he had no compunction about ending the lives of any of them. He only thought about it later, actually, and then there had been no real remorse, only anger at the situation in which he'd been placed to have to kill another. He had no remorse this time, either. Not even close. Just relief.

"Dammit, just die, Dickie," he said quietly.

And a few moments later, after a throat curdle and a body shiver, the man's eyes grew rigid and his chest grew still as his life ended.

Archer turned to Jackie and helped her up. "Are you okay?"

"Yes," she said shakily. "I'm fine. Just sore from where he hit me."

"Turn a light on," he said. He dropped his bloodied knife and raced over to Shaw, who was on the floor, his back against the wall.

Jackie turned on the nightstand lamp. Shaw was holding his arm where blood was leaching out. He had pulled the knife free, which might not have been a good thing.

Archer helped him off with his jacket and rolled up his shirt sleeve.

"Jackie, get me a towel. Do you have any bandages? And I'll need some hot water and soap. And some liquor. And some hydrogen peroxide if you got it."

Jackie rushed out of the room and returned with all of the items, including a bottle of brandy. Archer used his belt as a tourniquet above the wound, stanching the flow of blood.

"Give him the liquor," said Archer.

Jackie helped Shaw to drink it straight from the bottle.

Archer cleaned and bandaged the wound.

"We got to get you to the hospital," said Archer, helping the other man up. Shaw, gray faced, merely nodded.

"Jackie, get dressed and grab a few things. I'm taking you some place safe."

She looked over at the dead man and the unconscious man and didn't argue.

Shaw said slowly, "Got cuffs in my jacket pocket. You cuff that SOB over there so he can't get away."

Archer did as he was told, and when he turned the man over, he saw that it was Malcolm Draper. The man had finally turned up. He cuffed his hands behind his back and said to Jackie, who was getting dressed in her closet, "Throw me a belt."

She did so, and he hog-tied the man's legs with the belt, intersecting it through the handcuffs.

Archer drove the Buick straight to the hospital, which was a block over from the Derby. While the doctor attended Shaw, the detective had Archer call the police station and tell them what had happened at Jackie's. Deputies were sent over to secure the area and arrest Draper.

As Shaw lay on the gurney he stared up at Archer. "You saved my damn life, Archer."

"Just glad I was there. And you saved Jackie's life. Dickie woulda killed her for sure if you hadn't winged him. And you saved me, too, when you think about it. Not sure I could've got the upper hand with him if he hadn't been wounded. You rest easy now. I'll be back."

He left with Jackie and drove her over to Ernestine's, where he rapped hard on the door.

When a sleepy Ernestine opened the door, she looked confused when she saw Archer. But when she spied Jackie standing there, her features froze.

"Ernestine Crabtree, Jackie Tuttle," said Archer by way of introduction.

The women, Archer thought, looked like two prizefighters about to do business in the ring.

"Miss Tuttle," said Ernestine.

"Miss Crabtree," said Jackie.

He succinctly explained what had happened and what he wanted Ernestine to do with Jackie.

Ernestine's face had paled as Archer had described the horror at Jackie's home. He thought she might actually faint. His hand shot out and steadied her.

"Steady there," he said. "You okay?"

She composed herself and said, "I'm all right. My goodness. You poor thing," she said to Jackie, gently draping her arm around the other woman's shoulders.

"And Ernestine, you got your gun handy?" asked Archer.

"Yes."

"Keep it that way."

Jackie gripped Archer by the arm as he was about to leave.

"Thank you," she said.

"Just glad you're still with us, Jackie. And if it weren't for you, I'd be dead."

He hustled back to the Buick. As he started the car, he looked back to see the women turn and head into the house. Ernestine's arm was still around Jackie and the other woman was leaning into her for support. Then the door closed.

Well, thought Archer, that had gone better than he could have imagined.

However, as he thought about it some more, he began to grow worried. The women separately had gotten to know Archer fairly well. And he had slept with Jackie. If the two started comparing notes on him?

He let out a sigh. *Well, there's nothing perfect about life. But at least I still got a life after tonight.*

He drove off.

Shaw was sitting up and looking much better when Archer returned. The lawman had been placed in a private room and had bags of blood flowing into him.

"Deputies have been by. They got Draper. And they picked up Dill's body."

"Good," said Archer, sitting next to the man. "But you just rest easy now."

"Why do you think they went after Jackie Tuttle?"

"She knew Hank Pittleman as well as anyone did," said Archer. "They were afraid he told her something, I suspect. Like you said, tying up loose ends. That's what made me think to go over there in the first place. She asked me to stay with her last night for that very reason."

"Soon as I get outta this bed, I'm gonna ask Marjorie Pittleman point-blank what the hell is going on."

"Like to be with you when you do."

"Don't worry, you will. You earned that right tonight, son."

"And I think I'm retiring from the slaughterhouse business," said Archer.

"Good call," replied Shaw, looking drowsy.

Noting this, Archer said, "Now you need to get some sleep. And so do I."

Archer tipped his hat over his eyes and leaned back in his chair.

"What, you mean you're gonna sleep here?"

"'Course. Want to be around in case somebody wants to try to come after you to finish the job. Don't worry, I'm a light sleeper."

"You always been that way?"

"Nope. But something about fighting a war and spending time in prison just does that to a man."

He closed his eyes and fell asleep.

A minute later, so did Irving Shaw.

CHAPTER

33

IT WAS THE FOLLOWING DAY, around five. Shaw, his wound sutured, his blood levels fully restored, and his arm in a sling, had been pronounced to be out of danger. Now he was standing in front of Marjorie Pittleman's door with Archer next to him.

The elderly Agnes answered the door after Shaw knocked.

Shaw had wanted to question Draper, but he was still unconscious and had been transferred from a jail cell to the hospital. They feared his skull might be cracked.

"Now I wish I hadn't hit him so hard," lamented Archer when he heard this news.

Agnes led them down the hall to the conservatory this time. Marjorie was seated on a chaise lounge with silk upholstery reading a book when they were shown in. As usual, a tall glass of something on the rocks was on the small table next to her. Archer was concluding the mild-mannered woman perhaps drank all the time. And maybe he couldn't blame her.

"Yes, gentlemen, do you have news of my husband's killer?"

Shaw took off his hat with his good arm.

"My word, what happened to you both?" asked Marjorie, noting the sling and Archer's battered face.

Shaw pointed to two chairs. "May we?"

"Oh, yes, of course."

They sat, and Shaw stared at the placid woman.

"There *have* been developments, ma'am."

Marjorie closed her book, adjusted her pince-nez, and looked across at them.

"Such as?"

"Such as Sid Duckett getting fed to the hogs out at your husband's slaughterhouse. And two men trying to kill Jackie Tuttle last night."

Marjorie paled and dropped her book to the floor. "Excuse me!"

Shaw gave her a dead-eyed stare. "We also know about the life insurance policy on your husband, Mrs. Pittleman."

"That's right. It was Hank who insisted that we take it out on him."

"Oh, is that so?" said Shaw skeptically. "Why?"

"Well, we all have to die, Mr. Shaw. And Hank took out the policy, not me. You can ask the insurance person."

"But you knew about it?"

"Yes, of course. I was the beneficiary, after all."

"On the life insurance application, it said that your husband was in good health."

"Well, as far as I knew, he was."

Shaw's mustache twitched. "Is that right?"

"Yes."

"According to his doctor, you were with your husband when he told him he had incurable cancer in his brain. What do you say to that?"

"I didn't believe him."

"Excuse me?"

"I didn't believe the doctor. I told Hank to get a second opinion. As far as I was concerned, Hank did not have cancer."

"I doubt the insurance company will believe that."

"Then I will fight them to the very end," she snapped, her calm, refined expression gone in an instant. "I will not let them browbeat a poor, old widow, or cheat me out of money that is rightfully mine!"

"Okay," said Shaw, slowly glancing at Archer.

Marjorie calmed as quickly as she had grown angry. "I'm sorry, gentlemen, I'm sure you can understand how distressed I am about all this. But my money issues are not important. You said Sid Duckett is dead? And someone tried to kill Jackie?"

"One of her attackers was Malcolm Draper."

"Sid Duckett and Malcolm Draper! My God. They both worked for Hank."

"Which is why I'm here."

"You can't possibly think that I had anything to do with any of this. That…that is…I would never. How could you believe…?"

"Ma'am, look at it from my way. Your husband dies, you get a half-million bucks. Your husband was having a, well, an affair with Miss Tuttle. Lots of wives have killed their husbands *and* their husbands' mistresses. Just a fact of life."

Marjorie waved this off. "That is not how it was in this particular circumstance, Detective."

"Then why don't you tell me how it *was*, Mrs. Pittleman?"

"Jackie Tuttle was, well, an element of convenience for me."

Archer said, "She told me it was the same for her."

Marjorie said, "I'm sure. I can see how it would be, of course. I mean, Hank did financially support her."

"But why would you let that happen right under your nose?" exclaimed Shaw.

She looked at him with pity. "I really had no say in the matter. I mean, look at the French. The men there have mistresses. And the wives tolerate it."

"This ain't *France*," said Shaw.

She shrugged. "Women must do what we can. The fact is, Hank had control of everything. When he ventured to…seek out the affections of others, I struck a bargain with my husband. Jackie became a part of that bargain. If it were up to me, I would not have made that arrangement, but it was not up to me. So, there you are. It was not a perfect situation by any stretch, but it worked for us."

"But you might still want her dead," said Shaw.

"I never tried to harm her while my husband was alive. Why in the world would I wish to do so after he's dead and their…relationship must end?"

Shaw had no ready answer for this.

Archer said, "Can you think of anyone who would want to kill her?"

"No. I really don't know much about her

other than Hank wanted her by his side instead of me."

"And Mr. Draper?" asked Shaw.

"What about him?"

"We learned that he went out to the slaughter-house most nights. Do you know why?"

"He only came to work for Hank about a year ago. I can't say I really knew the man, although I was going to rely on him to help see me through this mess. I guess I'm on my own with that." She paused and said to Shaw, "Now, do you have any idea who killed Hank?"

"I thought I did, but maybe I'm wrong there. We'll keep working on it. But please don't leave the area."

"I can assure you that I have no intention of leaving my home. I have a lawyer working on the debts and the insurance policy and other things. I won't give up what Hank built without a fight, Detective."

"That's certainly within your rights, ma'am."

Archer said, "We saw Mr. Tuttle here the last time we visited."

"I know that. We talked about it." She hesitated. "But that was a little odd."

"What do you mean 'odd'?" said Shaw.

"Well, he came to pay his respects to me about Hank's death, as I said." She glanced at Archer.

"As you suggested before, most people knew the two did not get along. In fact, Hank hated Lucas Tuttle. He told me so."

"But he loaned him money," said Archer. "Five thousand dollars."

"Did he really?" said Marjorie, looking intrigued by this. "Well, Lucas must have indeed been in desperate straits to come to Hank for money."

"What was the beef between those two?" Shaw asked.

"You know what men are like—they never really grow up."

"Come again?"

Marjorie sighed resignedly. "Before Hank came to town, Lucas was the big shot in Poca City. But Hank's success left Lucas in the dirt," she added proudly. "Now, if there's nothing else?"

Marjorie pressed her bell, and this time Amy appeared and led them out.

"Mr. Archer, my goodness, what happened to your face?" she asked as they walked along.

"Ran into a wall. But I'll be fine."

She smiled. "Hope so. I like you all handsome." She actually winked at him before skipping off.

As before, Archer watched her go, until he felt Shaw tugging on his arm.

"Don't even think about it, Archer. That one is nothing but trouble."

In a way, aren't they all? thought Archer. *At least for me.*

They got back into the Buick. Archer was driving because of Shaw's bum arm.

The lawman said, "Well, that was not what I was expecting. The woman seemed to have an answer for every dang thing." He eyed Archer. "We got to hope Draper wakes up and tells us the truth. Drop me at the hospital so I can check on that. I can walk to the hotel from there."

"Okay. Then I'm gonna go see Jackie."

"Ask her if she knows anybody who wants to kill her."

"That's a tough thing to ask a person."

"Well, you got to because it's the only way we're gonna get to the truth, Archer."

"That seems a long way away right now."

"Hell, son, it always does, up until the moment you fall right over the damn thing."

CHAPTER

34

No enemies that I can think of, Archer," said Jackie.

She and Archer were sitting in the front room of Ernestine's bungalow. Ernestine had gone to the evening service at the Methodist church, but she'd left her gun with Jackie.

"You sure?"

"What, do you think I go around ruining people? Hank did that, not me."

"Which means there are a lot of folks who might have wanted to kill him."

She shivered. "I woke up and saw that awful man hovering over me with a knife."

"Dickie Dill standing over anybody, man or woman, would have been a disturbing sight."

He paused. "He, um, he didn't do anything to you before he tried to kill you, did he?"

"No, but—" Jackie started to weep and reached out to him.

Archer took the woman into his arms. "It's okay, Jackie, that man's not going to hurt anyone ever again."

She gently touched his damaged face. "Does it hurt?"

"Not compared to being dead, no."

She composed herself and sat up. "But why would they want to kill me?"

"You mentioned it yourself the other night. They maybe thought you knew something that they were afraid of. Did they ask you anything? I mean, about Hank or such?"

"No. I just heard a noise, woke up, and there he was. I started screaming."

"Lucky we were outside and heard it."

"How is Shaw?"

"He's fine. Tough man."

"It was sweet of Ernestine to let me stay here."

"Once you two get to know each other, I think you'll be friends."

"She's very nice."

"So, did you two gals talk about me?" He said this in a joking way, but underneath, a nervous Archer wanted some genuine answers.

"Talk about you? How do you mean?"

"I don't know. I guess how gals talk about guys."

She sat up straighter, pursed her lips, and said in a disapproving tone, "What, like comparing performances in the sack?"

"I never slept with Ernestine."

"Says you."

"It's the truth."

"Well, it's not like I would care, Archer. We're not married."

"Okay," he said, feeling a bit disappointed by her response.

"She thinks you're nice. And you saved my life, so you're okay in my book, too."

"You're a funny gal, Jackie."

"No, I'm just not what you're used to encountering in a 'gal.'"

"You speak the truth there," he said.

This seemed to defuse her standoffishness and she curled up next to him and said, "What about the debt that my father owes Marjorie Pittleman?"

"What about it?"

"In case you forgot, you were supposed to go out there again and get it paid."

"Hell, I had pretty much forgot about that."

"I don't see how you can afford to do that.

It's a lot of money, Archer. Unless you want to keep butchering hogs."

He mulled this over. "Well, the fact you're no longer with Pittleman is a good thing. Your daddy might pay based on that. Hell, Marjorie might need the money now."

"Five thousand plus interest," she said. "That *would* come in handy."

"You been giving this some thought, I see."

"What else do I have to do?" she shot back, but then smiled and kissed him on the cheek.

"But your daddy made it pretty clear that the only way he'll pay the debt, and me, is if you come back home, Jackie. And you've made it just as clear that you're not gonna do that."

She fingered his lapel. "But what if I agreed to...to meet with him?"

Archer glanced sharply at her. "Why would you do that?"

"He *is* my father. And you *do* need the money."

He held her at arm's length. "Jackie, don't base this on me getting paid."

"But I could meet with him. In fact, it might be best."

"Are you sure?"

"I don't know, Archer, but I think I have to try. Me almost getting killed? Well, it makes a person think, you know."

"Look, you don't have to worry about it now. You just need to stay here and rest and, well, just get right in the head. Somebody trying to kill you takes time to get over."

"No, I think I need to get this resolved, Archer."

"Okay, but how? Would you go out there to meet with him?"

He saw her perceptibly shudder.

"No, I can't go out there. But...but you could tell him that I can meet him at my house."

"You sure about that?"

"I am. Can you go tomorrow and tell him?"

"If that's what you want. What time do you want him to meet you?"

"Say around nine o'clock tomorrow night."

"Fine. I'll be right there with you."

"No, Archer, I don't want you there."

"But why? Why meet with the man alone?"

"I won't have to. Ernestine can come with me."

"But she doesn't know anything about this."

"Which is why I think she's the right person to be there. She won't have to be with us while we're meeting, just in the house."

Archer thought about Ernestine's skill with a gun, which might come in handy. But if Tuttle brought his shotgun...

"Look, if he has his shotgun, you don't let him in."

"He won't have his shotgun, Archer. Good Lord, he's my father."

Archer studied her for a moment. "Look, you're not thinking of doing anything to him, are you?"

She suddenly glared at him. "Why do you ask that?" she snapped.

"No…no reason."

"You *do* have a reason. What else did he tell you when you were in the car with him?"

"I already told you."

"Not everything."

"Jackie, you don't need to hear this now."

"Yes, I do," she snapped. "I'm tired of you keeping things from me, Archer."

"He said that you and your ma were a lot alike. Beautiful, but…"

"But what?"

"I guess you two butted heads a lot."

"We didn't see eye to eye on everything. There is nothing wrong with that."

"No, sure there's not."

"What else did he say?"

"Look, Jackie, I'm not…"

"Did he say we were unstable?" She grabbed his jacket. "Did he?"

He looked at her, searching the woman's eyes for what was really inside her head right now.

What he saw was a person who was starting to unsettle him. "He didn't use that word. But, like you just said, he told me you were both strong women. And that he was—"

"He said we were violent, didn't he? That he was afraid of us?"

"Look here, Jackie, won't you tell me how your mother died? Desiree said it was an accident, but she wouldn't say how."

"Did my father talk about it?"

"Yeah, a little."

"What did he say?"

"That...that maybe it *wasn't* an accident."

"Tell me exactly what he said. Now!"

Archer blurted out, "He said something about the truth destroying people and maybe it was better not knowing it, something like that."

"And what did you say to that?"

"I guess I come down on the side of knowing the truth is better than not knowing it."

Jackie said nothing for several long moments. She simply stared off.

"She fell."

"Fell? How?"

"From the barn, the second story where they winch the bales up to the hayloft. She died from the fall."

"Good Lord."

"I found her," said Jackie quietly. "I found her body."

Archer held her tight. "I'm really sorry, Jackie."

She abruptly pushed away from him. "I've gotten over it."

"I doubt you ever get over something like that."

"You're wrong, because I have. I'm…I'm going to lie down now. I'm tired." She rose, picked up her purse from the side table, and tossed him a set of keys. "For the Nash. Just leave them in the glove box when you're done."

He caught the keys and looked up at her. "Okay, Jackie."

She disappeared into the bedroom.

Very disturbed by what had just happened, Archer was about to take his leave when the door opened and Ernestine walked in. Her churchgoing clothes were charcoal in color and modest and demure in design. Her hat had a little veil, and her hair was once more done up in a tight bun.

When she saw him, she looked around. "Where is Jackie?"

"She just now went to lie down. How was church?"

"Soothing." She took her hat off and said, "Would you like some coffee?"

He eyed the bottle of Rebel Yell.

She followed his gaze, smiled resignedly, got two glasses and filled them with a finger each, and handed him one. They sat on the couch and sipped their drinks.

"Is Dickie Dill really dead?"

"Dead as they come. It was a close thing. Little man almost did me in."

He was surprised to see her lips tremble at this. "I'm so very glad that he did not."

He flashed her a grin to reverse her anxiety. "Hey, it's all good." He glanced in the direction of the bedroom. "Did Jackie talk to you at all?"

"About what?"

"I don't know. Anything, I guess."

"She was very frightened. And she was very grateful for what you and Detective Shaw did."

"Nothing about her father, maybe?"

"No, not about him."

"Okay. Uh, anything about me in particular?"

"Like what?"

"Just anything."

"She likes you. She's comfortable around you. She thinks you're a good person."

He nodded, feeling ashamed for trying to pry information from the woman.

"Can I ask you a question, Archer?"

"Shoot."

"Do you care for Jackie? I mean, do you love her?"

This was not what he had been expecting.

"I'm, uh, well, to tell the truth, I'm not sure what love really is, Ernestine. If it's feeling good with someone, liking how they look, and wanting to be around that person, then yeah." He paused, glanced down for a moment, and then decided to say it. "But that could apply just as much to how I feel about *you*."

A part of him wanted to keep looking away from her, but a stronger part of Archer compelled him to stare directly at her.

"I see," she said, eyeing her lap.

"I didn't mean to put you on the spot."

"I'm sure you didn't. And I know that I put *you* on the spot with my question. But your words were spoken with a great deal of sincerity."

"So, how do you feel about me?" he said quietly.

She glanced up at him, perhaps sensed the urgency, the necessity of having an answer showing clearly in his features.

"I like being around you too, Archer. Very much. But perhaps not in exactly the same way that you want to be with me."

He nodded slowly. "Well, a man can't ask for a straighter answer than that."

They fell silent for a few moments. Then Archer said, "Jackie wants to meet with her father at her house, tomorrow night. And she wants you to be there with her. I'm sure she'll talk to you about it, but I wanted to give you a heads-up."

"What will they be talking about?"

"Lots of things. Some I know, some I don't have a clue about. But are you okay with that?"

"I am. If that's what she wants."

He finished his drink, rose, and fingered his hat, looking nervous.

"Is there something else?" she asked quietly, peering up at him.

"My old man, rest his soul, was a good father. He, uh, he stood up for me a lot when I was a kid. I grew into my height and all later on. So some of the bigger kids would rough me up and such. But my dad was always there." Archer held up a fist. "He taught me how to fight proper and all."

"Why are you telling me this?"

"Sometimes my father would go too far, though. He beat up a couple older kids that had knocked me around. Police got called out on him. He almost went to jail, but in the end didn't. It was bad all around for everybody, and back then I got mad at my old man for doing it. But the thing I came to understand is that he did what he did because he loved me. It really was that simple."

Perhaps involuntarily, Ernestine glanced in the direction of her bedroom and where the scrapbook lay before her large and now sad eyes came to rest on him once more.

"Do you understand what I mean?" Archer said, his look unsure and anxious.

"I think I understand exactly what you mean, Archer," she replied.

She looked at him with an expression that Archer couldn't entirely fathom. It was sort of caught between hope and heartbreak, he supposed.

"Ernestine, you okay?"

"I'm fine, Archer, thank you. I hope everything works out for you."

"Yeah, me too. Well, good-bye."

"Good-bye," she said with something akin to finality, at least in his eyes.

Troubled by this odd impression, he left.

CHAPTER

35

THE FOLLOWING AFTERNOON, Archer ventured down to the Rexall drugstore, with the big orange-and-blue sign. Sitting at the counter he smoked a pair of Luckys while he devoured his bologna-and-cheese sandwich with a pickle, and drank down a lukewarm bottle of Coca-Cola. He bought some aspirin from the blue-smocked druggist standing behind the counter and downed a couple pills with the remnants of his soda pop. He idly watched a young, slender woman in geranium red coveralls loading *Life* and *Look* magazines into a wire rack next to a shelf of toiletries.

Finished with his meal, Archer ducked into the phone booth adjacent to the lunch counter, looked up the number in a phone book dangling from a chain, then dropped in a nickel and made the necessary call because he didn't want to surprise a man who answered his door with a shotgun. As he fingered the rotary dial and listened to the familiar clicks and whirls as it spun, he thought about what to say. He decided to make it short and sweet. When the call was answered, it wasn't Tuttle, it was his secretary, Desiree. The conversation went far more pleasantly than if Tuttle had been on the line.

Later, under a vast, blue sky, Archer pushed the Nash fast as he roared down the road leading to Lucas Tuttle's. The big, bulky car handled well and had plenty of power, like Shaw's Buick. Before taking the wheel of the Buick, Archer hadn't driven a car in years. For obvious reasons, the prison folks had not deemed it sensible to allow convicts to command heavy pieces of equipment.

He felt open and free, and part of him contemplated taking this Nash all the way to California, where he had heard the jobs were plentiful, the weather was always warm, and all the women looked like Rita Hayworth. Then the thought of Irving Shaw with his ribbon of mustache and indefatigable thirst for the truth made Archer ashamed he had even thought of making a run for it. Now he wanted to know the truth as much as the lawman did.

He turned past the leaning mailbox and hurtled down the road, cut to the right, and pulled up in front of the neat house a bit later.

He climbed out and looked around, thinking it had to have been something pretty bad for Jackie to forgo all this to take up with someone like Hank Pittleman. He didn't care how much money the man had. He had forsaken his wife and chosen a younger woman because Marjorie had the audacity to grow old. Well, Pittleman had gotten old, too. For Archer, who had never taken the plunge, marriage was for life, right or wrong, good or bad. You just didn't wake up one day and decide enough was enough because your mate had a few more wrinkles or a few more pounds.

Maybe that's why I never got hitched. Maybe I'm afraid I can't live up to the vows.

He put on his hat, angled it just so, and headed to the front door.

Rapping twice, he expected to see the door open and the Remington over-under appear in his field of vision. He braced himself for that in fact, but it wasn't necessary.

Desiree Lankford, dressed in a dark gray skirt and a three-button jacket with a pale blouse and sensible pumps, greeted him.

"Hello, Mr. Archer," she said. "You're right on time. This way."

She led him down a hall floored in two-by-two-foot terra cotta tile. As he gazed around, he noted once more the old wooden beams running along the ceiling and the walls plastered and thick. The place smelled of wood fires and age.

"You live here?" asked Archer.

"No, but I don't live too far away. I'm heading out now, in fact. I hope your meeting goes all right."

Desiree led him to a door and opened it.

Archer stepped through and she closed the door. He could hear her firm tread heading back down the hall. The room he was now in was large, comfortably furnished, and set up as an office or study of sorts, with shelves full of books and papers, a large weighing scale in one corner, and a map of the area with little pins stuck in it. A credenza stood against one wall with an ice bucket and scoop, and a line of liquor bottles and cut crystal tumblers behind that. Just the sight of it gave Archer a painful thirst.

Behind the desk was a stone fireplace, built of knobby gray-and-brown rock, that climbed to the arched ceiling. Next to the fireplace was a broad leafy plant on a wooden stand. In another corner was a hunter-green Mosler safe about six feet tall with a silver combination lock and matching spin wheel. Cigar and pipe smoke mingled aromatically in the air Archer was breathing. It actually made him want a Lucky Strike in the worst way.

On a console set next to the door were two revolvers: a .38 Long Colt double action with a three-and-a-half-inch barrel, and a Smith & Wesson .32 hammerless with a two-inch muzzle. He could see that both the wheel guns were fully loaded.

And sitting behind a large, paper-littered desk about the size of a dinner table set in front of the tall stone fireplace was Lucas Tuttle. The green eyes in the center of that face swiveled around and took hold of their target. He was holding what looked like a phone receiver in his hand, though it was hooked by a squiggly cord to a funny looking little machine.

"So you called for a meeting, huh? I wonder why?" said Tuttle, as he reached down, slid his Remington out from the kneehole, and laid it on the desk, the muzzle pointing in Archer's general direction.

Archer swept off his hat and came forward. "Told you I'd be working this thing. And like you told Detective Shaw, the matter *was* in my hands."

Tuttle's eyes indicated a wooden-backed chair with a nail-head upholstered seat on Archer's side of the desk. Archer took it, making sure he was not directly in front of the Remington's muzzle, not that it would matter much with the scattergun's shot field. He crossed his legs and perched his hat on his knee.

When Archer glanced at the double barrels, he thought he saw a bit of something that was white colored in one of them.

"Hello, Archer, you all there or are you drunk?" He looked up to see Tuttle staring at him.

"What's that thing?" asked Archer, indicating what Tuttle was holding.

"Called a Dictaphone. Records my voice. I can talk into it and then have Desiree type up what I said." He put the Dictaphone receiver down. "Has that Detective Shaw found out anything about who killed Pittleman?"

"No, but not for lack of trying. He's a good man. He'll get there."

Tuttle shook his head, not looking convinced. "I don't share your confidence. But then I don't get involved with the police as a matter of course."

"Then you're a smart man, but then again sometimes you can't get around it."

Archer fell silent and looked pointedly at the older man.

"Well?" said Tuttle. "You called and wanted to see me. I'm a busy man, so let's have at it, son."

"Two men tried to kill Jackie Saturday night."

Tuttle half rose from his seat. "What? Is she—?"

"She's fine. One was Malcolm Draper, he worked for Hank Pittleman. The other man was an ex-con named Dickie Dill who worked at the slaughterhouse."

Tuttle's eyes narrowed. "Why would somebody working for Pittleman want Jackie dead?"

"Well, it couldn't be Hank Pittleman's doing, since he was already dead."

"Wait, are you saying it was Marjorie? I can't believe that."

"Jackie *was* seeing her husband."

"Everybody knew that, including Marjorie."

"But still, it couldn't sit well with her."

"I told you before, I'm sure it did bother her. But Hank controlled the money. Without him she doesn't get to live in that big house."

"Fair point." Here Archer paused, considering some advice that Shaw had given him about revealing information. A smart detective had to have a good reason to do so.

"Turns out Pittleman had a cancer in his brain. He was dying and he had a lot of gambling debts. His money was running out."

He stopped talking and watched Tuttle carefully for his reaction to this.

Tuttle sat up and said, "But he was a rich man. The richest man around. So how could that be?"

"You're not rich if you spend more than you have. Then you're just like everybody else."

Tuttle leaned back in his chair. "Well, I can't argue with that logic. What does all that mean with regard to our meeting today?"

"Pittleman's dead. Do you take that as your debt to him no longer being valid?"

Tuttle shook his head. "No, I don't see it that way at all. Marjorie Pittleman will now become the holder of the debt. And from what you just told me, she can probably use the money."

"Did you talk to her about the debt when you were there?"

Tuttle looked at Archer as though he had a screw loose. "Good Lord, boy. I don't talk business with a woman. They don't have the sense for it. Certainly, Marjorie doesn't. Like I said, I was there to pay my respects, nothing else."

"With no Hank Pittleman around, the problem with your daughter goes away, too."

Tuttle said eagerly, "You've convinced her to come home then?"

"No, not exactly."

Tuttle frowned. "Then what are you doing here except wasting my time, son?"

Archer gazed at him. "How about if I can get Jackie to meet with you, to talk things out? You make your case to her. If I could make that happen, would it be enough for you to repay the debt *and* give me my commission?"

The green eyes blazed with curiosity. "Are you serious about her meeting with me?"

"First, is that a deal? Will that satisfy you to honor the debt and pay me my fee?"

Tuttle considered this for a moment and then nodded. "It's a deal."

"Okay, then. She'll meet you at nine o'clock tonight. At her house."

Tuttle glanced at him in surprise. "Is that a fact? And where is her house?"

"Number 27 Eldorado Street."

Tuttle wrote this down and then glanced up at Archer. "So you knew all along she was willing to meet with me? You could've just said so."

"I wanted to make sure you would agree to the deal *first*."

Tuttle looked at him in a new light. "You might make a pretty fine businessman, Archer."

"Well, let's just start my career off with this one, then."

Archer pulled out the note papers. "Got the documents right here. Good as cash, Pittleman told me. You give me the five thousand dollars plus interest and my two hundred dollars, and you get these papers and the meeting with Jackie."

Tuttle took his time getting up from his desk as Archer watched him closely, but keeping one eye on the Remington, too, just in case.

Tuttle walked over to the Mosler safe, worked the combination dial this way and that, and then spun the wheel and lifted the lever, and the heavy steel door slowly swung wide. Archer rose for a better look. Inside the maw of the safe were stacks of cash and coins, little cloth bags of something with string ties, what looked to be piles of stock and bond certificates, and a large stash of gold bars. It looked like what might be in a proper bank vault. It was more wealth than Archer supposed he would ever see again collected in a single place.

"Holy Lord," said Archer, which he followed up with an appreciative whistle.

Tuttle spun around and caught the wonder on the man's face. "This sort of thing doesn't come easy, Archer."

"I never thought it did, Mr. Tuttle."

He closed the safe and walked back to his desk with a bundle of money as Archer sat back down.

"The interest I calculated at one thousand five hundred dollars. All fair and square. Tell Marjorie I said so."

"Will do. Now, I got a question. With all that wealth you got in that safe, why did you need to take a loan from Pittleman in the first place?"

Tuttle pointed at the Mosler. "When I took out the loan, Archer, that safe was empty."

"What changed then?"

He next pointed to the map on the wall with all the pushpins in it. "What changed was they found oil on my land. Two of the largest oil concerns in this country are presently figuring out how best to bring it to the surface. And the contents of that safe reflect the value of their interest, with a great deal more to come, since I, like Hank Pittleman, drive a damn hard bargain."

"So you were near to broke before then?"

"Six straight years of drought, Archer, would challenge any farmer no matter how competent. Fact is, it nearly did me in. The oil is the only thing that saved me. And it was a damn close call. One month or two the other way, this house and land are gone from me. I had been engaged in discussions with the oil folks *before* I took out the loan. They just didn't have their reports back yet, and I needed the funds from Pittleman to keep things going, wages and bills to pay. Timing is everything in this world."

"Pittleman owned the bank, too. So why not just do a deal with those folks?"

"I would have preferred that, but Pittleman's bank turned me down for a loan. His doing, I'm sure. You see, he can charge a lot more interest if the loan was from him. And I believed he liked the fact that I had to come to him personally for my financial survival. He was just that sort of man. Loved nothing better than putting the screws to folks."

"I can see that."

"When the field reports came in better than anyone possibly thought they would, I struck my deal with the oil company and received initial payments. Being a savvy man, I diversified my holdings immediately: stocks, bonds, gold dust in those little pouches, along with cash and rare coins."

"And gold bars," added Archer. "Now you're rich again. Does your daughter know?"

"The oil companies cannot act with stealth in a place like this. But no one knows that the reports came back favorably. And I would appreciate it if you would not tell anyone, including Jackie."

"Okay."

"You see, I would not want my daughter to come back to me solely because she thought I was now rich. I hope you can understand that."

"If I had a daughter, I guess I'd feel the same way."

Tuttle slapped his desktop. "God, I sometimes think that that devil of a man hypnotized her or something."

"Don't know what to tell you there." He glanced at the envelope in Tuttle's other hand. He had put the cash from the safe in it. "Now, you added in my two hundred dollars to that sum, didn't you?"

"I actually made it three hundred, Archer."

Archer's eyes widened in amazement. "Why's that? Our deal was for two."

"Because I never really believed you would accomplish your task successfully. And I like to reward exceptional performance."

"She hasn't agreed to come home yet."

"But you've given me the opportunity to talk some sense into her, and that's good enough for me."

The men exchanged cash for promissory note.

Tuttle extracted a match from a box on his desk, struck it afire, and placed it against one edge of the papers. Both men watched the document flame up until Tuttle tossed the inferno into the fireplace behind him.

"I think that we're finished here, Archer. I need to get some work done," he added. "And if you see Jackie, tell her I will be at 27 Eldorado Street promptly at nine o'clock tonight."

"I'll do that."

Archer left the house, stepped off the front porch, and looked around.

A whirl of dust in the distance was coming closer and revealed itself to be a man on a farm tractor. He was heading for the barn that lay about a hundred yards behind the house. Archer glanced back at the house to see if anyone was watching him and then headed that way.

"Hey there," he said when he came within earshot. The man had parked the John Deere tractor, and was presently checking its engine.

It was the man who had driven Tuttle in the car. He didn't have his chauffeur's uniform on now. He wore dirty jeans, a checkered shirt, and a straw hat with a white band. Dusty, worn boots covered his feet, and his shirtsleeves were rolled up, revealing a mass of writhing muscles as he torqued a bolt with a long wrench.

The man looked up, then set down the wrench, took off his hat, and wiped his forehead with a greasy cloth lying on the engine cover of the tractor.

"Hey there, yourself."

"You were driving the Cadillac the other night."

"Sure was."

"Nice-looking car."

"It's a beauty all right. You're Archer, right?"

"Yep. I was just here doing some business with Mr. Tuttle." He put out his hand. "It's Bobby, right?"

"That's right. Bobby Kent. Nice to meet you, Archer."

The men shook hands.

Archer said, "Quite the farm he's got."

"Yeah, but it's been nothing but a pain in the ass for the last half-dozen years or so. Not nearly enough rain."

"But now I understand everything's okay." He gave Kent a knowing look.

"You mean the oil?"

"Didn't know if you knew about it."

"I been showing them boys from Texas all over the dang place for about ten months now. They dig a hole here, then run their tests and do their calculations. And then dig another hole fifty feet over from the last one and do it all over again. Drove me crazy. Just give me a tractor to ride all day and soil to tend, and I'm a happy man."

"Well, it paid off for Mr. Tuttle."

"Guess it did, yeah."

"How long you been here?"

"Hell, fifteen years if it's been a day."

"So you knew Isabel and Jackie?"

Kent put his hat back on and nodded, his expression turning somber. "Sure did. They're both gone now. Isabel's dead and Jackie left, oh, it's been about a year gone by now for both."

"An accident, I heard?"

Kent turned and pointed to the hay bale doors on the second story of the barn. "Happened right there. She fell out of there and got impaled on the upraised cone of a corn picker. It was damn awful. Bloody as all get out."

Archer thought back to the piece of equipment he had seen on an earlier visit here to one of the outbuildings while he was looking for the Cadillac.

"Allis-Chalmers Corn-picker?" he said.

Kent looked at him in surprise. "That's right. You a farmer?"

"I've done a little bit of everything over the years."

He wondered why Jackie had not added in

this detail of her mother's death, but then again, what did it matter? The woman was still dead, regardless of the exact particulars.

"Who found her?" He knew what Jackie had told him, but remembering Shaw's method, he wanted *corroboration*.

Kent's face twisted into disgust. "Poor Jackie did."

Archer looked over at the spot and imagined the daughter finding the bloodied corpse of her mother.

"Maybe that's why she left, huh?" said Archer, looking back at Kent.

"Could be. She loved her ma. All's I know is she was gone pretty soon after."

"Mr. Tuttle took her leaving hard, I understand. And he wants his daughter back."

"Don't know nothing about that."

"Okay, well, good talking to you."

"See you around, Archer."

Archer retraced his steps, climbed into the Nash, and drove off.

He felt the bulge of money in his pocket, which was a nice feeling. But what had happened to Jackie and her mother had left him with a level of sadness that he supposed was a little odd, since he'd never met Isabel and barely knew her daughter.

Yet maybe there was a reasonable explanation. *You might be an ex-con, Archer, but you kept your heart, despite a war and then prison. And that's something. As bad as things might get, don't ever sell yourself short on that.*

CHAPTER

36

HE DROVE FAST back to Poca City. The wind whistling through the open windows felt good, liberating, and about as far from Carderock Prison as a man could get and still be on this earth, he reckoned. He dropped the Nash off at the garage on Fulsome, leaving the keys in the glove box, as Jackie had requested.

Then he stood there in the heat of the falling sun, marveling at how he had snatched victory from the jaws of defeat. And it felt damn good. And he had one person he needed to tell first.

Jackie answered the door at Ernestine's house dressed in a pair of zippered white trousers and a pale blue short-sleeved blouse. Her Veronica Lake peekaboo had been clipped back, and her feet were bare. Her lovely features were fevered and anxious. "Well? How did it go?"

He held up the packet of money. "Your old man paid in full. Including *three* hundred for me instead of the two hundred," he added with a grin.

She hugged him tightly and then went up on tiptoe and gave him a congratulatory kiss on the cheek as he took off his hat. "This deserves a drink," she said, after coming back down to her heels.

She poured out two tumblers from the bottle of Rebel on the sideboard, and they sat and clinked glasses, then each took a drink.

"Talked to a man out at your father's today, Bobby Kent."

"Bobby has worked there a long time. He's a good person."

"He, uh, he told me about the corn picker."

This was such an asinine thing to say, and Archer regretted it as soon as his mouth closed on the last word of it.

Jackie's features veered from happy to neutral and then all the way to stark disapproval. "Did you go out there to collect a debt or to ask nosy questions about my family history?"

"I…It was stupid. I'm sorry. I'm not sure what I'm thinking."

He took a swallow of his drink and looked pensive.

She gave him another pointed look. "Is there something you want to say in there, but just can't work up the courage?"

"I don't know."

"Sure, you do know, Archer. A man like you always knows. You finished with your drink?"

"I suppose so."

She yanked it from him and stood. "Well, you have the cash, so there."

"Thing is, I was hoping you could take it over and give it to Marjorie. I mean, I've met her a few times, but I don't really know the woman."

She looked at him incredulously. "And you really think she'll be happy to see me?!"

"With six and a half thousand dollars as a peace offering?"

She studied him for an uncomfortably long moment, before holding out her hand for the envelope, which he gave to her. "I'll do it on the condition that you go with me."

"Why?"

"'Cause it's your job, Archer, not mine. I'm not being paid a dime to do this. In case you don't get the picture, with Hank gone, I've got nothing."

He thought about telling Jackie about her father's change in fortunes but decided against it. He had promised Tuttle, and he suspected that Jackie might make the wrong decision about going back home if she could be enticed by a mountain of wealth waiting for her. He didn't know Lucas Tuttle, but he had enough misgivings about the man to make him pretty certain he didn't want Jackie to go back to him.

"I can give you a cut of mine, then."

"I don't take charity, Archer, from you or any other man."

"Well, it wouldn't be charity."

She put a hand on her hip. "What then? I'm not a whore, either. Or do you think otherwise?"

"'Course not, the thought never entered my mind."

"Yes, it did. Don't lie to me. I'll put up with a lot from a man, you've seen that for yourself. But I don't tolerate lies. I just won't have it."

"You called yourself chattel, not me."

"And I can't believe someone who spent two damn years in college can be that stupid."

"How the hell did we go from celebrating to this, I wonder?" said Archer with a look of total bewilderment. "I mean, this is just a puzzle to me, truly."

"A puzzle? This is a man and a woman having a legitimate discussion about important things. But I'll let you off the hook for now." She opened the envelope, took out his three hundred, and handed it to him.

He didn't reach for it.

"Archer, you earned it. Take the damn money."

He slipped the bills into his jacket pocket.

She put the envelope with the rest of the cash into her pocket, then sat down, poured him another drink, and handed it to him.

Archer looked bewildered at the woman's mood swings but decided peace right now was preferable to what had just happened.

"You got a smoke?" he asked.

"Chesterfields."

"That'll do."

She passed across a cigarette and he cupped his hand around hers as she lit him up.

She stuck the burned match in an ashtray on the coffee table and watched him blow smoke sideways from his mouth. Then Jackie pulled a cigarette from her pack and lit up, too.

"What else did you hear today at my father's?"

"He believes that Hank Pittleman hypnotized you or something." Archer took the cigarette from his mouth. "*Did* he hypnotize you or something?"

"Yeah, Archer, if you clap your hands just right, I'll get on the floor and bark like a dog."

"I guess that means no."

"You miss being in the Army?"

His jaw went slack at this abrupt inquiry. "You trying to be funny?"

"No. I'm being serious."

"Why does that matter to you?"

"Remember I told you I was a psychology major? I like figuring people out."

"You said I was complicated even though I don't think I am."

"It's the complex ones who think they're simple, Archer. The simple ones think they have all this deep meaning in everything they do and say. And for the men it's mostly trying to get into a woman's bed."

"Well, I can certainly be guilty of that."

"But that's not all that makes you tick. Not by a long shot. So, the Army? Do you miss it?"

"You think I wanted to keep spending my days and nights killing and nearly being killed?"

She blew smoke out before answering. "You were part of something, Archer. Something big and important. Now?" She shrugged. "What do you have, really? What do any of us have?"

"I just got outta prison. Give me a chance. I mean to make something of myself."

"Must've felt good, though, being part of that."

"Didn't think about that while I was doing it. Then, when I got home, I started thinking about other things. So I must have missed that part."

"I'd like to be part of something like that. Bigger than any one person, I mean."

"Let's hope if you are, it has nothing to do with a damn war."

"What are you going to do now?"

"I need to find work."

"Why not try my daddy?"

Archer smoked his Chesterfield down as he thought about this. "He did pay me an extra hundred dollars. So he must've liked what I did."

Jackie tapped her ash into the ashtray and nodded. "He's a hard man to please, and don't I know it."

"What are you saying, that I should go back out there and ask for a job?"

"You got any other prospects?"

"Shaw is paying me a few bucks to help him on the case."

"Really? Is that allowed? I mean, you're not with the police. And you told me that he thought you might have killed Hank."

"Well, he doesn't think that anymore, thank

God. But he believes I might have the right qualities to be a good gumshoe."

"Is that what you want to do with your life?"

"How the hell do I know? Does anybody know what they want to do after the world went to war and everything got blown up? What do *you* want to do?"

She didn't answer right away. She took a final drag on her smoke, tapped it out, finished her Rebel Yell, and looked squarely at him.

"I just want to be happy, Archer. And every day I'm alive it seems like it's getting to be too much to hope for."

CHAPTER

37

ARCHER WISHED JACKIE LUCK with her father that night and then headed back to downtown Poca, making a stop at the Checkered Past for dinner, then taking another brief detour before he walked on to the Derby carrying a paper bag in one hand. He had gotten his things from Ernestine's and, using his newfound wealth, rented back his old room at the hotel. He took the stairs up to 610, cast his hat onto the bed, hung up his other clothes, and lifted the bottle of bourbon from the paper bag, along with a fresh pack of Lucky Strikes. Shaw had taken his drinking glasses, so Archer sat in a chair, put the heels of his new shoes up on the windowsill after opening the window, and drank straight from the bottle.

He lit a cigarette and blew smoke out the open window, tapping his ash onto the sill. He smoked down two cigarettes. Around eight o'clock, when the light was dimming, something happened that Archer had never once seen since he'd been here. An unholy storm came in, the sky turning to a mass of ugly, darkened clouds, and the winds fiercely picked up. A few moments later the heavens opened up and the rain poured down, forcing pedestrians on the street to make a run for it. After that the lightning flashed, and the thunder boomed. And it went on and on as Archer sat there and watched this spectacle of Mother Nature unleashed on Poca and its inhabitants. It was like she'd been saving up all her energy for the longest time to unleash it right this minute.

How much he drank, Archer wasn't sure. And he wasn't sure when he fell asleep in the chair. He did remember checking his watch at one point, and seeing it was about nine o'clock. He recalled praying that the meeting between father and daughter would go off without a hitch. He thought about going over there, but if Jackie spotted him it would not be good.

He woke much later due to the pounding on his door, not from the storm still raging unabated outside. His eyes popped open, his feet came down to the floor, and he looked around, momentarily disoriented. It was fully dark outside now, but a hint of light was emerging. He looked at his watch as the pounding on the door continued. It was nearly five in the morning.

"Archer?" the voice called out. "I know you're in there. Open this damn door or I'm going to break it down."

It was Irving Shaw.

Archer groaned, rubbed at his head and then his eyes, staggered over to the door, and opened it.

"What can I do you for, Mr. Shaw?" said Archer wearily.

Shaw looked as grim as he'd ever seen the man, and that was saying something.

Archer stiffened to attention when he saw this. "What's up with you?"

He cast a glance over Archer's shoulder. "You got anybody in here with you?"

Archer turned and waved his hand around the clearly empty room.

"Do you see anybody? Hey, how'd you even know I was here?"

"Because you were nowhere else. We got a problem. Sit down in that chair."

Shaw slammed the door shut behind him, pulled Archer over to the chair, and pushed him down on it.

"What the hell is going on?" asked a thoroughly rattled Archer.

Shaw eyed the half-empty bottle. "Are you drunk?"

"I might 'a been. I'm sure as hell not now."

Shaw went over to the window where the drenched drapes were flapping in the breeze and the floor was wet. He slammed the window shut, put his shoe up on the windowsill, placed his left elbow over his raised knee, turned his head, and cast a keen eye on Archer. "Tell me something, and I want the truth. Did you go out to see Lucas Tuttle yesterday?"

"Yeah, I did."

"Why?"

"To get the debt owed to Hank Pittleman paid."

"And did you?"

"Yes."

"Where is it?"

"I gave it to Jackie. Me and her were going over later today to give it to Marjorie."

"And did *you* get paid?"

"He put in three hundred for me. More than I asked for, but he said he respected what I had done."

"Why would he pay off the debt if he didn't get the note back? I understand it's the same as cash."

Despite the alcohol he had drank, Archer gathered his wits and formed his lie. "Pittleman gave me the note, so I could give it to Tuttle when he paid off the debt."

"Is that right?"

"Yeah, that's right."

Shaw's gaze sharpened. "Funny, you never mentioned that before now. And what did Tuttle do with the note?"

"He burned it with a match and threw it in the fireplace. I saw him do it."

"Did he now?"

"Yeah, he did."

"The thing is, Miss Tuttle told me earlier that Pittleman did *not* give you the note. That he would do so only when he'd gotten paid everything due to him. So, I'll ask you once more, where did you get the note?"

Archer let out an extended breath. "Okay, I took it from Pittleman when I found his body. But I didn't touch any of his cash."

Shaw shook his head the whole time.

"What?" asked Archer.

"I thought you and me had reached an understanding." He tapped his bad arm, which was still in a sling. "Hell, you saved my life. But now you just admitted to lying to me again, so that don't set too well."

"I would have liked to tell you the truth, but things kept getting in the way."

"I can't tell you how many men I've put in prison have said something similar. So you were going to deliver that cash to Marjorie Pittleman later today?"

"Well, yeah. It's owed to her."

"When did you get back from Tuttle's place?"

"Left there around four and got back to town about five o'clock or so."

"So you had plenty of time to go to Marjorie Pittleman's yesterday and give her that money back. Why didn't you?"

"Jackie wanted to have time to get ready to meet with her father last night. So I went and got some dinner, and then came back here, got my old room. I had something to drink, and I guess I just fell asleep. I just woke up now when you were pounding on my door."

"You been sleeping this whole time?"

"Off and on, yeah. Why? What the hell are you so riled up about?"

"I'll tell you, Archer. Mr. Lucas Tuttle was found at his home shot dead."

Archer leaned so far back in the chair, he

nearly toppled off it. "The hell you say. He was alive when I left."

Shaw let out a long sigh. "Please tell me that somebody can verify that."

"I talked to a man named Bobby Kent before I left."

"Was Tuttle with you?"

"No."

"Anybody else?"

"His secretary, Desiree Lankford, let me in the house yesterday."

"Did she let you out?"

"No."

"So you got no alibi?"

"Well, when was the man killed?"

"We don't know exactly. But he'd been dead a while, I can tell you that. Coroner will be working up a more exact time, but it won't be to the minute, I can tell you that."

"Hang on, Lucas Tuttle was supposed to meet Jackie at her house at nine o'clock last night. It was all arranged."

"I doubt he made that meeting, son."

"When did you find his body?"

"About two o'clock this morning. I just got back from there and came straightway here."

"Why'd you go out there that late?"

"That fella you mentioned, Bobby Kent,

phoned. He saw the front door of the house open last night. He went inside and found Tuttle dead. He called the police."

"How'd the man die?"

"He was shot dead with a bullet from a revolver. Right through the heart. Died instantly."

"There were two revolvers lying on the table in the man's office."

Shaw nodded. "Thirty-eight-caliber Long Colt and a Smith and Wesson .32 hammerless. But neither one of those was used to shoot the man." He eyed Archer. "What would a shamus make of that, I wonder?"

Archer thought about it and said, "The killing was planned because the murderer brought their own weapon. If it was a spur-of-the-moment thing, they wouldn't have brought a gun. They'd have snatched the Colt or the .32 to do the deed."

"Now you're thinking like a detective. How'd you get out to Tuttle's place?"

"Jackie let me use her car," said Archer. "I left it over at the garage on Fulsome."

Shaw looked at his watch. "Well, we'll go over and see Jackie Tuttle in a few hours. If her father was supposed to meet with her last night, then maybe she can explain why he was found dead at his house."

"You want me to go with you?"

"Hell, yes, Archer. In for a dime, in for a dollar."

"Hang on. Does Jackie even know her father's dead?"

"No. I told you I just found out myself and then came back here."

"You want a drink before you go?"

Shaw glanced thirstily at the bottle of bourbon for a long moment, but then decisively shook his head. "No. I *will* trouble you for a smoke," he said, eyeing the pack on the dresser.

Archer passed it over, and Shaw shook one out and lit up. "See you here at nine a.m. sharp."

After Shaw left the room, Archer stood there feeling like Joe Louis had just clocked him with a crushing left hook.

38

You nervous, Archer, about seeing this gal?" asked Shaw as they trudged along later that morning. The rain had passed, leaving a clear sky and crisp temperatures. They had decided to walk rather than drive.

"Not really. I *was* nervous when me and my company were surrounded by Germans who outnumbered us five to one at Salerno and we were running out of ammo."

"What'd you do?"

"Only thing we could think of. We charged their position because it was the last thing they'd expect us to do. Overran their right flank and got back to our lines."

"Your plan?"

"I admit I was the only one stupid enough

to come up with it, but my scouting revealed a weakness on that flank and a sliver of a path we could take to escape. And the captain okayed it."

"It worked, so how stupid could it be?"

"You'd think."

"I'm not sure how smart it was letting Jackie Tuttle go back to her house," said Shaw.

"But Dill's dead and Draper's still in the hospital unconscious."

"Yeah, but you're presuming that they attacked her on their own. My thinking is somebody paid them to try to kill her. Same as what happened to Sid Duckett."

"I never thought of that," conceded Archer.

"You really want to be a shamus, son, those are the very things you need to think about."

"But Ernestine Crabtree was going to be with Jackie when her father came. And I know she knows her way around a gun."

Shaw looked at him strangely. "Does she now?"

Archer couldn't figure out the look on the man's face, and he was afraid to ask.

The two trudged on.

* * *

"What do you two want at this hour of the morning?" asked Jackie at the front door of her house.

She was dressed in the same thick robe as before, and her hair was matted and her eyes were tired.

"I'm afraid we've got some bad news, Miss Tuttle," said Shaw, his hat in his hands. "Can we come in?"

She glanced quickly at Archer, saw his grim look, and stepped back for them to enter.

They sat in the front room. "What bad news?" Jackie asked anxiously.

"I'm afraid it's your father."

"Did something happen to him? Is that why he didn't show up last night?"

"So there *was* a meeting planned?" said Shaw, glancing at Archer.

Archer could sense what the man was thinking. He'd just gotten *corroboration* of what Archer had told him.

"Yes. Nine o'clock at my house. Archer arranged it. But he never came. I finally got mad and went to bed and Ernestine went home. So, is he ill? Is that why he never showed up?"

"No, ma'am." Shaw cleared his throat. "Fact is, someone shot him and he's dead as a doornail."

Jackie rose, wavered, and then looked like she might topple over.

Archer leapt up just in time as the woman went into a dead faint. He caught her, lifted her up, and set her on the couch. "See any brandy or anything around here?" he called out.

Shaw gazed frantically around the room. "No, but let me check the bathroom for some smelling salts."

"Yeah, and while you're at it, why don't you *check* yourself for another way of telling a daughter her daddy's dead as a doornail, Mr. Shaw? I mean, for Chrissakes."

Shaw looked suitably chagrined and rushed off in search of the smelling salts.

Archer sat down next to the unconscious Jackie, checked her fluttery pulse, and patted her hands and cheeks. When Shaw came back with the smelling salts, he applied them under her nose.

With a jerk she sat up and slowly looked around.

"I'm very sorry about that, Miss Tuttle," said Shaw nervously. "I should have found a more, um, delicate way to tell you." He shot Archer a quick glance.

"Somebody murdered my father?" she said, her eyes welling with tears.

"I'm afraid that's right. Did he have any enemies that you know of?"

She sniffled and said, "The only one I could think of is dead, too."

"You mean Hank Pittleman?"

Jackie nodded and gingerly put her feet on the floor. She leaned back against the sofa cushion, took out a hankie from her robe pocket, and wiped her eyes and then her nose, while Archer placed a protective arm around her shoulders.

"When did this happen?" she asked.

"Sometime late last night. We're not sure of the exact time of death, but he'd been dead a while when he was found."

"Who found him?"

"Bobby Kent. He called the police. It was around one a.m." He glanced at Archer. "Archer was out there to see your father yesterday, too."

"I knew about that. He borrowed my car to go."

"He said he was going out to try to resolve the debt held by Pittleman."

"I knew that too, and he did. Got three hundred for himself. He told me yesterday."

"He showed you the money?"

"Yes. And he gave it to me, too. We were going to take it to Marjorie's today."

Shaw looked at Archer once more.

Archer said, "Sounds like *corroboration* to me."

Shaw turned back to Jackie and said, "Well, what you might not know is that Archer here pilfered the promissory note from Pittleman's body."

"Well, he'd have to give that to my father, or he wouldn't have paid the debt," said Jackie defensively.

"I know that. But I don't like people lying to me, even if they are innocent." Shaw said this last part directly to Archer, who looked suitably chagrined.

"I can understand that," said Jackie.

"When did Ernestine go home?" asked Archer.

"Around eleven last night."

"And your father never showed up here?"

"No."

Archer looked at Shaw. "He has Bobby Kent drive him around in that big Caddy. He would know if Tuttle drove anywhere last night."

"No, he wouldn't," said Shaw surprisingly.

"What do you mean?"

"I talked to Kent last night. He was waiting at the house when we got there, of course."

"You think he had something to do with it?" blurted out Archer.

Jackie said, "Bobby wouldn't hurt a flea."

Shaw held up his hand. "No, he couldn't

have killed Tuttle *or* driven him anywhere last night."

"Why not?" asked Archer.

"Because he was out of town picking up a load of farm supplies. He had to get them last night or they were going to ship them back. He left around seven last night, picked up the supplies, and got back to the farm around one. He found the body and called us from the house phone a minute later. I've checked on his story and confirmed all of it. I got there around two, and your father had for sure been dead more than an hour. Coroner confirmed that. Kent's not the killer."

"But with Bobby out of town, my father would have had to drive himself here," said Jackie.

"That's right. Now, Miss Tuttle, you sure you don't know anyone other than Hank Pittleman who was at odds with your father? Anyone having a grudge?"

"I've been gone from my father's house for a year, Mr. Shaw. So I can't speak to what happened after that. Now, my father could be a hard man. Even his friends would say that. But I can't think of anyone who would want to kill him."

"Would anyone profit from his death?"

"I guess I would. I'm his only child. But he

only had the farm. And when I left he was having money troubles."

"Not anymore," said Archer. "The man had a safe full of cash and gold bars and such."

"What!" cried out Jackie.

"Come again?" said a stunned Shaw.

Archer explained about the contents of the safe and how the wealth had come via the companies finding oil on Tuttle's land. "They'd paid him an advance and he was expecting a lot more money from it."

"Why didn't you tell me that yesterday, Archer?" exclaimed Jackie, looking at him with a confused expression.

"Your father asked me not to."

"Why?" she snapped.

Archer looked deeply uncomfortable. "He... he didn't want you coming home just because he was rich."

When Shaw looked puzzled, Jackie said, "Most people didn't know this, but about a year ago my father was on the verge of bankruptcy. He kept up a strong front and all and probably robbed Peter to pay Paul to keep up appearances, but financially things were not good."

Archer said, "He told me he'd had six straight years of drought and he was hurting."

"I know that to be true," added Jackie.

Shaw looked at Jackie. "So you didn't know anything about that?"

"No, as I said, my father and I were estranged. I heard rumors around town that some oil companies were poking over his land." She glared at Archer again. "And Archer here apparently thought I'm so shallow that dangling money in front of me would make me go running right back to my daddy."

"Now look, Jackie—" Archer began.

She turned to Shaw. "Where is his body?"

"At the mortuary."

"You're sure it's him?"

"No question about it."

"I would like to see my father's body today, if that's permissible." She glanced at Archer. "Estranged or not, he's still my father."

"I can come get you around noon if that's all right," said Shaw.

"That's fine."

"And I'd like you to go out to your father's house with me at some point."

"All right, but I don't think I can manage that today." She wiped her eyes once more.

"I'm really sorry, Jackie," Archer said.

"My father and I were never really close. But he was the only family I had left. Now, if you'll excuse me." She rose and went into her bed-room and shut the door.

Out on the street, Archer found himself taking three deep breaths.

He glanced at Shaw, who was watching him closely.

"Well?" asked Archer.

"I don't know, Archer, I really don't. Either you're the dumbest man I ever met, or the unluck-iest. Or the smartest. Jury's still out on that."

"Right now, I'll take the unluckiest. And a close second would be the dumbest."

"I met a lot of infantry who were lucky. Lucky a bullet or a mortar round or bayonet missed its mark."

"I had my share of those. Why I'm still here, I suppose."

"You think you used up all your luck in the war, then?"

"Might be starting to look that way."

Shaw put on his hat. "Maybe more than starting."

"Hey, Shaw, didn't you see all that stuff in the safe when you were out there last night?"

"No. I saw the safe, of course, and I tried to open it to check."

"Why's that?"

"A dead man and a safe, Archer? Don't take a

genius to think there might have been a robbery. Matter of fact, the thing was locked, and I had no way to open it. Hopefully, Miss Tuttle will be able to open it when we go out there. If not, I can get into it another way."

The men started walking back to the Derby.

"Give it to me straight, Mr. Shaw. You think I killed the man?"

"No, I don't, Archer. That's as straight as I can give it."

"But I made money off him. And truth is, I met men in prison killed for less than what I got."

"You're building quite a good case against yourself. Congratulations."

"I'm not saying anything you're not already thinking, am I?"

"Now you're showing your smart side, as opposed to your unlucky and dumb side."

Archer gave him an odd look. "So, you're not jailing me then?"

"We both fought a war, Archer. But I don't necessarily feel like I owe you anything on that score, because most of us fought. As for your guilt or innocence? Well, you look at the big things—motive, opportunity—yeah, you're a suspect. But when I look at the little things, it don't add up to you being involved in the man's death. I been doing this long enough to see the difference." He paused. "But the thing is, Archer, I got people to report to. And sometimes they're not nearly so smart as me. So you ain't out of the woods yet, no matter what I think. Now I got some things to take care of." He tipped his hat. "See you around."

Shaw disappeared down the street, while Archer trudged on with all his troubling thoughts. He felt his confident gait fade to nearly a prison shuffle.

CHAPTER

39

ARCHER HAD SOME BREAKFAST, and then later he had his lunch, neither of which he really remembered eating. After that he went back to the Derby and sat on his bed trying to make sense out of all that had happened. Tuttle had never made the meeting with his daughter because he'd been murdered. Jackie had known nothing of the wealth in the safe until Archer had told her. Shaw didn't believe he was guilty, but others in the law might overrule him. So maybe he had to get himself out of this predicament.

Yet when Archer looked at the problem every which way, not a single answer or viable path of investigation reasonably presented itself. And he wasn't a shamus, anyway. Though Shaw had taught him a few things and said that Archer had good instincts, what did he really know about detecting? He found himself staring out the window of his hotel room for hours on end, his mind a muddle.

He checked his watch and wondered how Jackie had reacted to seeing her father's body at the mortuary. Jackie might have broken down and cried, despite being estranged from her father.

As day grew into night, he finally decided to act. And that act would take the form of his going back to where all this had started. So at nine o'clock sharp, his legs took him in the direction of the Cat's Meow. It was hopping at this hour, but he was able to wedge in at the bar.

The same string bean bartender came over to him. "What's your poison, son?"

"Rebel Yell. Straight up." Archer stacked *three* fingers one on top of the other this time.

The old man grinned. "I remember you now. You was talking to Mr. Pittleman." He shivered. "Damn shame what happened to him."

"Yeah," agreed Archer.

The man poured out the Rebel and slid it across to Archer, who slipped him a buck and told him to keep the change.

"Right kind of you."

"That night I was in here, you see anything funny?" asked Archer.

"Funny how?"

"Just funny."

"Naw, not that I can remember."

"You knew Hank Pittleman and Jackie Tuttle?"

"Sure, seen 'em in here many a time. Don't really know 'em though." The man grinned, showing multiple gaps in his teeth. "We don't really run in the same circles of high-falutin' society." He cackled at his little joke. "Did you know Mr. Pittleman owned this place?"

Archer nodded, edged his hat back, lit up a Lucky Strike, and blew smoke sideways out of his mouth. He took a swallow of the Rebel and said, "You know Lucas Tuttle?" Archer wanted to see if word had gotten around about the man's murder.

"Know *of* him. Never seen him in here. Apparently, he's not much of a drinker like his daughter. But I seen him around town sometimes in that big car 'a his."

"Ever seen him with Jackie Tuttle?"

"Not that I can say, no. Hey, why all the questions, fella?"

Archer handed him another dollar, which the man gripped and made disappear into his pocket. "I'm just trying to figure stuff out."

"You ain't been in town long, have you?"

Archer shook his head and continued to smoke down his Lucky Strike. "Want to know the truth? I'm an ex-con in from Carderock. On parole."

The man's features changed.

"What?" asked Archer, noting this.

"Now that *is* funny."

"What is?"

"You being on parole."

"Come again?"

"Made me think of that Ernestine Crabtree gal."

"What about her?"

"She runs the parole office. Why I thought of her just now."

"I know she does, friend. She's my parole officer."

"I figured that."

"So how do you know about her?"

"I got buddies who did time and got out not too long ago. They went to her, too."

"She's the only game in town when it comes to parolees, but what's funny about that?"

"The night you were in here before?" he began.

Archer looked at him through his cloud of cigarette smoke. "What about it?"

"Miss Crabtree was here, too. Sitting right

over there." The man pointed to his left, to a table against the far wall that would not really be in Archer's sight line at the bar.

Archer looked that way and then back at the man. "She was? Are you sure? Lot of people in here. And I don't recall seeing her."

"No, I saw her for sure. She comes in pretty regular. Hell, she was here the night before they found poor Mr. Pittleman dead."

"That's right, I saw her go inside that night. Said she was meeting somebody. You know who that was?"

"Oh yeah, it was her."

Archer stood up straight and gaped at the man. "*Her*? It was a woman? Do you know who it was?"

"You already said her name. Jackie Tuttle."

Archer stood there more stunned than he had ever been in his whole life. Even more than during the darkest days of the war, when it seemed every hour someone he knew and had fought alongside had been shredded by bullets, or else made to vanish from the earth by a well-placed mortar round.

"Hold on, mister, are you saying she was meeting up with Jackie? But Jackie was here with Pittleman."

"Well, yeah. But Mr. Pittleman started drinking

with some other folks he knew, and Jackie Tuttle went over and sat with Miss Crabtree."

"You sure they know each other?"

"Oh, yeah, they hung out a lot at the bar. Real good friends. I mean, real good."

"And Pittleman didn't mind?"

"Sometimes he got a little bent out of shape, but Miss Jackie, she knew how to handle him all right. And it's not like Miss Jackie was with another *man*."

Archer couldn't find any words to say.

"You okay, fella?" The bartender was studying him closely.

Archer nodded, drank down his remaining two fingers, passed the bartender another buck, and left. His long legs ate up the distance to Ernestine's house. When he reached it, he didn't go up to the door, but rather waited across the street and studied the place. He was on a scouting expedition now and intended to do it by the book, as he'd been trained.

There were no lights on, and he couldn't hear a sound coming from the place.

He finally walked over and knocked on the front door but got no response. He used the key the woman had given him to open the door. He went right to her bedroom and looked through her closet. It didn't take long. It was empty. All her clothes were gone and so was the scrapbook.

Archer sat on the woman's bed and, for one of the few times in his life, had no idea what to do.

CHAPTER

40

LATE THE NEXT MORNING, Archer was lying on his bed in his pants and undershirt, gazing at the ceiling and thinking hard about all that was troubling him, when someone knocked on his door. He opened it and found Irving Shaw leaning on the doorjamb and staring back at him.

"What?" said Archer.

"Got a problem."

"Dammit, Mr. Shaw, every time you come to see me you say something like that."

"Don't blame me. It sure as hell ain't my fault."

He barged past Archer and into the room.

Archer slowly shut the door and watched as the lawman paced the small footprint of the room.

"You gonna tell me or do I have to guess?" asked Archer finally.

"We went out to Lucas Tuttle's house this morning."

"Who did?"

"Me and Jackie Tuttle." Shaw sat down in the sole chair. "You been here the whole night?"

"Yeah. Man at the front desk can tell you that. Why?"

"Just wondering."

"Why, what did you find out there?"

"I'll tell you what we *didn't* find."

Archer sat on the edge of the bed. "Okay, shoot."

"We didn't find anything in the man's safe. I mean, not a damn thing."

Archer said nothing. He just gaped at the man like he'd been uttering Chinese.

"You look surprised."

"Well, that's because I am. There was all kinds of stuff in that safe, I'm telling you. Including gold bars. I never had the pleasure of carrying gold bars, but I imagine they're pretty damn heavy."

"They are."

"Well, where the hell did it all get to?"

"Now, that's the question."

"Did Jackie open the safe for you?"

Shaw shook his head. "She didn't have the

combination. I had to get a locksmith to come out and do it."

"Damn."

Shaw looked at him oddly. "You drove Jackie Tuttle's Nash out there?"

"I told you that already."

"And nobody's been there since you were up until Bobby Kent found the man's body."

"No, hold on, that's not right. Whoever killed Tuttle was there *after* I was. They must have cleared out the safe. You yourself said you couldn't look in it because it was locked. It might have already been empty when you got there."

"But the thing is, you're the only one who has admitted to being there on the day the man died. And by your admission he opened the safe to get the money to pay you."

"Whoa there. I don't like where this is headed."

"That's not all. I had the Nash searched just now over at the garage on Fulsome."

"What for?"

"For the contents of the missing safe, Archer! What else, son?"

"Hold on now, are you—"

"Just hush for a minute." Shaw fell silent for a moment, gathering his words. "We didn't find any of the items from the safe in the Nash."

"Well, of course you didn't because—"

"But we *did* find traces of them."

"What sort of traces?"

"Imprints of the gold bars on the carpet in the trunk. And a few grains of what turned out to be gold dust."

"But I was the only one to drive the Nash out there that day," Archer replied.

"That's true. And I was with Jackie Tuttle much of the day yesterday and I had a matron with her last night before I picked her up and we headed out to her father's place today."

"Hell, Jackie didn't have anything to do with this, if that's what you're thinking."

"I agree. Which is why I'm here, son." Shaw looked sad, painfully so.

"What are you getting at, Mr. Shaw?"

"Remember I told you folks not as smart as me in the detecting business might throw a monkey wrench in the works? Well, they have. I got my marching orders from the higher-ups. So, stand up."

"What?"

"Stand up."

Archer did so.

Shaw took out a pair of shiny handcuffs and put them on Archer's wrists after gently tugging them behind his back.

"You arresting me?"

"What was your first clue, son?"

"Arresting me for what?"

"That'll be put into writing down at the police station. You're gonna get your picture taken, have ink on your fingers, and then I'll want a statement."

"Hell, I'll give you a statement right here and now. I'm innocent."

"I know you are, Archer, but I got no choice. But let me work this, son. I know what I'm doing."

He grabbed up Archer's shirt and jacket and then led the man down the stairs and out the back door.

"Why not the front?" asked Archer.

"I'm trying to let you avoid the shame of being arrested. Bad enough for the guilty. Doubly so for the innocent."

The ride over to the police station took all of three minutes.

Archer was fingerprinted and photographed. Then he was allowed to wash his face and shave, and put on his shirt and jacket. Shaw even managed to find some hot coffee and cold eggs for Archer before he set him down in front of a recording machine in a small room with one table and two opposing chairs.

Shaw said in a low voice, "Now look, since I

have to record this, I got to go by the book. I'm gonna sound like you're guilty as hell. But you just stick to your guns, okay, son?"

"Listen, I'm not gonna do anything to get you in trouble, Mr. Shaw. And if this will, I don't want you to do it."

Shaw gave Archer a look that many of his fellow soldiers had right before they went into battle together. It was a cross between a sad smile and a dropped tear.

"I appreciate that, son, but we're gonna get through this. Just do what I said."

Shaw clicked on the machine, recited the date and time and their names. And then the crimes that Archer had been charged with, including the murder of Lucas Tuttle.

"Mr. Archer, if you want to tell the truth, now would be a good time to do so."

"Everything I know, I've already told you."

"If you tell us what you did with the stuff in that safe I can put in a good word for you with the court."

"Well, since I didn't take any of it, that's not really an option for me."

"So you deny all involvement in any crime hereabouts?"

"I lied to you about going into Mr. Pittleman's room and taking those debt papers. You can charge me with that if you want, and I'll confess to that. But not to another thing."

"You sure?"

"Hell yes. I'm innocent!"

Shaw clicked off the recorder. "That was fine, Archer."

"I hope so, because it's all the truth."

Shaw lit up a smoke. "Where were you last night?"

"At the Cat's Meow and then at Ernestine Crabtree's house. And then back at the Derby where you found me."

Shaw frowned. "At Crabtree's house, why?

"I was trying to figure out why she and Jackie lied and said they didn't know each other when the bartender at the Cat's Meow told me they were regulars there and knew each other really well."

"Come again?"

Archer told him what the bartender had shared.

"But as a parole officer if she saw you drinking at the bar, she should have turned you in for a violation."

"I know that! I'm wondering why she didn't. And why would they hide that they were friends and all? When I brought Jackie over to stay at Ernestine's I introduced them to each other. They acted like strangers till I did that."

"That is a puzzler."

"And now she's gone."

Shaw started. "What? Who's gone?"

"Ernestine. Her clothes are all gone from her closet. I think she's left town."

Shaw narrowed his eyes and rubbed his chin. "What else?"

"Look, you know about her father?"

Shaw shook his head, so Archer decided to fill him in on Carson Crabtree's history and also about what he had found in the scrapbook.

"So what do you think about that?" asked Archer. "Her father was a policeman. Then he ups and kills three men and confesses without giving any reason?"

"And one of them was a Peeping Tom," said Shaw thoughtfully. "You think?"

"Well, it's possible he was peeping on Ernestine. And maybe the others were too."

"But then why wouldn't her old man say that in his defense? Hell, he might've gotten off scot-free if he had. I could see a jury siding with him over that, especially if he had a bunch of fathers on the jury."

"I don't know," said Archer. "But her mother killed herself later."

"Damn. That woman's been through the wringer all right. Did she act surprised when she saw you at your first parole meeting even though she'd probably already seen you at the bar?"

"Not a jot, no."

"Good poker face then."

"And then some."

Shaw looked thoughtfully at Archer. "Sheila Dixon?"

Archer's face collapsed. "What about her?"

"She's the mayor's daughter you were charged and convicted with kidnapping, and false imprisoning and contributing to the delinquency of."

"Well, hell, I know that!"

"You got a pretty short sentence comparatively."

"I worked a deal so she wouldn't have to testify. And then I got paroled early. And dammit, for the record she told me she was twenty. I had no idea she was four days short of being sixteen. She didn't look it, I can tell you that. And I swear on a stack of Bibles, we didn't do anything. No fooling around or nothing. I just gave her a ride because she couldn't drive."

"I know all that, Archer."

Archer's jaw dropped perceptibly. "What! How?"

"I spoke by phone with the lady and she told me the whole story. How she loved you, but you were a real gentleman. That she lied about her age and the car and pretty much everything else to get you on her side. And that her father browbeat her into lying about you, because he was worried it would sully his reputation having, as she told me he called her, 'a slut' for a daughter. And by the way, she's still head over heels for you, though she's married now and just had a baby."

"Well, damn," said an astonished Archer. "Why'd you call her in the first place?"

"Because I wanted to know what sort of man you were, Archer. See, what you do in the past can matter to what you do in the present and in the future. I believed you, in my gut. But it's nice to have corroboration."

"You like your corroboration."

"In the detecting business, it's damn important. Now the fact that she was still hankering for you shows that you got a real way with women, Archer, but the thing is, son, that's not always good."

"What do you mean?"

"It's a two-way street. Meaning women can have *their* way with *you*."

Archer thought about this and nodded. "I believe you might be speaking the truth there, Detective."

"I think I am, Archer. I truly think I am."

"Did Jackie see her father's body?"

"She did."

"How'd that go?"

"Funny you should ask. I've watched many a family member view their kin's mortal remains. But I've never seen one who didn't shed a single tear while doing so until yesterday."

"So what now?"

"How much money you got?"

"Nearly three hundred dollars."

"Well, lucky you, your bail is going to be set at *two* hundred dollars. We'll go see the judge, you can enter your not-guilty plea, pay that amount over to the court, and you're free to go for now."

"Why are you really doing this? I understand that you believe I'm innocent. And I'm damn glad of that. But you're taking a chance here with me. You could torpedo your whole career over this. The easy thing would be to lock me up and throw away the key. Nobody would care."

"*I* would care, Archer. When I took a plane up in the air, I had a whole crew counting on me to make the right decisions. And I tried my best to do that very thing. And I signed up for this job to see that bad folks got punished. Putting the innocent in jail is something I have no interest in, because that would mean I made the worst decision of all. I might as well have put the damn plane in a nosedive."

"Well, I thank you for that."

"Don't thank me just yet, Archer. We got us a long row to hoe."

CHAPTER

41

AFTER PAYING HIS BAIL and entering his plea, Archer slept fitfully in his hotel room that night. His coming so close to being in a jail cell again had upset him more than he would have thought possible. But he had far too much in the troubling department to concern him.

He awoke at six in the morning and managed to snatch a two-minute hot shower in the bath down the hall. He dressed and headed out to the Checkered Past for breakfast and a formulation of his plan going forward. The eggs and coffee were hot, the toast burned, the sliced tomatoes passable, and the slice of strip steak would have been of more use nailed to the bottom of his shoe than being eaten. And he loved every minute and bite of it because he was right now a free man. And he had no idea how long that would last. That just made a fellow appreciate things.

He bought a five-cent newspaper and sat on a bench reading the headlines, learning nothing of interest and actually growing even more depressed than he currently was by some of the news stories. But he used the paper to also shield himself from folks passing down the sidewalk. He was hoping one of those would be Ernestine Crabtree, but he never saw her, even though where he was perched was directly on the path from her house to the Courts and Municipality Building.

For the second time since he'd been here, the sky was cloudy and it looked like it might start raining again. At two minutes to eight he got up and headed to the Courts building.

The front doors had just been unlocked, and he set up his surveillance post in the lobby behind a poster on an easel telling folks about a drive to aid war widows. Archer dropped fifty cents in the can attached to the poster.

Eight thirty came and went. So did nine o'clock. Then ten o'clock. Then eleven.

Finally, he took the stairs up to Ernestine's floor and headed to her office door. From the looks of her house, the woman had left town. But, like Shaw had taught him, he needed confirmation of that.

The parole office door was locked. And there was no sign on the door telling why the office was closed. He knocked several times and peered through the upper glass, but it was opaque, and the only thing he could tell was that there was no light on inside.

A matronly woman came out of the office across the hall carrying a bunch of file folders.

"Hello, ma'am?" said Archer.

"Yes?" she said, smiling.

"I was here to see Miss Crabtree, but she doesn't appear to be in. Door's locked."

The woman frowned at Archer. "Here to see Miss Crabtree, are we?" She might as well have tacked on, *You ex-convict, you.*

"Yes, ma'am."

The woman glanced at the door and then at the clock on the wall overhead and her expression changed to confusion.

"The door's locked, you say?"

"Yes."

"Did you try knocking?"

"I did indeed. I've been out here a while. I hope she's not ill in there or anything."

"Hmm. Wait just a minute."

She went inside her office and returned with a key in hand.

"I work in the court clerk's office, but this key will fit all the locks in the building."

"Well, that's handy," said Archer. "Wouldn't mind having a key like that."

"Hmm," she said disapprovingly. "What were you in for? And don't say some petty crime. I've heard it all before. And don't lie and say you're innocent or misunderstood."

"No, ma'am. Fact is, I was a bank robber."

She looked at him with a new level of respect. "Indeed? Well, that's where the money is, after all."

"Yes, ma'am."

She unlocked the door, swung it wide, and said, "Miss Crabtree? It's Mrs. Gibbons from across the hall. Yoo-hoo. Anyone in here?"

Clearly, the room was empty.

Archer also noted that the big, squat Royal typewriter was missing.

Archer said, "You want to check the ladies' bathroom down the hall, ma'am? I, uh, can't do that."

"What? Oh yes, of course."

As soon as she left, Archer looked in the wastebasket and searched the desk. Other than office supplies and parole office forms, the only thing in the drawers was a small book. He picked it up and read off the title: "*A Room of One's Own*."

He remembered it as being her favorite one of Woolf's works.

He slipped the book into his pocket when he heard the woman returning.

"She's not in the bathroom," she said when she appeared in the doorway.

"She might be sick at home."

"Well, if so, she should have let someone know. If this is your day to meet with her, tell me your name so you won't lose credit."

"No, ma'am, it's not my day. I was coming by to tell her that I got a job."

"Really, where?"

"Slaughterhouse."

"Hmm. Knocking in hogs' heads, I suppose."

"Yes, ma'am."

"You sure you were a bank robber?"

Archer held up two fingers in the form of a salute. "Scout's honor."

"Hmm."

He left her there and walked out of the building.

He sat on a bench and opened the book to a page whose corner had been turned down.

A sentence was underlined. He read it off: "A

woman must have money and a room of her own if she is to write fiction."

Archer kept staring at those words as though they would cause everything in his life to instantly make sense. It didn't work.

He imagined there were two ways to leave Poca City. A car or a bus. If she had left by bus, he might be able to check that, or Shaw certainly could. If by car, that would be more problematic.

Car?

He hoofed it over to Fulsome Street, hoping to beat the rain, which he did. Mostly. The heavens burst open just about the time he made it to the garage. He shook off the rain and slapped his hat against his thigh and watched as rainwater turned reddish brown by the dirt ran in meandering rivulets down the asphalt.

Well, this whole place could use a good cleaning.

The Nash sat in its space. And according to Shaw this vehicle was a veritable bastion of evidence. Mostly against him.

Now, he was no trained detective, it was true. But Archer had spent years of his life in another part of the world noticing little details that might save his life and that of his men. A machine gun muzzle barely visible under a mess of straw. A Panzer barrel edging out from the tree line. The too-intense stare of a villager who was trying to hide something. A wire leading to a bomb that looked like only a bit of plant vine. And then in prison it was sort of the same. A shiv sticking out from the cuff of a shirt, a guard clenching his baton a little too tightly before bringing it down on someone's skull, a group of cons edging a bit too close for comfort.

His realizing all these things before they could impact him, giving him a bare moment to react, and to live—those experiences had re-wired Archer's brain, bestowing on him a level of skillful observation to perhaps successfully accomplish what he was about to attempt.

Shaw had said that in the Nash's trunk were the imprints of what had appeared to be the gold bars, their weight pressing down on the soft carpet in the trunk. And along with that were grains of the gold dust. Clearly that had been the haul from Tuttle's safe. Shaw had told him on the way to the police station that pictures of all this had been taken and would be used as evidence in a trial.

In my *trial.*

He checked the car, which was unlocked, but the keys were not inside, and the trunk *was* locked. He managed to work the back seat free and was able to access the trunk that way. He used his Ray-O-Vac light to look at the trunk carpet. He could make out the bar impressions and a bit of sparkly particles in one corner; he concluded the latter represented fragments of the gold dust.

He climbed free of the car and shut the door.

He looked at the Nash's tires and lower half of the car and saw they were mud splattered. He felt the engine. It was cold. And the car couldn't have been driven during this latest rain because it had just started not five minutes ago. He peered under the car and saw the hardened and now dried mud caked there, too. That meant the Nash had been driven during the big storm, on the very night that Lucas Tuttle had been killed. He wondered where it had been driven to, and who had been driving it.

As far as I know, only one person has the keys. Jackie Tuttle.

But she hadn't mentioned going anywhere that night. She was at her house waiting for her father. Ernestine had gone home at eleven, and Jackie had gone to bed. Or so she had said.

She had asked him to leave the keys in the glove box when he returned the car that day, and he had done so. Now, there was no law against driving your own car whenever you wanted, but still. Yet with the keys in the glove box, anyone could have driven the car.

Including Ernestine Crabtree.

He could fathom no connection between the parole officer and Lucas Tuttle. But there had seemed to be no connection between Ernestine and Jackie, either. And now that he knew there was, that meant the connection between Ernestine and Lucas Tuttle would probably run through Jackie.

He walked around the car and stopped at the passenger side. He opened the door and sat in the seat. He rummaged in the glove box but found nothing useful. When he closed it back up, he looked directly down and saw it near his shoe.

It was a bit of a yellow flower bud on the floorboard. He picked it up and looked at it more closely. He couldn't be sure, of course, but it looked an awful lot like it could be from the flower beds at Marjorie Pittleman's place. That would make sense because Jackie knew her and had visited the place.

But why is the flower fragment in the passenger seat? Was it from my shoe when I was over there with her?

But if that were the case, the bud wouldn't have looked as fresh, he figured.

He drew a long breath and then stopped before he let it out. Then he drew two more breaths. He wasn't doing his combat ritual exercise. He was taking in a scent.

Ever since his time as a scout in the war, Archer's senses, particularly hearing and smelling, had been heightened. The bolt of a rifle sliding back or the collective breaths of a hundred men about to attack. Or the smell of cordite flung into the air from a brigade in arms marching. Or simply the scent of fear that oozed from anxious men at every deadly encounter.

He recognized the scent he was now inhaling. And it was not Jackie Tuttle's.

It was the same one Ernestine had been wearing when he had gone to his first parole meeting.

He climbed out of the Nash and shut the door.

He couldn't be certain that Ernestine had been in the car. She couldn't be the only woman in town to wear that perfume. But if it had been her, what was she doing in the Nash? Then again, he had just found out that the two were great friends. So maybe they had made a trip in this car to the home of Lucas Tuttle on the night he was murdered.

Archer left the garage and set off for Eldorado Street. He viewed Jackie's house from a distance, looking for any sign of her being there before heading up to the front door. He knocked and knocked and then called out. He went over to the window that she had been at before and rapped on the glass there. He peered inside a crack in the drapes.

He couldn't see or hear anything.

Archer looked around to see if anyone was watching him. He went around back and used his knife to unlock the woman's rear door. He called out when he got inside but heard nothing. He looked quickly through the house and found nothing. A search of Jackie's closet showed that her clothes, or at least a great many of them, were still there. But he didn't see a suitcase. Only he had never been in her closet before, and thus didn't know if she even had one.

He glanced at the bed where they had lain together.

Shaw's words—or warning, rather—came to his mind.

Women can have their way with you.

He *did* find the Nash's car keys hanging on a peg next to the back door.

That was convenient, because he couldn't exactly walk every place he needed to go.

As he was leaving by the back door, he pulled out his pack of cigarettes but saw that it was empty. He spotted the garbage can and lifted the lid. It was half full of rubbish. He tossed the empty pack in there and was about to put the lid back on when he saw the wadded-up paper next to an apple core.

He pulled the paper out and straightened it. On it were written a series of letters and numbers. He studied the paper a moment longer and put it in his pocket.

Next, he went to the houses on either side of Jackie's and knocked at the doors. No one was home at either place. Archer wanted to determine if anyone had seen Lucas Tuttle drive up to Jackie's house at nine that night. Well, he wouldn't get an answer to that right now. He wasn't sure anyone even lived in them.

Archer jogged back over to the garage on Fulsome, beating another furious bout of rain by about a minute, and then drove the car out onto the street. He had two places he could go and chose one by taking a quarter from his pocket and performing a coin flip. He punched the gas and the Nash leapt forward, its windshield wipers busily swishing the rain off the glass.

He hoped the clarity of his vision would be able to match that of the cleared glass. But right now that seemed like a stretch.

CHAPTER

42

NEARLY AN HOUR LATER, Archer pulled to a
stop in front of the gates to Marjorie Pittleman's home. This time Manuel didn't come
to open the gates, so Archer climbed out and
did the honors himself. He pulled the Nash
through and stopped in front of the enormous
house.

He made it to the door with three long strides,
knocked the rain off his hat, then rapped on
the door. He stepped back when he heard footsteps approaching. The door was opened by
Agnes, the same elderly woman in a maid's
uniform who had been there before. And her
look of disinterest had accompanied the woman
yet again.

"Yes?"

"You remember me? I was here with Miss Jackie?"

"Yes," said Agnes dully.

"Is Mrs. Pittleman in?"

"Yes."

Well, at least she hadn't vanished.

"Could I see her?"

"I will have to ask, please wait there," she said stiffly before walking rigidly off.

Ignoring her instruction, he stepped through and looked around.

Archer took a long whiff of the air to see if he could detect either Jackie's or Ernestine's perfumes. He couldn't. He paced in the front hall, shooting glances here and there. Through the broad, tall windows facing the rear grounds of the house, he saw a man working under the hood of a pickup.

He opened a door, stepped out, and hurried over to him. The rain had now weakened to a drizzle.

"Hey there," said Archer, walking over to him as the man looked up. "Just here to see Mrs. Pittleman."

The man nodded. "Okay."

"Bet you're glad to see this rain. Good for the crops."

"We'll take it when we can get it."

"Got a question."

The man finished turning a wrench on a bolt, wiped his hands off on a rag, and said, "What's that?"

"I was talking to another farmer hereabouts, and he said the last six years of drought just about wiped him out."

"It did a lot of folks around here, mister, that's no lie."

Archer eyed the lush fields of crops that stretched as far as the eye could see. "So how did you all buck those odds?"

"We got a large spring-fed pond on the property. We pipe water in from there. And if that wasn't enough, Mr. Pittleman had water trucked in for irrigation."

"Must have cost a pretty penny."

"Wasn't cheap. But we grew our crops and outlasted a lot of others round here."

"Probably didn't make him all that popular with his fellow farmers."

"You want the truth? I doubt the man cared. Just the way he was."

"Mister?"

Archer turned to see Agnes at the door calling out to him.

"Mrs. Pittleman will see you now."

Archer retraced his steps, and the maid led

him slowly down the hall to a small sitting room that was cozily furnished and had fine views through a pair of large French doors opening to the rear of the house. Marjorie Pittleman was ensconced like an aged portly queen on a chaise lounge, wrapped in a blanket even though the room was not cool. He wondered if the woman had poor blood or some other such ailment. Or maybe she thought the blanket could keep all her troubles at bay.

"Mr. Archer?"

"Yes, ma'am. Thank you for seeing me."

"Please sit down. Would you like a drink? Some lemonade or coffee?"

"Coffee would be fine, thanks."

She pressed a little buzzer on the wall behind her.

Archer thought it must be swell to have only to push a button to get what you wanted.

A few moments later Amy opened the door. She graced Archer with a coquettish smile before saying, "Yes, Mrs. Pittleman?"

"A coffee for Mr. Archer."

"Yes, ma'am. Right away. Do you take anything with your coffee, Mr. Archer?"

"Just a cup," he quipped.

Amy giggled, caught herself under the stern eye of Marjorie, and quickly retreated.

"What can I do for you, Mr. Archer?" she said impatiently.

"I was wondering if you'd seen Jackie lately?"

"Not since she was last here with you I haven't."

So that meant she hadn't been by to pay the woman the money owed to her.

"Okay. I suppose you heard about her father?"

"I did indeed. First Hank and now Lucas Tuttle. I don't know what Poca City is coming to. It's like a crime wave one associates with the likes of Al Capone and his ilk."

"Yes, ma'am. Do you happen to know a woman by the name of Ernestine Crabtree?"

Marjorie creased her brow. "Ernestine, what again?"

"Crabtree."

"I knew a Wanda Crabtree ages ago. But that was when I was a little girl, and that was nowhere near here."

"By the way, what brought you to Poca City?"

"Hank did." She let out a sigh. "I hated it when we first got here. There was nothing to this place. But I have to admit, Hank was right. He kept working at it, and people came. After the war things really picked up. He made a fortune. One that he will no longer enjoy, unfortunately."

He decided to throw out a remark and see what her response would be. "Well, even though I know things are complicated between you two, you still have Jackie as a friend."

She looked at him in a way that was both appraising and revealing, by degrees. "How well do you know Jackie Tuttle?"

"Not all that well, actually."

The door opened, and Amy brought in Archer's coffee and set it down on the table next to him.

"In a cup, just like you asked for, Mr. Archer," she said with an impish grin.

"Now all my wishes have come true," said Archer, grinning back.

"Thank you, Amy, that will be all," said Marjorie firmly.

Amy gave her employer a little curtsy and beat a hasty retreat, shutting the door behind her, but not before giving Archer a flirty look.

Marjorie said, "Now, back to Jackie. She is very cunning; did you know that?"

Archer took a sip of his coffee. "I know she's very smart."

"Her mother died in a horrific accident. I knew Isabel fairly well."

"What was she like?" Archer asked.

"She did not like living on a farm, for one. She and Lucas did not have a happy marriage.

When Jackie came along, it didn't help matters. It seemed to actually hurt them."

"How so?"

"Isabel was fiercely protective of her marriage, and it seemed, at least sometimes, that she perceived Jackie as an interloper."

"I thought they loved each other," said Archer.

"Sometimes love can, well, warp someone."

"Warp them how?"

"Now someone has killed Lucas Tuttle."

"Hold on, what are you suggesting?" exclaimed Archer.

"I am suggesting that you don't let your head be turned by every pretty face that happens by. Young men like yourself so often do."

"Like Jackie's, you mean?"

Marjorie said firmly, "Every pretty face. Now, why are you really here?"

"I can't seem to find Jackie. And Ernestine Crabtree seems to have left town."

"That is curious. Do you think it has anything to do with Lucas's death?"

Archer thought for a moment about what Shaw had said when Jackie had viewed her father's body.

Not a single tear shed.

"Jackie has her father's property to take care of. I'm assuming she's his sole heir."

Marjorie shrugged. "I have no idea, but possibly. He had no one else."

"So, it's not like she can just up and leave."

"She might have just gone for a drive. Perhaps on a visit to another town to clear her mind."

"She couldn't have. I drove Jackie's Nash over here."

This statement seemed to pique Marjorie's interest. "Did you now? Hank let her 'borrow' that car, you know, so I would appreciate if you would leave it here."

Archer's face went slack. "Then how will I get back to town?"

"I can have someone run you in, Mr. Archer," she said, smiling triumphantly. "Now finish your coffee. I have matters of importance to attend to."

He drank down his coffee and rose. "What are your plans now, if you don't mind my asking?"

"To make sure I keep my house and my dignity, or what's left of it." She paused. "Lucas Tuttle owed my late husband money. Five thousand plus interest. I expect to receive payment from his estate. If and when you see Jackie, you tell her that. I'll take it to court if I have to."

It seemed to Archer that the placid, refined lady was now firmly down in the dirt with the rest of them.

After Archer took his leave, he ran into Amy in the hall.

"How was your coffee, Mr. Archer?" she said anxiously.

"You make a nice cup of joe. You'll do a husband proud."

She smiled. "Is there anything else I can do for you? I'd be happy to."

"Well, seeing as how Mrs. Pittleman has sort of confiscated the automobile I drove here in, she said somebody could run me back to town."

"Oh, I can ask Manuel to take you in one of the trucks."

"That'd be great. Thanks."

He gave her a warm smile and she rushed off to accomplish this.

He once more watched her go and thought to himself, *Women are gonna be the death of you, Archer. Fighting a war was a damn sight safer.*

She came back a minute later and told him that Manuel would bring the truck around shortly.

"Thank you, Amy. Hey, I wonder if you could help me with something else."

"I'll sure try, Mr. Archer."

"You know Jackie Tuttle?"

"Yes sir, I mean, I know who she is."

"When was the last time she was here?"

"I think it was when she came to tell the missus about poor Mr. Pittleman. I think you were with her. I didn't see you, but I heard about the visit from Agnes."

"You sure she wasn't here more recently than that?"

"Not that I know of."

"How about an Ernestine Crabtree? You know her?"

"No, sir, I don't know nobody by that name."

"Okay, thanks."

The truck pulled up to the front with Manuel driving. He honked the horn, and Archer went out and climbed into the cab with him. They set off back to town.

"You worked for the Pittlemans for long?" Archer asked him.

Manuel nodded and said, "Seven years."

"Pretty sad what happened to him."

Manuel shrugged. "Mrs. Pittleman will keep things going."

"I left the Nash back there. Jackie Tuttle had borrowed it. Now Mrs. Pittleman wanted it back."

Manuel smiled at this.

"Something funny, friend?"

"Many things have changed since Mr. Pittleman died."

"You mean with respect to Jackie and Mrs. Pittleman?"

"Many things."

"You opened the gate for us when we came in the other day."

Manuel nodded. "And I opened the gate for her the night before last. It was very late."

Archer jerked his head so hard he almost hit it on the side of the truck door.

"You opened the gate for Jackie? Two nights ago? You're sure?"

"Yes."

"Was she here to see Mrs. Pittleman?"

"No. They could not see her that night."

"Wait a minute. *They*?"

"Miss Tuttle and the other woman."

"Describe her."

Manuel did so, outlining, unmistakably, Ernestine Crabtree.

"But if they didn't come to see Mrs. Pittleman, what then?"

Manuel shrugged. "It was not my place to ask."

"So they went into the house, then?"

"I don't know. I opened the gate, and then I went back to my little house. They must have opened the gate themselves when they left."

"You said it was late. When exactly did they get here?"

"It was nearly eleven."

"Did they say anything to you?"

"Miss Tuttle thanked me for opening the gate, as she always does."

Archer sat back. "Were they carrying anything with them? Did they take anything from the car?"

"Not that I saw. But, again, I did not stay out there. It was raining very hard. A very bad storm. I went back to my bed and fell asleep."

"I guess it must've been something important to bring them out in weather like that."

Manuel shrugged.

When Archer got back to Poca City, he went straight to the police station to see Shaw.

CHAPTER

43

ONLY SHAW WASN'T THERE and apparently no one had seen the man at all that day.

Archer ran into Deputy Bart Coleman in the hallway of the station and asked him about the detective.

Bart said, "Last I saw of him was yesterday." He suddenly put his hand on the butt of his revolver. "Hey, Archer, didn't you get arrested and charged with murdering Mr. Tuttle?"

"I did."

"What are you doing out then?"

"Made bail. You can check. Not like I escaped, right? And if I had, I sure as hell wouldn't have come back to the police station."

Bart reluctantly removed his hand from his gun. "No, I guess not."

"Look, if you see Shaw, can you tell him to come see me over at the Derby? It's important."

"Yeah, okay."

* * *

Archer sat down on the bed in his hotel room and contemplated things. He'd been rushing around so much, he hadn't had time to put together all that he had recently learned. He had wanted to tell Shaw and see the man write it all down in his notebook and maybe help him make sense of it. But that was not to be right now, apparently, so Archer instead went over it in his head.

It seemed likely that Jackie and Ernestine had some sort of understanding, and a plan. They had visited Marjorie Pittleman's home during the storm. That would account for the mud on the car and its tires. He didn't know if they had gone into the house or not, but Marjorie had said she hadn't seen Jackie since the time he had been there with her. And from what Marjorie had told him, it was clear that Jackie had not given her the money to repay her father's debt.

One thing Archer had concluded was that Jackie had cleared out her father's safe and loaded it into the large trunk of the Nash. And she had done so in the time between Archer's seeing all the wealth in there, and Jackie and Shaw going out to Tuttle's home. But now with Manuel telling him what he had, Archer could narrow that time frame down some.

She had arranged to meet her father at her house, probably using that ruse to make sure he wouldn't be home to stop her and Ernestine from ransacking the man's safe. But something had gone terribly wrong on that score because Tuttle had not been at Jackie's; he'd been at his house. But for the life of him, Archer couldn't fathom why the man hadn't kept the meeting with his daughter.

Jackie's emptying the safe and piling it into the Nash's trunk, at some point, was the only way the imprint of the gold bars and the transfer of the gold dust could have occurred. Then, Jackie and Ernestine had driven over to Marjorie's that same night. Why had they done that? To hide the loot? But why there? And what was even more confusing, why bother taking the things from the safe in the first place? As her father's only heir, they would have come to Jackie anyway after his death. And all that oil money on top of it. It just didn't make any sense.

And in addition to the emptied safe, someone had taken Lucas Tuttle's life. If Jackie had been the one to steal the items from the safe, she had to have been there that night. So had Jackie killed her father? If so, why?

His thoughts next turned to that last night with Jackie at Ernestine's house. She had been the one to bring the conversation around to the repayment of the debt, something Archer had admitted to her that he had forgotten about. And she had been the one to suggest the meeting with her father.

She used me. Set me up like the sucker I am.

He rose and was looking out the window when an idea occurred to him. At the same moment, he saw the dull, mustard-colored Hudson Hornet with the brown stripe and chrome side light parked at the curb. He put on his hat, pocketed his knife and flashlight, and rushed out.

He reached the street and ran over to the car, peering in the open window.

Bart Coleman, doughnut in hand, looked back at him, while Deputy Jeb was drinking his coffee and devouring a large, messy pastry.

"What do you want, Archer?" said Bart sharply. "I ain't seen Shaw to tell him you want to talk to him."

"That's why I'm here. He left me a note at the hotel and said to meet him out at Tuttle's place. Can you give me a ride?"

"We're working here, Archer," said an irritated Bart as he wiped a bit of doughnut powder off his mouth. "Hell, can't you see that?"

"Yeah, I can. Look, um." He pulled out a five-dollar bill. "How about this for gas? And maybe some more pastries?" he tacked on, eyeing Jeb eating away.

Bart looked at the fiver for a moment before snatching it. "All right, get in."

Archer climbed into the back seat and Bart pulled away from the curb. He drove fast, and in just under an hour they were at Tuttle's.

"Don't see Shaw's car here," noted Bart. "He drives a big Buick. Can't miss it."

"Yeah, I know. He might not have got here yet. He was coming from somewhere else, he said in the note. I'll ride back into town with him."

"Suit yourself."

Archer climbed out and the squad car drove off fast, trailing vortices of fresh dust in its wake. The recent rains had done nothing apparently to diminish *that* physical element of life around here.

Archer turned and faced the Tuttle house, which held no signs of life or light.

He walked around the place and noted that there was no activity in the adjacent fields. This was not surprising. It was getting on to supper

time now as the sun faded into the horizon.
Maybe with the man dead, all operations on the
farm had ceased.

A few minutes later, in the outbuilding, Archer
shone his light on the odd-looking piece of
farm equipment. It was the corn picker he'd
seen before.

Maybe this was the thing that Isabel had fallen
to her death on. It had four sharp-edged, cone-
shaped pods. They were all facing downward.
The woman couldn't have been impaled on one
of these things if they'd been pointed like that.
From his time in the military he was familiar with lots of different pieces of machinery,
and Archer quickly figured out how the thing
worked. He gripped a handle and started to turn
it. It was damn tough going and took a lot of
his strength. But one of the cones started lifting
upward. He stopped, panting slightly, when the
cone was finally pointing straight up.

So that was how the woman had died.

He next ventured to the barn and climbed
the ladder to the top landing. He went over
to the hay bale doors and opened them. He
eyed the winch used to haul bales up. Then
he looked down and imagined the corn picker
with the upturned cone on the ground directly
underneath. And then he visualized Isabel

Tuttle falling to her death, impaled on the damn thing.

And then Jackie finding her like that.

He thought about what Lucas Tuttle had told him about his daughter. And his dead wife. That they were both fiercely independent. Hotheaded. That he was scared of them. That mother and daughter had clashed repeatedly. And, that Isabel Tuttle's death might not have been an accident.

Well, I don't think it was an accident, either.

He suddenly had the awful vision of the woman falling to her death and Jackie being behind where her mother had stood, her arms stretched out after pushing Isabel to her death.

He felt a bit sick at that. Maybe more than a bit. But then something occurred to Archer. He was putting two and two together, like Shaw had taught him to do. But he needed to go further on that than he just had. He turned his head and looked in the direction of the outbuilding he'd just been in. After a few moments of thought, Archer smiled. Perhaps in relief. But it was a genuine feeling, that was for sure.

He returned to the home's front door and took out his knife, only this time it failed its mission. Undeterred, he moved over to a window, forced the latch back, and climbed through.

He walked down the hall and saw an open door.

He edged inside and shone his Ray-O-Vac around.

It was set up as a small office. Dead center on the desk was a typewriter. And next to that was a pair of earphones that were plugged into a little machine.

He assumed this had to be Desiree Lankford's office, where she did her typing.

He checked the wastebasket and then looked through the drawers. There were files and copies of correspondence and a small notebook. He looked inside it.

Under the *T*'s was Jackie Tuttle's name and her address on Eldorado and her phone number. That was interesting.

There was a little roll of tape next to the machine Desiree used to listen to Tuttle's dictation. He put it in the machine, figured out how it worked, and turned it on, listening to what was on the tape by slipping on the earphones.

Though he should have been expecting it, he nearly jumped when Lucas Tuttle's voice came on.

"To Sam Malloy, Attorney-at-Law. Dear Sam, Now that I've changed my will, disinheriting my traitorous and worthless daughter, and with all this new money coming in, I want to make a few more changes to everything. I would like you to come by next Friday to discuss them. Let me know a good time for you. Sincerely, Lucas Tuttle." There was a pause and the man next dictated a few other short business letters to various people.

The recording left off at that point and Archer tipped his hat back. So the old man had cut out his daughter. That explained a lot, but not in a good way for Jackie.

He pocketed the tape, left the room, moved down the hall to Tuttle's office, and opened the door.

Inside he once more shone his Ray-O-Vac light around.

There was some blood on the desktop, from where Tuttle had been shot. He next examined the console where the revolvers still lay side by side.

Archer walked over to the safe and swung open the door. It was indeed empty. He noted twin holes drilled into the door. The locksmith's doing, he figured. He next shone his light on some framed pictures lined up on the mantel. He had seen them on his prior visit here but couldn't make out who was in them. There wasn't a single picture of Isabel or Jackie.

Archer noted the large plant in a vase on a stand next to the fireplace. He had seen it before but paid it no attention. He poked around it and then shone his light behind the broad leaves of the plant. The light beam reflected off the glass. He pulled out the object that had been placed right behind the vase. It was a framed photo. Why would Tuttle have hidden this back there? When Archer looked at the photo, he thought he had his answer.

There were two men in the photo.

One was Lucas Tuttle. The other was Malcolm Draper.

What in the hell?

He slid the frame into his jacket pocket, stepped back, and looked over at the desk. There was nothing of particular importance on it except for the bloodstains. There were some on the floor, too, where the man had fallen. Archer looked through the drawers and wastebasket and came up empty. He figured Shaw had been all over this room anyway. But maybe he had missed something else besides the photo of the two men. Archer pulled out the drawers again and checked not in the drawers, but under them.

He found nothing.

He perched on the desk and his eyes alighted on the Remington over-under leaning against the fireplace stone. He picked it up, broke the breech, and saw that there were no shells inside. Then he turned it around and shone his light down the one barrel where he had previously seen something strange. There was definitely an object hidden in there.

He used a letter opener on the desk to work the item from the barrel. It was a curled-up piece of onionskin, a carbon copy of a typed letter. He uncurled it and started reading. It was from Tuttle and was addressed to Poca City's district attorney, a Mr. Herbert Brooks. As he read down the letter, Archer's insides turned to putty.

That son of a bitch.

He put the letter in his pocket. Well, at least the damn shotgun had been good for something.

He glanced at the device on the desk.

A Dictaphone, Tuttle had called it. The little receiver he had been holding when Archer had walked in here previously was lying on the desk, its squiggly cord attached to the machine.

As Archer kept staring at the thing, the image of Shaw's recording their talk at the police station popped into his head. He shone his light on the machine and, as he had with Desiree's machine, he quickly figured out the functions of the buttons.

He hit one and heard a whirring sound coming

from within the innards of the Dictaphone as the tape rewound fully. He also saw that the thing you spoke into had a little button that you held down, presumably when you were speaking into it. There was also a little catch that you could engage. This kept the speaking button down without having to use your thumb the whole time. Archer saw that this catch had indeed been set, keeping the button down.

When the tape stopped rewinding, he pressed another button. The whirring sound took up once more.

He flinched, as the dead man's voice suddenly filled the room.

He was dictating more letters to various people, methodically, without pause. Then there was a long gap. Then he heard the man say in connection with a letter to another gent, "Desiree, depending on how my meeting with Jackie goes tonight, we may have to make arrangements for her to move back in here. I will discuss those details when I return from my business trip next week." Tuttle went on with some more instructions for the woman, and then the tape fell silent. Archer turned the machine off.

It appeared that Tuttle had every intention of visiting his daughter that night. So what had happened? The thoughts were catapulting through his head like ack-ack fired at enemy planes. Because on the one hand it seemed that Tuttle was expecting his daughter to move back in. But then there was the letter to Herbert Brooks: What he had communicated in there did not mesh with having his daughter back home. But maybe it did somehow to Lucas Tuttle.

Desiree had typed up a letter from Tuttle where he had disinherited his daughter. He had a feeling that Desiree had let Jackie know about this. That would explain why Jackie would come here and clean out the safe. Otherwise, she would get nothing.

Next to the desk, he spied a small wooden box with a handle that the Dictaphone was evidently meant to be stored in. With a sudden thought, he wound up the machine's electrical cord and slipped it into the box. He wanted to know what Shaw would make of all this.

Overcome with all that he'd just learned, he eyed the little bar set up against the wall, went over, and poured himself a stiff one. He drank it down, planted his palms on the wood of the bar, hung his head down, and took three long breaths.

You survived the war, you can damn well survive this, Archer.

I hope.

CHAPTER

44

HE SET OFF DOWN THE ROAD carrying the wooden case on his hike back to Poca City proper.

It was a long walk, and the dusk grew into night as he went along. He would put out his thumb whenever a vehicle passed but no one even slowed down. Archer finally thrust out his thumb one more time as the headlights bore down on him. However, he held out no hope the vehicle would stop for him until he heard the gnashing of lowering gears and the slowing of an engine.

He turned around as the car pulled off onto the shoulder. The passenger's-side window came down with a jerky motion.

"Mr. Shaw?"

The detective was grinning at him through the opening.

Archer eyed the big Buick. "Where the hell have you been?"

"Drove over to Texas yesterday. Took me near to forever. Just getting back."

"Texas? Why?"

"Get in and I'll tell you all about it."

"And I'll do the same with what I found out."

Archer climbed in, and Shaw pulled the big Buick back onto the road.

"Guess your arm's okay," said Archer, noting the sling was gone.

"Aches a bit, but I'm fine. What's in the case there?"

"I'll show you when we get to town."

"Why don't you tell me what you found out first?" said Shaw.

Archer went through some of what he had learned. But he did leave out the details of the carbon copy letter he had found. He wasn't certain why he had, but his gut was telling him to keep that to himself.

"So Jackie and Ernestine Crabtree had something going together?" said Shaw, when Archer was done.

"That's right. And they went over to Marjorie Pittleman's that night. But Marjorie later told me she hadn't seen Jackie or the money I gave her."

"Good catch on the muddy car, Archer. I didn't see that one and I was staring right at the dang thing. And you think they emptied out the safe that night. Why?"

In answer, Archer told the detective about the recording where Tuttle had cut his daughter out of his will.

"That would give her a motive to steal what was in that safe," said Shaw. "Only how did she get it open? She didn't have the combination."

"No, I think she did."

He showed Shaw the slip of paper he'd found in Jackie's trash.

"Well, I'll be damned. Sure looks like a safe combo to me." He eyed Archer proudly. "You did good, son. Damn good. You got the makings of a fine detective." He paused as he watched Archer frown.

"What's wrong?"

When Archer didn't answer, Shaw did it for him. "You like these two gals. And you don't want to see them in trouble?"

Archer nodded. "You hit it right on the head."

"If they broke the law, Archer, nothing you can do about that."

"I guess."

"So Ernestine has up and gone. And you can't find Jackie?"

"I think they're both gone." He sat up straighter in his seat and stared out the windshield into the dark. "Now, tell me what you were doing over in Texas."

"After you told me what happened with Ernestine's father, I called a friend of mine at the Federal Bureau of Investigation."

"The FBI! You mean J. Edgar Hoover and those boys?"

"I do indeed. Anyway, this buddy of mine is assigned to Amarillo, Texas."

"Okay." Archer took the pack of Lucky Strikes out of his pocket. "You want one?"

"Hell, yes."

Archer shook a pair out, lit one up and passed it to Shaw, and then did the same for himself.

Shaw rolled down his window and blew his smoke out. "Anyway, I spoke with my buddy and he recalled the case. He phoned a friend of his in the Amarillo Police Department and put me in touch with him. I drove over to Amarillo yesterday shortly after I left you, and I'm just getting back now, like I said. They had a tornado come through there a few a months ago, wrecked half the damn town. Felt like I was back in the war."

"Damn. So what'd you find out?"

"Carson Crabtree was a fine police officer who everybody liked and respected."

"Except for the fact that he killed three people."

"Hold on, I'm getting to that." He puffed on his cigarette. "Thing is, those three men? They did have one thing in common."

"What was that?"

"They all knew Ernestine."

"And that never came out?"

"It did, but only *after* Carson was executed."

"Why only then? Didn't people investigate?"

"Why would they, Archer? Carson Crabtree confessed to the killings. What was there to investigate?"

"Right."

"Anyway, it *did* come out later when a curious reporter down there did a little digging. One of the men had been caught peeping on women."

"That was in that article I told you about."

"What you don't know is that he'd definitely been caught peeping on *Ernestine*."

"Okay. But how does that tie into what happened?"

"You know young men, Archer, being one yourself. Some think they can do what they want with the fairer sex. They start by peeping, then move on to something a lot worse."

Archer shot him a hard look. "Are you saying what I think you're saying?"

"The policeman I was talking to believed that the three men, well, they did things to Ernestine."

"You mean...?"

"They raped her, Archer, or so the man believed. And more than once."

"And that's why Carson Crabtree killed them?"

"Hell, if somebody did that to my little girl? I know I'm a lawman and all, but so was Carson Crabtree. I might just do what he did."

"But if he killed those men, he must've known what they did to her. He could have used that to not get electrocuted. Hell, he probably could've gotten off completely. You said that yourself."

"Now, there's the interesting part. The theory the man had is that Carson was guilt-ridden because, in his mind, he had failed to protect his daughter. And on top of that, if he used what they had done to his daughter as a defense, it would have to all come out. He probably thought the shame would have ruined her. So he confessed and went to the chair. For her sake."

Archer sat back. "I think the man might be right. Remember the letter in the scrapbook?"

Shaw nodded and said, "You think her mother knew and she was telling Ernestine not to dwell on it, not to blame herself for what her father did?"

"I think so. But then Ernestine's mother killed herself. I guess she couldn't heed her own advice." Archer rubbed his brow, tossed his cigarette out the window, and said, "Damn, I need a stiff drink."

"I'm with you there, son. Maybe more than one."

They drove on to Poca City.

CHAPTER

45

WHO DO YOU THINK killed Lucas Tuttle, then?" asked Shaw, over a glass of Rebel in Archer's hotel room. "You have any opinions?"

Archer refilled their tumblers he'd gotten from the hotel to replace the ones Shaw had taken to fingerprint. They'd purchased a cluster of roast beef sandwiches and pickles from a deli and brought them up as their dinner.

"Ernestine knows her way around a gun. But as far as I know Tuttle didn't know her. And I don't want to think she'd do something like that. She's a sweet gal. But I saw her turn the tables on a parolee coming after her. The lady has a spine of steel."

"And she's done a runner, too," said Shaw. "Innocent folks don't tend to do that."

"But what I don't get is, on the tape Tuttle is clearly intending on seeing Jackie that night. Only Jackie said he never showed up at her house."

"She could be lying," noted Shaw.

"The thing is, Jackie suggested that I go collect the debt. And then she said she'd agree to meet with her father, as a way, I thought, to help me get the money paid. But now I see it was a way for her to get her father out of the house, so she could get what was in that safe."

"But how'd she even know it was in there? You only told her after the fact. Remember? She was mad at you for withholding that."

Archer eyed the lawman in an amused fashion. "You're forgetting your own rule."

"What's that?"

"Don't believe anybody without *corroboration*. But I think I know how. Same way she knew that she'd been cut out of the will."

Shaw's eyes lit up. "The secretary, Desiree, could have told her."

"Right. She typed up all his letters. She'd sure as hell know what was going on with the man's business."

"You think Jackie promised her some of the loot in return for helping?"

"Could be. Hey, you think Desiree could've shot him?"

Shaw finished a sandwich, balled up the wax paper, and tossed it into the trash can. "I checked. She had an alibi. But that was a nice piece of deduction on your part, Archer."

Archer bit into his sandwich and took a swallow of his drink. "How'd you even come to be in the detective business?"

"My old man was a beat cop for forty years over in Kansas. I got married there and started a family, then moved out this way, became a patrolman, and later got promoted to detective for the state police. I was doing real well, had a knack for it and all. Then I volunteered for the war and flew planes. After I got out of uniform, I got my old job back."

"You obviously like the work. And you're good at it."

"Well, I see the utility in punishing bad folks. It preserves civilization as we know it. And both of us have seen the other side of that equation, when civilization gets shown the door, and the rule of law don't matter for shit, and the whole damn world gets set on fire. It's always closer than you think."

"So you got a family then? You mentioned a daughter?"

"Got me three kids. Two boys and a girl. Oldest is my son Johnny, near to grown now. He's going to join the Army. Serve his country."

"I wish him luck and that he gets to serve during peacetime. We don't need any more wars."

"Amen to that, brother."

They clinked glasses.

"I checked on you. You got no family left. Never married."

"That's right."

"Never found the right gal?" asked Shaw.

"I used to think that. No more."

"What changed?"

"Well, since I got here, I think maybe for all the ladies I met along the way, *I* wasn't the right man for *them*."

"That's pretty enlightened of you, Archer. But you must've wanted to settle down at some point."

"Can't say yay or nay on that. I grew up in a small slice of a big city and decided to see the country for a bit and then went on to college. Then they bombed Pearl Harbor, and I did my bit and came back. And took up my wandering ways again. Then Carderock Prison became my new home for a while. Hell, I'm not all that shy of thirty and part of me feels like I haven't started to even live my life yet."

"Maybe your day is coming."

Archer nodded, but he didn't really believe this was a viable possibility. He was thinking if he managed to survive Poca City, it would be a miracle.

Shaw said, "Now, why do you reckon they would go to Marjorie's house? What would they need from her? And why would she give them anything anyway? Is it just about money? People are that crass, you know. They'll kill for ten cents if they think it's worth it to them. And it's not a damn dime we're talking about here."

"But Jackie thought her father was going to be in town to meet with her. That was the whole point. So how did he end up dead at his place?"

"Maybe she called him *after* he recorded what he did on that machine and changed the plan. They could have arranged to meet him out there." Archer did not seem convinced by this. In fact, he felt even more troubled.

Shaw unwrapped another sandwich. "Now, you said something woke you the morning you found Pittleman's body. What was that?"

Archer thought back. "Loud noise or bang."

"Like maybe someone hit your door?"

"Yeah."

"Now, if I'm reading this right, whoever killed Pittleman was the one to bang on your door to get you up from your bed. Then they waited to hear you coming down the hall and they opened the door a crack to Number 615, and maybe went and hid in Number 617. You see, the plan was they wanted you to find the body and get your prints on that doorknob."

"I guess that could be." Archer smacked his forehead and pulled the small framed photo out of his pocket. "Hell, I forgot about this. There's Lucas Tuttle and Malcolm Draper together."

Shaw looked stunned. "But he worked for Pittleman, not Tuttle."

"Well, Marjorie said that Draper only came to work for them about a year ago."

"Hold on, wasn't that about the time Jackie left home?"

"Yes, it sure was."

Shaw squinted as he thought about this. "And Draper would go out to the slaughterhouse most nights, the clerk said. And then you told me they couldn't make payroll."

"That's right."

Shaw smiled in a self-satisfied way.

"What?" asked Archer sharply.

"I know this will sound like a long shot, but I was a pilot and you were infantry, Archer, so all we knew were long shots that paid off every night we went to bed still breathing." He paused. "What if Draper was a *plant* of Tuttle's?"

"A plant? How so?"

"Man gets Draper in there to do his bidding and mess up Pittleman's little empire. Draper might've been going out to the slaughterhouse to mess with the books, so to speak. Maybe skimming money off, things like that. And maybe that wasn't the only business of Pittleman's he was doing that to."

"You think?"

"Remember the past-due bills I found in the trash can behind the hotel? What if *Draper* took them from the office and tossed those in there? Thing is, the man was sort of Pittleman's business manager. He lived at the Derby Hotel. He could have had access to that office anytime he wanted. Hell, maybe Pittleman thinks the man is paying those bills, but instead he's tossing them. Wouldn't take long for Pittleman's businesses to be run into the ground and him not even know it before it was too late. And on top of that Pittleman had his own gambling problem."

Now Archer looked stunned as he recalled something Sid Duckett had told him. "Hold on. When I talked to Sid Duckett about what would happen to Pittleman's businesses since he was dead, the man said that Lucas Tuttle might buy them up, 'cause he had the money."

"But how would Duckett know that Tuttle had the money to do that? Everyone thought he had financial problems, including his own daughter."

"He would if Draper told him."

Shaw took all this in. "And the night we talked to Duckett at his cottage, and you mentioned payroll not being met at the slaughterhouse?"

"You think Duckett put two and two together and confronted Draper about what he thought was going on?"

Shaw nodded. "Maybe even tried to blackmail him over it. He could have threatened to tell the law what was going on unless they paid him off. And then he ends up fed to the hogs for his troubles."

"So Lucas Tuttle was getting his revenge on Pittleman."

"Come again?" said Shaw.

"When I met with him, Tuttle told me that Pittleman had this big plan to get Tuttle's daughter and then all his property. But I'm thinking that it was actually Tuttle who had that plan. To get all that Pittleman had. Like Marjorie told us, the two men were rivals."

"And Tuttle would get it on the cheap since Pittleman had all those past-due bills and such."

"And Marjorie would probably have to rely on Draper to tell her what a fair price for the business would be, and with the man working for Tuttle we know whatever price he told her was fair surely wouldn't be. Hey, how is Draper? We could ask him flat out about all of this."

Shaw shook his head. "Still not conscious. But when he does wake up, I'll be right there with all my questions."

Archer fell silent and looked out the window.

"What is it?"

"We fought a war for this? Conniving folks killing other folks over money?"

"Wars don't change how people are, Archer. They just kill a bunch 'a folks and when it's over, people go back to being how they always were. Most good, some not so good." He yawned and stretched. "Now, I'm all done in. Need some sack time. Been a long damn day."

"Okay."

Shaw gave Archer a thumbs-up. "We're going to get to the truth, have no fear. I got me some ideas."

After he left, Archer smoked another cigarette while he stared out the window.

Part of him wished he was back in prison, a thought he never believed he would have. This had all shaken his faith in a lot of things, but mainly in one thing.

Me.

During the war, during most of his life, in fact, Aloysius Archer had been able to trust his instincts. Not now.

A few minutes later he looked down at the framed picture. Pittleman was dead. Tuttle, too. Draper might never wake up and tell them the truth. He picked up the photo and absently tapped the frame against his knee, thinking about a million possibilities.

With his tapping, the backing fell off the frame and the freed paper fluttered to the floor. He reached down and picked it up. It was a letter. He read it through three times, each time growing more incredulous at what the words said.

He wanted to go and tell Shaw, but the man was no doubt already asleep. Well, it would keep until morning.

On impulse, Archer took out his knife and used it to cut the stitching on his hat's inner lining. He secreted the letter and the photo in there and put his hat on the bureau.

He lay back on the bed and closed his eyes.

When he woke up early the next morning, his life was about to totally change.

And not in a good way for him.

CHAPTER

46

ARCHER YAWNED, STRETCHED, and slowly came awake.

In the distance, he heard a sound that seemed, to his half-asleep state, partly familiar, and unrecognizable. As it grew closer, he sat up, because he now knew what the noise was.

The low-pitched wail-growl of a siren.

He lumbered over to the window, his legs stiff and heavy with sleep.

He lifted the glass, rubbed his eyes clear, and looked out onto a surprisingly cool, overcast day. He watched with interest as a long, white ambulance with red markings on the side raced down the street, its guttural siren shattering the otherwise peaceful commencement of another day in Poca City that at least for variety's sake did not hold clear skies and sun.

He was about to turn back when a second sound joined the first, another siren, but different from the ambulance's babble.

It was a police car, with the single roof light on and the siren cranked to an ear-numbing pitch—a one-note, one-instrument orchestra performing a banshee of a song with a troubling melody.

Archer slid out a Lucky Strike from a fresh pack and lit up as he continued to peer out and wonder what all the fuss was about. Ambulances he understood. But that coupled with a police car was disturbing.

The next moment he crushed the smoke out on the windowsill as both the ambulance and police car pulled up to the front of the Derby. He saw uniformed men leap from the patrol car, and men in white smocks and pants jump out of the ambulance. He slipped on his clothes and shoes, grabbed his jacket, and ran out of the room. He took the stairs two at a time to the lobby. He burst out of the fire door and saw that the lobby was half full of onlookers and a handful of anxious guests, some still in their pajamas.

He heard the elevator ding and watched the car ascend to and stop at the third floor.

Archer ran over to the front desk, where there was a different clerk, a young man with narrow shoulders and a pockmarked face.

"What the hell is going on?" he demanded.

The young man was pale and his eyes were large with fear. "They found somebody out in the hallway bleeding like crazy."

"Who is it?"

"I don't know. A maid found him."

Archer ran back to the stairs and sprinted up to the third-floor landing. He caromed out into the hall and looked in both directions. He saw nothing but heard something. He ran to his left and around the corner, where he stopped abruptly.

The police and ambulance men were gathered in a small knot around someone lying on the floor. Archer hustled over there to see. One of the officers heard his approach, whirled around, and put up a hand. "Stay back, this is police business!"

However, he had moved just enough for Archer to see who it was. Irving Shaw was lying there covered in blood.

"What happened to him?"

"Get out of here, sir," said the uniformed officer sternly, his face flushing red and the words catching in his throat. His partner turned, put his hand on the butt of his service revolver, and added, "Now."

Archer staggered back to the stairs, stumbled up them, and made it to his room before collapsing on the bed.

Shaw was wounded, or maybe dead. He had seen blood all over the man's shirt front. He didn't know if he'd been shot or stabbed or what, but it had to be one of them. He slowly sat up and covered his face with his hands. He felt sick and dizzy. He imagined he was back in combat and they were being called up to attack yet another enemy position, in an endless stream of them. Men would be praying, puking, writing letters good-bye, making sure their dog tags were on, even finalizing last wills and testaments on preprinted papers the army had conveniently provided, and for which your fellow soldiers were your witnesses and you theirs.

He got up and stumbled over to the open window, sucking in the fresh air like it was a gaseous version of Rebel Yell. He leaned out the window as more police stormed into the hotel, including pudgy Bart and long-legged Jeb.

As his thoughts cleared, Archer started to focus on what he needed to do. He and Shaw were supposed to talk this morning about how to get to the truth. Now it would be up to

Archer to do so alone. And maybe he had some ideas of his own.

Archer hustled down the stairs and out the back door of the hotel, avoiding the growing crowd in the front lobby.

Shaw had left his big Buick parked on a side street. Archer climbed into the driver's seat, popped open the glove box, and slipped out the keys. He had seen Shaw put them there the night before. He started up the Buick, geared it into reverse, made a U-turn, and drove off in the opposite direction to avoid all the activity at the front of the hotel. He came up on the main street two blocks from the hotel in time to see men carrying out a stretcher with Shaw on it, the sheet up to his neck.

But not over his face, so he's not dead, thank God.

Archer watched this until the rear doors closed on the ambulance. He took a whiff, and the scent of the man, imprinted in every pore of the Buick, came rushing into his lungs. A good man with maybe a bad ending. *It could happen to any of us*, Archer knew. Against enormous odds, the lawman had survived all those bombing missions fighting for his country only perhaps to come back and die in a two-bit hotel in Poca goddamn City.

And someone might've tried to kill him because he was looking for the truth and trying to clear my name at the same time.

This thought gave added fire to Archer's mission, not that he needed it. Avoiding a short drop with a rope around the neck should be incentive enough for any man, he thought.

He hung a left and drove out of town; his destination was Marjorie Pittleman's. Jackie and Ernestine had gone there, presumably with the loot from the safe. And he needed to find out why. And that also might provide a clue as to where the women had gone. And, most important, something had occurred to Archer that might lead him to the truth. Ironically, it was due in part to something Shaw had told him: It was a two-way street with the women. He was attractive to them, and they could, in return, bend him to their purposes.

He made it there in good time, parking the Buick down the road a bit and finishing the journey on foot. It was early enough that he could see no one out and about yet. The gates were chained shut, but he quickly clambered over and dropped to the ground inside.

From a crouch, he looked right and left, feeling back in his role of an Army scout.

He was not concerned with the main house

but flitted off to the left. He reached into his pocket and felt for it. He had not only taken Shaw's car; he had also popped open the compartment under the dash and taken the man's Smith & Wesson .38 Victory piece. Archer was hoping for a triumph of his own right about now. He could sure as hell use it.

He got the lay of the land while hunkered down and checked his watch. He imagined folks would be up and about soon. This assumption paid off when he saw Manuel come around a corner of an outbuilding with a bucket of something in hand.

He rose from his hiding position and approached the man, who stopped abruptly when he saw Archer.

"Hello, Manuel, how's doing?"

Manuel looked confused by this greeting.

"Doing?" He held up the bucket. "I am working."

"Got a question. Maid in the house named Amy?"

"What about her?"

"How long has she been working here?"

"Why?"

"I'm thinking of asking her out. I think she likes me."

Manuel smiled. "She is very…friendly."

"Yeah, I could see that. So how long?"

"Not long. Maybe six months."

"Any idea where she is now?"

"At this hour, probably in her room getting ready for work."

"Where is that?"

Manuel eyed him suspiciously. "Why?"

Archer patted his pocket where the gun was. "Got a present I want to give her and then ask her out. Don't like to let grass grow under my feet. Another fella might cut me out."

Manuel smiled again in understanding, nodded, and pointed to his left.

"The maids live in little cottages behind that barn. Amy's is the last one."

Archer pressed a dollar into the man's callused hand. "Thanks, friend, you have no idea how much that helps me."

"Good luck."

"I think I'm going to need it."

Archer hustled to the row of little one-room dwellings and reached the last one.

He knocked on the door and a girlish voice said, "Who is it?"

Doing a reasonably good impression of Manuel's baritone, Archer said, "Mrs. Pittleman needs you right now, Amy."

"Just a minute."

Less than a minute later the door opened
and there stood Amy. She looked up at Archer,
astonished beyond belief, and then she smiled
disarmingly. "What are you doing here, Mr.
Archer?"

She stopped smiling when Archer pulled out
the .38 and pointed it at her.

Terrified, she backed up, and Archer entered
and closed the door behind him. He looked
around the tiny dimensions of the room, which
was not much bigger than his prison cell had
been. It was furnished in a rudimentary fashion.
Cot, dresser with a washbowl and pitcher on
top. One wooden chair with a broken back.
Pegs on the wall for clothes, of which she had
few. A small square of tattered rug over the cold
plank floor. There was a chill in the air and the
distinct odor of mildew. He figured her bathroom would be a nearby outhouse.

"Sit down," he ordered, pointing to the cot,
while he took up residence in the chair.

She sat and looked at him fearfully. "Please
don't hurt me."

"I need you to tell me, right now, where Jackie
and Ernestine are."

She looked at him blankly and said nothing.
She just sat there with tears forming in her eyes
and her small face twitching.

He rose and roughly gripped her by the arm, jerking the woman to her feet. "Okay, let's just go to the coppers then. They'll be able to hang somebody, might as well be you, sister."

Amy's bloodless face collapsed, and she pulled against him and wailed, "Wait, wait, please. Don't. I—"

He looked around the room again. "They shake some cash in front of you? A way out of this dump. How much?" When she didn't answer he pointed the revolver at her again and said quietly, "I'm one desperate son of a gun, lady. So how much?"

"A...a th-thousand dollars."

Archer sat back down, took out his pack of smokes, flicked one out, and placed it, unlit, between his teeth. "Where's the crate?"

"Crate?"

"Box, crate, whatever the hell you want to call it. This is pretty damn simple, Amy, it was all about the dough."

When she didn't say anything, Archer nodded slowly. "Okay, let me just spell it out just so you know I'm not bluffing. They came that night in the Nash. Not to see Marjorie. No way Jackie's working a deal with a lady who hates her guts. So *my* gut tells me they came to see *you*. 'Cause you look like the sort that would do just about anything for money. And Jackie would be over here a lot because she was seeing Hank Pittleman. And I bet she sized you up real quick. And that other maid, old sourpuss Agnes, doesn't have the grit that Jackie needed. They had a trunk full of gold bars, cash, hell, maybe the damn crown jewels, for all I know. And they needed a way to get it outta Poca City." He glanced out the window in the direction of HP Trucking. "Is it in the warehouse over there?" When she didn't answer, Archer said very quietly, his gaze boring into her, "You willing to swing at the end of a rope for a thousand bucks, sister? Better give it to me straight, or that's where you're ending up."

She started to sob. "I just did what they told me to do. I didn't know nobody was going to get killed."

"Well, they did. And the law says ignorance is no excuse. You're just as guilty as they are. Now, take me to what they brought here that night."

They took the long way around to the Buick and drove directly over to the warehouse. There was no one yet there, it still being early. The big double doors were locked, but Archer found a window on the side that succumbed to his knife. He pushed Amy through and followed her in. He turned on his flashlight and aimed the beam around the huge interior of the place. It was piled high with merchandise ready to be shipped out.

"Where?" he demanded.

She led him to the very back corner where a number of boxes were piled high. Right behind this stack was the large metal four-wheeled trolley cart the men had used to bring the boxes in that Archer had loaded on Sid Duckett's truck. And behind that was something covered with a blanket. Archer slipped off the blanket and a wooden crate was revealed. He aimed his light beam at the shipping label on top and read off what was written there.

He looked at the quivering Amy. "I...I don't even know where that is," she said, eyeing the crate's final destination.

Archer said, "Well, I do. And it makes a lot of sense, actually."

He found a crowbar, popped open the top of the crate, and peered inside. He found the contents of Lucas Tuttle's safe underneath a great deal of folded-up women's clothes and shoes and blankets and sheets, probably for additional padding and also to fool anyone chancing to look inside that it was just full of such items and no hint to a king's ransom lurking there.

He thought that some of the clothing might have come from Jackie and Ernestine. In fact, he believed that he recognized a few items from Ernestine's closet. And they would want their personal things to also be delivered to where they were headed.

Then Archer found something stuck inside a pillow case that he had not been expecting. It was a sheaf of papers stapled together. He read down the first page and then flicked back to the last, eyeing the signatures at the bottom.

"Son of a bitch," he hissed.

"What's that?" Amy said in a trembling voice.

"Nothing." He put the papers in his jacket pocket, put the crate top back on, and pounded the nails back in using one end of the crowbar.

Next, he eyed the trolley, and his plan came together. Squatting down and using all his strength he heaved one end of the crate up on the trolley, and then squatted down once more and lifted the other end up. He rolled the trolley to the front doors, unlocked them, and managed to get the crate from the trolley into the enormous trunk of the Buick. He closed the warehouse door and pointed the .38 at Amy.

"You say one word to anyone about this, you're going to hang, do you understand me?"

Teary-eyed, and her hands gripping her white

apron, she nodded. "But I don't understand one thing."

"What?"

"I was nice to you. I was even…flirty with you. So why'd you ever think I was involved in all this?"

"You just answered your own question, lady."

"What?"

"I've discovered some gals like to play me for a sucker because I lose my good sense around them. Well, not this time."

He left her to walk back while he drove off down the road and hit the main strip. He had to find some place safe to hide the contents of the crate. Two miles down the road, the perfect place came to him.

He floored the Buick and shot down the road to where he needed to go.

CHAPTER

47

LATER THAT DAY ARCHER went back to his room at the Derby to do some serious thinking. He had taken the shipping label off the crate and stuck it between two pages of the Gideon Bible in his bureau drawer. He had just finished two cigarettes and a fifth of the bottle of Rebel when someone knocked on his door.

He muttered, "Who is it?"

"Front desk sir, you got a message."

"What? Who from?"

"She wouldn't say."

"She?"

Archer jumped up from the bed and hurried over to the door. As soon as he opened it, it flew inward, and Bart and Jeb plowed through the opening. They slammed him up against the wall.

"Well, good day to you, too," Archer said breathlessly.

"Your ass is under arrest," growled Bart.

"What for?"

"The attempted murder of Irving Shaw. And that's added to what you're already charged with, the murder of Lucas Tuttle. How the hell you made bail with that hanging over your head is beyond me."

"That's bullcrap. I had nothing to do with any of that. And I sure as hell didn't do anything to Mr. Shaw."

"So you say, Archer. We have it on good authority that you were seen with him last night right here at this hotel. Then he was found nearly bled to death early this morning three floors down from your ass."

"Is he going to be okay?"

"They moved him to the big hospital over in Garfield. He's still unconscious, not that you give a damn."

"We were working the case together."

"What case?"

"These damn killings."

"Again, so you say. We don't know nothing about that."

"But I'm out on bail."

"Not anymore you're not. Not after what happened to Lieutenant Shaw."

They hauled him out of his room and led him out the front in handcuffs.

Shortly after that he was behind bars in a holding cell.

They had found Shaw's spare gun on him, which did not help his cause in the least.

Indeed, when they had found the .38, Bart had eyed him triumphantly. "Shot the man and took his gun. Don't get any lower than that in my book."

"Well, maybe you should read some more books then, Bart."

That had cost him a heavy fist in the face and a bloodletting from his nose.

He sat on the bench against the wall of his cell, wincing from his shiner and pinching his nose. His facial injuries from his encounter with Draper hadn't even fully healed yet. Archer took a deep breath and contemplated his options. That didn't take long, because he really had none.

But then a tall, portly man in his late forties with slicked-back hair and wearing a gray three-piece suit and a tightly knotted blue tie appeared on the other side of the bars. He looked like a preacher or a politician, and Archer didn't really care to be jawing with either one right now.

"Mr. Archer?"

Archer looked up. "Who's asking?"

"I am Herbert Brooks, the district attorney for Poca City."

Herbert Brooks. Archer recognized the name from the letter that Archer had found inside Tuttle's shotgun barrel.

"That means you're no friend of mine."

"Maybe, maybe not."

"Come again?" said Archer, rising to his feet and coming over to the bars.

"It appears that Lieutenant Shaw's current condition was due, unfortunately, to a previous injury."

Archer's brows knitted together. "I'm not following."

"He was wounded in an altercation at Miss Jackie Tuttle's house."

"I know that, I was there. I stopped the bleeding and got him to the hospital."

"Yes, however, the doctors did not realize that that injury had nicked an artery. Either through some exertion or otherwise on Lieutenant Shaw's part, the nick turned into a partial tear of the artery. He nearly died from blood loss. He's still unconscious and still not out of danger.

We're speculating that he realized something was wrong and rushed out into the hall for help and collapsed."

"I hope to hell he pulls through. But then why did they arrest me for shooting him?"

"The police didn't know what had happened. He had blood all over him. They thought he had been freshly wounded."

"So am I free to go?"

"You are, and I'm seeing to that. But please keep in mind that you are still charged with the murder of Lucas Tuttle. And I must tell you in all fairness that I'm also thinking of charging you with the murder of Hank Pittleman. I can't imagine, after studying the evidence, that Lieutenant Shaw did not arrest you for that crime as well. But you are not to leave Poca City under any circumstances. I understand that you have made bail, which again strikes me as quite unbelievable. But Lieutenant Shaw did not go through me for that. He apparently talked one of my underlings into agreeing to it. And while I would like to revoke your bail, since you clearly did not attack Lieutenant Shaw, I have no grounds to go to court and seek that remedy. But because of the unusual conditions, I have ordered that you be kept under constant watch. If you attempt to leave town you will be immediately arrested."

"When will my trial come up?"

"Probably in a few weeks or so. I am putting together my case now and lining up my witnesses. It's a little more difficult, what with Lieutenant Shaw being incapacitated, but we must push on, and the notes he took during his investigation will be part of the trial record." He looked keenly at Archer. "And I must say, the evidence against you is quite compelling."

"Would one of those witnesses be Jackie Tuttle?"

"Yes."

"She's gone. Left town."

"So I understand. And while her testimony is not critical to our case, we have put out notices in as many places as we can think of for her to return and testify. I like to cover all bases."

"Well, good luck with that."

Brooks gazed at him suspiciously. "You haven't done any harm to her, have you?"

"Other way around, actually. And while you're at it, try to find Ernestine Crabtree."

"The parole officer?"

"Yeah, she's skipped town, too. I wonder why?"

Brooks looked at him skeptically and shook his head.

"Hey, Mr. Brooks, one more thing." From his pocket Archer drew out the onion skin copy of the letter he'd found in Tuttle's shotgun. He passed it between the bars to Brooks.

Brooks looked at it and then glanced sharply up at Archer. "Where did you get this?"

"Mr. Tuttle gave it to me. But he sent the original to you, right?"

"Yes."

"And what do you intend on doing about it?"

"I represent the law, Mr. Archer. So I intend on following it up. Mr. Tuttle was a very important man hereabouts and his word carries great weight. And that's the other reason I want her back here. And if she doesn't come back, I have ways to track her down. One way or another, justice will be served."

"Okay." Archer put out his hand for the letter.

"I'm not sure I should give this back to you."

"You already have the original of it, and I might need it for my defense."

"How so?"

"I don't need to tell you that, do I?"

"Well, actually no."

"Okay then."

He reluctantly passed the copy back to Archer.

Archer slowly put the paper back in his pocket and said, "Hey, do I get a lawyer, or what?"

"Yes, if you can afford one. If not, well…" He shrugged.

"Yeah, that happened to me last time. I didn't have a lawyer because I didn't have any money. Doesn't seem right that justice should depend on how much you have in your wallet."

"The U.S. Supreme Court has actually agreed with you, Mr. Archer. Under the Sixth Amendment a criminal defendant is entitled to a lawyer provided by the government if he can't afford one."

"Well, then?"

"But, at the current time, that rule only applies in *federal* court criminal prosecutions, not state court, except in very special circumstances—none of which you meet, unfortunately."

"Well, hell, I can be hanged if I'm convicted. What's more *special* than that?"

In the face of this, Brooks seemed to take pity on Archer. "I can recommend someone who comes relatively cheap."

"Okay. Thanks."

"Don't thank me, Mr. Archer. I'm going to do my best to see that you hang."

He walked off. Archer sat back down and leaned against the concrete wall, desperately wanting a smoke. But they'd taken his Lucky Strikes and matches along with the gun.

An hour later a stringy, beady-eyed, bald-as-a-billiard-ball gent in a dark blue worsted suit with a porkpie hat in hand walked up to the cell and peered through the bars. He had a battered leather briefcase in his other hand.

"Hey, Archer?" he said.

"Yeah?"

"I'm Jervis Donnelly. Hear you need a lawyer."

"Okay. What do you charge?"

"For you, my best rate, a hundred bucks."

"And what do I get for the C-note?"

"Got some ideas."

"I'm listening."

"Gonna plead you guilty and see if we can get you life in prison. That way you avoid the noose. A damn good deal, considering. I'm filling out the paperwork now. I'll take fifty bucks now and the other fifty when the court approves your life sentence."

"What's your next idea?"

"You being funny?"

"You see me laughing, mister?"

"Come on, Archer. You know you did it. Just take your medicine. This way you get three squares and a roof over your head till you croak. And they'll teach you how to make license plates. Most folks would love to have that deal."

"Well, I guess I'm not like most folks, then.

I came back from the war looking for something more than three squares and making damn license plates."

Donnelly shrugged. "You don't listen to my advice, what can I do?"

"You can get lost is what you can do. Go on, beat it."

Donnelly's beady eyes became beadier. "You need a lawyer, Archer. Nobody else will take your case. Me, I'm a nice guy. I got empathy."

"But you won't even put up a fight?"

"Hell, son, I'm not a magician. I can't change the damn facts. And you're a dirty ex-con on top of it. Plus, to me, you got a shifty look. They'll give you the noose sure as I'm standing here, or this ain't Poca City."

"Then I'll just represent myself."

"I would not advise that," said Donnelly gravely. "A man representing himself, particularly in a murder case, has not only a fool for a client, but a *damn* fool."

"The only damn fool around here is the one I'm looking at."

"Suit yourself, bumpkin," groused Donnelly, and he stalked off.

When Archer was released, he noted that two plainclothes men were trailing him as he headed back to his hotel before he changed direction and walked over to Ernestine's bungalow. He let himself into her house using the key she'd given him, went over to her shelf, and took out the law books she had there.

He walked back out and nodded to the pair of plainclothes dicks.

"Hey," said one. "You stealing?"

Archer held up one of the books. "I'm entitled to them for my legal defense. You read the Constitution? Says it right in there. Sixth Amendment. It's a good one."

The two men looked at each other and shrugged. One said, "It's your funeral, brother."

"Yeah, we'll have to see about that, friend."

He returned to his hotel room and put the books down on the bed. He went over to the chest of drawers, opened one of them, and looked at the Dictaphone case inside. Fortunately, they hadn't tossed his room and found it. Brooks probably thought he had all of the evidence he needed to hang Archer. He opened the case and looked at the papers he'd stashed in there. They were the ones he'd found in the crate at the trucking warehouse.

Both the tape and the papers told him a lot. He hoped he could put both to good use in his upcoming trial.

He stretched out on the bed and opened one

of the books. He commenced reading and taking notes using some stationery and a pen from the drawer next to the Gideon Bible. When his eyes grew tired and he couldn't read anymore, he started whistling a tune, a sad one he would perform after every battle when they were stacking, counting, and burying their dead. He'd fought for something he didn't entirely understand but had nonetheless believed to be the right thing to do. That had been followed by a stint in Carderock for something he didn't do. And now he was probably going to be hanged for something else he didn't do.

He drank some more of his bottle, and then took the Dictaphone out of the drawer, plugged it in, and turned it on. This time he just let the tape run. He lay back on the bed with his bottle and stared at the ceiling, whistled his tune, and wondered what death by hanging felt like.

He stopped his whistling when he heard something brand-new coming from the recorder. He had never let it run long enough to hear this part because there had been a long gap of silence, which made him think there was nothing else on it.

Archer sat up and his feet hit the floor. He looked down at the Dictaphone and listened to the sounds coming from there. And then he aimed his gaze out the window and to the sky.

After fighting a world war, he had no longer been a God-fearing man, because he firmly believed a loving, righteous god should have just stopped mankind from committing that egregious sin.

No, Aloysius Archer was not a God-fearing man.

Until right now.

"Thank you, Mister Jesus."

He pulled the shipping label out of the Bible, snatched up a piece of blank paper, and took about a half hour to carefully compose a letter. He ran down to the front desk, got an envelope, wrote the address down on it, and carried it over to the post office to mail it. The plainclothes men followed him every step of the way. After that, he went back to his room, lay on his bed, and prayed that what he'd written in that letter worked its magic.

But Archer also had to smile. He had stopped believing the best in people because he so rarely saw it. Now? His faith had been renewed. Just in the nick of time.

48

ALL RISE," said the heavy-set bailiff with a stern gaze and a widow's peak etched sharply into his dark hair.

It was several weeks later and a goodly portion of the town of Poca City, along with the empaneled jury, rose as one inside the first-floor room in the Courts and Municipality Building. This included Archer, in his new suit and spit-polished shoes. His hat rested on the table in front of him. Next to that were Ernestine's law books and some handwritten notes alongside the books.

A squirrel of a judge with rounded shoulders, a bald head encircled by gray hair, and a skinny, corrugated neck augmented by a wattle of flesh scampered out from a door behind the high bench and took his seat. He stared down imperiously over his little domain behind horn-rimmed spectacles.

"Be seated," bellowed the bailiff.

The collection of bottoms hit the wooden seats, and Judge Theodore Richmond called the court to order in a high, reedy voice. He looked down at a paper in front of him and said, "Mr. Aloysius Archer, you are on trial for the murders of Mr. Hank Pittleman and Mr. Lucas Tuttle. And you are representing yourself, is that correct?"

Archer stood. "That's correct, Judge."

The judge eyed him severely. "Just so you know, it is highly unusual for a man to be defending himself against murder charges."

"Well, Judge, me and the lawyer they sent didn't see eye to eye. He thought a life sentence was a good deal. And I couldn't afford anybody else."

"Considering the alternative, he might well be right about that life sentence." He turned to the DA. "Mr. Brooks, you ready to go on your end?"

Brooks, resplendent in a blue three-piece pinstriped suit and dark red tie, with cufflinks on his starched shirt and his hair combed precisely so, rose and cleared his throat. In an impressive baritone he said, "Yes, Your Honor."

"Defendant?" said the judge, giving Archer a patronizing look.

"Uh, the defense is ready, Judge," said Archer, half rising from his seat. As he looked at the stack of law books next to him, he suddenly reached out and tapped the volume on top.

If good fortune is ever going to shine on me, let it be now.

After legal proceeding preliminaries were dispensed with, Judge Richmond said, "Call your first witness, Mr. Brooks."

Brooks called a series of people to help lay out the state's case. Archer declined to cross-examine any of them.

The judge finally looked over at him. "Mr. Archer, just checking to see if maybe you've fallen asleep over there."

The crowd tittered at this.

"No, Judge, just biding my time," replied Archer.

"Well, don't wait too long. You might find your 'time' has run out, son."

Finally, Archer perked up when Brooks said, "The state calls Miss Jacqueline Tuttle."

Archer turned to see Jackie Tuttle rise from the back row and head to the witness box set directly next to the bench. She was dressed in a modest dark blue dress, low heels, black stockings, a matching turban with a little veil attached, and a string of fake pearls around her neck. She was sworn in by the bailiff and took her seat. Jackie took a moment to lift her veil and fix it to a hook on the turban.

Brooks approached. "You are Jacqueline Tuttle, the daughter and only child of Lucas Tuttle?"

"I am."

"Do you know the defendant, Aloysius Archer?"

Jackie gave a searching look at Archer. He stared back at her, impassively.

"I do."

"What can you tell us about the events that led up to the death of your father?"

"I was there when Mr. Hank Pittleman, who was a friend of mine, employed Mr. Archer to collect a debt owed by my father. Mr. Pittleman was going to pay him one hundred dollars when the debt was paid, but Mr. Archer asked for and received a forty-dollar advance."

"Why was that?"

"He said he might have some expenses in collecting the debt and needed some money up front. I thought it made sense, actually."

"And did he use some of the money?"

Jackie hesitated.

"Miss Tuttle, did he use some of the money?" Brooks asked again.

"He bought himself some new clothes."

Brooks held up a piece of paper. "New clothes that we have determined cost about thirty-five dollars."

"He looked good in them."

"And did the time come when Mr. Archer sought to collect this debt?"

"Yes. He told me that he'd had a good first meeting with my father and that he intended to keep working away at it."

"Was he successful?"

"At first, no."

"Can you walk us through that, please?"

"Hank wanted Mr. Archer to take back a Cadillac that my father owned and that he had assigned as collateral for the loan."

"Did Mr. Archer secure this collateral?"

"No, he later told me that my father had burned it up."

"And what happened after that?"

She glanced at Archer before replying. "Mr. Archer was worried because he'd already spent most of the money Hank had advanced and he was concerned that Hank might come after him for it."

Brooks looked over at the jury and saw them hanging on every word of this testimony.

"And what *was* Mr. Pittleman's reaction to Mr. Archer having spent the money?"

"He told Archer if he didn't get the car back, he was going to make Archer pay somehow."

"How did Mr. Archer take that?"

"Like anyone would have. He was worried about it."

The jury and the crowd started mumbling about this until the judge restored quiet with smacks of his gavel.

"Thank you for making things so clear, Miss Tuttle. Now, did there come a time when Mr. Archer met with your father again?"

"Yes, I let him drive my car out there to meet with him."

"And what happened?"

"Archer convinced my father to pay back the debt."

"How much money did he come back with?"

"Um, five thousand dollars plus another fifteen hundred dollars in interest."

"Wasn't Mr. Archer paid as well?"

"Yes. My father also paid him an additional three hundred dollars as his commission."

These large sums caused whistles and musings

from those gathered until the raps of the judge's gavel ended the distraction.

"So just to be clear, this three hundred dollars paid by your father was in addition to the amounts promised to Mr. Archer by Mr. Pittleman?"

"Yes."

"Do debtors ordinarily pay the men collecting their debts?"

"Well, I thought it was strange. But it happened."

"But you don't know that it did, Miss Tuttle. You only had Mr. Archer's word for it that your father paid him the three hundred dollars. Isn't that correct?"

"But why would he lie about that?"

Brooks glanced at the jury. "Oh, I think most people could think of a few reasons."

He refocused on Jackie. "Now, your father was murdered the very same day that Mr. Archer went out there, correct?"

"Well, yes, but—"

"Wasn't his safe also emptied?" asked Brooks, interrupting.

"His safe?"

"Yes. His safe was cleaned out. Can you tell us what was in it?"

"No. The last time I was there, the safe had nothing in it."

"But what did Mr. Archer *tell* you was in the safe?"

Jackie glanced at Archer, but he looked down at his hands.

She looked back at Brooks, who was waiting patiently for her answer.

"Miss Tuttle?" he prompted. "Didn't Mr. Archer tell you what was in the safe?"

She nodded but said nothing.

"Can you share what you know with the court?" he said pleasantly but firmly.

She sighed and said, "He told me that it was full of cash, stock and bond certificates, and even gold bars."

"And where did this wealth come from?"

"He said that my father had told him that the reports of oil on his land had come back favorably, and that was where the money had come from, with more to follow once they commenced drilling."

"And you weren't aware of this until he told you?"

"That was the first that I had heard of it. I had been gone from home for a year."

The crowd once more verbally fussed over all this until the judge's gavel smacked down again.

"And then?" prompted Brooks.

"And then I went out to my father's house with Mr. Irving Shaw, the detective on the case. He had the safe opened, but it was empty."

"What else did Mr. Shaw tell you? About your car specifically and traces of things inside it?"

Brooks had now moved so that Jackie's sight line to Archer was blocked. "Mr. Shaw said that the trunk of my car had residue of gold dust and the imprint on the carpet of the gold bars."

Brooks said to the jury, "Although unfortunately Lieutenant Shaw is still in the hospital and cannot be here to testify, we have photographs and other evidence of all this, which will be entered into evidence." He turned back to Jackie. "Again, to be clear, you had given Mr. Archer permission to use your car that day to drive out to your father's home to meet with him?"

"Yes, that's right."

"So to clarify for the jury, Mr. Archer went to see your father, collected the debt, and your father ended up dead that very same day. Then his safe was emptied and the wealth from the safe was placed in the car that Mr. Archer was driving." He paused. "That is correct, isn't it?"

"That is correct," she said quietly.

Brooks glanced over at the jury. He smiled because every single one of them was nodding and, Brooks could tell, connecting the dots. "And even though we never found the murder weapon, a gun can easily be disposed of. And a former soldier like Mr. Archer would no doubt know how to do so."

Archer didn't bother objecting to this or looking at the twelve men who would decide his fate; he kept his gaze on Jackie.

Brooks continued. "And the, let's call it, *treasure* that Mr. Archer told you that he had seen in the safe? That meant that it must've been opened by your father while he was there?"

"Yes."

"And, again, just to clarify, all this treasure was then loaded into the trunk of your car? The car that Mr. Archer had been driving that very day?"

"Yes."

"Gold bars are very heavy. Would you say a man like Mr. Archer was strong enough to carry them out to the car?"

"Yes," she said resignedly.

"And the contents of the safe are nowhere to be found today?"

"Nowhere to be found," she repeated, keeping her eye on the lawyer.

"Now, as to your friend, Mr. Hank Pittleman?"

"Yes?"

"Did there come a time when Mr. Archer helped carry Mr. Pittleman to his room at the Derby Hotel, a room that was virtually contiguous with Mr. Archer's?"

"That is correct."

"Tell us about that."

"Hank and I were at the Cat's Meow. Hank had too much to drink, as he often did. I was helping him out of the bar when suddenly Mr. Archer turned up."

"Suddenly? You had not expected to see him there?"

Jackie looked confused. "No."

"Go on."

"Then he volunteered to help me get Hank to the hotel. He actually carried him into his room and put him on the bed. That's how I knew Mr. Archer was strong."

"What happened after that?"

"We left and went to Mr. Archer's room, where we had a drink."

"And that was all?"

Jackie flicked a quick glance in Archer's direction. "We might have fooled around a bit. After that I left and went home. It was the next day that I found out Hank had been killed." She took a handkerchief from her purse and dabbed at her eyes. "Poor Hank."

Archer eyed Marjorie Pittleman, who sat in the front row looking just like a pillar of the community except for the fact that she was shooting venomous tipped daggers at the younger woman.

"What did Mr. Shaw tell you about fingerprints on the doorknob to Mr. Pittleman's room?"

Jackie slowly removed the hanky from her face. "He told me that Mr. Archer's fingerprints had been found on the doorknob of Hank's room."

"Did that surprise you?"

She didn't respond.

"Miss Tuttle, I know that you were, well, friends with Mr. Archer, but you took an oath to tell the whole truth. Please do so."

She sat up straighter, her features firmed up, and she placed her hands on the front rail of the witness box. "Look, the thing is, when we went into the room, *I* opened the door because Mr. Archer was carrying Hank. And I closed the door after us when we left the room."

"So you're saying that Mr. Archer's fingerprints having been found on the doorknob could only have occurred if he had gone back later and entered the room?"

"Yes, and he later conceded to me that he'd done so."

"So he went back into the room later. When was that?"

"He said it was after Hank was dead."

"*He* said it was *after* Mr. Pittleman was dead?"

"Well, yes."

"Could anyone corroborate that?"

"Um, no."

Brooks again eyed the jury. "Indeed, Mr. Shaw could not as well. The facts will show that taking into account the time of Mr. Pittleman's death, the accused would have had ample time to kill him, as his room was only a short distance away. His prints were found on the doorknob, for which he has no explanation, and he had a motive to kill the deceased, because of money owed." Brooks glanced questioningly back at her. "And perhaps there was another motive for him to murder Mr. Pittleman."

"I don't know what you mean," she said.

"Oh, come, come, Miss Tuttle. Isn't it a fact that Mr. Archer was sweet on you? He's a good-looking man around your age. And you just testified that you and he went back to his hotel room and, well, to use your words, 'fooled around'?"

The courtroom chatter went up several notches after that until the judge beat it back down with his gavel.

"Well, yes we did. But—"

"So presumably Mr. Archer could have seen Mr. Pittleman as a rival for your affections."

"I don't think Mr. Archer thought that at all."

"Really?" said Brooks, once more gazing at the jury, this time with an incredulous look that was mirrored by the majority of the men there.

He turned back to her. "What else can you tell us about Mr. Pittleman's death? Specifically about the papers representing the debt of your father to Mr. Pittleman? Please be as precise as you can. And keep in mind that we have your earlier statements to Detective Shaw on this subject."

This time Jackie did not glance in Archer's direction. Her gaze downcast, she said, "Mr. Archer told me that he had taken the papers representing my father's debt from Hank's pocket while he was lying there dead. And he said he gave these papers to my father when the debt was paid."

"And the sixty-five hundred dollars your father gave to Mr. Archer in repayment of the debt? What happened to it?"

Jackie now glanced in Archer's direction. Brooks had shifted positions, allowing her to do so. Archer looked back stoically.

"I have no idea."

"Did he pay the money over to Mrs. Pittleman?"

"Not that I know of."

All eyes turned to Marjorie, who slowly shook her head.

"So Mr. Archer kept it then?" offered Brooks.

Archer, who had been feverishly turning the curled down pages of one of the law books, rose and said in a tremulous voice, "O-objection, um, spec-speculation on the witness's part, um, Your Honor."

"Overruled," snapped Judge Richmond. "Witness may answer the question."

"I don't know. He might have," she added, half-heartedly.

Brooks said smoothly, "So to sum up your testimony and those who have come before you, Mr. Archer was the only person who was with both men at around the times they died. And he gained a great deal of money by their deaths. Isn't that right?" When she didn't answer, he added, "Miss Tuttle?"

"Yes, I guess that's right," she replied, her features frustrated.

"And did Mr. Archer tell you that he had killed plenty of men during the war?"

"What?"

"You mentioned to Detective Shaw that you

had spoken to Archer about his military service."

"That's right."

"Did he tell you that he had killed during the war? With a gun, a knife, his bare hands even?"

"I suppose most of the men who fought did that." She glanced at Archer. "I mean, that was sort of the point of them being over there, right?"

There were a few guffaws from the crowd at her response, and Archer noted that a few of the jurors were nodding and looking almost sympathetic now.

Brooks also seemed to have noted this. "But that also means he knows how to kill someone with a knife and a gun, correct?"

To this Jackie said nothing, and Brooks did not persist.

"Nothing further, Your Honor," said Brooks, who retreated to his table.

"Mr. Archer, would you care to cross-examine this very informative witness?" said Richmond tauntingly, holding up his gavel like a broadsword ready to strike.

"I would," said Archer, who had once more been consulting a few pages in one of the books.

He closed his eyes and took three deep breaths because he was once more going into battle. And just as he had known as a scout, one mistake here and he was a goner.

This is it, Archer. For all the marbles.

He rose, picked up a piece of paper with scribblings on it, and walked toward the witness box and the woman sitting there.

CHAPTER

49

ARCHER CAME TO STAND directly in front of
Jackie, who looked back at him impassively.

"Where have you been all this time, Miss Tuttle? You just disappeared right after your father
was killed, and no one's seen hide nor hair of
you till now."

"I had nothing left in Poca City. Hank was
dead. And my father, too. I went to stay with
some friends, so I could think things over about
what to do going forward."

"So why in the world did you come back
here then?"

"I...I heard what was happening here, and
that my presence was required. So I came back.
To do my civic duty."

"Okay, can you tell us what your real relations with Mr. Hank Pittleman were?"

Brooks shot to his feet. "Objection! Relevancy?"

"Goes to motive, Judge," said Archer sharply, as he gazed at the paper in his hand. This comment drew an astonished look from Brooks.

"How so?" asked Richmond incredulously.

Archer glanced at his paper with the notes on it and then approached the jury.

"Well, the standard for guilt in a criminal case, my law books say, is beyond a reasonable doubt. So it makes sense that if I can show that others had a motive to kill Hank Pittleman, that creates doubt and helps my case, doesn't it? Consequently, for a man in danger of swinging from a hangman's rope, I'd say that's about as *relevant* as you can get." Archer turned to look at Richmond. "You agree, Judge?"

Richmond glanced at Brooks, who shrugged and sat back down.

"Okay, go ahead then, but I'll be watching you sharp," admonished the judge.

Archer walked back over to Jackie. "Your relations with the man?"

"He was a good friend."

"And he gave you a house to live in, a car to drive? Cash money in your pocket?"

"He was a very generous…father figure."

"A father figure? Okay, did you go to bed with him?"

The courtroom exploded in muttered discussions over that one, until Richmond restored order by bangs of his gavel. "Don't be disgusting, Mr. Archer," roared the judge, but Jackie put up her hand.

"It's all right, Your Honor, I'll answer." She had kept her gaze on Archer this whole time. "I did what Hank asked me to do, so long as it was something a lady could reasonably commit to doing."

"Now, was Marjorie Pittleman okay with this relationship?"

"I don't know. Hank never said."

"You've been to their home? You know her?"

"Yes."

"How would you say your relations are with Mrs. Pittleman?"

Jackie glanced over at the older woman, who was making no effort to hide her true feelings for the witness. "Right this minute? I'd say mine are nonexistent and hers are homicidal."

Marjorie looked around at everyone watching her and quickly attempted a weak smile that lapsed into a well-practiced placid expression.

"You may well be right about that, since

Mrs. Pittleman suggested to me that you were quite cunning and had perhaps killed your own mother and father."

Now *Jackie* looked at Marjorie with a homicidal expression.

"Stop badgering the witness, mister, right now," ordered Richmond.

Archer put his hands on the witness box rail. "Do you recall that Mr. Shaw and I saved your life when a man named Dickie Dill and another fellow named Malcolm Draper attempted to murder you in your bedroom?"

"Yes, of course I do. You were both very brave and nearly died helping me." Jackie's features softened. "I would be dead but for what you did."

Archer's features also relaxed. "Well, I have to say the same about you. Without your well-placed lamp against Dickie Dill's head, I don't think I'd be here today."

The two shared a meaningful look before Archer said, "Now, did your father employ Malcolm Draper at some point in time?"

She looked confused. "Mr. Draper? No, he worked for Hank."

From his jacket pocket Archer took the photo of the two men.

"Can you identify the men in this picture?"

"Objection," said Brooks. "I've never seen that photo."

Archer walked it over to him and held up the photo. "You recognize these two men?"

Brooks looked mightily confused but nodded.

"Then can I show Miss Tuttle?"

Brooks glanced at the judge, curtly nodded, and sat down.

"Go ahead, Archer," said the judge.

Archer walked back to the witness box and showed the picture to Jackie.

"It's my father...and Malcolm Draper." She blanched and gazed up at Archer. "I don't understand."

Archer took the photo back. "Let me see if I can clear it up for you. Malcolm Draper went to work for Hank Pittleman right about the time that your father took out the loan from him, correct?"

"Yes, I believe that's what Hank told me. He thought he was a good man."

"But what if Draper was actually working for your father while he was also employed by Hank Pittleman?"

"But why would that be the case?"

"Your father told me that he wanted to take the loan out from Pittleman's bank, but the man refused him."

Brooks jumped to his feet. "Objection. Your Honor, the defendant is testifying without the benefit of being under oath."

"Sustained," barked the judge.

"Okay," said Archer. "Let me put it this way then. Based on what you know of the two men, would it strike you as possible that Mr. Pittleman wanted the loan to be a personal debt, so he could charge more interest and because he liked your father owing him directly?"

"That sounds like Hank, actually. But it still doesn't explain why Draper would be working for my father while also working for Hank."

"Did you know that Mr. Draper would go out to the slaughterhouse most nights?"

Richmond said, "Hey now, we're getting far afield here."

"I'm gonna bring it back around, Judge, I swear," said Archer. "And Mr. Shaw had that in his notes."

"Well, hurry it on up, then."

"No, I didn't know," said Jackie.

"I worked out there butchering hogs. And on payday they could only make half wages. Now, I wondered about that because it looked like the hog business was doing fine. But what if Mr. Draper was going out there to cook the books, so to speak? And maybe he was doing that to Pittleman's other businesses, too."

Archer saw Brooks jump to his feet to object, but forestalled this by saying, "That was actually Mr. Shaw's idea. It's in his notebook where he wrote everything down. And Mr. Brooks said those notes are part of the official record, so I can use what's in there as part of *my* defense, just like he's been doing this whole time to make the jury believe I'm guilty."

All eyes went to a helpless-looking Brooks.

"Well, Mr. Brooks?" said the judge, who was regarding Archer in a somewhat more favorable light.

Brooks said, "That is … correct. And … I waive any objection I might have made."

Archer continued his questioning. "And Mr. Shaw found a mess of unpaid bills that he thought Draper had tossed in the trash so Mr. Pittleman wouldn't see them."

"And you think my father had him do this? Why?"

"Well, let's look at your father for a minute. He'd had bad farming years due to the drought. But Mr. Pittleman, he had water on his property and had the cash to truck in more if needed. I think maybe that didn't sit well with Lucas Tuttle. And then he has to borrow money from the man. That must've stung his pride. And then, what does Hank Pittleman do? He starts using you as his—what did you call yourself again?"

Jackie looked down and said something.

"I couldn't quite get that, Miss Tuttle."

"I was his *chattel*," she said sharply.

"That's right. Like his property. Must've made your old man mighty upset. And then, someone goes into Hank Pittleman's hotel room and cuts his throat."

"So who do *you* think killed Hank, Mr. Archer?" she asked.

"Maybe the same pair who tried to kill you—Dickie Dill and Malcolm Draper."

Brooks shot to his feet. "Your Honor, really! He's doing it again."

Archer grinned and said, "Well, hell, I was just answering the lady's question."

Archer and Jackie once more shared a look and exchanged tiny smiles as folks in the courtroom laughed over his remark.

Richmond said to the jury, "You are hereby instructed to not listen to any of what the defendant has just said. There's not an ounce of proof in any of it."

Archer turned to the jury and said, "You folks remember reasonable doubt? I just need to let you good people see that others had a reason to kill Hank Pittleman, not just me, and Lucas Tuttle had a damn good reason. A lot more than me."

He turned back to find Jackie's gaze upon him. Archer leaned against the witness box, folded his arms over his chest, and said, "You moved out of your father's house. Why?"

"I wanted to make my own way in the world."

"Your father approved of this?"

"I don't know if he did or not."

"But he wanted you back home, didn't he?"

"Yes, but so what? I wasn't going back. I told *you* that."

"Your mother died in an accident out at the farm right before you left home, correct?"

Jackie looked startled by this abrupt segue. "Y-yes."

"Can you describe what happened?"

Brooks got to his feet. "Judge, what does this have to do with anything?"

"Good question," said Richmond. "You care to answer that, Mr. Archer?"

"I've got a theory of the case, Judge, and this one goes to motive on both the murders I'm accused of."

Richmond looked at Brooks, who finally shrugged.

"Okay, proceed."

"Your mother's death?"

"She fell out of the hay bale in the barn and was impaled on a corn picker that was down below."

"How do you get impaled on a corn picker?"

"One of the cones was pointing upward. The ends are very sharp, almost like the point of an arrow. That's what she fell on."

"Do you know how to raise the cone on that machine?"

"No. I've never had a reason to do it."

"Well, I do—and before anybody objects to me testifying again, I got Mr. Bobby Kent sitting over there who will back up everything I have to say on the matter."

Kent, who was sitting in the second row and dressed in an old suit, shyly waved his hand and nodded.

Brooks looked put out by this, but the judge finally nodded. "Go ahead, Mr. Archer."

"While I was preparing for the trial I talked to Bobby Kent, and he told me the corn picker there now is the same one your mother fell on. There's a little turn handle. Now, as you already testified to, I'm pretty strong, but it took a lot of my strength to turn that thing and point that cone upward. Kent said it's always been that way."

"So what are you getting at?" asked Jackie.

"Would it surprise you to learn that your father tried to suggest to me that you murdered your mother?"

The court broke into pandemonium over this until Richmond shattered a gavel bringing back order. He pointed the broken gavel at Archer and said, "You better get to your dang point, but fast, son."

Here, Archer turned and looked over at Brooks. "A woman couldn't have turned that handle to make the cone point upward. It would take a fairly strong man. So I think your father killed your mother by pushing her out of the hay barn and onto that corn picker, which he had set just underneath, because why else would it have been there with one of the cones pointing up?"

While Archer and Brooks exchanged a long, probing look, the whole courtroom went into such an uproar over this that it took a full minute for Richmond this time to restore order, using his fist against the wood of the bench and his high-pitched voice as he searched through the drawers of his bench for a fresh gavel.

The judge barked, "We are not interested in what you *think*, Mr. Archer. Is there a question in there somewhere for the witness?"

"Yes, Judge, and here it is." He looked at Jackie. "Did you see your father kill your mother?"

The courtroom went quiet. Even Richmond seemed mesmerized, waiting for her to answer.

Archer and Jackie were locked in a stare-down. When it seemed apparent that Archer was not backing down, Jackie said quite firmly, "Yes. I saw him do it."

"But you never told anyone?"

"No."

"Why?"

Jackie dabbed at her eyes, and this time Archer could see that these were real tears.

"Because he told me if I did, that no one would believe my word over his and that he would then make me pay a tremendous price."

"He threatened to harm you?"

"He told me he would blow my head off with his shotgun."

Surprisingly, the courtroom remained quiet at this. Brooks and Judge Richmond were watching all this openmouthed, along with everyone else.

"Why would he want to kill his own wife?" asked Archer.

"I...I don't know."

"I think I might be able to help with that." Archer went back to the table, picked up his hat and took the letter out of the liner. He held it up to Brooks. "I'm going to get her to identify this and then you can take a look." He didn't wait for Brooks to respond. He walked back to the witness stand.

He held the letter out. "You know your mother's handwriting?"

"Of course I do."

"I found this letter in the back of the picture frame that held the photo I showed you." He held it up for her to see. "Is that Isabel Tuttle's handwriting?"

Jackie stared at the letter for a few seconds and then nodded. "Yes, it is."

Archer took the letter over to Brooks and let him read it. He looked shaken and handed the letter back to Archer.

"You okay with me asking her about this, Mr. Brooks?"

Brooks seemed to waver for a moment but said, "Go ahead, Archer. I...I think this needs to come out."

"Thanks."

He returned with it to the witness stand.

"Do you want to read this letter for the jury?" asked Archer.

"No, I do not."

"Okay, but to sum up what it says, your

mother was going to divorce your father, leave, and take you with her. She was doing this because he had physically and mentally abused you and your mother for many years, and she was not going to allow him to do that anymore. And here're the last lines of her letter." Archer held it up and read, "'And, Lucas, if anything happens to me, you will have done it because you've threatened to kill me so many times, I've lost count. But if you end up killing me before I can leave with Jackie, rest assured that my beautiful daughter will know what really happened, and she will be free of you at last. May you rot in hell, you sick bastard.'"

Archer lowered the letter and then left it on the rail of the witness box. He stood there in silence while Jackie tried to compose herself.

Archer waited patiently while she did so. When her tears began to flow more freely, he handed her his handkerchief. She used it to dry her eyes. When she gave it back, he gripped her hand for a moment. She looked up at him, her eyes wide and probing.

A few seconds later Archer said slowly, "So your father never showed up the night he was murdered to meet at your house as was arranged?"

She glanced up at him and held his gaze. "Not while I was there, no."

"That makes sense, since he later ended up dead at his place. But you *did* go out that night, didn't you? When he didn't show up?"

"How do—"

"It was the mud on your Nash. That meant it was driven during that hard rain." Archer glanced at the judge. "Mr. Shaw took photos of it and wrote notes about it, so it's included in the record." He turned back to Jackie. "You went over to the Pittlemans', didn't you? Around eleven or so?"

Jackie looked hesitant and glanced around the room. "I—" Here, she faltered.

But right away Archer said, "You went over there to have it out with Mrs. Pittleman, about her husband, about a lot of things. Only you couldn't see her. Isn't that right? You two didn't meet?" When she didn't answer, he leaned in closer, held her gaze. "Isn't that right? You two *didn't* meet? All you need to tell us is the truth about that, Jackie. *Just* that."

One of her hands was clenched on the box's rail. Archer put his hand over hers and gently squeezed it. Her guarded and suspicious look fell away as their gazes comingled. "Yes, that's right. I went over there, it's true. But I didn't see her that night. And that *is* the truth."

He removed his hand and looked at Richmond. "No more questions, Judge. And I'd like to thank Miss Tuttle for coming back here and telling us the real deal."

With a questioning look, Jackie got up from the witness stand. Archer put out a hand to assist her. As their flesh touched, more was communicated between them than a physical helping hand.

Jackie walked down the aisle with her head held high, and perhaps a lightness in her heart that had not been there for a long time.

CHAPTER

50

Brooks presented physical evidence of the two men's deaths, elicited the testimony of some police officials, and methodically questioned several other witnesses with knowledge of the affairs.

Then he called Marjorie Pittleman to the stand.

She took her time getting there and then settled in, her gloved hands placed primly on her broad lap and her wide-brimmed, old-fashioned hat with a bird attached set at an angle on her head.

"Mrs. Pittleman, you are the deceased's widow?"

"I am."

"And you are aware that your husband hired

the defendant to collect a debt from Mr. Lucas Tuttle?"

"I am."

"Was your husband happy about the defendant's work?"

"Not at all. He was most displeased. I could see that Mr. Archer was very worried that Hank would do something to him if he couldn't get that car from Lucas Tuttle."

"Did Mr. Archer visit you on other occasions?"

"Yes, once with Miss Tuttle and twice with that detective fellow, Shaw."

"Do you think Mr. Archer had a problem with your husband and Miss Tuttle's relationship?"

Archer stood. "Objection, that calls for speculation."

The judge looked at him severely. "Considering you been up here basically testifying without once putting your hand on the Bible, you can just sit down and keep quiet." He smacked his gavel and nodded at the witness. "You go right ahead, Marjorie."

The woman smiled and said, "I think Mr. Archer was very fond of Jackie Tuttle. I mean, what young man wouldn't be? You heard that they were *fooling around* in his hotel room right before my poor Hank was murdered. We all know what that means. And I've heard tell he's been to her house early in the morning and maybe sleeping over there for all I know." She shook her head and looked repulsed by the thought.

"Perhaps the only thing that stood in the way of Mr. Archer being with Miss Tuttle was your husband?"

Marjorie took out a hanky and blew her nose. "So I believe." She glared at Archer. "But if I were her, I would watch myself. He was flirting with my maid right in front of me."

"My, my," said Brooks, looking appalled. "Anything else?"

"I can tell you that Hank came into my room one night and told me that if anything happened to him, to tell the police to look at Mr. Archer. He said he was one dangerous man. He took a gun out when Mr. Archer came over by himself the first time because he told me he was afraid for his life. You all heard that Mr. Archer had done a lot of killing overseas. And the police told me that he'd just gotten out of prison in Tartupa." She shivered a bit. "I can't believe I had that man in my house."

"I think you were quite fortunate, Miss Pittleman. No further questions."

Brooks retreated to his table, and Marjorie started to get up.

"Hold on there, Mrs. Pittleman," said Archer, coming forward. "Now I get to ask my questions of you."

Marjorie looked up at the judge in a bewildered fashion.

Richmond nodded solemnly and said apologetically, "I'm afraid he's right." He glared at Archer. "For once."

Archer walked up to the witness box as she sat back down, looking very irritated. "So you think your husband was scared of me?"

"I do."

"Is that why he had that nickel-plated Smith and Wesson belly gun with the hair trigger on the table when I came in?"

"Yes!"

"You know where that gun is now?"

Marjorie, who had looked like she was falling asleep, appeared startled. "The gun?"

"Yeah, where is it?"

"I...I don't know."

"Why is that important?" Brooks protested.

"We can come back to that," said Archer. "Now, you knew your husband was dying of cancer, right?"

"As I told you, I didn't believe that."

This brought more gasps from the crowd, but Archer plowed on. "And that he was a gambler who owed two hundred thousand dollars to the boys in Las Vegas?"

More gasps.

"Yes."

"And that you and your husband tried to defraud the insurance company by taking out a half-million-dollar policy, even though you both knew he was dying?"

"That has nothing to do with why we're here," she retorted. "And I didn't defraud anyone, young man!"

"And that your husband's business bills were being unpaid and that he owed a ton of money to vendors and creditors. You knew that?"

"Only because that detective told me so," she snapped. "For all I know it was a load of hooey."

"So maybe your husband wasn't as rich as he made himself out to be. And then neither will you be."

"I think I'll be fine."

"Is that right? Why's that?"

She looked imperiously at him. "I may be a woman, Mr. Archer, but I do have a head for business, though Hank didn't think so."

Archer reached into his jacket pocket and pulled out the sheaf of papers he'd found in the crate at the trucking warehouse. "Speaking of business, would you identify this for the court?"

Brooks shot to his feet. "I have not seen this document, Your Honor."

"Oh, you will, Mr. Brooks, I promise you that," said Archer.

Brooks slowly sat back down as the judge eyed Archer. "Go on ahead, but this is pretty unorthodox, son."

"Well, not being a lawyer and all, I'm doing the best I can, Judge."

Archer gave the papers to Marjorie. She looked down at the document like it was a load of dung heaped in her hands.

"Where did you get that?" she snarled.

"That's not important. What is important is that this is a contract between you and Lucas Tuttle. It has both your names and signatures on the last page." Archer turned to the page and held it up for her to see. "Now, do you want to tell the court what's in here or do you want me to do it?"

She shook her head and remained silent.

"Okay, not to beat about the bush, you agreed to sell all of your husband's businesses and assets to Lucas Tuttle for a half-million dollars, but you get to keep your big house and a bit of the land around it."

The crowd started murmuring at this and the judge did nothing to quell it. He was too busy listening to this exchange.

Marjorie said, "So what? I had every right to do so."

"But on page six, paragraph H, it says that the purchase price can be reduced by any unpaid debts owed by your husband to others, personal or otherwise. Even if Mr. Tuttle didn't have to pay these debts." He paused. "I don't know much about contracts and such, but that sounds unusual. Did it to you?"

"I...I..."

"I'll take that as a no. Did you even have a lawyer look at this thing?"

When she didn't answer, he said, "I'll take that as another no. Now, when you signed this agreement, you didn't know that your husband had all these debts, did you? Because Mr. Shaw only told you *after* you signed the agreement with Mr. Tuttle. Because I saw him coming out of your house with these papers before we went in to see you."

Marjorie merely stared stonily at him.

"Now, I'll take that as a yes. Mr. Shaw had all the numbers down very accurately. So when I add up what your husband owed in debts, including the gambling debts, I figure that you

were due basically *nothing* from Mr. Tuttle for
that vast empire that your husband built, while
you got stuck with all the bills." He paused and
added, "I'd say Mr. Tuttle played you for the
biggest sucker in the world."

He looked at her sitting there, seething in the
witness chair.

When he glanced up at Richmond and then
over at Brooks, both men were staring openmouthed at the woman.

"When Mr. Shaw and I came to see you and
tell you about the debts, you got upset about the
gambling, but not *too* upset. But when he told
you about the unpaid business bills that were
much larger, then I could see you were truly
bowled over. And you glanced at the door. The
same door Lucas Tuttle had probably walked
out of not that long ago. See, I think you already
knew about the gambling debts, but you had no
idea about all the other money he owed. Now,
since you didn't understand that part of the
contract I just read out, you thought with the
half-million bucks from Tuttle you could pay
off the Vegas boys and live happily ever after
in your big house. But you couldn't do that
with the other debts, they were far too high,
even if Mr. Tuttle paid you the full half-million.
And then when Mr. Shaw told you about the

insurance policy, you got really agitated and said you would fight it. Like you testified here, you just flat out said you didn't believe the doctor and that would somehow make it okay for the insurance company to shell out all that dough to you. I think you were desperate at that point and were looking for anything to hang your hat on, even playing the poor old widow role and hoping that would be enough to shame the insurance company into giving you something. And you did that because it suddenly occurred to you that you *needed* that insurance money. And then you put the idea into Mr. Shaw's head that maybe it was the Vegas boys who had killed your husband. It was a real good performance. I mean, you shoulda gone into the pictures, ma'am. But in the end, it didn't fool me. I don't go to the pictures much, but I do read a lot of detective novels."

Archer walked over and handed the contract to Brooks before returning to the witness box. "But that's just money. That's really not why we're here. Now, when I went over to your house one time, that Manuel fellow who works for you told me something." Archer pointed to the back of the courtroom where Manuel sat looking nervous. "I spoke with Manuel in preparing for my trial and, if need be, he'll testify.

Now, he said that Jackie Tuttle came to your house on the night Lucas Tuttle died, just as Miss Tuttle testified that she did."

"So what?" Marjorie said sharply.

"Only he said she *couldn't* meet with you. And in fact Miss Tuttle also testified that no meeting took place that night between you two."

Marjorie looked blankly at him. "Again, so?"

"*Couldn't.* That's the word Manuel used. I wondered why. Even if you were asleep, they could always wake you up. The only way you *couldn't* meet with Jackie Tuttle is if you weren't there. And if you weren't there, I wonder where you and that big Cadillac Coupe de Ville were on the night Lucas Tuttle died. Care to tell us?"

Marjorie looked exceedingly put out by all of this. "I have no idea what you're talking about. This whole thing is ridiculous. I'm saying nothing more. Nothing more, you…you vile, disgusting *criminal*! I hope when they hang you, it takes you a long time to die!"

Archer turned to Richmond. "Your Honor, I got one more witness to call."

"Does that mean you're finished with Mrs. Pittleman?"

"Oh, no, she can sit right there."

"But where will your next witness sit?"

Archer slapped the rail of the witness box. "Right here."

Brooks rose. "And who is this witness?"

"That would be Mr. Lucas Tuttle," said Archer.

A gasp went up from the courtroom and was immediately followed by the collective murmurings of speculative and excited conversation.

"Excuse me?" bellowed Brooks, even as Richmond slammed down his fresh gavel repeatedly to quiet the crowd.

Brooks exclaimed, "The man is dead, Mr. Archer. Unless you plan on holding some type of séance."

"No, sir. But just because a man's dead doesn't mean he can't be heard. You just have to have the right equipment."

Archer turned and motioned to a uniformed sheriff sitting near the courtroom door. He rose and came forward carrying something.

It was the wooden case with the Dictaphone. He set it on the table in front of Archer.

"What is that?" demanded the judge.

"Mr. Tuttle's recording machine," answered Archer. "From his office. It's called a Dictaphone."

"How do we know it belonged to Mr. Tuttle?" demanded Brooks.

"You know what Mr. Tuttle's voice sounds like?" asked Archer.

"Yes, of course. I knew him well."

"Well, proof's in the pudding. So can I go ahead? See, I'm just trying to get to the truth, which I think is the whole point of why we're here."

Richmond looked at Brooks, who again resignedly shrugged, but who also looked awfully curious about what Archer was planning to do.

"All right," said the judge grudgingly. "But fair warning. If anything on there is out of bounds, you are good as gone from my courtroom."

Archer carried the case up to the witness box, took the Dictaphone out, and placed it on the rail of the box while Marjorie sat there and stared fiercely at him. Then he plugged the machine in using an outlet on the floor next to the bench. He rewound the tape to a certain spot and turned to the courtroom.

"What you're about to hear will clear up not one, not two, but *three* murders."

He hit the button, and the first sound that could be heard was the squeak of a door opening. It was almost like listening to a radio show. Everyone in the courtroom, young and old, leaned forward to hear.

Lucas Tuttle said, "What the hell are *you* doing here?"

The next voice to be heard seemed to suck all the air out of the large room.

Marjorie Pittleman bellowed, "You cheated me, you son of a bitch!"

"I cheated you?" screamed Tuttle. "Look at that! My safe is empty. Someone stole everything in it."

"I don't care about that. Malcolm Draper was working for you! He drained Hank's businesses."

Tuttle laughed. "That brain tumor must have dulled old Hank's senses. It was easy as taking candy from a baby. Not just failing to pay bills but making some singularly bad business decisions that proved costly for him. Very costly. But he was too far gone to see it. He just drank his whiskey and had *my* daughter on his grubby arm."

She shrieked, "You took all the money and left unpaid bills for me. I had a lawyer look at that contract after I signed it. He told me because of all the debts, you're getting Hank's businesses for nothing!"

"Well, then we're even because he took my Jackie from me. And he made me take out a loan *personally* so he could rub my face in it. Well, look who won: I did."

"Your daughter is a slut, and everyone knows it. She waltzes in and becomes my husband's concubine! That's why I—"

"That's why you what?" demanded Tuttle in a mocking tone.

"After I learned about Hank's debts, I confronted Draper. I had figured out what was going on, you see. That detective told me about the bills not being paid. I told Draper he had to kill her or else I was going to the law. But he couldn't even manage to do that! The idiot!"

There was a moment of silence until Tuttle said, "Well, part of me is sad they didn't kill her. But now that I got the slaughterhouse, I'll do to her what I had my boys do to Sid Duckett. Did you know he tried to blackmail me when he found out Draper was working for me? Well, it cost him, all right. Hogs had a nice dinner on him," he added gleefully.

"You cheated me! The contract I signed is worthless! Where is it? I want you to tear it up. I'm not selling."

"Too late for that, Marjorie. And you should have read the fine print, it was all right there. But then again, you wouldn't think to do that, only being a woman."

"You bastard!"

"You should be thanking me. I got rid of your

husband for you, didn't I? If Hank's gambling had kept up, those Vegas boys would have come and taken your house and more. That's why you begged me to have him killed, wasn't it, so you could sell out? Even though he was already dying? Because a dying man can still gamble, but a dead one can't." He grew quiet for a moment. "Only you didn't know about all his other debts. That equaled a lot more than two hundred thousand dollars." He paused. "But I'm a fair man. You get to keep the house."

"But I can't afford to live there!" she wailed. "And I have no money to pay the debts!"

"Then sell it. I'll give you a couple of bucks for that monstrosity. But in the future, Marjorie, try to remember that size does not equal good taste."

On the tape, Marjorie didn't respond to this barb. The real Marjorie was sitting as motionless as the fox around her shoulders.

The room was so quiet that not only could one hear a pin drop, one could probably hear the air being propelled along by the pin as it fell.

Then the whole courtroom nearly jumped out of their seats at the next sound.

The single gunshot cut through the room like one had actually gone off in their midst. As though not only had someone cried out fire inside a crowded room, but there actually *was* an inferno. And then came the sound of a body falling to the floor.

When these sounds ceased, on the tape Marjorie said, "How's it feel, Lucas? Being killed by 'just' a woman?"

On this, Archer turned off the machine and looked at Marjorie. "Well?" he asked.

She was silent for a few moments.

When she spoke, the woman's voice was tranquil, even...happy.

"That's the most fun I've had in my whole life, killing that man."

Archer looked up at the judge and said, "I rest my case."

CHAPTER

51

ARCHER STOOD next to Irving Shaw's hospital bed. The detective was sitting up, looking far better than the last time Archer had seen him. Herbert Brooks, the district attorney, walked in and came over to the bed.

"They told me back in Poca City that you had driven over to see Lieutenant Shaw," said Brooks to Archer. He looked keenly at the detective. "And how is the patient?"

Shaw gingerly moved his damaged arm. "Not bad. Want a smoke bad, but they said no. They got oxygen around."

Brooks eyed Archer. "Now, a few things. I've spoken with the DOP and they have agreed that in light of, well, recent developments, you are deemed to have completed your three-year parole and may freely move about as you desire." He added, "I would imagine that you have no wish to remain in Poca City."

"I think it's time for me to head on."

Then he held out to Archer an envelope.

"What's that?" asked Archer.

"Two thousand dollars, from the city government. This was deemed to be fair compensation for all that you endured."

Archer didn't move to take the money until Shaw nudged him. "Go on, Archer. You earned it, son. You solved three murders on your own. You need to hang out your gumshoe shingle. Use the money as a stake to get started."

Archer reluctantly took the envelope. "I wouldn't have solved anything if it weren't for you, Mr. Shaw. You should get half of this."

"No can do. I'm a public servant. It's my job." Shaw looked over at Brooks. "Any word on Draper?"

"He passed away the other night. But he would've been hanged anyway. Marjorie Pittleman talked like a canary, though we heard most of it already on the recorder. Draper killed Pittleman on Lucas Tuttle's orders after he and Marjorie agreed on the sale of the businesses. And then they tried to frame Archer for it. And

Dill and Draper killed Sid Duckett, and they tried to kill Jackie Tuttle, at Marjorie's direct request." He shot Archer a glance. "And you were right. We found Hank Pittleman's Smith and Wesson in Marjorie's home. It was the gun she used to kill Tuttle."

"What'll happen to her?" asked Archer.

"I doubt the state has the stomach to hang a widow. But she'll die in prison."

"And that fancy house of hers?" asked Shaw.

Brooks shrugged. "Maybe someone can turn it into a hotel."

Archer looked at Shaw. "You called it, Mr. Shaw. You said early on that Marjorie was involved in her husband's death."

"Well, unfortunately, between husband and wife, it's usually one or the other doing the killing."

"Reason enough to stay single," said Archer.

Shaw said, "So Lucas Tuttle killed his wife and scared his daughter into keeping silent?"

Archer glanced at Brooks. "I guess a man's word is worth more than a woman's? You sorta told me that before."

Brooks said quietly, "I guess you could say that was the case, yes."

"There's nothing right or fair about that."

Shaw cleared his throat. "There's some more

information about Ernestine Crabtree's past, Archer. Thought you might want to hear it."

"What's that?"

"Those men *did* rape her." He added in a far more somber tone, "In fact, she could never have children after that because of her injuries."

There was an awkward silence until Brooks said, "I have to say the way you handled yourself in that courtroom was truly remarkable, Mr. Archer, particularly so for a person with no legal training."

"When a man's fighting for his life, what choice does he have except do what he has to so he can survive?"

Shaw said, "Amen. Every man who fought in the war damn sure knows that."

Archer eyed Brooks and said, "So you have no reason to go after Jackie, right? You're convinced that Lucas Tuttle killed his wife?"

Brooks nodded. "I *am* convinced, Mr. Archer. She has nothing to worry about from me. It was a terrible thing for her to endure. Even more so for a young woman. They are very delicate."

Archer's gaze at the man sharpened. "You married?"

Brooks looked surprised at the question. "Well, yes."

"You work, and your wife stays at home?"

"She has no head for matters outside of the home."

"You might be surprised about that, Mr. Brooks. I mean, I don't see much logic behind men being the breadwinners and all except it's just the way it's always been, and for no good reason. Everybody deserves a fair shake."

Brooks shook his head and smiled. "A woman's place is in raising children and keeping the home and assisting her husband. But it's still important work nonetheless and quite proper for someone with their fairer sensibilities. It's a hard world out there, Mr. Archer, and men are designed to thrive in that world, not our women. I mean, that's why they're referred to as the weaker sex, after all."

"Well, by the time I'm an old man, maybe the world will see things differently."

After Brooks left, Archer said to Shaw, "You taught me a lot."

"I can say the same about you. So what's next for Aloysius Archer?"

"Maybe a bit of wandering."

"Would that wandering take you to see a couple of gals far away from here?"

"Couple of gals?"

"Yeah."

Archer smiled. "I'm not sure. As you know, I'm sort of susceptible to the spell they can cast over me."

"Hell, boy, we all got that problem. Ain't enough reason to stay away, though, so I say go for it. Hey, you got a smoke, Archer?"

"I thought you said—"

"Come on, son, don't make me pull my gun." Archer shook out a Lucky and lit the man up.

Shaw gratefully blew the smoke out and looked up at Archer with a bemused expression. "I wonder what happened to all that money in Lucas Tuttle's safe?"

"Never could really figure that out. I thought maybe I knew, but I'm probably wrong." He paused. "You gonna dig into that?"

"Archer, I catch killers. I don't waste no time with people taking stuff from people who already got too much."

"That's good to know."

"Thought you'd see it that way."

Archer put out a hand for the lawman to shake.

"You let me know how you get on," said Shaw.

"You can count on that."

"Take care, *shamus*."

As Archer walked out, he met a woman and three teens—two young men and a girl—coming down the hall to Shaw's room. He figured he knew who they were and introduced himself to Shaw's family.

"He thinks the world of you, Mr. Archer," said Shaw's wife.

"It's mutual. Oh, and one more thing." He took out the envelope and counted out half the money in there. "The folks in Poca City took up a collection for Lieutenant Shaw." He handed her the money. "I wouldn't mention it to your husband. I know how proud he is. Maybe you can use it for the kids' education and such."

"Thank you so much, Mr. Archer."

Archer eyed the oldest boy. "Hear you're going into the Army?"

"Yes, sir."

"Good man. You stay safe and make your parents proud." He gave the young man a crisp salute and then headed on his way.

As Archer walked down the hall, the spring was fully back in his step.

CHAPTER

52

THE SEA VOYAGE was rough for much of the way because of gale-force winds clustered along the shipping channels. But it seemed the more hostile the ocean was, the more soundly Archer slept in his first-class berth. It was perhaps fitting that a man who had done his hardest fighting on land and even lost his freedom there could find peace in such chaotic waters.

He would venture out to the top deck from time to time to admire the vastness and calamitous pitch of the ocean, while most passengers and even some of the crew were below decks vomiting into buckets. For him, this trip symbolized many things. Yet chief among them was redemption. Not for him, though he could use a fair amount of it, he supposed. No, this journey was not about him. It was about others.

During the war, Archer had one chief goal: to survive. Wedded to that enterprise was his desire to survive with as many of his fellow soldiers as possible. In that spirit, one looked out for the other. Sometimes you risked your life to save another. Sometimes you succeeded and sometimes you didn't, and sometimes all died in the collective effort. But there was profound risk in not trying. Then what sort of a world would one have? Not to be too mushy about it, thought Archer, but thinking only of yourself as you trudged through life was a lonely journey indeed.

He finally reached Brazil and immediately made his way inland to São Paulo. To an address that he had taken off the crate in Hank Pittleman's warehouse and stuck in the Gideon Bible in his room at the Derby. It was a small house on a low rise of earth with expansive views just outside the city's main footprint. It was painted a deep eggplant and had yellow shutters. There were exotic flowers in terra cotta pots thriving in the warm air and hot sun, in a place where rain bursts were plentiful and welcome.

Archer had purchased a new wardrobe; his three-piece suit was beige and made out of lightweight summer cloth that was comfortable for where he was right now. He wore a Panama hat and brown lace-up leather shoes, and his face was tanned and weathered from the ocean trip.

Archer walked up the steps to the front door and knocked. He almost instantly heard approaching footsteps.

When the door opened, he had to look twice to recognize Jackie Tuttle. Her hair was dyed blond, for one thing, and cut short in a gamine style, the peekaboo all gone. And instead of the clingy and expensive dresses he was used to seeing her in, she had on a pair of faded coveralls, like those the factory women would wear during the war. Under that was a loose-fitting blue cotton shirt. No gloves, hat, jewelry, or makeup in sight. On her feet were a pair of clogs.

"You don't look surprised to see me," he said.

"That's because I'm not."

She stepped back to allow him passage.

He walked through and into a small front room.

It had three chairs and a small settee resting on threadbare carpet. In one of the chairs was Ernestine Crabtree, looking as physically modified as her companion. Again, he had to look twice to make sure that it was her. Her blond hair was styled in an urchin cut and partially covered by a plum-colored beret. She was also dressed as plainly as Jackie.

He sat down with his hat perched on his knee and looked around. "You like it here?"

"It's warm, sunny, and beautiful, and the people are friendly," said Jackie as she sat next to Ernestine. "And we've got some money to live on—the remains of the cash my father paid on the debt to Hank. But I'll have to get a job at some point." She paused and eyed Archer with a bemused look. "Maybe I can find a Hank Pittleman down here."

"How'd you come by this place?" asked Archer.

"This used to belong to my mother's family. It passed to me when she died. I used to travel here with her when I was younger. I can speak the language, which comes in handy. And I've been teaching Ernestine."

Archer nodded as he took this in and then looked at Ernestine. "I'm sorry for what happened to you back in Texas," said Archer.

She glanced sharply at him. "How did—"

"I...saw your scrapbook," he said. "And Mr. Shaw checked into some things."

Staring down at her lap, she said, "When

my father was arrested, he told me he would only go to jail for a few months. He had me and my mother move away and then he said he would come and join us." She halted here, the tears clustering in her eyes. Jackie put a supportive arm around her. "And then...and then...."

"I know, Ernestine," said Archer quietly.

She suddenly sat up straight and brushed away the tears. "I couldn't believe it. I was so furious with them both. I didn't care if my father told everyone what those men had done to me. I just wanted him to be with us. I...I didn't want him to die on my account. And I said things to my mother, things I regretted." She paused once more as her eyes filled with fresh tears. "And then she was gone, too."

After she composed herself, Archer looked around and said, "So where's the Royal type-writer?"

She glanced up and said quietly, "I...I have a little room in the back of the house."

"For your scribblings?"

"She's working on a novel, Archer," said Jackie. "I've read parts of it. It's really good."

"'A woman must have money and a room of her own if she is to write fiction,'" said Archer, quoting Virginia Woolf.

"Y-yes," said Ernestine. "So I believe, too."

"Maybe you can take everything you had to endure in life and put it on those pages, Ernestine. And I think you'll have a fine book. Because sometimes, you just have to be rid of it, and move on."

A few moments of silence passed.

And then Jackie took a letter from her pocket and held it up. "You wrote to me here and asked me to come back and testify."

"And if you did, I said everything would be okay, for both of you, and me. I gave you my word."

"But why was that so important? You had Marjorie Pittleman dead to rights with that recording. And my father, too. He confessed to killing Hank and Sid Duckett. You didn't need me to win your freedom."

"It wasn't about *my* freedom, Jackie. It was about yours."

He took out the onionskin carbon copy and handed it to her. "I found this curled up inside your father's Remington. I don't think this went through Desiree Lankford, or else she would have told you."

She read quickly through it and then looked up at him in shock. "My father was accusing me of killing my mother. He said he had evidence and he wanted Brooks to prosecute me for murder. He wanted to see me hang."

"That's about the size of it."

"Even after everything he did, he still wasn't done hurting me." She handed back the letter and said quietly, "I don't know why I'm surprised."

"You left home because of what he did," said Archer.

"I wanted to kill him. I wanted to throw him on that corn picker. But he just laughed at me. Said I was just a girl, no one would believe me."

"He tried to make out to me that you were the crazy, violent one."

She gazed at him with wide, probing eyes. "I guess with how I acted around you, you might have been justified in believing that."

"You wear your heart on your sleeve, Jackie. I could see that. Nothing devious there. Your father, on the other hand, he was way too manipulative. Way too slick. Those are the ones you have to watch out for."

"I guess your reading all those detective novels came in handy," interjected Ernestine.

Archer said, "I wanted to put you on the stand and show Brooks that you didn't kill your mother. I didn't want you to have to worry about that ever again. And now you don't. I confirmed that with him."

Jackie looked shaken by this news and said, "Thank you, Archer. That was very kind of you."

"But you didn't know that was my reason. I didn't put that in my letter to you."

"And so I didn't have to come back."

"But you did, Jackie. Why's that? It *was* risky for you. You had to trust me." He paused. "And for a few seconds in the courtroom, I'm not sure you did."

She looked away for a moment before focusing on him. "Remember I was asking you how it was in the war?"

He frowned. "You mean the killing part?"

"No, about being part of something bigger than yourself. Well, I guess that bigger something was you, Archer. I...I couldn't leave you to fight that battle alone. That's why I came back."

Ernestine leaned forward and said, "We had no idea you were going to be implicated in what happened. With the evidence from the safe in the Nash and all. I had already left town, and Jackie soon followed. But we never meant to hurt you, Archer, never."

"I believe you," he said simply.

Jackie said, "When I was on the witness stand, my trust in you *did* waver at one point."

"But?" said Archer.

"But in the end, I figured I had to count on a man at some point in my life. And it might as well be you. I think you earned that right."

He nodded and said, "I thank *you* for that."

A few moments of silence passed.

"Archer, how did you know I had seen my father kill my mother?"

"I didn't know for sure. But in prison I hung around a lot of guilty people, so I know what that looks like. But I was innocent, so I know what that looks like, too. You loved your mother and you butted heads with her, nothing wrong with that. But Lucas Tuttle tried to convince me you had killed her, while you wouldn't even talk about it, or got agitated when you did. And then you left home to be Pittleman's chattel. You never struck me as the type that would do that unless you had a really good reason. And that reason was you couldn't live with a man who had killed your mother, and you wanted to punish him in the only way you could, by being with Pittleman."

"That was very perceptive of you, Archer," she said quietly. "Because that's exactly why I did it. I knew it would drive him crazy, and I wanted to hurt him for what he'd done."

"I would have too, if I were you." He paused.

"But now it's time to let it go, Jackie. You can't let your hate for the man dictate the rest of your life. He's gone now. You need to get on with living, on your own terms."

Ernestine smiled and patted Jackie's hand. "I've been telling her that ever since we got here."

Jackie said, "But why did you really ask Marjorie all those questions on the witness stand? You could have just played what was on the recorder. That would have been enough."

"I was lucky Tuttle had forgotten the machine was on. But sometimes people won't believe what's right in front of them. And Marjorie is a good liar. I wanted to lay out the reasons why she would kill your father and pin her down on the stand before I played what was on that recorder. Mr. Shaw would call that corroboration, of a sort." He paused. "And I wanted to make that pious-looking woman squirm, after all the terrible things she'd done."

"I can see that," said Jackie.

"Now I got a question."

She smiled and wearily shook her head. "You still like your questions."

"I never figured out exactly *why* you needed that maid, Amy."

"The man who ran the warehouse for Hank was sweet on her. He gave her a key to the building, so they could meet up there sometimes and be alone, and...you know."

"Good to know I'm not the only man who got taken in by a pretty lady."

"Trust me, Archer, you'll never be alone in that regard."

"Desiree tipped you off about Bobby Kent not being around to drive your father to town that night?"

Jackie nodded. "It's why I picked that time. Desiree has always been a good friend. I gave her some of the money from my father's repayment to Hank. I...I feel like I earned it more than he did."

"I think you're right about that. Now, you must've seen that contract that Marjorie signed that was in the safe?"

"We did. But we were moving so fast, Archer, we never looked at it. We just grabbed everything quick as we could. It took the both of us to carry each of those gold bars out. I was terrified my father was going to show up before we were finished."

"And good thing you got out of there before Marjorie showed up with Hank's gun." He grew quiet and studied both. "I take it you and Ernestine were good friends back in Poca?"

Jackie said, "We were drawn together. We

found that we had some..." Her voice suddenly faltered.

Ernestine finished for her. "We found that we both had some *challenges* in our past that drew us together."

Archer gave each of them a searching look. "I can understand why you might not want to trust any man for the rest of your lives. But I want you to know that I wish you no ill will." He took one of their hands in each of his. "Life can make suckers of us all. I'm a young man in years, but an old one inside after the war and prison." He directed his gaze at Jackie and then Ernestine. "During the war, I guess we were all part of something bigger than ourselves. Then the war was over, and it just left us with what we started with, but wanting something more than what we had before. But I think to really be part of something special, you have to find something special in yourself first. Now the three of us have a second shot at something and maybe we'll mess that up, too, I don't know. But what I *do* know is I'm a lot better off for having met both of you."

The women looked back at him, and tears clustered in not only their eyes, but in Archer's as well. Maybe for the first time in his life.

After a few moments of silence, Jackie said

quietly, "What you just said was pretty insightful, Archer. You sure you didn't graduate from college?"

"Yeah, I did. The college of hard knocks." He rose and drew two pieces of paper from his pocket. "I also came down here to give you these." He handed one to Jackie and the other to Ernestine.

They were two cashier checks.

Both women gasped when they saw the enormous amounts the checks were drawn for.

"What in the world, Archer?" cried out Jackie.

"Good God," chimed in Ernestine.

He said, "That's your shares from what was in the safe."

"Why did you take it from the warehouse?" Jackie asked.

He smiled in an embarrassed fashion. "After you left me high and dry, I did it partly out of anger. But maybe part of me was thinking you would have more incentive to come back if you thought I had the money."

Jackie returned the smile. "You didn't trust me to do the right thing for altruistic reasons?"

"I never expect more from others than I expect from myself," Archer replied diplomatically.

"But why give it to us?" asked Ernestine.

"I considered it a debt that needed to be repaid

to you both. And you know I'm really good at collecting debts."

"But you deserve some of it," said Jackie.

"The good folks of Poca City compensated me fairly for my troubles." He ran his hand along his suit lapel. "How do you think I could afford these duds or the boat passage here?"

A few seconds passed, and Archer watched Ernestine reach out for Jackie's hand. And then they hugged. And in that hug Archer saw two people who were perhaps more than friends. This made him smile. Because everyone should have someone like that in their lives.

When they had drawn apart, Jackie said, "Now I got a question for *you*. Where'd you hide the stuff from the safe after you took it from the warehouse?"

"You know that place you told me about? Where you used to play as a kid and imagine yourself to be anything you wanted to be when you grew up? Well, I buried it there for safe-keeping under that burned-up Cadillac. Didn't think anybody would bother looking there."

Archer put his hat on, cocked it at an angle, and turned to the door.

Jackie quickly rose and said in a disappointed tone, "You're leaving? Already?"

"Well, if you're willing, I thought I might take

you two ladies out to dinner and drinks before I shove off and commence wandering again. And who knows, I might make something of myself. Mr. Shaw thought I could make a decent shamus."

"I think you can make of yourself anything you want, Aloysius Archer," said Ernestine.

"We'll need to change," said Jackie, looking at her plain outfit.

Archer shook his head and said, "I think you both look fine just as you are."

He put out an arm to each of them, which they immediately took.

The three walked out the door into the bright sunshine of a new world that held an abundance of possibilities.

ACKNOWLEDGMENTS

To Michelle, here we go again, this time to the 1940s. Thanks for your encouragement on this one.

To Michael Pietsch, for your vision.

To Andy Dodds, Elizabeth Kulhanek, Brian McLendon, Karen Kosztolnyik, Beth deGuzman, Albert Tang, Bob Castillo, Kristen Lemire, Anthony Goff, Michele McGonigle, Cheryl Smith, Andrew Duncan, Joseph Benincase, Tiffany Sanchez, Morgan Swift, Matthew Ballast, Daniel Modlin, Jordan Rubinstein, Alison Lazarus, Rachel Hairston, Karen Torres, Christopher Murphy, Ali Cutrone, Tracy Dowd, Martha Bucci, Rena Kornbluh, Jeff Shay, Thomas Louie, Sean Ford, Laura Eisenhard, Mary Urban, Barbara Slavin, Kirsiah McNamara, and everyone at Grand Central Publishing, for always being by my side no matter the path I take.

To Aaron and Arleen Priest, Lucy Childs, Lisa Erbach Vance, Frances Jalet-Miller, John Richmond, and Juliana Nador, for always being so supportive.

To Mitch Hoffman, for paying your dues on this one!

To Anthony Forbes Watson, Jeremy Trevathan, Trisha Jackson, Katie James, Alex Saunders, Sara Lloyd, Claire Evans, Sarah Arratoon, Stuart Dwyer, Jonathan Atkins, Anna Bond, Leanne Williams, Natalie Young, Stacey Hamilton, Laura Ricchetti, Charlotte Williams, and Neil Lang at Pan Macmillan, for being a great publisher, and the nicest group of people.

To Praveen Naidoo and the team at Pan Macmillan in Australia, for consistently taking me to #1!

To Caspian Dennis and Sandy Violette, for being the absolute best.

To Bob Schule, for your great insights.

To Mark Steven Long, for good copyediting.

And to Kristen White and Michelle Butler, for doing all the things I can never manage to do!

ABOUT THE AUTHOR

David Baldacci is a global #1 bestselling author, and one of the world's favorite storytellers. His books are published in more than forty-five languages and in more than eighty countries, with over 130 million sales worldwide. His works have been adapted for both feature film and television. David Baldacci is also the cofounder, along with his wife, of the Wish You Well Foundation, a nonprofit organization dedicated to supporting literacy efforts across America. Still a resident of his native Virginia, he invites you to visit him at DavidBaldacci.com and his foundation at WishYouWellFoundation.org.

CPSIA information can be obtained
at www.ICGtesting.com
Printed in the USA
LVHW042341060721
692046LV00008B/37/J